The Log Of The Flying Fish

A Story of Aerial and Submarine Peril and Adventure

by

Harry Collingwood

Double 9
BOOKS

The Log Of The Flying Fish
A Story of Aerial and Submarine
Peril and Adventure
by Harry Collingwood

ISBN: 978-93-67145-84-5

Published by

DOUBLE 9 BOOKS

2/13-B, Ansari Road
Daryaganj, New Delhi – 110002
info@double9books.com
www.double9books.com
Tel. 011-40042856

ABOUT THE AUTHOR

Harry Collingwood (1851-1922) was an English author known for his adventurous novels and stories, particularly those set in maritime environments. Born in London, Collingwood was a prolific writer whose works often centered around themes of adventure, exploration, and nautical life. Collingwood's literary career was marked by his fascination with the sea and maritime adventures. His background and experiences as a sailor heavily influenced his writing, contributing to the authenticity and excitement of his stories. Some of his notable works include: The Pirate Island (1887): One of his most famous novels, it tells the tale of a group of pirates and their adventures. The book combines elements of high-seas adventure with thrilling escapades and daring heroism. The Congo Rovers (1893): This novel explores the adventures of a group of characters navigating the Congo River, mixing elements of exploration and adventure with a focus on the African landscape. The Madcap of the School (1901): A novel set in a school environment, focusing on the humorous and adventurous escapades of its young protagonist. Collingwood's novels are characterized by their engaging plots, vivid descriptions of maritime life, and well-drawn characters. His writing often reflects his enthusiasm for adventure and exploration, capturing the excitement of the unknown and the allure of the sea. Harry Collingwood's legacy lies in his ability to captivate readers with tales of adventure and exploration. His novels remain a testament to his passion for maritime life and his skill in crafting engaging and adventurous stories.

CONTENTS

Chapter One
Professor Von Schalckenberg
makes a startling Suggestion

The "Migrants'" Club stands on the most delightful site in all London; and it is, as the few who are intimately acquainted with it know full well, one of the most cosy and comfortable clubs in the great metropolis.

It is by no means a *famous* club; the building itself has a very simple, unpretentious elevation, with nothing whatever about it to attract the attention of the passer-by; but its interior is fitted up in such a style of combined elegance and comfort, and its domestic arrangements are so perfect, as to leave nothing to be desired.

Its numerous members are essentially wanderers upon the face of the earth—that is the one distinguishing characteristic wherein they most widely differ from their fellow-men—they are ceaseless travellers; mighty hunters in far-off lands; adventurous yachtsmen; eager explorers; with a small sprinkling of army and navy men. Their visits to their club are infrequent in the extreme; but, during the brief and widely separated intervals when they have the opportunity to put in an appearance there, they like to be made thoroughly comfortable; and no pains are spared to secure their complete gratification in this respect.

The smoke-room of the "Migrants'" presented an appearance of especial comfort and attractiveness on a certain cold and stormy February evening a few years ago. A large fire blazed in the polished steel grate and roared cheerfully up the chimney, in rivalry of the wind, which howled and scuffled and rumbled in the flue higher up. An agreeable temperature pervaded the room, making the lashing of the fierce rain on the window-panes sound almost pleasant as one basked in the light and warmth of the apartment and contrasted it with the state of cold and wet and misery which reigned supreme outside. A dozen opal-shaded gas-burners brilliantly lighted the room, and revealed the fact that it was handsomely and liberally furnished with luxurious divans, capacious easy-chairs, a piano, a table loaded with the papers and periodicals of the day, an enormous mirror over the black marble mantel-piece, a clock with a set of silvery chimes for the quarters, and a deep, mellow-toned gong for the hours, and so many pictures that the whole available surface of the walls was completely covered with them. These pictures—executed in both oil and water-colour—represented out-of-the-way scenes visited, or incidents participated in by the members who had executed them, and all possessed a considerable amount of artistic merit; it being a rule of the club that every picture should be submitted to a hanging committee of distinctly artistic members before it could be allowed a place upon the smoke-room walls.

The occupants of the room on the evening in question were four in number. One, a German, known as the Professor Heinrich von Schalckenberg, was half buried in the recesses of a huge arm-chair, from the depths of which he perused the pages of the *Science Monthly*, smoking meanwhile a pipe with a huge elaborately carved meerschaum bowl and a long cherry-wood stem. From the ferocious manner in which he glared through his spectacles at the pages of the magazine, from the impatience with which he from time to time dashed his disengaged hand through the masses of his iron-grey hair, and from the frequent ejaculations of "Pish!" "Psha!" "Ach!" and so on which escaped his lips, accompanied by vast volumes of smoke, it seemed evident that he was not altogether at one with the author whose article he was perusing. He was an explorer and a scientist.

Near the Herr Professor there reclined upon a divan the form of Sir Reginald Elphinstone, sometimes called by his friends "the handsome baronet," said to be *the* richest commoner in England. At the age of thirty-five, having freely exposed himself to all known sources of peril, except those involved in a trip to the Polar regions, in his eager pursuit of sport and adventure, Sir Reginald seemed, for the moment, to have no object left him in life but to shoot as many rings as possible of cigar-smoke through each other, as he lay there on the divan in an attitude more easy than elegant.

Square in front of the fire, dreamily puffing at his cigar and apparently studying the merits of a painting hanging behind him, and on the reflected image of which in the mirror before him his eyes lazily rested, sat Cyril Lethbridge, ex-colonel of the Royal Engineers, a successful gold-seeker, and almost everything else to which a spice of adventure could possibly attach itself.

And next him again, on the side of the fire-place opposite to the Herr Professor, lounged Lieutenant Edward Mildmay, R.N.

The lieutenant was skimming through the daily papers. Presently he looked up and remarked to the colonel:

"I see that some Frenchmen have been making experiments in the navigation of balloons."

"Ah, indeed!" responded the colonel, with his head thrown critically on one side, and his eyes still fixed on the reflection of the picture. "And with what result?"

"Oh, failure, of course."

"And failure it always will be. The thing is simply an impossibility," remarked the colonel.

"No, bardon me, colonel, id is not an imbossibilidy by any means."

This from the professor.

"Indeed? Then how do you account for it, professor, that all attempts to navigate a balloon have hitherto failed?" asked the colonel.

"Begause, my dear zir, the aeronauts have never yed realised all the requiremends of zuccess," replied the professor, laying down his magazine as though quite prepared to go thoroughly into the question.

The colonel accepted the challenge, and, rousing himself from his semi-recumbent posture, said:

"That is quite possible; but what *are* the requirements of success?"

The professor knocked the ashes out of his meerschaum, refilled it with the utmost deliberation, carefully lighted it, gave a few vigorous puffs, and replied:

"The requiremends of zuccess in balloon navigation are very zimilar to those which enable a man to draverse the ocean. If a man wants to make a voyage agross the ocean he embargs in a ship, not on a life-buoy. Now a balloon is nothing more than a life-buoy; id zusdains a man, but that is all. Id drifts aboud with the currends of air jusd as a life-buoy drifts aboud with the currends of ocean, and the only advandage which the aeronaud has over the man with the life-buoy is thad the former can ascend or descend in search of a favourable air currend, whereas the ladder is obliged do dake the ocean currends as they come."

"Very true," remarked the colonel; "and what do you deduce from that, professor?"

"I deduse from thad thad the man who wands to navigade the air musd do as his brother the sailor does, he musd have a *ship*."

"Well, is not a balloon a sort of air ship?"

"You may gall it zo iv you like, colonel, I do nod; I call it merely a buoy," returned the professor. "A *ship* is a zomething gabable of *moving* in the elemend which zustains it; a balloon is ingabable of any indebendend movement in the air; it drifts aboud at the mercy of every idle wind that blows. Id is like a ship on a breathless sea; withoud any means of brobulsion the ship lies motionless, or drifts at the mercy of the currends. Bud give the ship a means of brobulsion, and navigation ad once begomes bossible. And zo will it be with balloons."

"Well, that has already been tried," remarked the colonel; "but the buoyancy of a balloon is too slight to permit of its being fitted with engines and a boiler."

"My vriendt," said the professor impressively, "whad would you think of the man who tried to pud the engines and boilers of an Atlantic liner in a leedle boad?"

"I should think him an unmitigated ass," retorted the colonel.

"Jusd so. Yed thad is whad the aeronauds have been doing; they have been drying to make the leedle boad-balloon garry the brobelling bower of the aerial ship. In other words, they have not made their balloons large enough."

"Then you think they have not yet reached the practical limit to the size of a balloon?" asked the colonel.

"They have—very nearly—if balloons are do be made only of silk," was the reply. "Bud if *navigable* balloons are to be gonsdrugded, aeronauds musd durn do other maderials and adobd another form. As I said before, they musd build a *shib*, and she musd be of sufficiend size to float in the air and to garry all her eguipments."

"But such an aerial ship would be a veritable *monster*" protested the colonel.

"Zo are the Adlandic liners of the presend day," quietly answered the professor.

"Phew!" whistled the colonel. The baronet rose from the divan, flung away the stump of his cigar, and settled himself to listen, and perhaps take part in the singular conversation.

"And of what would you build your aerial ship, professor?" asked the colonel when he had in some measure recovered from his astonishment.

"Of the lighdesd and, ad the zame dime, sdrongesd maderial I gould find," answered the professor. "Once get the aeronaud to realise thad greadly ingreased bulk and a differend form are necessary, and id will nod be long before he will find a suitable building maderial. Iv I were an aeronaud I should dry medal."

"Metal!" exclaimed the colonel. "Oh, come, professor; now you are romancing, you know. A ship of metal would never float in the atmosphere."

"A zimilar remarg was made nod zo very many years ago when id was suggesded that ocean shibs could be buildt of medal," retorted the professor. "Yed there are thousands of medal shibs in existdenze do-day; and there can be no doubt as do the facd thad they fload. And zo will an aerial shib. The gread—in facd the *only* diffiguldy in the madder is thad air is eight hundred dimes lighder than wader; and an air shib of given dimensions musd therefore be ad leasd eight hundred dimes lighder than her ocean sisder do enable her do fload in the atmosphere. The broblem, then, is this: How are you to gonsdrugt a medal shib, of given dimensions, sdrong enough do hold dogether and withsdand the shock of goming do earth, yed of less weighd than her own bulk of air? With the medals hitherdoo ad our disbosal, I admid thad the dask is a diffiguld one; bud I maindain thad id is by no means an imbossibilidy. An ocean shib musd be buildt sdrong enough nod only do susdain the weighd of her gargo— often amounding do upwards of a thousand dons—bud also do withstand the dremendous and incessandly varying sdrain do which she is exbosed when garrying thad gargo through a moundainous sea. This enormous sdrength necessidades the use of a gorresbonding thickness—and therefore weighd—of the medal used in her gonsdruction. Such brovision would of gourse be unnecessary in the gase of an aerial shib; begause no one would dream of garrying an ounze of unnecessary weighd through the air; and there are no moundain seas in the admosphere to sdrain a shib. A vasd saving in weighd would resuld from these zirgumsdances alone; and a further saving—zufficiend, I believe, to aggomblish the desired object— gan, no doubd, be effecded by skilful engineers, one of whose greadesd driumphs id is do design sdrugdures in which the maximum of sdrength is zecured with the minimum of weighd. Id musd nod be forgodden, either, thad an air shib musd, in one imbordand bardigular, be dreated exactly like her ocean sisder. An ocean shib gonsdrugded, say, of sdeel, will sink if filled with wader, begause sdeel is heavier than wader, bulk for bulk; bud bump oud all the wader from her inderior, and if she be proberly gonsdrugded, she will fload on the elemend she is indended do navigade. And the same with an air shib: bump out all or nearly all the air which she gondains, and if she be gonsdrugded in aggordanze with the brincibles I have indigaded, she will fload in the lighder elemend."

"Upon my word, professor, you have argued your case extremely well," exclaimed the colonel. "I can see only one difficulty in the way; and that is in the matter of *weight*."

"Which diffiguldy I have gombledely gonquered," triumphantly exclaimed the professor, rising excitedly from his seat with flushed cheeks and flashing eyes. "Do me, Heinrich von Schalckenberg, belongs the honour and glory of having made dwo mosd imbordand disgoveries, disgoveries of ingalgulable value do the worldt, disgoveries which will enable me do soar ad will indo the highesd regions of the embyrean, do skim the surface of the ocean, or do blunge do ids lowesd debths."

"Bravo, professor; that was positively dramatic!" exclaimed the baronet. "You have mistaken your business, my dear sir; you were undoubtedly born to be an actor. But what are these two most important discoveries of which you so exultantly speak?"

"They are a new medal and a new power," exclaimed the professor. Then, fumbling in his breast-pocket, he drew forth a wallet from which he extracted a small rectangular plate of—apparently—polished silver. It measured about five inches long by four inches broad, and was about a quarter of an inch thick.

"There, Sir Reginald," he exclaimed, offering the plate to the baronet, "dell me whad you think of thad."

"Very pretty indeed," commented Sir Reginald, as he held out his hand to take it. "What is it? Silver? Phew! No; it can't be that," as his fingers closed upon it; "it is far too light for silver. Why, it seems to be absolutely devoid of weight altogether. What is it, professor?"

"Thad, my good sir, is my new medal, which I gall '*aethereum*' begause of ids wonderful lighdness. See here."

There was a very handsome cut glass water-jug, full, standing on the table in a capacious salver of hammered brass. The professor took up the jug and emptied it into the salver, almost filling the latter. Then he laid the glittering slab of metal down on the surface of the water, where it floated as buoyantly as though it had been an empty box constructed of the lightest cardboard. The professor raised the salver from the table and agitated the water, to show that the metal actually floated.

"Why, it floats as lightly as a cork!" exclaimed the colonel in the utmost astonishment.

"Korg!" exclaimed the professor disdainfully, "korg is *heavy* gombared with this. This is the lighdesd solid known. Loog ad this."

The professor lifted the plate of metal out of the water, and, wiping it dry very carefully with his silk pocket-handkerchief, held it suspended, flat side downwards, between his finger and thumb. Then, when he had poised it as nearly horizontal as he could guess at, he let it go. It wavered about in the air as a thin sheet of paper would have done, and finally sailed aslant and very gently to the ground, amid the astonished exclamations of the beholders, by whom it was immediately examined with the utmost curiosity.

"You have seen for yourselves and gan therefore judge how marvellously lighd this medal is," continued the professor when the plate had been handed back to him; "bud ids *sdrength* you musd dake my word for, as I have no means ad hand do illusdrade id. Ids sdrength is as wonderful as ids lighdness, being—zo var as I have had obbordunidy do desd id—exactly one hundred dimes thad of the besd sdeel."

"If that be the case, professor, then I should say you have solved the problem of aerial navigation," remarked the colonel. "But you spoke of having also discovered a new power. What is it?"

The professor once more instituted a search in his pockets, and at length produced a small paper packet, which, on being opened, was found to contain about a table-spoonful of green metallic-looking crystals.

"There id is," he said, handing the packet to the colonel for inspection.

"Um!" ejaculated the colonel, turning the crystals over slowly with his finger. "Quite new to me; I don't recognise them at all. And what is the nature of the power derivable from these crystals?"

"Dreated in one way they give off elegdricidy; dreated in another way they yield an exbansive gas, which may be subsdiduded for either gunbowder or sdeam," answered the professor.

"Are they explosive, then?" asked the colonel.

"Nod in their bresend form. You mighd doss all those crysdals indo the fire with imbunidy; but bowder them and mix indo a baste with a zerdain acid, and whad you now hold in your hand would develop exblosive bower enough to demolish this building," was the quiet reply.

The professor's little audience looked at him incredulously; a look to which he responded by saying:

"Id is quide drue, I assure you," in such convincing tones as left no room for further doubt. They knew the professor well; knew him to be quite incapable of the slightest attempt at deception or exaggeration.

"Then, if I have understood you aright, you will construct your aerial ship of your new metal, and apply your new power to give motion to her machinery?" said the colonel.

"Yes. Thad is do say, I *would* if I bossessed the means do build such a ship as I have described. Bud I am a scientist, and therefore boor. Never mind; I have no doubt thad, when I make my discoveries known, I shall find some wealthy man who, for the sake of science, will find der money," said the professor hopefully.

"How much would it cost to build an aerial ship such as you have been speaking of?" asked the baronet.

"Oh! I cannod say. Nod zo very much. Berhabs a hundred thousandt bounds," was the reply.

"Phew! That's rather 'steep,' as the Yankees say. But—'a fool and his money are soon parted'—if you are convinced that your scheme is really practicable, professor, I will find the needful," remarked the baronet.

"Bragdigable! My dear sir, id is as bragdigable as id is to build a shib which will navigade the ocean. I have thoughd the madder oudt, and there is nod a single weak boindt anywhere in my scheme. Led me have der money and I will brovide you with the means of zoaring above the grest of Mount Everest, or of exbloring the deepest ocean valleys," exclaimed the professor enthusiastically.

"Good!" remarked the baronet quietly. "That is a bargain. Meet me here at noon to-morrow, and we will go together to my bankers, where I will transfer one hundred thousand pounds to your account. And—what say you, gentlemen?—when this wonderful ship is completed will you join the professor and me in an experimental trip round the world?"

"I shall be delighted," exclaimed the colonel.

"Nothing would please me better," remarked the lieutenant.

And so it was agreed.

"Well," remarked the baronet reflectively, and as though he already began to feel doubtful as to the wisdom of his agreement with the professor, "if it has no other good result it will at least afford employment to a few of the unfortunate fellows who are now hanging about idle day after day."

The professor looked up sharply.

"What!" he exclaimed. "Of whom are you sbeaging, my dear Sir Reginald?"

"I am speaking of the unfortunate individual known as 'the British Workman,'" was the baronet's quiet reply.

"Am I do understandt thad you make the embloymend of English workmen a gondition of the underdaking?" asked the professor somewhat sharply.

"By no means, my dear sir," answered Sir Reginald; "I shall not attempt to impose conditions of any kind upon you. But I should naturally expect that, if English workmen are as capable of executing the work as foreigners, the former would be given the preference in a matter involving the expenditure of say a hundred thousand pounds of an Englishman's money."

"Quide zo," concurred the professor; "and you would be perfectly justified in such an expegdation *if* the Bridish workman was the steady, indusdrious, reliable fellow he once was. Bud, unfordunadely, he is *nod* the same, zo var ad leasd as *reliabilidy* is concerned. You gannod any longer debend ubon him. Id is no longer bossible to underdake a work of any imbordance withoudt the gonsdand haunting fear that your brogress will be inderrubted—berhaps ad a most cridical juncture—by a 'sdrike,' The greadt quesdion which, above all others, do-day agidades the British mind is: 'Do whadt cause is the bresendt debression of drade addribudable?' And, in my obinion, gendlemen, the answer to that quesdion is thad id is very largely due do the consdandly recurring sdrikes which have become almosdt *a habid* with the Bridish workman. The 'sdrike' is the most formidable engine which has ever been brought indo oberation do seddle the differences bedween embloyer and embloyed; and, whilst I am willing to admid thad in certain cases id has resulded in the repression and redress of long-sdanding oppression and injusdice, id has been used with such a lack of discrimination as do have almost ruined the drade of the goundry. With the invention of the 'sdrike' the workman thoughd he had ad lasd discovered the means of enriching himself ad the expense of his embloyer, or of securing his fair and righdful share of the brofids of his labour, as *he* described id; and, udderly ignorand of the laws of bolidigal egonomy, recognising in the 'sdrike' merely an insdrumend for forcing a higher rade of wages from his embloyer, he has gone on recklessly using id undil the unfordunade gabidalist, finding himself unable do produce his wares ad a cost which will enable him do successfully gompede with the manufagdurers of other goundries, has been gombelled to glose his works and remove his gabidal and his energies to a spodt where he gan find workmen less unreasonable in their demands. There is no more capable or valuable workman in existence than the English artisan, if he gould only be induced to do his honest *best* for his embloyer; there is hardly any branch of industry in which he is nod ad leasd the equal, if not very greadly the suberior of the foreigner; and id is even yet in his power to recover the command of the world's market by the suberior excellence of his broductions, if he could only be brevailed upon do abandon sdrikes and do be satisfied with a wage which will allow the cabidalist a fair and moderade redurn for the use of his money and brains and for the risks he has do run. If the British workman would gollecdively make up his mind to do this, and would acquaindt the gabidalist with his decision, we should speedily see a revival of drade and embloymend for every really capable workman. Bud in the meantime there unfordunadely seems do be very little chance of this; and in so delicade a madder as the gonsdrugdion of this ship of ours, it would be nod only unwise, but also unfair to you to run the risk of a failure through the embloymendt of untractable or unreliable workmen; and if, therefore, you had insisted on my embloying Englishmen, I should have been relugdandly gombelled do wash my hands of the whole affair. Ad the same dime I feel id due do myself do say thad, even had you nod mendioned the madder, I should have done my best to secure Englishmen for the work, as of course I shall now; bud I do nod feel very sanguine as do the resuldt."

"My dear professor!" exclaimed the baronet, smiling at the intense earnestness of the German, "are you not laying on the colour rather thickly? I admit with sorrow that your portrait is only *too* truthful—as a portrait— still I cannot help thinking it rather highly coloured. They are surely not *all* as despicable as you have painted them?"

"No," answered the professor with enthusiasm, "no they are nod. Id was only a few weeks ago thad I read of the workmen of a cerdain firm bresending their employers with a full week's work *free*, in order to helb the firm out of their beguniary diffiguldies. Now, *they*, I admid, were fine, noble, sensible fellows; they had indelligence enough to regognize the diffiguldies of the siduation, and do grabble with them in a sensible way. I warrand you *they* always worked honesdly and efficiendly whether their embloyer's eye was on them or nod. And they will find their reward in due time; their embloyers will never rest until they have recouped the men for their generous sacrifice. But where will you find another body of men like them? They are only the one noble, grand exception which goes do brove my rule."

"Well, professor, though what you have said is, in the main, only *too* true, I cannot agree with you altogether; I believe there are a few good, intelligent, reliable men to be found here and there, in addition to those splendid fellows of whom you have just told us," said the baronet. "But," he continued, "I will not attempt to constrain you in any way. If you cannot find exactly what you want here, import men from abroad, by all means. I have a great deal of sympathy for want and suffering when they are the result of misfortune; but when they are brought on by a man's own laziness or perversity he must go elsewhere for sympathy and help; I have none to spare for people of that sort."

Chapter Two
The Realisation of a Scientist's Dream

Punctual to the moment, Professor von Schalckenberg opened the door of the smoke-room at the "Migrants'," and entered the apartment as the deep-toned notes of Big Ben were heard sounding the hour of noon on the day following that upon which occurred the conversation recorded in the preceding chapter. Sir Reginald Elphinstone was already there; and after a few words of greeting the two men left the club together, and, entering the baronet's cab, which was in waiting, drove away to the banker's, where the business of the money transfer was soon concluded.

The pair then separated; and for the next fortnight the professor was busy all day, and during a great part of the night, with his drawings and calculations. At the end of that time, having completed his work on paper to his satisfaction, he took advantage of a fine day to make a little excursion. Proceeding to London Bridge, he embarked in a river steamer, about ten o'clock in the morning, and indulged himself in a run down the river. He kept his eyes sharply about him as the boat sped down the stream; and just before reaching Blackwall he saw what he thought would suit him. It was a ship-building yard, "for sale, or to let, with immediate possession", as an immense notice-board informed him. Landing at the pier, he made his way back to the yard, and, having with some difficulty found the man in charge of the keys, proceeded to inspect the premises. They turned out to be as nearly what he wanted as he could reasonably hope to find, being very spacious, with a full supply of "plant," in perfect working order, and with enough spare room to allow of the laying down of the special "plant" necessary for the manufacture of his new metal. Having satisfied himself upon this point, he next obtained the address of the parties who had the letting of the yard and works, and proceeded back to town by rail. The parties of whom he was now in search proved to be a firm of solicitors having offices in Lincoln's Inn; and by them, when he had stated the object of his call, he was received with—figuratively—open arms. The premises had been lying idle and profitless for some time; and they were only too glad to let them to him upon a two years' lease upon terms highly advantageous to him and his client the baronet.

This important business settled, the next thing was to lay down the special plant already referred to; and so energetic was the professor in his management of this and the other necessary preliminaries that six months sufficed to place the yard in a fit state for the commencement of actual operations.

And now the professor's troubles began in real earnest. Impressed with the idea that he was perhaps wrong after all, and the baronet right, in his judgment of the British workman, Herr von Schalckenberg determined to run the risk of giving the Englishmen another trial. He had no difficulty whatever in engaging an efficient office staff; but when it came to securing the services of foremen, mechanics, and labourers, the unhappy German was driven almost to despair. He advertised his wants widely, of course, and, in response to his advertisements, the applications for employment poured in almost literally without number. The great entrance-gates of the works were fairly besieged, and the roadway outside blocked by the great army of applicants, who were admitted into the presence of the professor in gangs of twenty at a time. The professor had set out with the resolve that he would deal as liberally with his employés as he possibly could, consistently with justice to his client, the baronet; and with this object he had spared no pains to ascertain the rate of wages then ruling for such men as he wanted. With the data thus obtained he had drawn up a scale of pay which he was prepared to offer, and beyond which he had resolved not to go. Armed with this, he interviewed the countless applicants as they presented themselves before him; and the result was enough to drive to distraction even a more patient man than Herr von Schalckenberg. The applicants proved to be, almost without exception, trades-unionists, out on strike because their employers had declined or had been unable to accede to the exorbitant demands of the workmen. These workmen had in many cases been idle for months; yet they now unhesitatingly refused employment, and refused it insolently too, because the wages offered by the professor, though fully equal to those paid by other employers, were less than they chose to consider themselves entitled to. Their wives and children were, by their own admission, naked and starving, and here was an opportunity to clothe and feed them, yet they rejected it scornfully. And naked, starving though the families of these wretches might be and actually were, almost every man of them, bearing out the professor's criticism of them, had a short dirty pipe in his mouth and smelt strongly of drink. There were a few exceptions to this rule—about one in every fifty applicants, perhaps—and they were almost all non-union men, who eagerly and thankfully accepted employment, careless of the sneers, gibes, and threats of the others; and these proved to be, with scarcely a single exception, steady, reliable, honest, and capable men, who soon worked themselves into leading positions. The professor wanted about two hundred men, and he succeeded in securing twenty; after which his overtasked patience gave out, and in despair he obtained the remainder from Germany.

All this took time; and it was not until nearly eight months after the conversation in the "Migrants'" smoke-room that the professor was actually able to commence work in the building yard. Then, however, the operations proceeded apace. Day after day long mineral trains jolted and clanked noisily along the siding and into the yard, where they disgorged their loads and made way for still other trains; day after day clumsy steam colliers hauled in alongside the yard wharf and under the fussy steam-cranes to discharge their cargoes; and very soon the lofty furnace chimneys began to belch forth a never-ending cloud of inky smoke. Very soon, too, the belated wayfarer might possibly, had he been so disposed, have obtained a chance glimpse, through accidental chinks in the close palisading, of a long range of brilliantly lighted buildings, wherein, if the doors happened to be inadvertently left open, he would have witnessed huge outpourings of dazzling molten metal, which, after being subjected to the action of certain chemicals, and passing through divers strange processes, was passed as it solidified through a series of powerful rolling mills, which relentlessly squeezed and flattened it out, until it finally emerged, still glowing red with fervent heat, in the shape of long flat symmetrically shaped sheets, or angle-bars and girders of various sections. And, a little later on, an inquisitive individual, could he have obtained a peep into the jealously boarded-in building shed, might have seen a far-reaching series of light circular ribs of glittering silver-like metal, of gradually decreasing diameter as they spread each way from the central rib, rearing themselves far aloft toward the ground-glass skylight which surmounted the roof of the building. But perhaps the strangest sight of all, could one but have gained admission into the forge to see it, was the huge main shaft of the ship, which, after having been mercilessly pounded and battered into shape by the giant Nasmith hammers, was coolly seized by only a couple of men, and by them easily carried into the machine-shop, there to receive its finishing touches in the lathe.

And so the work went on, steadily yet rapidly, until at length it so nearly approached completion that the professor was every week enabled to dispense with the services of and pay off an increasingly large number of men. Finally, the day arrived when the score or so of painters and decorators, who then constituted the sole remnant of the professor's late army of workmen, completed their task of beautifying the interior of the aerial ship, and, receiving their pay, were dismissed to seek a new field of labour. The official staff now alone remained, and to these, after making them a pleasant little complimentary speech expressing his appreciation of the zeal and ability with which they had discharged their duties, Herr von Schalckenberg announced the pleasant intelligence that, although he had now no further need of their services, Sir Reginald Elphinstone had, upon his—the professor's—earnest recommendation, successfully used his influence to secure them other and immediate employment. The professor then handed each man a cheque for his salary, including three months' extra pay in lieu of the usual notice of dismissal to which he was entitled, together with a letter of introduction to his new employer, and, shaking hands with the staff all round, bade them good-bye, wishing them individually success in their new posts. Then, watching them file out of the office for the last time, he waited until all had left the premises, when he turned the key in the door, and making his way into the interior of the building shed, found himself at length alone with his completed work.

How the professor spent the next few hours no man but himself can say; but it is reasonable to suppose that, man of science though he was, he was still sufficiently human to regard with critical yet innocent pride and exultation the wonderful fabric which owed its existence to the inventive ingenuity of his fertile brain. It is probable, too, that when he had at length gratified himself with an exhaustive contemplation of its many points of interest, he went on board the ship, and with his own eyes and hands made a final inspection and trial of all her machinery, to satisfy himself that everything was complete and ready. At all events, however the professor may have passed those few hours of precious solitude, when he finally handed over the keys to the yard watchman and bade him "good-night" late on that summer evening, his whole bearing and appearance was that of a thoroughly happy and satisfied man.

Chapter Three
The "Flying Fish"

During the whole of the following week stores of various kinds necessary to the comfort and sustenance of the voyagers were being constantly delivered at the building yard, where they were received by the valet and cook of Sir Reginald Elphinstone—the only servants or assistants of any kind who were to accompany the expedition—and promptly stowed away by them, under the direction of the professor, who was exceedingly anxious to accurately preserve the proper "trim" of the vessel—a much more important and difficult matter than it would have been had she been designed to navigate the ocean only. By mid-day on Saturday the last article had been received, including the personal belongings of the travellers, the stowage was completed, and everything was ready for an immediate start.

At three o'clock on the following Monday afternoon the voyagers met in the smoke-room of the "Migrants'" as a convenient and appropriate rendezvous, and, without having dropped the slightest hint to anyone respecting the novel nature of their intended journey, quietly said "Good-bye" to the two or three men who happened to be there, and, chartering a couple of hansoms, made the best of their way to Fenchurch Street railway station, from whence they took the train to Blackwall. On emerging from the latter station they placed themselves under the guidance of the professor, and were by him conducted in a few minutes to the building yard. The professor was the only one of the quartette who had as yet set eyes on the vessel in which they were about to embark; and the remaining three naturally felt a little flutter of curiosity as they passed through the gateway and saw before them the enormous closely-boarded shed which jealously hid from all unprivileged eyes the latest marvel of science. But they were Englishmen, and as such it was a part of their creed to preserve an absolutely unruffled equanimity under every conceivable combination of circumstances, so between the whiffs of their cigars they chatted carelessly about anything and everything but the object upon which their thoughts were just then centred.

But the baronet's equanimity was for a moment upset when the professor, after a perhaps unnecessarily prolonged fumbling with the key, threw open the wicket which gave admission to the interior of the shed, and, stepping back to allow his companions to precede him, exclaimed in tones of exultant pride, in that broken English of his which it is unnecessary to further reproduce:

"Behold, gentlemen, the embodiment of a scientist's dream—the *Flying Fish!*"

The baronet advanced a pace or two, then stopped short, aghast.

"Good heavens!" he ejaculated. "What, in the name of madness, have you done, professor? That huge object will *never* float in the air; and I should say it will be a pretty expensive business to get her into the *water*, if indeed it is worth while to put her there."

The other two, the representatives of the army and of the navy, though probably as much astonished as the baronet, said nothing. They knew considerably more than the latter about the capabilities of science; and though they might possibly entertain grave doubts as to the success of the professor's experiment, they did not feel called upon to express an off-hand opinion that it would prove a failure.

The baronet might well be excused his hasty expression of incredulity. Towering above and in front of him, filling up the entire space of the enormous shed from end to end and from ground to roof-timbers, he saw an immense cylinder, pointed at both ends, and constructed entirely of the polished silver-like metal which the professor had called aethereum. The sides of the ship from stem to stern formed a series of faultless curves; the conical bow or fore body of the ship being somewhat longer, and therefore sharper, than the after body, which partook more of the form of an ellipse than of a cone; the curvilinear hull was supported steadily in position by two deep broad bilge-keels, one on either side and about one-third the extreme length of the ship; and, attached to the stern of the vessel by an ingeniously devised ball-and-socket joint in such a manner as to render a rudder unnecessary, was to be seen a huge propeller having four tremendously broad sickle-shaped blades, the palms of which were hollowed in such a manner as to gather in and concentrate the air, or water, about the boss and powerfully project it thence in a direct line with the longitudinal axis of the ship. Crowning the whole there was a low superstructure immediately over and of the same length as the bilge-keels, very much resembling the upper works of a double-bowed vessel such as are some of the small Thames river steamers. This was decked over, and afforded a promenade about two hundred feet long by thirty feet wide. And, lastly, rising from the centre of this deck there was a spacious pilot-house with a dome-like roof, from the interior of which the movements of the vessel could be completely controlled. The entire hull of the vessel, excepting the double-bowed superstructure, was left unpainted, and it shone like a polished mirror. The superstructure, however, was painted a delicate grey tint, with the relief of a massive richly gilded cable moulding all round the shear-strake and the further adornment of a broad ribbon of a rich crimson hue rippling through graceful wreaths of gilded scroll-work at bow and stern, the name *Flying Fish* being inscribed on the ribbon in gold letters. Altogether, notwithstanding her unusual form, the aerial ship was an exceedingly graceful and elegant object, and, but for her enormous proportions, looked admirably adapted for her work.

Under other circumstances the professor would probably have been seriously offended at the baronet's incredulous exclamation; but as it was he was so confident of his success—so gratified and triumphant altogether—that he could afford to be not only forgiving but actually tolerant. He therefore replied to Sir Reginald only with a mute smile of amused compassion for the baronet's lamentable ignorance and unbelief.

The professor's smile somewhat reassured Sir Reginald, though he still continued to eye his novel possession very dubiously.

"You once spoke of Atlantic liners," he at last remarked to the professor; "but surely this craft is larger than the largest Atlantic liner afloat. What are her dimensions?"

"She is six hundred feet long, by sixty feet diameter at the point of her greatest girth," quietly replied the professor.

"And do you mean to tell me that such a monster will ever float in the air?" ejaculated the baronet, his incredulity returning and taking possession of him with tenfold tenacity.

"I do," answered the professor firmly, his self-love at length becoming slightly ruffled. "In that ship you shall to-night soar higher into the empyrean than mortal has ever soared before; and after that you shall, if you choose, sleep calmly until morning at the bottom of the English Channel. By and by at the dinner-table I will endeavour to demonstrate to you, my dear friend, that it is her immense proportions alone which will enable her to float in so thin a fluid as air."

"Very well," said the baronet in the tones of a man still utterly unconvinced; "if you say so, I suppose I must doubt no more. Now, please, introduce to us the novel details of this wonderful craft of yours."

"With pleasure," answered the professor, his brow clearing and a gratified smile suffusing his countenance. "A few minutes will suffice to show you all that can be seen from the outside. Those small circular pieces of glass which you perceive let into the hull here and there are, as you have no doubt already surmised, windows to enable us to observe what is passing outside. The larger windows at the bow and stern protect powerful electric lamps, and are exclusively for the purpose of lighting up our surroundings when we are at the bottom of the sea. This," — pointing to what looked like a circular trap-door in the bottom of the ship, some fifteen feet from the centre on the port side — "is the anchor recess; and this," — pointing to a corresponding arrangement on the starboard side — "is the door through which we shall obtain egress from and access to the ship when she is at the bottom of the sea."

"Do you mean by that, that we are going to leave the ship and walk about on the bed of the ocean?" asked the baronet.

"Certainly," answered the professor with a look of surprise. "Our exploration of the ocean's bed will probably be one of the most interesting incidents of the expedition."

The baronet shrugged his shoulders and the professor continued:

"These bilge-keels serve a threefold purpose; they enable the ship to rest steadily and firmly on the ground, as you see, which, from her peculiar form, she could not otherwise do; they also form the sheaths, so to speak, of four anchors to fasten her securely to the ground either above or beneath the water—a most necessary precaution, believe me; and they also add considerably to the cubical contents of the water-chambers, with which they communicate, which will help to sink the ship to the bottom. Lastly, there is the propeller, the only peculiarities of which are its great diameter—fifty feet—its enormous surface area, and the fact that it is attached to the hull in such a way as to admit of its being turned freely in any direction, thus dispensing with all necessity for a rudder."

"Why have you left the hull unpainted, professor? I suppose you had some good reason for so doing?" remarked the colonel, chiming into the conversation.

"I had no less than *three* good reasons for leaving the hull of the ship unpainted," answered the professor. "In the first place, aethereum is quite insensible to the attacks of air and water—it never oxidises, and paint was therefore unnecessary for its preservation. In the next place, the quantity of paint necessary to cover that enormous surface would weigh something considerable; and, as I have throughout the work taken the utmost pains to keep down all the weight to the lowest ounce consistent with absolute safety, I rejected it on that account. And lastly, I take it that we are anxious to avoid all unnecessary observation; and I believe this cannot be better accomplished than by preserving the brilliant metallic lustre of the hull, which, especially when we are floating in mid-air, will reflect the tints of the surrounding atmosphere, and so make it almost impossible to distinguish us."

"Except when the sun's rays fall directly upon us, eh, professor?" remarked Mildmay.

"In that case," returned the professor, "observers will see a dazzling flash of light in which all shape will be indistinguishable."

"And we shall thus be mistaken for a meteorite," exclaimed the baronet somewhat sarcastically. "Excellent! admirable! I really must congratulate you, professor, upon the wonderful foresight with which you seem to have provided for every possible and impossible emergency. Now, what is the next marvel?"

"There is nothing more down here. We will now proceed on board, if you please, gentlemen," said the professor; and he forthwith led the way up a ladder which leaned against the vessel's lofty side. This conducted them as far as the upper curve of her cylindrical bilge, at which point they encountered a flight of light ornamental openwork steps permanently attached to the ship's side, up which they passed to the gangway in the stout metal railing which served instead of bulwark, and so reached the spacious promenade deck. Looking down into the yard from this coign of vantage, they seemed to be an enormous height from the ground; and the baronet shrugged his shoulders more expressively than ever as he glanced first below and then around him, realising more fully than ever, as he did so, the immense proportions of his new possession. He said nothing, however, but turned inquiringly to the professor.

"This way, gentlemen, if you please," said the German, in answer to the look; and he led them aft to what may be styled the quarter-deck.

"You spoke about the weight of a coat of paint on the hull just now, but I see you have planked the deck. The weight of all this planking must be something considerable," remarked Mildmay.

"A mere trifle; it is only a thin veneering just to give a secure and comfortable foothold," remarked the professor. He paused at what looked like a trap-door in the deck and said:

"We shall not be always soaring in the air nor groping about at the bottom of the sea; we shall sometimes be riding on the surface; and I have therefore thought it advisable to provide a couple of boats. Here is one of them."

He stooped down, seized hold of and turned a ring in the flap, and raised the trap-door, disclosing a dark pit-like recess of considerable dimensions. Letting the flap fold back flat on the deck, the professor then stooped down and grasped the handle of a horizontal lever which lay just below the level of the deck, and drew it up into a perpendicular position, and, as he did so, a pair of davits, the upper portions of which had been plainly visible, rose through the aperture close to the protecting railing, bringing with them a handsomely modelled boat hanging from the tackles. The professor deftly turned the davits outward, and there hung the boat at the quarter in the exact position she would have occupied in an ordinary ship.

"Bravo, professor; very clever indeed!" exclaimed Mildmay. "But what is the object of those four curved tubes projecting through the boat's bottom?"

"Those tubes," answered the professor, "are the boat's means of propulsion. You see," he explained, "being built of aethereum, the boat is extremely light, and draws so little water that a screw propeller would be quite useless to her. So I have substituted those tubes instead. One pair, you will observe, points toward the stern, and one pair toward the bow. The boat's engine is a powerful three-cylinder pump, and it sucks the water strongly in through the tubes which point forward, discharging it as powerfully out through those which point astern; thus drawing and driving the boat along at a speed of about twelve knots per hour, which is as fast, I fancy, as we shall ever want her to go. If you want to go astern the movement of a single lever reverses the whole process. There is a similar boat on the other side."

The boat having been returned to her hiding-place, the professor next led his friends to the structure which occupied the centre of the deck. It was a perfectly plain erection, with curved sides meeting in a kind of stem and stern-post at its forward and after ends, with a curved dome-like roof, several small circular windows all round its sides, and no apparent means of entry.

"Why, how is this, professor? You have actually built your pilot-house—for such I suppose it is—without a door," exclaimed the baronet with returning good-humour as he perceived that, even in the event of the *Flying Fish* failing to fly, he would still have a very wonderful ship for his money.

"As you have rightly supposed, this *is* the pilot-house," answered the professor, with one hand pressing lightly against the gleaming wall of the structure. "But as to its being without a door, you are mistaken, for there it is."

And as he spoke a door, hitherto unnoticed in the side of the building, flew open.

"Why, you are a veritable magician, professor! How on earth did you manage that?" exclaimed the colonel.

"Easily enough," answered the professor. "Just look here, all of you. This is a secret door which it is necessary you should all know how to open. Now, there are four of us, are there not? Very well; find the fourth rivet from the bottom in the fourth row from the after end of the building—here it is—push it to your left—*not* press it; pressing is no good—and open flies the door. Push the rivet to the *right* when the door is open, and you shut it—so," suiting the action to the word. "Now, Sir Reginald, let me see if you can open that door."

The baronet opened and closed the door without difficulty; and then the other two essayed the attempt with similarly successful results.

"That is all right," commented the professor. "Now step inside, please; and close the door—so: when you want to open it from the inside you simply turn this handle—so, and open it comes."

The quartette now found themselves inside the pilothouse, which proved to be two stories in height. On their right hand they beheld the companion-way leading to the interior of the ship, with a wide flight of stairs of delightfully easy descent, handsomely carpeted, and a magnificent massive handrail and balusters of gleaming aethereum. The square opening to the companion-way was also protected by a similar handrail and balusters, producing an exceedingly rich effect and seeming to promise a corresponding sumptuousness of fitting in the saloons below.

Just clear of the head of the companion staircase and leading up one side of the pilot-house was another light staircase of open grid-work leading to the floor above, which, at a height of seven feet, spanned the building from side to side. This floor was also of light open gridwork, affording easy verbal communication between persons occupying the different stories in the pilot-house. Through this open grid-floor could be seen various apparatus, the objects of which the new-comers were naturally anxious to learn; and to this floor the professor accordingly led his companions up the staircase.

The first object to which he directed attention was a long straight bar of aethereum handsomely moulded into the form of a thick cable, and finished off at the outer end with the semblance of a "Matthew Walker" knot. This bar issued at its inner end from a handsomely panelled and moulded casing which extended down through both floors of the pilot-house, presumably covering in and protecting the mechanism with which the bar was obviously connected.

"This," said the professor, laying his hand on the bar, "is the steering apparatus—the tiller as you call it—of the ship. It moves, as you see, in all directions, and communicates a corresponding movement to the propeller— as you may see, if you will take the trouble to look out through one of those windows."

The trio immediately did so, and saw, as the professor had stated, that with every movement of the tiller, right or left, up or down, the propeller inclined itself at a corresponding angle. A handsome binnacle compass stood immediately in front of the tiller, but the professor did not call attention to it, rightly assuming that his companions were fully acquainted with its use and purpose.

On the professor's right, as he stood at the tiller, was an upright lever working in a quadrant, and communicating, like the tiller—and indeed all the other apparatus—with the interior of the ship.

"This," said the professor, directing attention to the lever, "is the lever which controls the valves of the main engines. I have fashioned and arranged it exactly like the corresponding lever in a locomotive. Placed vertically, thus, the engines remain motionless. Thrown forward, thus, the engines will turn ahead. And thrown backward, thus, they will turn astern. That is simple enough. And so is this," directing attention to a dial on his left hand which stood facing him. The dial had a single hand which was obviously intended to travel over a carefully graduated arc of ninety degrees painted on the dial-face, and which, in addition to the graduations, was marked in the proper positions with the words "Stop;" "Quarter speed;" "Half speed;" "Full speed;" and also with two arrows pointing in opposite directions marked "On" and "Off" respectively. Just beneath the dial was a small wheel with a crank-handle projecting from one of its spokes, and on this crank-handle the professor now laid his hand.

"This," he said, "regulates the valve which admits vapour into the engine; and the dial-hand shows the extent to which the valve is opened. Turn the wheel in the direction of the arrow marked 'On'—thus, and you admit vapour into the engine. You will observe that, as I turn the wheel, the hand on the dial travels over the arc and indicates the extent to which the valve is open. There; now it is fully open, and the cylinders are full of vapour." Then he quickly reversed the wheel and sent the index hand back to "Stop," keeping a wary eye on his companions as he did so.

"These are dangerous things to meddle with," he remarked apologetically. "The engines are of one hundred thousand horse-power; and, full as the ship now is of air at the atmospheric pressure, they would drive her irresistibly along the ground and through all obstacles. I must beg that none of you will meddle with the machinery until you are fully acquainted with its tremendous power."

"What is this pendulum-looking affair, professor?" asked the colonel, pointing to a pendulum the point of which hung in a shallow basin-like depression thickly studded with needle-points which the pendulum just cleared by a hair's-breadth.

"That," explained the professor, "is a device for automatically regulating the balance, or 'trim' as you call it, of the ship when she is floating in the air. You will readily understand that when freed of air, and thus deprived of weight, as it were, the most trifling matter will suffice to derange her equilibrium; one of us, walking from side to side, or from one end of the deck to the other, would very seriously incline her from the horizontal, and thus alter the direction of her flight, possibly with disastrous results; so I have devised this little apparatus to prevent all that. This pendulum, as you see, is so delicately poised that it will instantly respond to the slightest deviation from a horizontal position, and, swaying over one of these needle-points, will send an electric current to the air-pump, causing it to promptly inject a sufficient quantity of air into the proper chamber to restore the equilibrium. But, as we may desire occasionally to direct the flight of the ship in an upward or a downward direction, I have so arranged matters that the apparatus shall be thrown out of gear when the tiller is sloped in either direction out of the horizontal; and as we shall not require it when the ship is on or below the surface of the ocean, I have here provided a small knob by pressing which inwards the apparatus can also be thrown out of gear until it is again wanted."

"Excellent!" exclaimed the baronet. "I must again congratulate you, professor, on your truly wonderful forethought. And what is this, pray?"

"That," said the German, "is the controlling lever of the air-pump. When we want to sink into the depths of the ocean, I thrust this lever over — so; and the pump at once begins to pump air into the air-chambers."

"*Out* of them, I suppose you mean," interrupted the baronet.

"*Into* them, I mean," insisted the professor. "You must understand," he continued, noting the baronet's look of astonishment, "that air, like everything else, has *weight*. Feathers are light; but you may pack them so tightly into a receptacle as to make them very weighty; and so is it with air: the more air you force into a receptacle of given size the heavier you make that receptacle; and, provided that both your forcing apparatus and your receptacle are strong enough to endure the tremendous pressure, you may at last force enough air into the receptacle to sink it. And that is precisely what we shall do; we shall force air into our air-chambers until the ship is on the point of sinking, and we shall then close the valves, stop the air-pump, and, opening the sea-cocks of the water-chambers, admit water enough into the ship to send her to the bottom like a stone."

"Well! you astonish me, I freely admit," gasped the baronet. "This is the first time I ever heard of a ship being sunk by filling her with air. And then the cool way in which you talk of our 'sinking to the bottom like a stone!' I undertook this enterprise because I wanted to experience a new sensation; and it appears to me that there are a good many of them in store for me. However, it is all right; go on with your explanations, my dear sir."

"These," said the professor, indicating several levers marked with distinguishing labels ranged all along one side of the pilot-house, "are the levers opening and closing the valves of the air and water chambers, and need no further description. This," he continued, pointing to a small box with a little knob projecting out of the top of it, "is the apparatus for firing our torpedo shells."

The baronet glanced mutely round at his companions, and shrugged his shoulders expressively, as who should say, "What next?"

The colonel and the lieutenant nodded approvingly, however, and the latter said:

"That is capital, professor; we ought to have the means of fighting the ship, if necessary; but I was beginning to fear you had overlooked that matter, having seen no provision for anything of the kind. But where is your torpedo port? you omitted to point that out to us when we were under the ship's bottom."

"There was nothing to show," replied the professor, "and I can explain the matter just as well up here as I could have done when we were down below. The conical point which forms the extreme forward end of the ship is solid and movable. Under ordinary circumstances it remains firmly fixed in position; but when it becomes necessary to fire a torpedo-shell the solid point is made to slide in along a grooved tube for a certain distance; the shell is then placed in the tube and fired, when the solid point follows it out and becomes again securely fixed in its former position. In addition to this arrangement, I have two large guns which can be worked through ports in the dining-saloon, and six wonderful magazine rifles invented by a Mr Maxim, a friend of mine. They are perhaps the most wonderful pieces of mechanism in the ship, for when the first shot has been fired they will go on firing themselves at the marvellous rate of six hundred shots per minute so long as you keep them supplied with cartridges. Then I have also provided an ample supply of ordinary guns and rifles, swords, pikes, pistols, and in fact everything we are likely to require for the purposes of sport or defence. These small knobs afford the means of lighting the electric lamp in the lantern on the top of the pilot-house and those in the bow and stern of the ship. And that is all to which I think I need direct your attention here at present. Now, if you please, we will go down and look at the machinery."

The party accordingly left the pilot-house and directed their steps below by way of the grand staircase. At the bottom of this they found themselves upon a spacious landing magnificently carpeted, and lighted at each end by a circular window in the side of the ship. In front of them as they descended the staircase, and at a distance of about twelve feet from its base, a partition stretched from side to side of the ship, evidently forming one of the saloon bulkheads. Along the face of this a series of Corinthian pilasters, supporting a noble cornice at the junction of wall and ceiling, divided up the partition into a corresponding number of panels, which were enriched with elegant mouldings of fanciful scroll-work and painted in creamy white and gold. In two instances, however, at points which divided the partition into three equal parts, the panels were replaced by handsome massively moulded doors of unpainted aethereum, imparting a very rich and handsome effect. These doors were, however, closed, and the curiosity of the new-comers as to what was to be seen on the other side of them had to remain for a short time ungratified.

Passing round to the back of the grand staircase (in which direction lay the sleeping apartments, bath-rooms, and domestic offices) they found themselves at the head of another staircase much narrower than the former. The one now before them was only about four feet wide, winding cork-screw fashion round the tube which encased the communications between the pilot-house and the engine-room, etcetera, and it was in its turn encased in a cylindrical bulk-head, in which, on their way below, they passed several doors giving access, as the professor explained, to the different decks.

Winding their way downward for a considerable distance they at length reached the foot of the staircase and passed at once through a doorway marked

"Engine Room." The first sensation of those who now visited this apartment for the first time was disappointment. The room, though full of machinery, was small, absurdly so, it seemed to them. So also with the machinery itself. The main engines, consisting of a pair of three-cylinder compound engines, though made throughout of aethereum, and consequently presenting an exceedingly handsome appearance, suggested more the idea of an exquisite model in silver than anything else, the pair occupying very little more space than those of one of the larger Thames river steamers. The impression of diminutiveness and inadequacy of power passed away, however, when the professor informed his companions that the vapour would enter the high-pressure cylinder at the astounding pressure of five thousand pounds to the square inch, and that, though the engines themselves would only make fifty revolutions per minute, the propeller, would be made, by means of speed-multiplying gear, to revolve at the rate of one thousand times per minute in air of ordinary atmospheric pressure.

"But how on earth do you manage to get your vapour up to that tremendous pressure?" asked the colonel.

"Oh!" answered the professor, "that is a mere matter of mixing. According to the proportions in which the crystals and the acid are mingled together, so is the pressure of the vapour."

"And how do you mingle them together?" asked the lieutenant.

"This," said the professor, leading them up to a small boiler-like vessel, "is the generator. The crystals are placed in a hopper at one end, and the acid in that small tank at the other, from whence they are respectively conducted along tubes into a small well in the bottom of the generator, where, their proportions being regulated by the size of the tubes through which they pass, they mingle and generate a vapour having a pressure of five thousand pounds on the square inch. See, there is the gauge, and it is now registering a pressure of five thousand pounds."

"Good Heavens, man!" exclaimed the baronet, starting back; "you don't mean to say that your generator is *now*, at this moment, subjected to that enormous pressure of more than two tons per square inch? Supposing it exploded, what would become of us?"

"We should be consumed in an instant by the fierce heat of the liberated vapour," replied the professor calmly. "But," he continued, "you need have no apprehension of an explosion. When that generator was being made I had a second one constructed at the same time, precisely similar in every respect, and this second one I tested to destruction, with the satisfactory result that it endured without distress a pressure of thirty-five tons per square inch, showed the first signs of weakness when it became subjected to a pressure of thirty-eight tons, and burst at a joint when under a pressure of forty-three tons per square inch. You may therefore feel quite satisfied that the generator is fully equal to a continuous pressure of at least fifteen tons, instead of the trifle over two which it will have to sustain."

The remainder of the machinery possessing no very startling or novel features, it was passed by with merely an admiring glance at its exquisite finish; and the quartette, leaving the engine-room, passed round on the other side of the spiral staircase to a room marked "Diving Room."

Entering this they found themselves in an apartment about twenty feet square, one side of which was wholly occupied by four cupboards labelled respectively "Sir Reginald Elphinstone," "Colonel Lethbridge," "Lieutenant Mildmay," and "Von Schalckenberg."

"This," explained the professor, "is the room wherein we shall equip ourselves for our submarine rambles; and here," opening one of the cupboards, "are the costumes which we shall wear upon such occasions."

The opened cupboard contained an ordinary indiarubber diving-dress, a sort of double knapsack, a number of heterogeneous articles, and, lastly, a suit of armour.

"Why, professor, what, in the name of all that is comical, is the meaning of this? Are we to walk forth among the fishes equipped like the knights of old?" asked the baronet, pointing to the armour.

"I will explain," said the professor. "In an ordinary diving-dress a man can only descend to a depth of something like fifteen fathoms. Instances have certainly occurred where this depth has been exceeded, a Liverpool diver named Hooper having descended as far as thirty-four fathoms, if my information is correct; but this was quite an exceptional circumstance; and, as I have said, fifteen fathoms may be taken as the average depth at which a man can move about and work in comfort. The reason for this limit is that beyond it the pressure of the water on the exposed hands is so great as to drive the blood to the head and bring on a fainting fit, if nothing worse; besides which, the volume of air inside the dress necessary to counteract the outside pressure of the water would be so great as to speedily result in suffocation. Now, if our explorations were limited to a depth of fifteen fathoms only they would hardly be worth the undertaking; so I have devised these suits of armour, in which we may safely explore the profoundest depths of the ocean to which the *Flying Fish* can penetrate. The armour is, as you see, composed of a number of small scales or plates of aethereum, and is so constructed that, whilst it is perfectly flexible, permitting the utmost freedom of movement to the wearer, it is also absolutely water-tight and incompressible, no matter how great the exterior pressure to which it is subjected. The wearer of it will consequently be perfectly protected at all points from the enormous water pressure; and he will be able to breathe in comfort, his air being supplied to him at the normal atmospheric pressure. In equipping himself the diver will first don the india-rubber diving-dress in the usual way. Then he will assume this double-haversack, the larger chamber of which, worn on the back, will contain a supply of air, whilst the smaller of the two, worn on the chest, is charged with a supply of chemicals for the purification of the air after it has been breathed. The two are connected together by a pair of flexible tubes, as you may perceive, and the mere expansion and contraction of the chest, in the act of breathing, sets in motion the simple apparatus which produces the necessary circulation of air between the two chambers. Having secured this haversack in position the diver next dons his body armour, and straps about his waist this belt, with its electric lamp and its dagger. The dagger, as you see, is double-bladed; it has a haft of insulating material, and the blades have connected to them this insulated wire at the point where the blades and the handle unite. You thus have a weapon which, on being plunged into the body of a foe, not only inflicts a severe wound, but also administers an electric shock of such terrible intensity as must result in instant death. The last portion of the armour to be assumed is the helmet, on the top of which is securely fixed an electric lamp, which, with the aid of the one at the belt, will give us, I imagine, as much light as we are likely to need.

"Having donned our armour we pass out of this chamber into the next, which I call the chamber of egress, carefully closing the door behind us."

The professor, suiting the action to the word, ushered his companions into the next chamber, closing the door behind him, and they found themselves in a small room some ten feet square by seven feet in height. This room, in common with the diving-room, was brilliantly lighted by an electric lamp inclosed in a lantern of abnormally thick glass.

"Arrived here," continued the professor, "we are all ready to sally forth upon our submarine explorations; all we have to do therefore is, first to fill the chamber with water by means of this valve, then open the trap-door and step forth upon the bottom of the sea."

As the professor said this he released the fastenings of the door, and it fell down, forming a sort of inclined plane, over which they passed, to find themselves once more on the solid earth, under the ship's bottom, with the starboard bilge-keel rising like a wall of silver before them. They passed along the lane formed by this keel and the cylindrical bottom of the ship, and then stepped back with one accord to take another glance aloft at the huge bulk of the ship as she towered high above them. They now became conscious of the sounds of vigorous hammering and of men's voices in the direction of the river gable of the building shed, and on looking in that direction they saw that the contractor, whom the professor had engaged for the purpose, was already at work with his men removing the boarding which had hitherto concealed the *Flying Fish* from passers-by on the river, thus making a way for the exit of the ship a little later on.

The little party had re-entered the hull by way of the trap-door, and the professor had just made the fastenings once more secure, when, far away aloft from somewhere within the recesses of the ship, they heard the loud, sonorous, sustained note of a gong.

"Ah, that is good!" exclaimed Herr von Schalckenberg, rubbing his hands; "that is the dinner gong; and I am hungry. Come, my friends, to the dining saloon, and let us partake of the first of, I hope, many pleasant meals on board the *Flying Fish*."

Chapter Four
The Novel Beginning of a Singular Voyage

On reaching the head of the spiral staircase the professor paused for a moment to direct the attention of his companions to a long passage which extended apparently along the middle of the ship to the fore-end of the superstructure. The passage was about five feet wide, and the ceiling was of ground glass, through which a flood of light streamed brilliantly down.

"In that direction," said the professor, "are to be found, first, the kitchen, pantry, larder, and store-room; then next to them come my laboratory and workshop, with the armoury and magazine on the opposite side; then the quarters of the cook and the valet; next these again are the bath-rooms and lavatories; and finally, at the extreme end of the passage, there are the state-rooms or sleeping apartments, eight in number—four for ourselves and four spare ones."

George, the valet—whose duties, however, on board the *Flying Fish* were to be rather those of steward and general handy man—stood during the progress of this brief explanation with his hand on the handle of the saloon door; and now, as the professor turned and nodded, he flung the door wide open and stood aside for the baronet and his friends to enter.

They now found themselves in the dining-saloon, an apartment thirty feet square and about ten feet high to the lower edge of the cornice. The walls, of unpainted aethereum, were broken up into panels by fluted pilasters with richly-moulded capitals, each panel having a frosted border covered with delicate tracery, whilst the central portion of the panel was left plain and polished, serving the purpose of a mirror, in which the room and its multiplied reflections on the opposite wall was again reflected in a long perspective. The floor was covered with a rich Turkey carpet, into which one sank ankle deep; the chairs, sofas, the massive sideboard, the wide table, in fact all the furniture in the room, was constructed of aethereum and modelled after the choicest designs, the upholstery being in rich embossed velvet of a delicate light-blue shade. The table glittered with a brilliant array of plate and glass; and the entire apartment was suffused with rich, soft, rainbow-tinted light, streaming down through the magnificent coved skylight of stained glass, which served instead of ceiling to the saloon.

"Superb!"

"Magnificent!"

"Exquisite!"

Such were the exclamations which burst from the professor's companions as they paused to look about them and take in all the details of the splendidly furnished and decorated apartment. A dozen eager questions rushed from their lips; but Herr von Schalckenberg was hungry, and the dinner was served, he therefore contented himself with bowing profoundly and pointing to the dinner-table.

"Come, gentlemen," exclaimed the baronet laughingly, "take your seats, I beg. It is evident that we have quite exhausted both the professor's patience and his strength, and that we shall get no more information out of him until both have been restored by a good dinner."

With which remark Sir Reginald set the example by taking his place at the head of the table, as he was entitled to do in virtue of his ownership of the *Flying Fish*.

The dinner was an admirable one, in all respects quite worthy the exceptional nature of the occasion; and under its genial influence, and that of the choice wines which accompanied it, the conversation soon grew extremely animated. The topic was, of course, the aerial ship and the novel and interesting character of her various equipments. The professor speedily redeemed his afternoon's promise to the baronet, and at length succeeded in completely convincing that hitherto sceptical individual that, so far from the enormous proportions of the *Flying Fish* being detrimental to her, they constituted the principal basis upon which he was justified in his anticipations of her success as an *aerial* ship.

Having at length made this perfectly plain, he was next called upon by Lieutenant Mildmay to explain a certain peculiarity in the binnacle compass, which had attracted that gentleman's notice and excited his curiosity.

"I observed," he said, "that the compass-card bore round its outer rim, at every quarter point, a small upright needle. As everything on board here, however apparently insignificant, seems to have its own especial purpose, I should like to know the purpose which those small needles are designed to serve."

"Ha, ha, my friend! so you noticed them, did you? I quite expected that, as a seaman, you very soon would," said the professor. "Well, I will tell you what they are. They form part of a little device of mine to render the ship self-steering, or, more correctly, to make the compass itself steer her in any given direction. Having noticed those needles, you doubtless also noticed that across the 'lubber's mark' there was a small slit some six inches long in the side of the compass-box?"

The lieutenant nodded.

"Good!" ejaculated the professor. "Had you looked outside the box you would also have observed two long slender arms pivoted close together, their outer and longer extremities being united, and carrying a small needle which travels, point downwards, along the arc of a circle. Now the action of the instrument is this. Supposing that you wish the ship to travel along, say, a southerly course, you manipulate the helm in the usual manner until the south point of the compass-card swings round to the lubber's mark. The moment that these two accurately coincide you pull toward you a small lever within easy reach of your hand, and the two arms glide in through the slit in the side of the compass-box, passing one on each side of the needle on the edge of the card, and your apparatus is then connected up ready for action. Now, so long as the ship's bows remain pointed accurately to the south, the south point on the compass-card continues coincident with the lubber's mark, and nothing happens. But should the ship deviate ever so slightly from her   proper course the heavy, yet sensitive, compass needle at once swings round in sympathy; the small needle on the edge of the card moves the two slender arms which embrace it; the downward-pointing needle at the further extremity of these arms travels along the arc; and electric communication is at once established with the steering machinery, which promptly acts in such a way as to bring back the ship to her original course."

AT DESSERT BEFORE THE START.

"Capital! Admirable!" ejaculated Sir Reginald and the lieutenant together, the former continuing:

"Upon my word, professor, you are a veritable wizard—a magician with powers exceeding those of the most potent of your brethren referred to in the 'Arabian Nights.'"

The professor made a laughing disclaimer. "No, no, my dear sir," said he, "I am no magician, but only a poor scientist. Nevertheless, the wonders of science far exceed those of the 'Arabian Nights,' and will well repay the man who cares to patiently study them."

Enlivened by conversation of a character so interesting to all present, the sitting was prolonged to quite an inordinate length, and though no one, except perhaps the professor, noted the fact, it was past midnight when the adventurous quartette rose from the table, and taking their wine and cigars with them, moved into the music-room, at the same time dismissing the patient George for the night.

The music-room was a much larger apartment than the dining saloon, being, like the latter, the full width of the superstructure, and measuring forty feet between the fore and the after bulkheads. It was the next room abaft the dining saloon, and was even more elaborately furnished and decorated than the latter. The walls, divided up in the same manner as those of the other apartment, were adorned with choice pictures, and exquisite statues of frosted aethereum were grouped on pedestals at frequent intervals all round the room. A coved and panelled ceiling of decorated aethereum sprang from the upper edge of the richly moulded cornice; and a skylight of magnificent stained glass, somewhat similar to that of the dining saloon, surmounted the whole. A grand piano and a noble chamber organ, both in superbly modelled aethereum cases, occupied opposite sides of the apartment; a very handsome clock, with a set of silvery chimes for the quarters and a deep rich-toned gong for the hours, occupied a conspicuous position on a wall bracket; chairs, couches, and divans of seductive shape and ample capacity were dotted here and there about the rich carpet; and a handsome table occupied the centre of the room, supporting and reflecting in the silvery depths of its undraped top a noble épergne of choice hot-house flowers.

"Why, how is this?" exclaimed the colonel as he sank into the luxurious depths of a most inviting arm-chair; "my watch must be all wrong, and your clock there is also wrong, professor; they both assert that it is half-past twelve o'clock, yet the sun has not yet set," pointing aloft to the skylight, through which a brilliant flood of sunshine was streaming down into the magnificent apartment.

"The sun has not yet set? Then we will soon make it do so," laughingly remarked the professor, rising from his seat and approaching one of the walls of the apartment, whilst the baronet and the lieutenant stared in dismay at their own watch-faces. The German began to manipulate a couple of tiny knobs which occupied unobtrusive positions in the base of one of the pilasters, and the sunlight gradually deepened into a rich orange hue, then changed to a soft pearly grey, which gradually deepened into a dim delicious twilight in which little was visible save the pictured glass in the skylight above; then it gradually brightened again, and presently a flood of glorious silvery moonlight streamed down through the skylight and suffused the room. Finally, with an instantaneous change, the brilliant sunlight was again restored. "Another wonder!" exclaimed Sir Reginald. "How do you manage it, professor?"

"Oh! that is a very simple matter," was the reply; "it is merely a cunning arrangement of variously tinted glass shades interposed between the electric light above the centre of the skylight and the mirrors which reflect the light down through the stained glass into the room. As you probably noticed when on the deck, there are no actual skylights in the usual acceptation of the term; ours are only make-believes; but they struck me as affording an agreeable means of lighting the saloons, so I introduced them."

In further conversation, diversified by music, the time slipped rapidly away; and at length the clock on the bracket proclaimed that it was two hours after midnight.

As the sonorous strokes of the gong announced the fact, the professor rose to his feet, and in a voice tremulous with sudden nervous excitement, said:

"Gentlemen, the hour for our departure, the hour which is to witness the success or failure of our grand experiment, has arrived. The river and the streets of the great city are by this time nearly or quite deserted; and we may therefore hope that our movements will attract little or no notice. Are you ready?"

"Ready!" ejaculated the baronet; "of course we are, my dear sir. Is not this the moment to which we have all been anxiously looking forward for more than two years? Proceed, professor, we will follow you; and whatever orders you may give us shall be obeyed to the letter."

"Come, then," said the professor; and he led the way through the dining saloon and up the grand staircase to the lower compartment of the pilot house, and thence out on deck.

To their eyes, fresh from the brilliantly lighted saloons, the night appeared intensely dark; but in a minute or two, becoming accustomed to the gloom, they were able to perceive that the ladder had been taken away from the ship's side, and also that the contractor had completed his task of removing the planking at the river end of the shed, thus clearing a way for the exit of the great ship. They walked to the after extremity of the deck, and from that point were not only able, in the breathless stillness then prevailing, to distinctly hear the gurgle and rush of the river, but also to dimly make out the shining, swirling surface of the water as the flood-tide swept past them.

"The air is absolutely motionless," said the professor. "No more favourable moment could possibly have been chosen for the difficult task of moving the *Flying Fish* out of her present cramped quarters, and we will at once avail ourselves of it. Lieutenant, I will ask you to return here presently on the 'look-out,' as you sailors term it. Your duty will be to see that when we move out of the shed we do not come into collision with anything. Perhaps you, colonel, will kindly go to the other end the deck, also on the 'look-out;' and, as for you, Sir Reginald, I must ask you to stand on the deck just outside the pilothouse, to see that the electric lamp on the top of it does not come into collision with the roof-timbers, and so drag the roof off the shed. But as it is necessary that you should all become acquainted with the working of the ship, you had better be with me in the pilot-house until we are actually ready to move."

"Now," continued the professor when the quartette had made their way to the upper floor of the pilot-house, which was moderately illuminated by an electric lamp of small power, "the first thing to be done is to place the tiller of the ship in a horizontal position, and thus bring into action the automatic balancing gear. So! It is done. The next thing is to expel the air from the entire hull of the ship, excepting, of course, the comparatively insignificant portion reserved for habitation, and this I do by injecting vapour into the several compartments. The vapour drives out the air, and then, condensing like steam, creates, if required, a perfect vacuum. This large wheel controls the valve which we now want to open. I turn it this way, so—and now we shall see what will happen."

Two large dials were attached to the side of the pilothouse, close together; and upon these the professor now intently fixed his gaze. The index-hands of both were seen to be moving. A period of perhaps half a minute elapsed, and then the professor, suddenly shutting off the vapour, went over and closely inspected both dials.

"Good!" he exclaimed, after a single keen glance at each of them. "Gentlemen, let us congratulate each other. Our experiment is a *Signal Success !*"

"How do you know that, professor? How can you tell?" eagerly asked his companions.

"Look at these two dials; they will tell you," replied the professor. "This dial," tapping one with his finger, "indicates the weight of the ship, or the pressure with which she bears upon the ground. This one," indicating the other, "shows the pressure of air inside the hull of the ship. The first, as you see, shows that the ship is now pressing upon the ground with a force of less than a single ton—in other words, she now weighs less than one ton. The air-gauge shows that there is still an air pressure of six pounds per square inch inside the hull, and we therefore have, as I expected we should, a large margin of buoyancy. Now, lieutenant, do me the favour to turn on the vapour once more, very cautiously. Steady! *Stop!* There, Sir Reginald, the index has reached zero, and your ship is now as nearly as possible without weight; and if a man were now underneath her, he might, notwithstanding her gigantic proportions, easily raise her upon his shoulders. Now comes the delicate part of our operation. To your stations on the deck quickly, gentlemen, if you please."

The professor's companions, just a trifle excited, perhaps, hurried away to their posts, and the scientist was left alone. The circular windows in the sides of the pilothouse were all left open, and in through them presently floated the voice of the lieutenant shouting:

"All ready abaft, professor."

"All ready at this end," replied the colonel.

The professor reversed the engines, turned on the vapour *very* cautiously indeed, and simultaneously, with the engines below only just barely moving, the huge propeller began to whirl round at a speed of some sixty revolutions a minute.

A breathless pause of perhaps two seconds followed, and then the professor, his forehead damp with nervous perspiration, heard:

"Hurrah! She's away!" from the lieutenant.

"She moves; she moves!" from the colonel.

And, "By Jove, she is actually moving!" from the baronet.

Slowly but surely the *Flying Fish* backed out of the building-shed, until nearly half her immense length projected beyond the walls. Then the voice of the baronet was heard exclaiming:

"Ho! stop her! The electric lamp will not clear the roof, I am afraid. Can you give us a little light on the subject, professor?"

By way of reply the professor pressed a knob, and the lamp itself flashed its dazzling light upon the scene, when it became apparent that the ship had gradually risen from the ground, bringing the top of her lamp just above the level of the last tie-rod of the roof.

"Can you drop her a little? Six inches will do it," said the baronet.

The professor opened the air-valve and the ship at once began to settle down.

"So! That will do; all clear. You may go astern again now as fast as you please," said the baronet.

Once more the great propeller began to revolve, and presently the baronet, from his position under the foremost end of the pilot-house, remarked:

"Now she is all clear, professor; the whole of the pilothouse is outside the shed. A bold dash astern now and we shall be clear fore and aft in another moment."

The professor extinguished the electric lamp; gave the wheel connected with the vapour-valve another turn; the engines increased their speed; and the great ship at once shot rapidly out over the stream and clear of everything. Then the professor stopped the engines, turned a thin stream of vapour into the air chambers, and the huge fabric began to slowly rise perpendicularly in the air. Herr von Schalckenberg waited until he saw that they were fairly above the level of the roofs on both sides of the river; then he left the pilot-house and, joining the baronet on the deck outside, said, in a voice of undisguised exultation:

"Well, Sir Reginald, what think you *now* of the *Flying Fish?*"

"I think her, professor, a wonderful creation of a still more wonderful man. I see that we are steadily rising in the air, as you assured us would be the case, but I cannot yet fully realise the fact; I feel like a man in a dream; you must give me time to become familiar with this new marvel—this new triumph of science. But there can no longer be any doubt as to the success of your labours; and I accordingly offer you my most hearty thanks and congratulations."

The colonel and the lieutenant also hastened to offer theirs, and then the whole party sauntered to the side, and, leaning upon the guard-rail which took the place of bulwarks, stood gazing upon the scene below. Not that there was very much to see; the sky was obscured by a thin almost motionless canopy of cloud, and the moon, in her last quarter, had not yet risen; the darkness was therefore profound. At the same time it was novel and interesting to watch how, as the huge ship rose steadily higher in the air, the long lines of lighted gas-lamps in street after street became visible, until gradually the whole of the great city lay spread out below them like a map, with the thoroughfares indicated by faint twinkling lines of fire. And, as they continued to rise, the various disjointed sounds which, even at that early hour, pervaded the city, began to reach their ears: the rumbling of a wagon or the rattle of a cab over the stone-paved streets, the barking of a dog, the crow of some unnaturally wakeful rooster, the clank of shunting trucks at one or another of the many goods stations dotted here and there all over the metropolis, the distant whistle and rattle of a train speeding along in the open country beyond; all floated up to them with almost startling distinctness at first, then fainter and fainter, until at length they died completely away as the *Flying Fish* gradually attained a higher altitude. Then they entered the bank of cloud which overspread the city, and the air, which had hitherto been warm, became suddenly chill and damp.

"Now, my friends," said the professor, "there will be little or nothing more to see until we again descend; I therefore propose that we return to the pilot-house, shut ourselves in, and at once test the soaring powers of the ship by rising to the highest attainable altitude."

"Agreed!" said the baronet. "But why shut ourselves in?"

"Because," answered the professor, "it will not only grow rapidly colder as we rise, but, if we remain outside, we shall also find it increasingly difficult to breathe as we reach the more rarefied air; whereas, by remaining inside, we shall be sheltered from the cold and shall be able to breathe the denser air which we shall take up with us."

They accordingly entered the pilot-house, shutting the door after them, and closing all the windows; then the professor turned a full jet of vapour into the air-chambers for a moment, producing a perfect vacuum therein, and the ship at once began to mount into the ether with greatly accelerated speed, as they could easily see by watching the barometer, the bulb of which, completely protected, was situate outside the walls of the pilot-house.

It was no very easy matter for cold to penetrate through the thin yet obdurate walls of the pilot-house; but by the time that the barometer had fallen to fifteen inches the voyagers experienced a distinct sensation of chilliness, whilst the windows of the pilot-house were thickly coated with a delicate frost tracery. Still the barometer continued to fall steadily, though not so rapidly as at first, indicating that the ship was still soaring upward; and with every inch fall of the mercury the professor became an increasingly interesting study of mingled delight and anxiety. At length the mercury, still falling, registered a height of eleven inches only, and the professor gave vent to a great sigh of relief. And when it further dropped to ten inches he could no longer contain himself.

"Gentlemen," he exclaimed, "rejoice with me. The conquest of the mountains is ours. We are now as nearly as possible on a level with the topmost peak of Everest, the most lofty projection on the earth's surface; and in due time I hope we shall have the unique felicity of planting our feet on that as yet untrodden spot, and of leaving a record to that effect behind us."

At length the mercury fell to a little below eight inches, and there it stopped; the limit of the *Flying Fish's* buoyancy was reached.

The professor stood intently regarding the barometer tube for some time; then he turned and said to his companions:

"Gentlemen, behold the indisputably lowest reading of the barometer which man has ever witnessed, and which indicates that we are at this moment farther from our mother earth than mortal has ever journeyed before. Humboldt and Bonpland ascended Chimborazo to a height of eighteen thousand five hundred and seventy-six feet. Gay-Lussac rose in his balloon to the much higher elevation of twenty-three thousand feet, only to be eclipsed by your own countryman, Green, who soared to the astounding height of twenty-seven thousand six hundred feet. But it was left for *us*, my friends, to achieve the crowning feat of aeronautical science, by attaining to the extraordinary altitude of thirty-four thousand six hundred feet, or more than six and a half miles of perpendicular elevation above the sea-level. *Now*, Sir Reginald, what think you of your latest acquisition, the *Flying Fish*?"

"I think her by far the most wonderful creation of which I have ever heard or read, and," (with a bow to the professor) "every way worthy of the truly remarkable man to whom she owes her existence. If her power to penetrate the hitherto unexplored depths of the ocean is at all commensurate with her ability to reach the higher regions of the air, I foresee that our voyage is likely to be fruitful in startling incident and in the discovery of many hitherto unsuspected secrets of nature. Now, what do you propose that we shall next do, professor?"

"I propose," said von Schalckenberg, "that, having tested the *Flying Fish's* capabilities of merely rising into the air, we should now ascertain what she can do in the way of *navigating* the atmosphere; after which we will try her powers as a submarine ship. The lowest depression in the English Channel is to be found in a submarine valley called the 'Hurd

Deep;' it is situate about six miles north of the 'Casquets,' and lies ninety-four fathoms (or five hundred and sixty-four feet) below the surface of the water. I propose (subject to your approval) to make for this spot and there sink to the bottom, taking advantage of our presence there to make a first trial of our diving armour. Does this meet with your approval?"

The baronet and his companions thought it a very capital idea, and the professor took immediate steps for carrying it out. Opening a case he produced therefrom a chart of the English Channel, and, directing his companions' attention to the spot which he proposed to visit, requested Lieutenant Mildmay to lay off the course and measure the distance in a straight line. The latter was found to be about one hundred and fifty miles.

"Which distance," remarked the professor, "I expect we shall accomplish, in the present calm state of the atmosphere, in about an hour and a quarter. This high rate of speed will necessitate our remaining in the pilothouse; but it will, perhaps, be worth while to put up with that temporary inconvenience on the present occasion, since we have so exceptionally favourable an opportunity of testing the actual speed of the ship through the air. If, however, you prefer to be on deck in the open air, we can of course moderate our speed sufficiently to render such a mode of travelling pleasant."

It was unanimously decided, however, to remain inside and give the speed of the ship a fair trial. The professor accordingly turned the vapour into the engines, slowly at first, but in gradually increasing volume, until they were revolving at full speed, and the ship's head was pointed in the proper direction, the automatic steering gear being at the same time thrown into action to test its capabilities. This done the professor opened the main air-valve, gradually admitting a certain quantity of air into the ship's interior, and she at once began to drop once more earthward.

"We will descend to within about a thousand feet of the sea level," said the professor. "This will restore us to a more genial temperature, will give the propeller a denser atmosphere in which to work, and will also enable us to see somewhat of the country over which we are flying; whilst our elevation will be ample to take us clear of everything. Leith Hill, nine hundred and sixty-seven feet in height, is the greatest elevation at all near our path; but we shall pass some three miles or so to the westward of it, if the air remains calm; and Saint Catherine's Point, over which we shall pass, is only seven hundred and seventy-five feet high. So that we have nothing to fear."

In a few minutes the *Flying Fish* had dropped to within the proposed distance of the earth; and, on clearing the windows of the accumulated frost, it was discovered that the moon (then in her third quarter) had risen and was suffusing the earth with her feeble ghostly light, which, slight as it was, enabled the voyagers to perceive that they were skimming through the air at a tremendous speed. The engines, though working at their full power, were perfectly noiseless; and the propeller, though revolving at a rate of fully one thousand revolutions per minute, caused not the slightest perceptible vibration in the hull of the ship. A loud humming sound, however, proceeded from it, audible even above the rush of the air against the sides of the pilot-house.

Leith Hill was soon passed, the waters of the Channel—distinguished in the faint light only by a thin tremulous line of glimmering silver under the crescent moon—were sighted, and, almost before they had time to realise the fact, they had skimmed over the anchorage at Spithead, across the Isle of Wight, and were floating above the waters of the Channel. By this time the eastern sky had begun to pale perceptibly before the coming dawn; the lights of Saint Catherine behind them and the Casquets ahead gleamed with steadily diminishing power in the gathering daylight; the half-dozen or so of ships and steamers in sight, one after the other extinguished their signal lamps; and, just as they reached their destination and settled lightly as a snow-flake upon the glassy surface of the water, up rose the glorious sun, flashing his brilliant beams over land and sea, and awakening all nature into light and life once more.

As the *Flying Fish* alighted on the surface of the water, the professor pulled out his watch and remarked, with evident satisfaction:

"One hundred and fifty miles in just one hour and a quarter! That is good travelling, and proves the speed of our ship to be exactly what I estimated it would be. We will now set the force-pump to work; and I hope, that by the time we are ready to descend, that brilliant sun will have enshrouded our movements in a concealing mist. We are surrounded by fishing-boats, as you see, and I have no doubt that we have also been observed by the light-keepers on the Casquets. It will never do to disappear before so many curious eyes; they would be filled with horror at the supposed catastrophe. In the meantime we may as well go out on deck to enjoy the fresh morning air. As for me, I propose to indulge in the luxury of a swim."

The main engines had, in the meantime, been stopped, and the force-pump put slowly in motion, so that the submersion of the hull might be sufficiently gradual to escape notice.

Five minutes later the professor and his three companions were gambolling round the ship like so many porpoises—or dolphins, if they would prefer the latter metaphor—enjoying to the full the invigorating luxury of their bath in the cool, pure sea-water.

By the time that they were on board again and dressed, the intelligent George had arranged for them on deck a nice little light breakfast of chocolate, biscuits, and fruit, for which their swim had given them an unbounded relish. The meal was partaken of at leisure, and followed by a cigar, over which they dawdled so long that the *Flying Fish* was submerged to the deck before the last stump had been reluctantly thrown away. The mist which the professor had prognosticated having, meanwhile, gathered sufficiently to cloak their movements, a cast of the lead was taken and the ship was found to be in ninety fathoms of water. The professor, for reasons of his own, deemed this sufficiently near the deepest point to justify an immediate descent. They accordingly entered the pilot-house forthwith, closing the door securely after them—the air-pump was stopped, the sea-cock communicating with the water-chambers was opened, and the *Flying Fish*, with an easy imperceptible motion, sank gently beneath the placid waters, to rest, a minute or two later, on a bed of gravel at the bottom of the Channel.

"Now," said the professor, looking at his watch when the ship had fairly settled into her strange berth, and had been securely anchored there, "it is just eight o'clock. We are all somewhat fatigued, and our bath and breakfast have prepared us nicely to enjoy a few hours' repose. I therefore propose, gentlemen, that we retire to our sleeping apartments until two o'clock p.m. George shall call us at that hour and have a bit of luncheon ready for us, after which we shall have ample time to test our diving apparatus before dinner."

This proposal met with a very cordial reception, and was duly carried out, with the result that, half an hour later, the four adventurous voyagers were sleeping as calmly in their novel resting-place as though they had been accustomed from their earliest infancy to take their repose at the bottom of the sea.

Chapter Five
A Submarine Excursion

At the appointed hour the imperturbable George, who never could be betrayed into the slightest exhibition of astonishment at finding himself in any extraordinary situation which he might happen to be sharing with his somewhat eccentric master, duly aroused the four sleepers, and when they were ready, laid luncheon before them with the same indomitable *sangfroid* which he would have exhibited had the transaction been conducted on *terra firma*.

The meal over, the professor led the way below to the diving chamber, where the adventurous four carefully donned their diving dresses, inclusive of the armour which Sir Reginald felt so strongly disposed to ridicule. As this was the first occasion of inducting themselves into their novel costume, they were rather a long time about it; but when once they were fairly encased, they were fain to admit that, strange as might be their appearance, they felt exceedingly comfortable. The professor was the last to assume the dress, having busied himself in the first instance in assisting the others; but at length all was ready, and they filed into the exit chamber, carefully closing the door behind them. This chamber was illuminated by an electric lamp, the light of which clearly revealed the whereabouts of the sea-cock, and of the fastenings to the trap-door, all of which the professor pointed out to his companions, at the same time explaining the method of working them. The sea-cock was then opened, and the chamber began to slowly fill with water.

"Now," explained the professor, "please listen to me. If now, or at any future time, either of you should experience the slightest sensation of discomfort as the water rises round you, all you have to do is simply to open this air-cock, which communicates with the air-chambers, and the condensed air will at once rush in and expel the water again; then close the sea and air cocks; open this relief valve, which will allow the condensed air to disperse itself in the habitable portions of the hull, and you can at once open the door of communication to the diving chamber, and disencumber yourself of your dress, remembering always to close the door behind you. Now, do either of you feel at all uncomfortable?"

The exit chamber was by this time full of water, and its occupants were, therefore, completely submerged, and subject to the same pressure of water as they would be outside, but the armour proved fully equal to its work in every respect, and its wearers were able to move with just as much freedom and ease as if they had been on dry land. They accordingly replied to the professor's inquiry with a brisk negative.

"And can you hear distinctly what I say?" continued the professor.

They replied that they could hear every word perfectly, only realising when the question was asked that they were completely sheathed in metal from head to foot, and that, consequently, the fact of their being able to hear at all was somewhat singular.

"That is all right," exclaimed the professor. "I thought it would be convenient if we could communicate freely with each other under water, so I introduced a couple of small microphones into each helmet, hoping they would answer the purpose. Mine are simply perfect, but I was anxious to know if yours were also. Now, if you are quite ready I will open the door."

The next moment the trap-door fell open, and a great black aperture yawned before them.

"Light both your lamps," exclaimed the professor, "and pick your footsteps. Remember, you are about to tread on strange ground."

The professor led the way, his armour-clad figure looming up black and gigantic against the two overlapping discs of illuminated water before him, and the other three followed closely in his footsteps. On emerging from the trap-door they turned sharp to the left, and made their way toward the bow along the tunnel-like passage between the ship's bottom and the starboard bilge keel. This was soon traversed, and they then found themselves on a tolerably firm, level, gravelly bottom. Emerging from underneath the ship's bottom, they now extinguished their lamps for a moment by way of experiment, and found that so clear was the water that even at the great depth of ninety fathoms it was not absolutely dark, a sombre greenish blue twilight prevailing in which the hull of the ship towered above them vast and shadowy, yet with tolerable distinctness. This twilight, however, was strongly illuminated at both ends of the ship by the powerful electric lamps at the bow and stern, all of which the professor had taken the precaution to light before descending to the diving chamber.

"Those are our beacons," said the professor, pointing to these lamps, "and we must be exceedingly careful not to stray beyond the reach of their rays, otherwise we might experience great difficulty in finding our way back to the ship. Are you all pretty comfortable in this great depth of water?

We are now five hundred and forty feet beneath the surface of the sea, or three hundred and thirty-six feet deeper than man has ever reached before. Why, if we were to accomplish nothing more than this, we have already achieved a great triumph! Now, let us make our way toward the deepest spot in this submarine valley; I have an idea that we shall see something curious when we reach it. This way, gentlemen; our course is about due west, and we cannot well lose our way if we descend the slope which seems to commence yonder."

The little party pressed forward, experiencing no inconvenience or difficulty whatever, save that of making their way through water of such a density as that which enveloped them, and soon reached the edge of a rather steep declivity, evidently leading down to the lowest part of the depression. Before venturing down this declivity they paused to glance backward, and saw that, though the ship herself had become invisible in the sombre twilight, all the electric lights were distinctly visible, the very powerful one on the top of the pilot-house especially gleaming like the illuminated lantern of a lighthouse. So far, therefore, all was well; they were still within range of the lights, and they at once turned and plunged fearlessly into the depression. They had not far to go, the sides of the depression being steep, and in about two minutes they found themselves at the bottom, and standing before an immense confused heap of wreckage of almost every imaginable description. Shattered stumps of spars, waterlogged and weighed down with a thick incrustation of barnacles, the accumulated growth of years of immersion; part of the hull of a ship, so overgrown with "sea grass" as to be distinguishable as such only from the fact that the channels and channel irons with their dead-eyes, and even the frayed ends of the shroud lanyards still remained attached; a twisted and tangled-up mass of iron rods which looked as though it might at some distant period have been the paddle-wheel of a steamer, and near it the evident remains of a boiler and some machinery; the beam of a trawl-net, and bales, boxes, packing-cases, barrels, and, in short, every conceivable description of covering in which ships' cargoes are usually stowed were mixed up in inextricable confusion with heaps of coal, large stones, and other anomalous substances.

"Just as I anticipated," exclaimed the professor, pointing to the heap and addressing his companions. "And this, I expect, is the sort of thing which we shall see in every depression of the ocean's bed which we may visit. All these matters have been swept hither and thither over the ground by the action of the tidal and other currents, until they have happened to drift over this spot, and here they have finally settled owing to the inability of the currents to move them up the steep sides of the depression. Let us walk round the heap; we may see something of interest before we have completed the circuit."

And so they did, though the interest was hardly the kind of which the professor had been thinking when he spoke. For, whilst standing on the opposite side of the heap, contemplating the remains of an ancient and grass-grown wreck, they were startled by the appearance of a sharp snake-like head with a pair of fierce gleaming eyes which was suddenly protruded from a gap in the ship's side, and in another moment the creature—a conger-eel of truly gigantic proportions—emerged from its hiding-place, and, possibly attracted by the brilliancy of the electric lights which the party carried, swam boldly toward them.

"What a horrible monster!" ejaculated the colonel, at the same moment that Lieutenant Mildmay, struck with the savage look of the creature, exclaimed:

"Why, I believe the brute means to attack us!"

"And, by Jove, here come some more of them!" exclaimed the baronet, pointing to the hole from which the creature had emerged.

"Draw your daggers, gentlemen!" shouted the professor. "And be not dismayed; they and our armour are quite sufficient for our protection."

It was perhaps just as well that the professor had sufficient presence of mind at that moment to say what he did; for his companions, though their courage had been proved a thousand times before, were now in a new and strange element to which they had scarcely had time to accustom themselves; and, moreover, the aspect of the fierce fish as they rushed forward with open jaws, disclosing their formidable teeth, was sufficiently weird and uncanny to at least momentarily dismay the stoutest heart.

Lieutenant Mildmay's anticipation as to the intentions of the fish proved quite correct. On they came, some thirty or forty in number; and before the attacked could quite recover from their confusion they found themselves fairly in the clutches of the snake-like creatures. The attack was made with the utmost determination and ferocity, the eels twining themselves so powerfully about the bodies of their foes that it was almost impossible for the latter to move hand or foot; whilst the sharp teeth rasped strongly but ineffectually against the scales of the aethereum armour. The fight, however, though fiercely waged on the part of the assailants, was soon over, a single stroke of the keen double-edged dagger—as soon as the assailed could get their hands free—proving sufficient to instantly destroy the individual fish upon which it happened to fall. But so fierce were the eels that the conflict ended only with the slaughter of the last of them. The fish were of truly enormous size, two or three specimens measuring, as nearly as could be estimated, fully eighteen feet in length, whilst none were less than ten feet long. The tour of exploration was then completed without further adventure; the powerful electric lights of the ship enabled them to find her without difficulty the moment that they climbed up out of the depression; and they made good their return with no worse result than that of excessive fatigue due to their unwonted efforts in forcing their way through so dense a medium as water of ninety fathoms depth.

So novel an experience as theirs had that day been naturally furnished the chief topic of conversation at the dinner-table; the professor especially entertaining his companions with many interesting anecdotes of strange adventures which had happened to, and curious sights witnessed by divers at various times and places. At length, during a lull in the conversation, he said:

"There still remain two trials to which the *Flying Fish* must be subjected before we can say that we are fully acquainted with her powers, namely, a trial of her speed through the water when fully submerged; and a trial of her behaviour as an ordinary ocean-going ship. And these trials, I think, should—if you approve, Sir Reginald—be carried out before we do anything else."

The baronet gave his willing assent to the professor's proposal; and it was finally arranged that the trials, or, at all events, one of them, should take place on the morrow.

It having been arranged that early rising should be the order of the day throughout the voyage, they were aroused at seven o'clock on the following morning, and sat down to breakfast at eight prompt. By nine o'clock the meal was over, and the party, pipe or cigar in mouth, mustered in the pilot-house. Here the first thing the professor did was to produce a chart, to which, on spreading it open on the table, he called Lieutenant Mildmay's attention, saying:

"Being a seaman by profession, you are undoubtedly the most skilful navigator of the party; and I therefore propose—with Sir Reginald's full approval, which I have already obtained—to confide the navigation of the *Flying Fish* to you. Now this,"—making a pencil mark on the chart—"is our present position; and this,"—pointing to another pencil mark off Cape Finisterre, which presented the appearance of having been very carefully laid down—"is the point to which I wish you to navigate us in the first instance."

"Very good," said Mildmay. "I undertake the charge with pleasure. Only I must stipulate, that when making long passages you will rise to the surface occasionally, in order that I may be enabled to take the observations necessary to verify our position."

"Of course, of course," answered the professor. "Now, are we all ready to start?"

An answer in the affirmative was given; and von Schalckenberg thereupon moved the lever which actuated the simple machinery controlling the four anchors in the bilge keels. The ship being thus released from the ground, he next opened the cocks connecting the air and water chambers; a stream of compressed air at once rushed into the latter, forcing out a certain quantity of water, and the ship began to rise.

"We will so adjust our position that the top of the lantern surmounting the pilot-house shall be submerged to a depth of six fathoms; at which depth we shall not only be enabled to pass clear of all ships, but shall also, if the water be clear, be enabled to see pretty well what is before and above us," said the professor, fixing his eyes upon a gauge before him. "There," he continued, closing the air-cocks as the index pointed to six fathoms, "now we shall do very well. Are you ready to set the course, Mildmay?"

"A run of six hundred and fifty miles, upon a west-south-west course, will take us to about the spot you have indicated," answered Mildmay.

"Which is a trifle less than five and a half hours' run, if our speed under water is equal to what it was through the air. But I anticipate that we shall do better than that; the resistance of water is considerably greater than that of air to the vessel's passage through it, I admit; but I anticipate that this will be more than counterbalanced by the greater power of the propeller in the denser fluid. We shall soon see."

So saying, the professor set the engines in motion, and the *Flying Fish* began to glide smoothly yet soon with marvellous rapidity through the water.

"My surmise was correct, you see," said the professor some ten minutes afterwards, as he pointed to another gauge on the wall of the pilot-house. "We are now running steadily at a speed of one hundred and fifty miles per hour; and we have already travelled twelve miles from our starting-point. The gauge is, as you see, self-registering, and shows on that piece of paper the exact distance run through or along the surface of the water (but not through the *air*) between any two given points. When the ship's course is altered, or you desire for any other reason to commence the register afresh, all you have to do is, press that ivory knob, and the instrument will draw a line across the paper and, at the same moment, spring back to zero."

The water, at the depth at which they were travelling, proved to be almost as transparent as crystal, of a dark olive-green tint beneath them, merging by imperceptible gradations to a faint greenish-blue above; the surface being discernible by the shifting lace work of gold incessantly playing over it where the sun's beams caught the ridges of the faint rippling wavelets raised by the languid summer breeze. Even small objects, such as medusae, and fragments of weed floating in mid-sea, were distinguishable at a considerable distance; and fishing-boats could be clearly made out at the distance of a mile. A very novel and curious effect was witnessed when objects floating on the surface (such as ships, fishing-boats, or aquatic birds) came into view, the submerged portions of them being as clearly defined as though they were floating in air, whilst the parts *above* the surface were wavering and indistinct. A flock of diving gulls, for instance, which they passed at no great distance, presented the curious spectacle of little more than dark dots furnished with pairs of quickly-moving webbed feet whilst they floated on the placid surface; but directly a bird dived its whole body became distinctly visible, with a long stream of air-bubbles trailing behind it.

At length it became apparent that they were approaching a large fleet of ships making their way up channel.

A smile passed over the professor's features as he gazed out at them, and turning to his companions he remarked:

"I feel mischievously inclined this morning. I think we will give the crews of those ships a little surprise, and furnish them with a new topic for conversation."

"Ah, indeed!" said the baronet. "How do you propose to do it?"

"By rising to the surface in the midst of the fleet. Our engine power is quite sufficient, I believe, to send us to the surface or to plunge us several fathoms deeper than we now are without our interfering with the water chambers or altering in any way the weight of the ship. There is a nice clear space just ahead, with ample room in which to show ourselves and to make a downward plunge again beneath that large ship, the barnacle-covered bottom of which seems to tell of a long voyage through tropic seas. Now take up your stations of observation, gentlemen, and note the consternation which our unexpected appearance will produce."

The professor's companions placed themselves at the windows of the pilot-house, and Herr von Schalckenberg at the same moment suddenly pressed the end of the tiller vertically downward. Obedient to the helm, the *Flying Fish's* sharp snout immediately swerved upward, and with a tremendous swirl and commotion of the water the great ship rushed to the surface, throwing half her length out of the sea, only to disappear again the next moment with a graceful plunging motion and a still greater disturbance of the water by her immense rapidly revolving propeller.

A single swift glance around them was all that the travellers were able to obtain of the state of affairs above water; but that sufficed to show them that their appearance, sudden though it was, had attracted a considerable amount of notice. They saw that the *Flying Fish* had broken water in the very centre of a large fleet of ships, most of which were making their way up channel under every stitch of canvas they could spread before a very light westerly air. Many of these ships were evidently, from their weather-beaten appearance, traders from far-distant foreign ports; and their crews, taking advantage of the beautifully fine weather and smooth water, were either occupied on stages slung over the sides in giving the hulls a touch of fresh paint to brighten up their appearance previous to going into port, or aloft, scraping, painting, and varnishing the spars, or tarring down the rigging, with a similar object. All eyes seemed to be directed toward the apparition which had made its sudden appearance in their midst; and the shouts of astonishment and dismay evoked by that sudden appearance were distinctly audible to the occupants of the *Flying Fish's* pilot-house. The hurried way in which the crew of the large ship immediately ahead of them sprang to their feet and scrambled in over the bulwarks from the stages on which they were working, or slid down the freshly-tarred backstays to the deck as they saw the immense object rushing directly toward them, was particularly amusing, and drew a hearty laugh from the beholders on board the *Flying Fish*. Another moment, and the cause of all this commotion was plunging fathoms deep beneath the keel of the last-mentioned ship, to reappear on the surface a minute later, beyond the farthest outskirts of the fleet. A judicious manipulation of the helm kept the *Flying Fish* this time on the surface for perhaps a quarter of a minute, just long enough, in fact, to satisfy the wondering beholders that their eyes had not deceived them, when she once more disappeared, this time finally, from the view of the fleet.

"That escapade of ours will produce a tremendously sensational paragraph for the newspapers, and we must keep a look-out for it," said the colonel. "I wonder what they will make of it!"

Sure enough, the paragraph appeared in due course, to the following effect, as copied from a cutting which is still preserved in the professor's scrap-book:—

Appearance Of A Gigantic Sea Monster In The English Channel.

Extraordinary Story.

"On Wednesday morning last, the 27th instant, a fleet of some hundred and fifty sail of vessels was off the Start and about in mid-channel, making its way to the eastward before a light westerly air, the weather at the time being fine, the water smooth, and the atmosphere perfectly clear. A portion of the crews belonging to several of the craft in question were at work in the rigging when their attention was attracted by a curious commotion which suddenly appeared on the surface of the water at a considerable distance to the eastward. The disturbance was in the form of a long wedge-like ripple, the appearance being very pronounced and distinct at its forward or pointed extremity, but less so at its rear end, where it spread widely out and became gradually merged and lost in the gentle ripple caused by the wind. It was travelling directly towards the fleet at a speed far exceeding that of the fastest express train, and it bore all the appearance of being the 'wake' of some enormous body moving at no great distance beneath the surface. While the seamen were still watching it in wonder and perplexity, mingled with no little alarm, it had reached the fleet, the rippling swell spreading out on each side and curling over into a breaker which dashed against the sides of the several vessels, causing the smaller craft to rock and toss perceptibly. It clove its irresistible way to the very centre of the fleet, where there happened to be a large open space of water, and here there suddenly shot into view above the surface a gigantic fish, the length of which is variously estimated by those who saw it as from four hundred to eight hundred feet, with a girth of between one and two hundred feet. The creature, apparently startled at finding itself in the midst of so many vessels, immediately dived below the surface again, passing directly beneath the keel of the barque *Olivia*, of London, from Bangkok, William Rogers master. The crew of this ship had a most distinct view of the monster, as it broke water at not more than half a cable's length (or some three hundred feet) from them, and immediately afterwards shaved the keel of the ship so closely as almost to touch it. Captain Rogers, who was on deck at the time, describes the creature, and his description tallies perfectly with that of the other witnesses, as being somewhat like a saw-fish, without the saw, in general shape, but with a proportionately longer and more sharply pointed head, in which *four* eyes, two in the upper and two in the lower part of the head, were distinctly seen. The body was a beautiful silvery white, glistening in the sun like polished metal. On the back of the immense fish was a curious flat protuberance, above which rose another in the form of a dome-shaped hump, with, if we may venture to repeat so incredible a story, eyes all round it, and surmounted by an object having a very marked resemblance to a silver crown. This extraordinary creature had no fins so far as could be seen, but propelled itself solely by its tail, which it moved with such wonderful rapidity as rendered it utterly impossible to detect the shape of it. The creature was evidently an air-breather, for it had no sooner completely cleared the fleet, which it did in about one minute, the distance travelled in that time being fully three miles, than it rose once more to the surface, remaining there for perhaps half a minute, evidently for the purpose of getting a fresh supply of air, when it again dived and was seen no more."

Chapter Six
In Search of a Submerged Wreck

To return to the *Flying Fish*. It was exactly two o'clock p.m. when Lieutenant Mildmay announced that, according to his "dead reckoning," they were now on or very near the spot indicated on the chart by the professor, and that, if there was no objection, he should like to rise to the surface in order to obtain the astronomical observations necessary to verify the ship's position. The engines were accordingly stopped, and the water being ejected from the water chambers, the travellers once more found themselves above water, advantage being taken of the opportunity to throw open the door of the pilot-house and step out on deck.

The first discovery made by them was that a moderate breeze was blowing from the westward, with a corresponding amount of sea and a very long heavy swell, which, however, to their great gratification, affected the *Flying Fish* only to a very trifling extent. When end-on to the sea she pitched a little, it is true, but when broadside-on she simply rose and fell with the run of the sea, being as completely free from rolling motion as though she had still been on the stocks.

Their next discovery was that a large steamer was in sight, some seven miles distant; and, whilst they stood watching the way in which the craft plunged along over the heavy swell, pitching "bows under" occasionally, she suddenly altered her course and steered direct toward them, her crew having apparently only that moment sighted the *Flying Fish*, and being evidently in great perplexity as to what she could possibly be.

"Be as quick as you can with your observations, Mildmay, and let us get under water again," said the baronet. "We shall perhaps be expected to explain who and what we are if that steamer gets within hail of us, and I am not particularly anxious to do that."

The sights were taken, and, whilst the steamer was yet some five miles distant, the *Flying Fish* quietly sank once more beneath the waves; doubtless to the intense astonishment of those who were making such haste to get alongside her.

Rapidly, yet steadily, and with a perfectly level deck, the craft sank lower and lower, the light diminishing momentarily, until it at length vanished altogether, and the darkness became so intense that it was impossible for the occupants of the pilot-house to discern each other; whilst the silence which prevailed around them was first oppressive and then awe-inspiring in its intensity.

Suddenly a light shuffling sound arose within the pilot-house, and in another moment the inky depths through which they were descending became brilliantly illuminated with a clear white penetrating light, in which every detail of the ship's hull fore and aft stood out distinctly visible, whilst here and there, above, below, and on either side of them, a momentary gleam revealed the presence of some startled and hastily retreating denizen of the deep. The professor had lighted up the electric lanterns, the especial purpose of which was to illuminate the sea around the ship, leaving the interior of the pilot-house still in darkness, in order that its occupants might enjoy, to the fullest extent, the novelty of the scene thus suddenly revealed to them, and also that, on reaching the bottom, they might the better be able to distinguish external objects.

Lower and lower sank the *Flying Fish*, and at length, after what seemed to the travellers an almost interminable descent, she reached the bottom.

"Now, gentlemen," exclaimed the professor, with some slight evidences of excitement in the tones of his voice, "look around you, and see if you can discover anything unusual in our neighbourhood."

The persons addressed did as they were requested, the professor himself also peering eagerly out of each of the pilot-house windows in turn, but without result; the electric lamps, though they brilliantly illuminated the scene on all sides for fully fifty yards, and rendered objects distinguishable for at least three times that distance, revealed nothing but a plain completely covered with rocks and boulders, some of which were of enormous size, and all thickly overgrown with sea-weed.

"What is it you expected to find down here, professor?" asked the colonel, when it had become perfectly evident that nothing but rocks lay within their range of vision.

"The hull of a ship," answered the professor. "She foundered on or near the spot indicated by me, and cannot be far off; unless, indeed, we are out in our reckoning. Have you worked out your calculations, Mildmay?"

"Not yet," answered the lieutenant, "but I soon will do so if you will oblige us with a little light inside here."

"Ah, true! I had forgotten," murmured the professor apologetically, and he lighted the lamp which hung suspended above the table in the pilot-house.

The lieutenant sat down and rapidly worked out his observations, with the resulting discovery that they were exactly two miles north-east of the spot they were seeking, having doubtless been swept that much out of their proper position by the tide. The *Flying Fish* was accordingly raised some fifty feet from the bottom, her engines were once more set in motion, slowly this time, however, and the ship's head laid in the proper direction, the occupants of the pilot-house stationing themselves at the windows and peering out eagerly ahead on the look-out for the object of their search.

The engines being set to work dead slow and stopped at intervals when the speed became too high, the speed of the *Flying Fish* was kept down to about twelve knots per hour, at which rate she would occupy ten minutes in traversing the required distance. She had been under weigh exactly nine minutes when Mildmay exclaimed:

"Sail ho! That is to say, there is a large object of some kind dead ahead. Port *hard*, professor, or we shall be into it."

The professor, who was not absolutely ignorant of nautical phraseology, promptly ported his helm and at the same moment stopped the engines, by which manoeuvre the *Flying Fish* glided close past the object so slowly that it was easily distinguishable as a huge pinnacle of rock.

They were now on the exact spot indicated by the professor on the chart, but nothing in the slightest degree resembling the hull of a ship was in sight. Rocks in the form of pinnacles, huge fantastic boulders, and boldly-jutting reefs appeared all round, as far as the powerful lamps of the ship could project their rays, but no ship was to be seen. They rose some fifty feet higher, in order to see over the more lofty rocks, some of which intercepted their view, but with no more successful result.

"There is no ship here, professor," at last remarked the baronet, after all hands had carefully inspected the whole of the ground within their ken. "Are you quite sure of the accuracy of your information?"

"My information has reference only to an *approximate* position; the ship is hereabout—within a few miles of this spot—and I considered that our best chance of discovering her lay in coming here first, and, if necessary, prosecuting our search with this position as a starting-point."

"Very good. Then, as the object of our quest is manifestly not here, I propose that we proceed with our search at once."

By way of reply the professor put the helm hard over, and once more set the engines slowly in motion, thus causing the ship to travel in a circle about the spot; all hands going, as before, to the windows of the pilot-house on the look-out.

The circle described by the *Flying Fish* was a very small one—not more than two hundred feet in diameter—and the inmates of the pilot-house were therefore able to carefully examine every inch of ground within its circumference. One complete circuit having been accomplished without result, the helm was very slightly altered, and the ship then went on in a continually widening spiral which must necessarily at length take her to the object of her search, if indeed it actually existed.

That it did so was ultimately demonstrated, the professor himself being the first to make its discovery.

The wreck, when first sighted, was distant about one hundred yards on their starboard hand, and only just within range of the circle of electric light. The ship's head was at once turned in that direction, the engines being at the same time stopped, to permit of a very gradual approach.

All eyes were of course intently fixed upon the strange object; and they had neared it to within about one hundred feet, when Lieutenant Mildmay exclaimed in a low, awe-struck voice:

"Just as I suspected! It is the *Daedalus!*"

"Yes," replied the professor very quietly; "it is that most unfortunate ship. And now, gentlemen, with your permission I will anchor the *Flying Fish*, and pay a visit—unaccompanied—to the wreck."

It was evident, from the extreme gravity of the professor's demeanour, that his proposed visit was prompted by some other motive than that of mere idle curiosity; his companions therefore simply bowed in token of acquiescence, and permitted von Schalckenberg to follow undisturbed the bent of his own inclinations.

The *Flying Fish*, meanwhile, had been caused to descend to the bottom, to which she was at once secured by her four grip-anchors; immediately after which the professor, with a somewhat hurried and incoherent apology, left his companions and descended to the diving-room.

Left to themselves, the trio occupying the pilot-house had ample leisure to note the position and surroundings of the ill-fated steamer.

She had settled down upon a flat ledge of level rock, and rested, keel downwards, in a perfectly upright position, having apparently recovered herself whilst settling down. She was greatly damaged, both in hull and rigging; the spar-deck and forecastle being swept away, and her main deck blown up in midships, very possibly through the explosion of her boilers. Her bowsprit and mizzen-mast were gone, as was also her fore topmast; and the mainmast, with topmast and all attached, was leaning aft, and so far over the side that the observers would not have been surprised to see it fall at any moment. Loose ropes were trailing in all directions; and the tattered remains of sails still hung from some of the yards and stays, swaying occasionally in a slow, weird, ghostly manner, with the mysterious intermittent under-currents of the sea.

The trio were still discussing the particulars of the sad disaster, which, on a stormy September night, had resulted in the drowning of nearly five hundred people, and the plunging of the ship herself to the depths wherein they had so strangely found her, when the figure of the professor, clad in his suit of diving armour and dwindled in apparent dimensions by his great distance below them, was seen to emerge from the black shadow of the *Flying Fish's* hull and make his way slowly and laboriously over the rocky bottom toward the wreck. A couple of minutes sufficed him to perform the short journey; and; scrambling up the side by the aid of some of the dangling gear, he entered the poop cabin and disappeared.

The party in the pilot-house finished their chat; and then sauntered down into the music saloon, of which they had seen nothing since the night of their departure from London—actually only two nights before, but they had since then been so satiated with novel sights and experiences that it really seemed as though at least a month had elapsed since they last passed the threshold. Here they beguiled the time so effectually with music, vocal and instrumental, that it was not until George appeared announcing dinner that it occurred to either of them that the professor had been out of the ship nearly three hours.

"Where can the man be? Surely some accident must have befallen him!" exclaimed the baronet, starting up in alarm.

"Not necessarily," replied the colonel. "The professor is pretty well able to take care of himself. It is much more probable that he has discovered some object of exceptional interest on board the wreck, or has fallen into a scientific reverie as to the actual cause of the disaster—the cause, I mean, from a *scientist's* point of view. Sound the gong, George; water is a good conductor, and he may possibly hear it and be awakened to a consciousness that time flies."

The gong was accordingly struck, and the three companions hastened to the pilot-house to watch for results. The call proved effectual, for in less than five minutes afterwards the professor made his appearance on the deck of the wreck, soon afterwards rejoining his friends on board the *Flying Fish* in the vestibule outside the saloons. He carried in his hand a small compact package, which he deposited carefully on the sideboard, and then, with a much more cheerful mien than he had worn when setting out upon his solitary journey, took his accustomed place at the table, apparently quite prepared to do full justice to the meal which was about to be served.

The soup and fish were discussed in silence; a glass of wine was then imbibed with much apparent enjoyment, and this unlocked the professor's lips.

"I feel it to be due to you, gentlemen—and more especially to *you*, Sir Reginald—to offer some explanation of the motive which influenced me in my proposal that we should come hither," he remarked, setting his wine-glass down on the table. "I had a threefold object in view. In the first place, I felt curious to know whether it would be possible to find, *at the bottom of the sea*, an object the position of which is only approximately known. In the second place, I was anxious to secure a relic. And in the third place, I was almost equally anxious to recover a most valuable document which I was convinced had gone down in the unfortunate *Daedalus*. With regard to the first-named object, you have already witnessed our complete success. I have also been successful in the remaining two."

The speaker paused here; but it was so evident from his manner that he had not yet said all he had to say upon the subject that his companions contented themselves with mere simple monosyllabic murmurs of polite congratulation, and then awaited in silence a further communication.

The professor continued silent and evidently plunged deep in a somewhat sombre reverie for several minutes; then he lifted his head and said somewhat hesitatingly:

"You will perhaps be surprised to learn that my life has not been left wholly ungilded by the halo of romance. Five-and-twenty years ago, when Science had perhaps not obtained so light a grip upon me as she now has, it was my fate to meet the loveliest woman I have ever beheld. She was an only daughter, of English parentage; and chance threw us somewhat more intimately together than is usual with people who become acquainted casually and informally. I fell blindly, madly in love with this peerless creature; and, gentlemen, I have since—and alas, too late!—had reason to believe that, strange as such a circumstance may appear to you, she did not altogether escape a reciprocal passion. But my studious habits had brought with them one serious disadvantage—I was indescribably diffident and shy; so much so that when the time arrived that I must either unbosom myself or let her pass away out of my life, perhaps for ever, I found myself without the courage to make the necessary declaration. We parted without a word of love having passed between us. She remained single for five years—to give me an opportunity of declaring myself, as I now know—and then married a man far more worthy of her than I could ever have proved. Gentlemen, her only child, a lad of fifteen, went down with the ill-fated *Daedalus*; and the mother is to-day breaking her heart because, by some perverse chance, she does not possess a single memento of her lost boy. My visit to the wreck, however, will remove that source of grief; for I shall have the melancholy satisfaction of transmitting to the dear lady, by the first safe conveyance which offers itself, the watch and chain and the signet-ring which he wore when he bade her a final farewell. In the moment that I conquered the last difficulty connected with the construction of this ship, and felt assured that she would prove a success, I vowed to myself that, by the courtesy of our amiable host, I would avail myself of the means she would offer for securing some memento of that poor lad; and I have to-day at once performed my vow and passed through scenes of such surpassing horror as probably no mortal has ever witnessed before, and which language has no words to describe.

"The third object of my visit to the wreck is before you in the shape of yonder package. It is a manuscript book filled with jottings and memoranda, the result of some thirty years of profound research in the many bypaths of science. It was the property of an officer of the ship with whom I had corresponded for many years; and, knowing how greatly I coveted the book, he left it me in his will, probably little thinking, poor fellow! that it was fated to go with him to the bottom of the sea. On being made acquainted with the circumstances of his death, and also with his bequest, I surmised at once that the precious volume must have been in his immediate possession when the ship foundered. And having visited him on board, as well as had occasion to notice the place in which the book was ordinarily kept, I had very little difficulty in placing my hand upon it."

"I suppose matters are in a very terrible state on board the wreck?" asked the baronet.

"So bad," was the reply, "that, knowing what I now know, I cannot think of any motive powerful enough to induce me to repeat my visit. I had two very strong motives for going on board the ship; and, as each successive horror presented itself, I thought, surely there can be nothing worse than this; and I pressed onward, only to encounter greater and still greater horrors at every step. But I would not go there again even to achieve what I have achieved to-day."

"Ah!" said the baronet, "I have a great curiosity to see what the ship herself looks like after such a tremendous catastrophe; but, if the sights to be witnessed on board her be one-tenth part so bad as your words would lead one to suppose, I would not go near her for the world."

"Nor I," said the colonel.

"Nor I," added Mildmay.

"You are wise, gentlemen," remarked the professor. "I can quite understand your curiosity; but, were you to gratify it, your pleasure would be effectually destroyed for the remainder of the voyage."

"That reminds me to ask the question, Where are we going next?" said Sir Reginald.

The professor shrugged his shoulders and spread out his hands, palms upwards.

"The world is all before you where to choose," he replied. "You have only to name a place, and it will be strange indeed if we cannot get there."

"Well, for my own part, I am of opinion that it will be wise for us to devote this trip as far as possible to the visiting of such spots as it is difficult or impossible to reach by any other means. What say you, gentlemen?"

This from the baronet.

The others expressed their full coincidence in this opinion.

"Very well, then," continued Sir Reginald; "my proposal is that, as the days are now at their longest, and this is therefore the most favourable time for such an expedition—and as, moreover, the *Flying Fish's* stores have as yet been barely broached—we make the best of our way forthwith *to the North Pole*, there to enjoy a little of the choice sport which we may reasonably hope to find among animals that have never yet seen the face of man."

"A most admirable proposal, and one which we are especially well adapted to successfully carry out," exclaimed the professor enthusiastically. The colonel and Mildmay also gave their cordial assent to the plan.

"Very well, then; that is settled," remarked von Schalckenberg. "Now, to revert for a moment to the subject of the wreck. You have not been on board her, as I have; but, even with the comparatively distant view you have had of her, I think you must have seen that she is injured beyond all possibility of repair; to say nothing of the fact that she is lying in a spot from which it would be difficult—quite impossible, indeed, without our assistance—to recover her. Now, it has occurred to me that, all things taken into consideration, it would be a good deed to destroy her. What say you, gentlemen? It would afford us an excellent opportunity for making trial of one of our shells."

"Destroy her, by all means," said the baronet.

"I can see no possible objection," observed the colonel.

"Nor I," remarked Mildmay. "As to assisting in her recovery, I would not stir so much as my little finger to do it; she has already drowned some five hundred human beings, which is quite enough mischief for one ship."

"Quite so," coincided the professor. "Then we will do the deed after dinner."

Accordingly, half an hour later, the party rose from the table and made their way to the pilot-house, where the professor delivered a little lecture on the mode of firing the shells. Then, accompanied by the colonel, who had proffered his assistance, von Schalckenberg proceeded to the fore end of the ship to make the requisite arrangements. It being a first experiment, the preparation occupied fully ten minutes—or ten times as long as he should allow himself in future, the professor remarked. Then, all being ready, a return was made to the pilothouse; the anchors were withdrawn from the ground, and the *Flying Fish* was got under weigh. The monster circled once or twice round the doomed wreck, seeking the most suitable point of attack, which having been decided upon, the sharp nose of the submarine ship was pointed straight at the *Daedalus*, and the professor touched a knob. At the same instant—so it appeared, so rapid was the discharge—there was a blinding flash of light on board the wreck, a terrific concussion, but no sound, and the wreck *vanished*; that is the only word which adequately describes the suddenness and completeness of her destruction. The concussion was so violent that it jarred the *Flying Fish* throughout the whole of her vast frame; indeed, but for her tremendous strength she would in all probability have herself been destroyed. As it was, no damage or harm whatever was done on board beyond throwing the four occupants of the pilothouse somewhat violently to the floor, and terrifying the cook and the hitherto sedate George almost out of their senses.

But perhaps even they were less frightened than were the captain and crew of a small Levant trader which happened at the moment to be almost directly above the scene of the explosion. All hands felt the jar; the watch below frantically sprang on deck under the impression that they had collided with another vessel; and the skipper, who happened to be standing near the taffrail, was horrified beyond expression to see an immense cone of water some thirty feet high rise out of the sea just astern of his vessel, to fall next moment with a deafening splash and an accompanying surge which tossed the little vessel as helplessly about for a moment or two as though she had been the merest cockle-shell. It took that skipper nearly half an hour to fully recover his faculties; and when he did so, his first act was to go below and solemnly make an entry in his official log to the effect that, on such and such a date at such an hour, in latitude and longitude so and so, the weather at the time being fine, with a moderate breeze from S.W., the schooner *Pomona* had experienced a terrific shock of earthquake with an accompanying disturbance of water which nearly swamped the ship. This entry he signed in the presence of the mate, secured that officer's signature to it also, and then, reviving his courage with a glass of grog stiff enough to float a marlinespike, he retired to his bunk.

Chapter Seven
En Route for the North Pole

The destruction of the wreck having been effected, the *Flying Fish* moved a few miles northward until she reached a small level sandy patch affording a good berth for the night, and there she was once more placed upon the ground and anchored.

Nothing whatever occurred to disturb the repose of the travellers; and, after passing a tranquil night, they assembled at the breakfast table punctually at eight o'clock on the following morning. An hour later, having finished their meal, the quartette rose, and made their way to the pilot-house, where preparations were at once commenced for an ascent to the surface. On this occasion the professor being anxious that the other members of the party should become conversant with the method of handling the ship, the baronet placed himself at the tiller—from which post the entire apparatus controlling the movements of the vessel could be reached—and, with von Schalckenberg at his elbow to correct him in the event of a possible mistake, the ascent was begun. This, from prudential motives, was slowly accomplished, and at a distance of five fathoms from the surface a pause was made for the purpose of taking a good look round and thus avoiding all possibility of inflicting damage on passing ships in the act of breaking water. It was well that this precaution was observed; for their first glance revealed to them the bottom of a large steamer close at hand and coming rapidly straight toward them; and had the *Flying Fish* continued to rise she would have broken water directly under the stranger's bows. As it was, by backing astern a few yards they gave the steamer good room to pass; and it was both interesting and novel to see the great mass go plunging heavily past with the long sea-grass waving and trailing from her bottom, and the great propeller spinning rapidly round, now completely immersed, and anon lifted almost entirely out of the water. Once clear of her, the *Flying Fish* sank to a depth of ten fathoms, and after a ten-mile run at full speed, once more paused to reconnoitre. This time the sea was clear for at least a mile in every direction—which was as far as they could see in the then condition of the water—and they at once rose to the surface.

The horizon proved to be clear in every direction save to the southward, in which quarter the upper spars of the steamer they had so lately encountered were still visible. The wind was blowing a moderate breeze from S.S.E. — almost a dead fair wind for the *Flying Fish* — the weather also was delightfully fine and clear; it was therefore promptly resolved to take to the air once more and thus wing their way northward.

The valves of the air-chambers were accordingly thrown open to their full extent, when, with a screaming roar, the highly compressed air at once rushed forth, and in less than half a minute the huge bulk of the ship was lying poised as lightly as an air-bubble on the surface of the heaving water. The main vapour-valve was then cautiously opened, and a partial vacuum produced, when, as easily as a sea-bird, the *Flying Fish* rose at once into the air. The engines were next turned ahead, the helm adjusted, and the northward journey was fairly begun.

The wind was blowing at the rate of about fifteen miles an hour, and nearly dead fair; the engines were therefore set so as just to turn round and no more; this gave the ship a speed of about twelve knots through the air, which, added to the rate of the wind, gave a total speed of twenty-seven knots over the ground — or rather over, the water — and at this pace they calculated that, after making the necessary allowance in their course for the set of the wind, they would reach the Irish coast, in the vicinity of Cape Clear, at about five o'clock the next morning. Their reason for not travelling faster was that, as the baronet said, they were on a pleasure cruise, and having been pent up inside the hull for fully thirty-six hours, they felt that a few hours in the open air would be an acceptable change.

They pursued their flight throughout the day at an altitude of only a thousand feet above the sea, except when they encountered a ship — which happened only once during the hours of daylight — and when this occurred they rose, on the instant of sighting her, to the highest attainable distance, in pursuance of their resolve to attract as little attention as possible, descending again to their former level as soon as they had passed beyond her range of vision. At this latter elevation they were able to enjoy to the full the health-giving properties of the pure sea-breeze, and to revel in a prospect — though it was only that of the restless sea — of nearly forty nautical miles on every side; the horizon, that is to say, forming a circle of little less than eighty miles diameter round about them. And though it may be hastily thought that, with a sea bare of craft there was little or nothing to interest the travellers, this was by no means the case; for at their height the water was clear and transparent for a long distance below the surface, and the gambols of the fish, of which there were great numbers visible, including several schools of porpoises and a solitary whale, could be seen distinctly, affording a most interesting sight; and when they grew tired of this they promenaded the spacious deck, or lounged about in chairs, smoking their cigars or pipes, and discussing with much animation their future prospects. And now, for the first time, a fact in connection with the automatic balancing apparatus brought itself under their notice. It was this. They found that, let them walk about the ship where and as much as they chose, the balance of the ship always remained perfect; but the little jets of air which, at their every movement, were admitted into the hull to maintain its equilibrium, soon had a perceptible influence on the vessel's buoyancy, causing her to slowly but steadily descend toward the surface of the sea, thus necessitating periodic visits to the pilot-house to renew the vacuum. This set the professor's brain to work, and by nightfall he succeeded—with the aid of a second barometer having a small piece of highly magnetised steel floating on the top of the mercurial column, and a couple of magnetised steel bars—in constructing a somewhat rude but thoroughly efficient apparatus for automatically maintaining the ship at any desired height, unaffected by the movements, be they few or many, of those on board.

By the time that this apparatus had been fixed, and subjected to the test of an hour's conscientious walking fore and aft the deck by the entire party, the dinner-hour had arrived, and they retired below with such appetites as only a day's exposure to the tonic effects of a sea-breeze—minus all uncomfortable motion—could produce. The fullest justice was consequently done to the meal, after which they made their way once more to the deck, and there, under a brilliant star-lit sky, gave themselves up to the soothing influence of *the weed* and the renewed enjoyment of their novel position. Midnight found them quite ready for their state-rooms, and at that hour they accordingly retired; the professor first of all, as a matter of precaution, increasing the ship's altitude to four thousand feet above the sea-level, and then paying a visit of inspection to the engine-room. Matters were found to be all right there; the engines were working smoothly and noiselessly, the bearings were quite cool, and the automatic feed was doing its work to perfection. The ship, then, being at such a height as to be clear of all danger, and steering herself in the required direction, with all the machinery in perfect working order, the weather also being fine and wearing a settled aspect, von Schalckenberg told himself that there was not the slightest necessity for the maintenance of a look-out, and he therefore also retired. A quarter of an hour later the whole of the crew were sunk in profound repose, and the *Flying Fish*, left to herself, was leisurely wending her way northward at a height of nearly a mile above the earth's surface.

The first of the quartette to put in an appearance on deck next morning was the professor, who was awakened just as day was breaking by the faint sound of a steam whistle. Springing hastily from his very comfortable couch, he rushed up the companion way and into the open air, without even pausing to don his nether garments. Springing to the guard rail he looked around and below him, and the half-formed fear that something had gone amiss, and that the ship was in danger, was at once dissipated. He saw that the *Flying Fish* was moving rapidly along with the land beneath her, the breeze having freshened during the night, whilst still blowing from the same quarter, causing them to reach the Irish coast sooner than had been anticipated. The mercury stood at the same height in the tube as it had done when they retired to rest on the preceding night; the ship had consequently maintained her approximate height above the sea-level, the only variation being that due to the greater or lesser density of the atmosphere; which was eminently satisfactory, as it showed that the professor's hastily constructed apparatus for maintaining an uniform level had been faithfully performing its duty.

These facts ascertained, von Schalckenberg cast his glance over the scene spread out beneath him, in order to ascertain, if possible, his position. The morning was beautifully clear, the atmosphere being entirely destitute of clouds, and the only obstacle to uninterrupted vision was a thick mist which overspread the earth outstretched below him like an immense map. This, to a certain extent, rendered prompt identification of the locality difficult; but a lake of very irregular triangular shape was immediately underneath the ship, and from S. round to about W.S.W., at a distance of about eight miles, extended a range of hills which, from their height, the professor easily identified as Macgillicuddy's Reeks, the lake below being Killarney. Other hills towered up out of the mist all round the ship, and, at a distance of some twenty miles straight ahead, appeared the Stack Mountains. Towns, villages, farm buildings, and solitary cabins were dotted about all over the country, and beyond all, from S.S.E. round by S. and W. to N., could be seen the blue sea, dotted here and there with the brown sails of the fishing craft or the scarcely whiter canvas of the coasters.

Satisfied that all was right, the professor returned to the pilot-house, and, closing the doors to exclude the intense cold of the higher atmospheric region, perfected the vacuum in the air chambers, causing the ship to immediately soar aloft to the enormous height of thirty-five thousand feet; having done which he made his way below again and plunged into his bath.

On meeting his companions at the breakfast-table, von Schalckenberg informed them of the position and elevation of the ship, and they at once expressed an ardent desire to go out on deck immediately after breakfast to view the magnificent prospect spread out around and beneath them.

"You will have to put on your diving suits then, gentlemen," remarked the scientist, "for you would find it quite impossible to breathe in the extremely rarefied atmosphere which now supports us; moreover, it is so intensely cold that, unless exceedingly well protected, you would soon freeze to death. But I quite agree with you that the prospect, embracing as it does a circle of—let me see," and he made a hasty calculation on the back of an envelope—"yes, a circle of very nearly four hundred and sixty miles in diameter, must be well worth looking at."

Accordingly, on the completion of the meal, the quartette descended to the diving-room, and there donned their armour, taking the additional precaution of adding a flannel overall to their ordinary inner diving dress. Thus equipped, they made their way to the pilot-house, carefully closing all doors behind them on the way, and sallied out on deck.

The spectacle which then met their gaze was novel beyond all power of description, and can only be feebly suggested. The sky overhead was of an intense ultramarine hue, approaching in depth to indigo, gradually changing, as the eye travelled downward from the zenith toward the horizon, to a pallid colourless hue. The stars—excepting those near the horizon—were almost as distinctly visible as at midnight; whilst the sun, shorn of his rays, hung in the sky like a great ball of molten copper; the moon also, reduced to a thin silver thread-like crescent, had followed the sun into the sky, and hung a few degrees only above the eastern horizon.

So lost in wonder were the travellers at this most extraordinary sight that it was several minutes before they could withdraw their gaze from the heavens and allow it to travel earthward. When at length they did so a scarcely less enchanting spectacle greeted them. They were hovering just over the inner extremity of an arm of the sea, which the colonel—who was well acquainted with the south-west of Ireland—at once identified as Dingle Bay. Westward of them stretched the broad Atlantic, its foam-flecked waters tinted a lovely sea-green immediately below them, which gradually changed to a delicate sapphire blue as it stretched away toward the invisible horizon (the atmosphere not proving sufficiently clear to allow of their seeing to the utmost possible limits of distance), the colour growing gradually fainter and more faint until it became lost in a soft silvery grey mist. Northward lay the Dingle peninsula, and beyond it again could be seen Tralee Bay, the mouth of the Shannon, and Loop Head; then Galway Bay and the Isles of Arran, and, further on, just discernible in the misty distance, the indented shore and hills of Connemara. From thence, all round to the eastern point of the compass, could be seen, with more or less distinctness, the whole of county Clare, with part of county Galway, the Doon Mountains, and a considerable portion of Tipperary; the Galtee and Knockmeledown Mountains, and, in the extreme distance, a faint misty blue, which the colonel declared was the sea just about Dungarvan harbour.

And from thence, round to the southward, the sea and the southern coast-line became more and more distinctly visible as the eye travelled round the compass, Cork Harbour being just discernible, whilst Cape Clear Island, Bantry Bay, and the Kenmare river seemed little more than a stone's-throw distant. Altogether it was perhaps the most magnificent prospect upon which the human eye had ever rested; it certainly exceeded anything which the travellers had ever witnessed before, and their expressions of admiration and delight were unbounded.

When at last they had become somewhat accustomed to even this unique experience, and had found leisure to take note of themselves, as it were, the baronet remarked to the professor:

"But how is this, professor? The engines are working, yet we do not appear to be making any headway. So far as I can judge we seem to be simply drifting bodily to the westward and more toward the open sea."

"It is so," answered the professor. "We have risen above the range of the variable winds, and are now feeling the influence of an adverse air current, which, in this latitude, invariably blows *from* the northward; and if we were to maintain our present altitude, for which, however, there is not the slightest necessity, we should have to struggle against it for the next eight or nine hundred miles, in fact until we reach the neighbourhood of the Arctic circle. There, or thereabout, we should again have a fair wind, of which we may possibly yet be glad to avail ourselves. In the meantime, however, we will increase our speed, if you please—at all events, until we are clear of the land, when we can once more descend into a favourable current. And as, until then, our rate of travelling will be such as to make it difficult, if not impossible, to maintain our footing on the deck, I would suggest the advisability of a retreat to the pilot-house."

This suggestion having been promptly carried out, the speed of the ship was increased to its utmost limit, whereby the rate of progression over the ground was raised from nothing to about one hundred and eight miles per hour. This rate of travelling—the adverse wind fortunately remaining moderate—enabled them to reach Erris Head, the north-western corner of county Mayo, in an hour and a half, or about eleven o'clock A.M., at which hour they found themselves just running clear of the land, with the bay and county of Donegal on their right hand, and the broad expanse of the North Atlantic ahead.

At this point the professor turned to his companions and said:

"It now becomes necessary that we should come to a definite decision as to the course to be steered. All routes are of course equally open to us; but there are two which especially commend themselves to our preference. One is the direct northerly route to the Pole, which will take us to the eastward of Iceland, straight to the island of Jan Mayen, and thence, between Greenland and Spitzbergen, into an icy sea which has been but little explored. And the other is the usual route taken by nearly all the great Arctic explorers, namely, up Davis Strait, through Baffin's Bay, and thence, by way of Smith Sound and Kennedy Channel, into the open Polar Sea, if such should actually exist. By the one route we shall have an opportunity of surveying the eastern coast of Greenland, and thus accurately determining much that is at present mere matter of conjecture; and by the other we shall have an opportunity of beholding with our own eyes many spots of interest associated with the researches of former explorers. Now, which is it to be?"

The colonel and Mildmay naturally glanced at Sir Reginald, as an intimation that he, in his character of founder of the expedition, was entitled to the first expression of opinion; and, thus appealed to, the baronet, after a short pause for reflection, replied:

"Well, so far as I am concerned, if I have a preference at all, I think I am inclined to favour the Baffin's Bay route. I confess I should like to go over the ground traversed so painfully by former explorers, and see for myself the nature of the obstacles with which they have had to grapple. And I should also like to look with my bodily eyes upon the spots where they sought refuge during the rigours of the Arctic winter, and those other spots where, the forces of nature finally proving too great for them, they were reluctantly compelled to abandon further effort, and, confessing themselves beaten, turn their faces once more southward. But if either of you happens to have a preference for another route, I beg that you will say so, uninfluenced by my remarks."

The colonel and Mildmay now looked at each other interrogatively; and at length the latter said:

"My predilections are naturally in favour of the route proposed by Sir Reginald, that being the one followed by so many of my distinguished predecessors in the service. But what says the professor? Which route does he, as a scientist, think would be the most interesting?"

"Exactly; that, it seems to me, is the point of view from which we ought to regard the question," exclaimed the baronet and the colonel in a breath.

"From a purely scientific point of view they would probably prove equally interesting," answered the professor. "But, taking the other circumstances into consideration, I am inclined to record my vote in favour of Sir Reginalds suggestion."

"Then let that decide it," remarked the colonel; "I am sure we shall have no cause to regret the choice."

The Baffin's Bay route was accordingly agreed upon; and the ship's head was forthwith laid in a west-north-westerly direction for Cape Farewell.

For the next hour the ship's altitude above the sea-level was maintained unaltered; but at noon, the ocean proving clear of ships as far as the eye could reach, a descent was made to within one thousand feet of the sea, at which height a favourable breeze and a clear atmosphere was again met with. On returning to the pilothouse after luncheon, or about half-past three o'clock in the afternoon, three icebergs were discovered, two ahead and one astern; but they were very small, and it was therefore deemed hardly worth while to pause and examine them. At the same time a large steamer was observed, steering east, on the extreme verge of the southern horizon; and by the aid of their very powerful telescopes the travellers were able to identify her as one of the Atlantic liners. Half an hour later a sail was discovered on the starboard bow; and, from the fact that she was heading to the northward under easy canvas, they rightly concluded that she was a whaler. They passed this vessel within a distance of a dozen miles, and at this point were able to so minutely examine her with their telescopes that they could distinctly make out the figure of a man perched aloft in the "crow's nest" on the look-out, as well as the figures of her crew moving about the deck; but, although within such comparatively close proximity to her, they were quite unable to detect any sign of their being observed, which the professor attributed to the almost total absence of colour about the hull; indeed, he gave it as his opinion that, unless the rays of the sun happened to be reflected from the polished surface of the aethereum directly toward an observer, the *Flying Fish* might easily pass within half a dozen miles unnoticed.

Before this whaler had been left out of sight astern other icebergs had risen into view above the western horizon, and within half an hour they found themselves flying above a sea thickly dotted with ice in every direction, showing that they were rapidly nearing the entrance to Davis Straits. At six o'clock the sound of the gong summoned them below to dinner; and just as they were on the point of leaving the pilot-house, Mildmay, who, with the instinct of the seaman, had paused to take a last look round, sighted a faint blue cloud-like appearance on the horizon, about a point on the starboard bow, and raised a joyful shout of:

"Land, ho!"

The professor glanced at the clock, and, muttering to himself, "Yes, it is about the right time," took his telescope and carefully examined the distant cloud-like appearance

"You are right, Mildmay," he exclaimed, as he closed the instrument, "that is the land; it is Cape Farewell, the most southerly point of that great *terra incognita*, Greenland. With your permission, Sir Reginald, I will reduce the speed of the ship to about twenty miles per hour, and slightly alter her course; and, from the look of the weather, I think I may promise that, when we go on deck to smoke our cigars after dinner, you will see a sight well worth looking at."

Chapter Eight
A Superb Spectacle

Upon one pretext or another the professor purposely delayed the rising of the party from the table until nine o'clock; and when they at length reached the deck they found the somewhat rash promise made by von Schalckenberg abundantly fulfilled. A scene of surpassing loveliness met their delighted gaze, and, to enjoy it more fully and completely, it was promptly decided to descend to the ocean's surface. The sea on all sides was thickly covered with detached masses of floating ice, from the diminutive fragment of drift-ice, measuring not more than two or three square yards in area, to gigantic bergs, measuring, in one or two instances, from a half to three quarters of a mile long, and towering from two to three hundred feet above the surface of the water. The sun was nearing the horizon, and, with his golden beams falling full upon them, these huge masses of ice glittered against the rosy grey of the horizon like burnished metal or solid flame. Two of these bergs in particular were the objects of the travellers' especial wonder and admiration. One, at a distance of some six miles to the eastward, resembled an island of crystal capped with an assemblage of marble ruins. Its perpendicular sides were rent here and there with deep fissures, and in the centre there yawned an immense cavern, the interior of which displayed every conceivable shade of the most lovely green, from the transparent tint of the emerald to the opaque colour of the malachite, a projecting bluff near at hand casting a strangely-contrasting shadow of the deepest, purest ultramarine. The ruined pinnacles on the summit of the berg gleamed with every tint of the rainbow, from palest yellow, through orange and crimson, to a blue varying from the most delicate cobalt to a deep violet, almost undistinguishable from black. And, to complete the fairy-like beauty of the picture, the body of the berg, a pure marble-like white in the centre, gradually assumed a translucent appearance toward the edges, in which the rays of the sun gleamed and sparkled so brilliantly that the mass resembled nothing so much as a gigantic opal.

The other large berg, which in the first instance was only remarkable for its enormous size, lay on the western horizon at a distance of some eleven miles, and, when the travellers first directed their gaze upon it, presented the appearance of a vast mass of a uniform very pale tint of opaque blue rising above the rosy waters. But as they looked upon it the setting sun drew round toward its rear, and then the pale blue opaque tint gradually quickened into translucency and quivered here and there with sudden golden and roseate gleams of indescribable beauty. As the sun neared the berg these gleams and flashes deepened in tint and became mingled in the most bewildering and delightful manner with rays of rich sea-green, warm violet, and delicate purple. Finally the sun, just skimming the edge of the horizon, passed behind the berg, when it at once flamed out into a dazzling blinding blaze, as though the berg had taken fire. For a space of perhaps half a minute this dazzling spectacle continued with scarcely diminished brilliancy; then the blaze deepened from gold to crimson, momentarily subsiding in intensity and increasing in depth of colour until it stood out against the horizon an immense mass of blood-red hue. The red deepened into purple, the purple into violet, and at last, probably when the sun had entirely sunk beneath the horizon, the violet faded gradually to a pale cold lifeless grey.

"Superb!"

"Magnificent!"

"Delightful!"

"Beautiful as a dream!"

Such were the exclamations which burst from the lips of the travellers as they turned away with a sigh at the transitory nature of the beauties they had just been witnessing, when lo! the scene to the eastward had donned new glories. The sun had vanished below the horizon, and the lower portions of the bergs were therefore in cold blue shadow; but as the glance travelled upwards the blue became merged by imperceptible degrees into a delicate amethystine tint, which, growing gradually warmer and more ruddy, passed by a thousand gradations through the richest rose and orange tints to the purest golden-yellow, out of which the projecting points and pinnacles of ice flashed and sparkled like living flame. This fairy-like spectacle lasted for a short time only, however; the golden flashes vanished one by one; the yellow became orange, the orange deepened into crimson, and the crimson in its turn slowly merged into a cold cobalt blue as the light died out of the western sky; and finally the stars came out one by one until the entire firmament was thickly studded with them. It was "nightfall on the sea."

Enthralled by the surpassing witchery of the scene, some time elapsed before either of the travellers cared to break the silence. At length, however, the baronet turned to the professor and said:

"I owe you a debt of never-dying gratitude, professor, for having been the means of introducing me to a scene of such indescribable beauty as that which we have just witnessed; I have looked upon many a fair scene during the course of my wanderings, but never upon anything to equal this. We must have been exceptionally fortunate to-night, have we not? for surely the Polar world can have no spectacle more enchanting than the one which we have just witnessed?"

"We *have* been fortunate; there is no doubt about that," was the reply. "But you have not yet seen the midnight sun nor the aurora borealis, both of which sights far exceed in beauty what we have looked upon to-night. But it grows chilly and an insidious fog is gathering round us; we must take measures for passing the night in safety, for, were we by chance to be caught between two icebergs of even ordinary size, not even the enormous strength of the *Flying Fish* would save her from destruction."

"And what do you propose to do, then, professor, in order to ensure our safety?"

"There are two courses open to us. One is to sink to the bottom of the sea, which is here deep enough to secure us from all danger of being struck by floating bergs. And the other is to ascend into the calm belt, where the night can be passed in a state of absolute safety."

"Very well, then; let us ascend into the 'calm belt,' by all means," said the baronet. "And, by the way, I should feel extremely obliged if you would kindly explain to us what the 'calm belt' is; I for one never heard of it before."

"I will do so with pleasure," replied the professor. "You must know, then, in the first place, that there are certain atmospheric currents as regular and precise in their action as those of the ocean, both being created by the same cause—namely, the tendency of a warm fluid to rise and of a colder one to flow into the vacated space. Thus the air on the equator, being heated by the vertical rays of the sun, rises, creating a partial vacuum which the cold air from the poles rushes equator-ward to fill, the warm air moving toward the poles to restore the balance. Thus at a few degrees north of the equator the upper stratum of air will always be found to be travelling northward. And it continues so to do until it reaches the vicinity of the thirtieth parallel of latitude, when, having lost most of its heat by constant exposure to open space, it becomes cold enough to descend, taking the place of the polar current, which meanwhile has been warmed by passing over the temperate zone. The equatorial current, though it has descended to the surface of the earth, still makes its gradual way northward, as well as local circumstances will permit, in order to replace the southward-flying polar current; and by the time that it reaches the Arctic circle, it has again, by contact with the earth, become the warmer of the two currents, when it once more rises into the upper regions of the atmosphere, to descend no more until it reaches the vicinity of the pole, when it sinks, and at the same time turns southward as the polar current. And the same thing happens in the southern hemisphere. Thus in each hemisphere we have two great atmospheric currents—one flowing from the pole to the equator, and the other flowing from the equator to the pole. The lower current, or that which sweeps along the surface of the earth, meets with so many disturbing local influences that it is frequently deflected greatly from its proper course, sometimes so much so that its course becomes completely reversed for a time; but in the upper regions of the atmosphere these disturbing influences are very little if at all felt. Now, if I have succeeded in making this plain to you, you will readily understand that where the top of the lower current and the bottom of the upper current touch each other there will be so much friction that a neutral or 'calm belt' will occur in which the air will be motionless. And it is in this calm belt— which occurs between the altitudes of three thousand and twelve thousand feet above the earth's surface—that I propose we should take refuge to-night."

The professor's small audience duly expressed their thanks for the extremely interesting lecture to which they had just been treated, and then the party retreated to the pilot-house; the door was closed to exclude the cold air of the upper regions which they were about to visit; and an ascent was made to an altitude of eight thousand feet, where the night was passed in an atmosphere so completely motionless that, on their descent next morning, Lieutenant Mildmay's observations showed them to be in the exact spot which they had occupied on the previous evening.

It was decided over the breakfast-table that morning, that the journey northward should be prosecuted, as far as possible, upon the surface of the sea; and the *Flying Fish* was accordingly put in motion on the required course immediately upon her descent. Their rate of progress was particularly slow, not exceeding, on the average, a speed of six miles per hour, as drift ice was remarkably abundant, mostly in small detached blocks, though they occasionally encountered a floe of several acres in extent; and, far away to the northward, quite a large assemblage of bergs were seen. This slow rate of progress would have been wearisome to a veteran Arctic navigator in possession of such means for the accomplishment of a quick passage as those enjoyed by the inmates of the *Flying Fish's* pilot-house; but to them everything was novel and interesting, and, almost before they knew it, they found themselves in the immediate vicinity of the bergs. These varied greatly in size, some of them being no larger than a dwelling-house of moderate dimensions, whilst others fully equalled, if, indeed, they did not exceed, the proportions of the monsters seen on the previous evening. They were grouped so closely together that a passage between them seemed to be not wholly unattended with danger; and the party were in the act of discussing the question which channel it would be most prudent to take, their eyes being meanwhile fixed on the huge towering cliffs of ice before them, when a gigantic overhanging mass was seen to detach itself from its parent berg and plunge, a distance of some two hundred and fifty feet, with a terrific splash into the water and disappear. The deep thunderous roar of its plunge smote the ears of the watchers next moment, and they looked on with breathless interest to see what would follow. The mass, from its enormous size, would weigh, they considered, fully five thousand tons; and they were not surprised to see that the loss of so much weight had seriously disturbed the balance of the berg, which at once began to rock ponderously to and fro, creating a terrific commotion in the water when conjoined with that caused by the plunge into the sea and the reappearance a second or two later of the detached mass. The sea was seen to heap itself up in a long well-defined ridge, similar—though, of course, on a tremendously magnified scale—to that caused by the plunge of a stone into the water. This ridge spread out in a circular form all round the spot where the mass had fallen, and at once began to travel outward in the form of an immense breaker some six or seven feet in height. Onward it rolled, its smooth glassy front capped with a foaming crest presenting a singular and somewhat alarming spectacle. The fears of the beholders, however, if they had any, were groundless, for, though the threatening wave swept forward with a velocity of some twelve knots per hour, it swept harmlessly enough over and along the cylindrical sides of the *Flying Fish*, hissing and roaring most ominously, but failing to throw so much as a single drop of spray on her deck. This wave was quickly followed by several others, each of which, however, was less formidable than the preceding one. Meanwhile, the drama, it appeared, had only begun. The oscillation of the parent berg, though it was probably quite unaffected by the portion of the circular wave which dashed furiously against its sides, became momentarily more and more violent, accompanied by a rapidly increasing agitation of the sea in its neighbourhood, an agitation so great that the surface of the ocean soon assumed the appearance of a boiling cauldron, the foaming surges leaping wildly hither and thither with a continuous roar like that of the surf beating on a rocky shore, and soon assuming such dimensions that they even broke over the deck of the *Flying Fish,* and dashed themselves into a cloud of spray against the strong walls of the pilot-house. Other fragments now began to detach themselves with dull heavy roaring crashes from the rocking berg; and, as though the action were contagious—or more probably, in consequence of the jarring vibration of the air from such a strong volume of sound—one after the other, the remaining bergs began to go to pieces. Then, indeed, the sight and the accompanying sounds became truly awe-inspiring. The air resounded with the continuous roar of the dismembering bergs; the eye grew dizzy and bewildered as it watched their swaying forms; and the surface of the ocean was momentarily stirred into a wilder frenzy as the surges swept madly hither and thither, and, meeting in mid-career, shattered each other into a wild tempest of leaping foam, in the midst of which huge masses of ice were seen every now and then to be tossed high into the air as though they had been fragments of cork. So mad was the commotion, and so furiously were even the larger masses of ice dashed to and fro, that it was deemed prudent to remove the *Flying Fish* out of harm's way; and she was accordingly raised a few fathoms above the surface of the raging commotion which leaped and roared around her. Scarcely had this been accomplished—the whole of the drama occupying not one-tenth part of the time which it takes to describe it—when the largest of the bergs was seen to roll completely over, raising in the act so awful a surge that it visibly affected even the immense masses of the other bergs, which, in their turn, rolled slowly over one after the other, to the accompaniment of one long loud echoing roar of rending ice as their dismemberment thus became accelerated. The resulting ocean disturbance was, as may easily be imagined, appallingly grand and utterly indescribable; and it no doubt contributed in no inconsiderable degree to the total destruction of the bergs, which, once started, continued to roll over and over, every lurch causing a further dismemberment until the fragments became so small as to be incapable of further division. Then ensued comparative silence, the only sounds being those of the hoarse roar of the angry surges and the grinding crash of ice-blocks dashed violently together. Gradually these too subsided; and, in half an hour from the commencement of the spectacle, the ice-strewn waters were again rippling crisply under the influence of a moderate breeze, and no sign remained to tell a new arrival upon the scene—had there been one—what an awful tempest of destruction had raged there so short a time before.

Pushing northward, the travellers sighted the coast of Greenland about noon; the land made being a lofty snow-covered mountain, the conical summit of which gleamed like silver in the brilliant sunshine. As they neared the coast the water became more open; and at length they emerged into a broad channel completely free of ice, up which the *Flying Fish* was urged at a trifle less than half-speed, or at the rate of about sixty miles per hour. At eight o'clock that night they crossed, according to their "dead reckoning," the Arctic circle; and midnight found them abreast of Disko Island, gazing with delighted eyes upon the glorious spectacle of the midnight sun, the lower edge of his ruddy disc just skimming the northern horizon.

At this point the channel between the Greenland coast and the pack-ice narrowed very considerably; and their rate of progress northward next day was reduced to a speed of between two and three miles per hour; the engines needing to be just started, and then stopped again for a few minutes in order to keep the speed down to this very low limit. But they were all as yet so new to Arctic scenery—everything was so entirely novel to them—that even this snail's pace failed to prove wearisome, especially as the weather continued gloriously fine.

Strange to say, up to this time they had not set eyes on a single Arctic animal; but now, as they were busily threading their way through a narrow channel in the ice, a white bear was seen about half a mile ahead rapidly making his way across the pack toward them, whilst, a quarter of a mile nearer, an animal which they at once took for a seal was seen basking in the sun on the ice close to the water. It speedily became evident that the bear was after the seal, which, seemingly all unconscious of the proximity of its enemy, raised its head now and then as though in keen enjoyment of the warm glow. The colonel hurried below for rifles, as eager as a schoolboy, to obtain a shot at one or both of the animals; and when he returned to the pilot-house with the weapons both the seal and the bear were within range. He raised one of the rifles to his shoulder, and was covering the seal with it, when Sir Reginald, who was watching the animals through a telescope, said:

"Do not fire, Lethbridge; there is something very curious about this; *that seal is armed with a bow.*"

The colonel stared incredulously at his companion, and then, dropping the rifle, took and applied to his eye the telescope which Sir Reginald handed to him.

"By George, you are right!" he exclaimed. "What a very extraordinary thing. Why," he continued, "it is not a seal at all, it is a man, an Esquimaux. Now, look out and you will see some sport; the fellow is fitting an arrow to his string, and how cautiously he is doing it, too. It is my belief that he has got himself up as a seal and has been simulating the actions of the animal in order to entice that deluded bear within range. There! he has shot his arrow and hit the mark, but the bear does not seem to be very much the worse. Aha! now you have to run for it, my good fellow. By Jove, the matter grows exciting!"

The Esquimaux had indeed been compelled to "run for it," the only apparent effect of the arrow being to irritate the bear. The man ran fairly well, although hampered with an immense amount of clothing, but the bear proved the faster of the two. He rapidly gained upon the man, and seemed about to spring upon him when the party in the pilot-house poured in a general fusillade from their rifles. There was just a perceptible click from the locks of the weapons, but neither fire nor smoke appeared, neither was there any report. At that moment the bear rose upon his hind-legs and, reaching forward with his fore-paws, aimed a terrific blow at the flying hunter. The man, who had been intently watching his enemy all the while, nimbly leaped aside, and, quick as thought, plunged a light lance fairly under the creature's armpit and deep into his body. The bear uttered a single roar of pain and baffled rage, staggered a moment, and fell upon the ice, dead.

"Bravo! very cleverly done, indeed," exclaimed the colonel, apostrophising the distant Esquimaux; "that was a lucky stroke for you, my man. But, I say, professor, what in the world is the matter with these wretched rifles? Every one of them missed fire, and, so far as we are concerned, that unfortunate Esquimaux might have been killed."

"He might—yes, that is quite true," answered the professor with provoking composure; "but if he had been it would have been our fault, not that of the rifles; it was we who missed, not they. Every one of them duly discharged its bullet, and we simply missed our mark. But had we—or rather had I—preserved my presence of mind, I could still have saved the man, for each of these weapons is a magazine rifle, firing twenty shots—a fact which I had forgotten for the moment, and which it now seems I have never yet explained to you. Fortunately, the poor man has proved quite able to take care of himself; but the shameful way in which we all missed the bear, and our failure to fire again, is a lesson on the folly of using untried weapons in an emergency. We must practise, gentlemen; we must practise."

And, without troubling themselves further as to what became of the Esquimaux and his game, the deeply mortified party set themselves forthwith first to listen to the professor's explanation of the peculiarities of the weapons, and next, to practise diligently with them for a full hour; at the expiration of which, as the rifles were really a splendid arm and simple enough to handle when their action had been clearly explained, the quartette had fully regained their confidence in themselves and each other, having done some most excellent shooting.

Meanwhile the channel hourly grew more narrow and intricate; and, to add still further to the difficulties of the passage, the wind shifted round and began to blow freshly from the northward, bringing with it a dense and bitterly cold fog. The travellers struggled gallantly against these adverse circumstances as long as any progress northward was at all possible, being desirous of realising, as fully as might be, for themselves the difficulties experienced by explorers in these high latitudes; but at length they found themselves so completely hemmed in by vast floes and drifting masses of pack-ice that to prolong the struggle would only be endangering the ship, and they were reluctantly compelled to own themselves beaten and to rise into the air.

They rose to a height of five hundred feet above the sea-level, and, at this elevation, found themselves entirely free of the fog. So far this was well, but the dense masses of heavy grey snow-laden cloud which obscured the heavens above them, and the threatening aspect of the sky to windward, told them that their holiday weather was, at all events for the present, gone, and that they were about to experience the terrors of a polar gale. The temperature fell with astounding rapidity; and they were compelled to beat a rapid retreat to their state-rooms, there to don additional garments. This done, they sallied out on deck, to find that during the short period of their retirement a heavy snow-storm had set in, the air being so full of the great white blinding flakes that, standing abreast the pilot-house, it was impossible to see either end of the ship. Floating in the air as they were it was, of course, impossible for them to estimate the strength of the gale, the only apparent movement of the atmosphere being that due to their own passage through it. Though heading to the northward, with the engines making a sufficient number of revolutions per minute to propel them through still air at the rate of thirty miles per hour, it was quite on the cards that the adverse wind might be travelling at a higher speed than this, in which event they would actually be driving more or less rapidly astern, notwithstanding their apparent forward motion. It thus became necessary to post a look-out at each end of the ship, in order to avoid all possibility of collision with some towering iceberg, unless they chose to rise high enough in the air to be clear of all danger; and this they were reluctant to do, as they wished to experience, for at least once in their lives, all the terrors of a polar gale. The baronet accordingly volunteered to look out forward and the colonel to do the same aft, and they hastened at once to their respective stations, Mildmay and the professor superintending meanwhile the engine levers and other appliances controlling the motion of the ship. It was well for them that these precautions were so promptly taken, for the colonel had scarcely reached his post when, through the thick whirling snow which scurried past him, he descried a huge white ghostly mass looming vaguely up in the semi-darkness directly astern, and before he well had time to make up his mind that he actually saw something, the top of a gigantic berg revealed itself close at hand, and his prompt warning cry was only raised in barely sufficient time to prevent the *Flying Fish* driving stern foremost into it, when the loss of her propeller must inevitably have resulted. Mildmay, however, whose quick ear first caught the sound, promptly sent the engines at full speed ahead, and the danger was averted.

Meanwhile, though the snow whirled so thickly around them and the fog was so dense beneath that they were unable to see anything, they were not allowed to remain entirely in ignorance of what was happening in their near proximity. The howling of the bitter blast over the frozen waste beneath resounded in their ears like the diapason of some huge organ played by giant fingers, and mingled with these deeper tones there rose up to them a constant grinding crunching sound with occasional rifle-like reports, telling of the tremendous destruction going on among the ice-floes beneath.

Suddenly the snow ceased, the fog was swept away upon the wings of the gale, and the entire scene in all its terrific grandeur burst at once upon their gaze. They were hovering immediately over the spot where two immense floes had come into collision, and for miles to the right and left of them the contiguous margins were being ground to pieces by the enormous pressure, and the splintered fragments heaped up one above another in the wildest confusion, to a height of from fifty to eighty feet above the surface of the floe. The ice, which was about fifteen feet thick, crumbled away like fragile glass, and it was only by observing the manner in which masses weighing hundreds of tons were wildly tossed hither and thither like corks that even an approximate idea of the tremendous power at work could be obtained.

A mile ahead another grand sight presented itself. The northern and larger of the two floes, acted strongly upon by the gale, and opposed by the smaller floe, was slowly but irresistibly swinging round, and in its sweep it had come into contact with a very large berg, which, influenced apparently by some undercurrent, was with equally irresistible force actually making its way to windward in the teeth of the gale. The result was a scene of wild chaos and confusion and destruction compared with which that upon which they had just looked was as nothing. The berg simply tore its way through the floe as a plough does through a furrow, splitting up the thick ice before it, and tossing the huge fragments hither and thither until its path through the field was marked by a black band of open water churned into fleecy froth by the breath of the tempest, and bordered on either side by an immense wall of ice-blocks, each of which constituted a small berg in itself.

The cold had by this time so increased in intensity that the colonel and the baronet were only too glad to abandon their posts, now that there was no further necessity for maintaining them, and retreat to the friendly shelter of the pilot-house, where they lost no time in closing themselves in.

Chapter Nine
An Exciting Adventure and a Rescue

It was at this moment that Mildmay caught a momentary glimpse of an object far away on the northern horizon, which his practised eye at once told him was a sail of some sort. He instantly seized one of the telescopes suspended in the pilot-house, and brought the instrument to bear in her direction. For nearly a minute he was unsuccessful in his endeavour to find her; but at length she reappeared from behind an intervening berg; and it appeared to him that she was in a situation of considerable peril. She was a barque, under close-reefed topsails, reefed courses, fore topmast staysail, and mizzen; and she appeared to be embayed in the bight of a huge floe, with a whole fleet of bergs in dangerous proximity and apparently bearing down upon her. Perhaps the strangest peculiarity about her was that, notwithstanding her perilous position, she was dressed with flags, from her mast-heads downward, as though it were a gala day on board.

Mildmay's anxious attitude and expression of face, together with his earnest devotion to his telescope, soon attracted the notice of the rest of the party; and the baronet asked him what object it was that so riveted his attention.

He withdrew his eyes for a moment from the instrument, and, pointing out the small and scarcely distinguishable dark spot on the horizon, said:

"Do you see that object, gentlemen? Well, that is a barque embayed in the ice, and evidently making a supreme effort to free herself—an effort which to me, and at this distance, appears quite hopeless. It is my opinion that, unless the wind changes, or something equally unforeseen occurs, she will within the next half hour be smashed into matchwood—unless, indeed, *we* can help her."

"Help her? Of course we can," said the professor; and without waiting for further discussion, he laid his hand on the engine lever and sent the machinery ahead at nearly half-speed.

The *Flying Fish* darted forward like a swallow in full flight; and the professor, leaving the baronet in charge of the engines and the steering-gear, summoned Mildmay and the colonel to follow him. The trio hastened to the after part of the deck, and, raising a trap-door which the professor indicated, withdrew therefrom a thin pliant wire hawser—made, like almost everything else in the ship, of aethereum—which, having secured one end of it to a ring-bolt in the after extremity of the deck, they coiled down in readiness for use as a tow-line.

"There!" ejaculated the professor in a gratified tone of voice, "we will give her the end of that rope; and it shall go hard with us, but we will tow her into some place of at least temporary safety."

"That is all right," responded Mildmay; "but how are we going to get it on board her? Its weight is a mere nothing, it is true, but it is rather too bulky to heave on board. Have you nothing smaller that we can bend on to the eye of the hawser and use as a heaving-line?"

"Certainly I have," replied the professor. "I had not thought of that. 'Every man to his trade.'" And, diving down the hatchway, he rummaged about for a few minutes and finally reappeared with a small coil of very thin light pliant wire line, which Mildmay, pronouncing it to be exactly the thing, proceeded at once to attach to the eye of the hawser.

Meanwhile, the baronet had been anxiously watching the barque through the telescope, and had seen so much to increase his anxiety for her safety that, forgetful of the exposed situation of his companions, he had gradually increased the pace of the *Flying Fish* until he had brought it up to full speed. This, of course, created so tremendous a draught that not only was it quite impossible for the party aft to make headway against it and thus regain the pilot-house, but they actually had to fling themselves flat on the deck to avoid being blown overboard; and even thus it was only with the utmost difficulty that they were able to save themselves.

And this, unfortunately, was not the worst of it. The light hawser, acted upon by so powerful a draught, was for an instant slightly lifted off the deck, and that slight lift did the mischief. The next moment the coils went streaming away astern one after the other, and, almost before those who witnessed the accident could tell what had happened, the propeller had been fouled and the hawser snapped like a thread.

The powerful jerk thus occasioned caused the baronet to turn his head; and he then saw in a moment what mischief he had done. He, luckily, had presence of mind enough to stop the engines at once; the *Flying Fish's* course was stayed, and she immediately began to drive swiftly astern in apparently a dead calm, but actually swept along upon the wings of the gale.

The professor at once scrambled to his feet, and, followed by his companions, hurried to the pilot-house, where, without wasting time in useless words, he at once set himself to look out for a suitable spot upon which to alight, it being absolutely necessary to clear the propeller before again moving the engines, lest in doing so a complete break-down should result.

A favourable spot was at length found—but not until they had drifted completely out of sight of the apparently doomed barque—and the *Flying Fish* was carefully lowered to the surface of a large floe, her anchor being first let go in order to "bring her up" and prevent her being driven along by the wind over the smooth surface. It was a task more difficult of accomplishment than they had anticipated, the anchor for some time refusing to bite, but it caught at last in a crevice, and immediately on the vessel touching, the grip-anchors were extended and the ship secured.

No sooner was the *Flying Fish* fairly settled on the ice than Mildmay, who knew exactly what ought to be done, descended to the lower recesses of the ship, and, opening the trap-door in her bottom, made his way out on the ice, dragging with him a ladder which was always kept in the diving-room. He soon reached the stern of the vessel, and, rearing the ladder in a suitable position against the propeller, nimbly ran aloft and began to throw off the convolutions of the entangled hawser. Twenty minutes sufficed, not only to complete the work, but also to assure him that no damage had been done to the hull of the vessel; and, his three companions having followed him and removed the hawser to the interior of the vessel, he re-entered the hull, secured the trap-door after him, and ascended to the deck. He here found Sir Reginald and the colonel busily engaged in adjusting a new hawser ready for use, and, with his assistance, this task was completed in another five minutes, and the ship was once more ready for service.

As the *Flying Fish* was in the act of rising from off the ice, Sir Reginald asked:

"Should we not make better speed by taking at once to the water, professor?"

"Undoubtedly we should," was the answer. "Such a course would also have the additional advantage of enabling us to immerse the hull to the proper depth as we go along, thus giving us that hold upon the water necessary to cope successfully with the weight of a large ship like the one of which we are going in search. We *might*, whilst floating in the air, be able to tow her out of danger, but I am a little doubtful on the point; and, as this is a case in which it will not do to incur any risk by trying experiments, we will take to the water as soon as we can discover a suitable channel. It appears to me that there is something of the kind about six miles ahead and a little to our right."

There certainly was a channel through the ice at the point indicated by the professor, but whether it was a true channel, or merely a *cul de sac*, they were for the moment unable to decide. On nearing it to within a mile, however, they found it to be the latter; but about a couple of miles beyond it another streak of water was seen extending, unbroken, as far as the eye could reach. For this they steered, and in a very few minutes afterwards the *Flying Fish* was once more afloat, with her water-chambers full and her air-compressor working to the full extent of its power.

The hawser being this time temporarily secured in such a manner as to render a repetition of their late accident impossible, and the entire party being, moreover, safely ensconced in the pilot-house, there was no hesitation about again pressing the ship forward at full speed, the channel, luckily, being straight enough to allow of this; and very soon the group of icebergs in which the unfortunate barque was entangled once more appeared in view. Mildmay was at the helm, with the professor standing by the engines; but Sir Reginald and the colonel no sooner saw the bergs than they seized their telescopes and began at once to look out for the barque.

At first they could see nothing of her, but presently she glided into view from behind an intervening berg, and a single glance was sufficient to assure them that another five minutes would decide her fate. She had gradually set down into the triangular extremity of the bight in which she was embayed, so that every tack she made became shorter than the one preceding it, and very soon the water space would become so circumscribed as to leave no room for her to manoeuvre. But this was not the worst feature of the case. As desperate diseases are sometimes combated with desperate remedies, so in her desperate condition the hazardous and almost hopeless expedient of berthing her alongside one of the edges of the floe might have been attempted. But this last resource was denied to the despairing seamen, from the fact that two enormous bergs, the vanguard of the fleet, had already reached the edge of the floe, on opposite sides of the bay, to windward of the entrapped barque, and were rapidly rasping their way down toward the apex of the triangle where the whaler was already shooting into stays for what must evidently be her last tack. This would be so short that she could scarcely fail to miss stays on her next attempt, when she would drift helplessly down into the corner of the bight, and be ground out of existence by the berg which first happened to reach that point.

It was at this critical moment that a cry of dismay arose simultaneously from the lips of the party in the *Flying Fish's* pilot-house. A slight turn in the channel had revealed to them the appalling fact that it, also, terminated in a *cul de sac*, a neck of solid ice, some fifty yards in width, dividing it from the open water in which the barque was still battling for her life.

What was to be done? There was no time to discuss the question; but a happy inspiration flashed through the baronet's brain.

"We must *leap* the barrier!" he exclaimed.

"Right! I understand," was the professor's brief reply; and, turning the compressed air into the water-chambers, he forced out the water and succeeded in raising the sharp nose of the *Flying Fish* just above the level of the floe a single instant before she reached it.

It was a tremendous risk to run—one which would never have been thought of in cold blood, as the ship was rushing forward at full speed, and there was no knowing what might happen; but the sympathies of the party were now so fully aroused by the awful peril of the barque—which, in the midst of all her danger, was still gaily dressed in flags—that they never paused to think of the possible consequences, but sent the ship at the barrier as a huntsman sends his horse to a desperate leap. For an infinitesimal fraction of time the four adventurous travellers were thrilled with a feeling of wild exultation as they held their breath and braced themselves for the expected shock. Then the smooth polished hull of the *Flying Fish* met the ice, and, rising like a hunter to the leap, slid smoothly, and without the slightest jar, up on to the surface of the floe, across the narrow barrier, and into the water beyond.

"Stop her!" shouted Mildmay, checking the exultant cheer which rose to the lips of his companions. "Sheer as close alongside the barque as you can go, Sir Reginald, and give me a chance to get our heaving line on board. Then, as soon as I wave my hand, go ahead gently until you have brought a strain upon the hawser, when you may increase the speed to about twelve knots—not more, or you will tear the windlass out of the barque. Steer straight out between those two bergs, and remember that *moments* are now precious."

With these words the lieutenant hurried out on deck and made his way aft, where he at once began to clear away the heaving line and make ready for a cast.

The engines meanwhile had been stopped in obedience to Mildmay's command, his companions intuitively recognising that he was the man to cope with the present emergency, and the *Flying Fish* answering the helm, which the baronet, an experienced yachtsman, was deftly manipulating, shot cleverly up along the weather side of the barque.

"Look out for our line, lads!" hailed Mildmay to the crew of the vessel, who were gaping in open-mouthed astonishment at the extraordinary apparition which had thus abruptly put in an appearance alongside them.

"Ay, ay, sir; heave!" answered one smart fellow, who, notwithstanding his surprise, still seemed to have his wits about him. Mildmay hove the line with all a seaman's skill, and a couple of bights settled down round the neck and shoulders of the expectant tar.

"Haul in, and throw the eye of the hawser over your windlass bitts," ordered Mildmay; "we will soon have you clear of your present pickle."

"Thank you, sir," hailed the skipper; "haul in smart there, for'ard, and take a turn *anywhere*; those bergs are driving down upon us mighty fast."

With a joyous "hurrah" at the timely arrival of such unexpected assistance, the men roused the hawser on board, threw the eye over the bitts, passed two or three turns of the slack round the barrel of the windlass, and adjusted the rope in a "fair-lead" with lightning rapidity. Mildmay, who was intently watching their movements, waved his hand as a signal to the baronet the instant he saw that the hawser was properly fast on board the barque, and the *Flying Fish* immediately began to glide ahead. The baronet was evidently bent on retrieving his character and making up for his past carelessness, for he handled his strangely-shaped vessel with most consummate skill, bringing the strain upon the hawser very gradually, and, when he had done so, coaxing the barque's head round until her nose and that of the *Flying Fish* pointed straight toward the rapidly narrowing passage between the bergs. Then, indeed, the thin but tough hawser straightened out taut as a bow-string between the two vessels as the baronet sent his engines powerfully ahead; the barque's windlass bitts creaked and groaned with the tremendous strain to which they were suddenly subjected; a foaming surge gathered and hissed under her bows, and as her harassed crew, active as wild-cats, skipped about the decks busily letting go and clewing up, away went the two craft toward the closing gap.

It was like steering into the jaws of death. The two bergs were by this time within a bare cable's-length of the *Flying Fish's* conical stem; and as they swept irresistibly onward, their pinnacled summits towering five hundred feet into the air, their rugged sides rasping horribly along the edges of the floe with an awful crushing, grinding sound, and their contiguous sides approaching each other more and more nearly every moment, there was not a man on either of those two vessels who did not hold his breath and stand fascinated in awestricken suspense, gazing upon those menacing walls of ice and waiting for the shock which should be the herald of their destruction.

Rapidly—yet slower than a snail's pace, as it seemed to those anxious men—the space narrowed between the bergs and the ships; the grinding crash and crackle of the ice grew momentarily more loud and distracting; the freezing wind from the bergs cut their faces like an invisible razor as it swept down upon them in sudden powerful gusts, apparently intent upon retarding their progress until the last hope of escape should be cut off; the gigantic icy cliffs lowered more and more threateningly down upon them; and at last, when the feeling of doubt and suspense was at its highest, the *Flying Fish* entered the gap. The channel had by this time become so narrow that for the *Flying Fish* to pass through it seemed utterly impossible; indeed, it looked as though there remained scarcely room for the barque with her much narrower beam; and as the towering crystal walls closed in upon them every man present felt that the final moment had now come. Everything depended upon Sir Reginald; if at this critical instant his nerve failed him there was nothing but quick destruction and a horrible death for every man there. But the baronet's nerve did *not* fail him. With a face pale and teeth clenched with excitement, but with a steady pulse and an unquailing eye, he stood with one hand on the tiller and the other on the engine lever, guiding his ship exactly midway through the narrow gorge; and precisely at the right moment, when the *Flying Fish's* sides were actually grazing the ice on either side, he increased the pressure of his hand upon the lever, the engines revolved a shade more rapidly, and the flying ship slid through the narrowest part of the pass uninjured, but escaping by the merest hair's breadth.

But would the barque also get through? She was fully two hundred feet astern of the *Flying Fish*, and the bergs were revolving on their own centres in such a manner that ere many seconds were past they must inevitably come together with a force which would literally annihilate whatever might happen to be between them. And as for the barque—the way in which her bows were burying themselves in the hissing wave that foamed and surged about her cutwater, and the terrified looks of her crew as they glanced, now aloft at the formidable bergs, and now at the straining hawser—from which they stood warily aloof lest it should part, and in so doing inflict upon some of them a deadly injury—told the baronet that he must not increase by a single ounce the strain upon the rope, lest something should give way on board the whaler and leave her there helpless in the very grip of those awful floating mountains of ice.

It was a race between the bergs and the barque; and Mildmay, standing there by the after rail, told himself, as he breathlessly watched the progress of events, that the bergs would win. The contiguous sides of these monsters were slightly concave in shape; and whilst the whaler, still some dozen yards or so within the passage had a foot or two of clear water on either side of her, the projecting extremities of the bergs had neared each other to within a distance of twenty feet, or some five feet less than the breadth of the imprisoned ship.

Suddenly a tremendous crash was heard, and the party on board the *Flying Fish* looked to see the unfortunate barque collapse and crumple into a shapeless mass of splintered wood before their eyes. But, to their inexpressible astonishment, nothing of the sort occurred. There was a reverberating sound as of muffled thunder, which echoed and re-echoed in the confined space between the two bergs; a series of tremendous splashes just astern of the whaler; the bergs recoiled violently from each other; the baronet, more by instinct than anything else, threw the engine lever still further forward, and before anyone had time even to draw a breath of relief, the apparently doomed vessel was dragged, with a foaming surge heaped up round her bows as high as the figurehead, out from the reopened portal and clear of all danger a single instant before the two gigantic masses of ice again closed in upon each other with a horrible grinding *crunch* which must have been audible for miles.

It was not until the barque had been dragged, almost bows under, some fifty or sixty fathoms away from the still grinding and rasping bergs, that her crew were able to realise the astounding fact of their safety, but when they did so they sent up a wild cheer which was as distinct an expression of gratitude to God for their deliverance as ever issued from human lips. Their escape, though it could easily be accounted for, might indeed well be called miraculous, for at the moment when their last hope was extinguished — apparently their last chance gone — two huge overhanging projections on the summits of the bergs had come into contact with such violence that both the projecting masses of ice had become detached and had gone thundering down into the water, fortunately at some few yards' distance astern of the whaler, and the shock of collision had been so great as to compel the momentary recoil of the bergs, with the fortunate result already described.

Directly it was seen that the barque had indeed escaped, the *Flying Fish's* engines were slowed down to their lowest speed, and the whaler, relieved of the enormous tugging strain upon her, once more floated on her normal water-lines. The two craft were now in comparatively open water, the channel being between two and three miles wide, and still widening ahead of them, with a few small bergs in their vicinity, it is true, but with no ice at hand likely to cause them immediate peril. The barque was towed to windward of all these, and then the baronet stopped the *Flying Fish* altogether, and hailed the skipper of the whaler to know whither he was bound. Upon this the worthy man lowered one of his boats and pulled alongside his strange consort to return thanks in person for his recent rescue.

He was a very fine specimen of a seaman, not very tall, but bluff and hearty-looking in his manifold wraps surmounted by a dreadnought pilot jacket, sealskin cap, and water boots reaching to his thighs; and it was amusing to see his look of surprise as he came up the *Flying Fish's* side-ladder and stepped in upon her roomy deck unencumbered by anything but the pilot-house. The four companions of course stepped out on deck in a body to meet him, and after they had all heartily shaken hands with him and deprecatingly received his thanks for the important service rendered in the rescue of his ship from the ice, he was invited to accompany them below to cement the newly-made acquaintance over a glass of grog. And if the worthy seaman was surprised at the exterior of the strange craft he was now visiting, how much greater was his astonishment when he entered her magnificent saloons, revelled in their grateful warmth, and looked round bewildered upon the rich carpets, the handsome furniture, the superb pictures and statuary, and the choice *bric à brac*, all glowing under the brilliant but cunningly modified electric light. And if he was surprised at all these unwonted sights, his astonishment may be imagined when he was informed that the four refined and cultured men who welcomed him so hospitably, constituted, with the exception of the cook and the steward, the entire crew of the immense craft, and that the owner of all the magnificence he beheld had dared the terrors of the polar regions solely by way of pastime.

"Well, gentlemen," he remarked, "it's an old saying that tastes differ, and what you've just told me proves it. I've been a whaler for nigh on to twenty-five years, but it has been a case of necessity, not choice, with me; and after the first two or three years of the life—when the novelty had worn off a bit, as you may say—I've looked forward to only one thing, and that is the scraping together of enough money to retire and get quit of it all for ever. I took to it first as a hand before the mast, and have regularly passed through all the grades—boat-steerer, third, second, and chief mate, master, and at last owner of my own ship, always with the same object ahead. And when, little more than a year ago, I put the savings of a lifetime into the purchase of the old *Walrus* there, I thought that the dream of my life was soon to be realised, and that one trip more to the nor'ard would bring me in a sufficiency to last me the remainder of my days, and enable me to enjoy 'em in the company of my wife and my little daughter. God bless the child! if she's still alive she's five years old to-day."

"Ah!" interrupted Mildmay, "then that, I suppose, accounts for the flags flying on board you, and the meaning of which we were so utterly unable to guess?"

"That's it, sir," was the reply. "I 'dressed ship' at eight o'clock this morning in honour of my little Florrie's birthday, and I hadn't the heart to haul down the flags even when we found ourselves in such a precious pickle amongst the ice yonder. I thought that if so be it was God's will that we was to go, we might as well go with the buntin' still flying in Florrie's honour as not."

"And what success have you met with, captain?" asked Sir Reginald.

"Precious little, sir. We've been out now more'n a twelvemonth, and we've only killed three fish in all that time. Got jammed up here in the ice all last winter. I stayed in hopes of doin' something in the sealing line, and only got some three hundred skins after all. It's been a bad speculation for me. An old friend of mine came this way the year before last, and, the season being an open one and not much ice about, he reached as far north as Baffin's Bay and through Jones' Sound, fillin' his ship with oil and bone in a single season. He was lucky enough to hit upon a spot where the sea was fairly alive with whales, and he filled the ship right up in that very spot. The fish seemed tame, as though they hadn't been interfered with for years; and bein' an old friend, as I said before, he gave me the latitude and longitude of the place as a great secret, and I've been trying to reach the spot ever since we came north, but have been kept back by the ice and the contrary winds. If I could get there, even now, it would make the trip profitable enough to serve my purpose; but I see no chance of it, and the men are getting disheartened."

"Never mind, captain, cheer up; all may yet be well," exclaimed the baronet. "We can't drag your ship *over* the ice, but if there is only a passage for her we can drag her *through* it, and for little Florrie's sake we will. If it is in our power to get you to the spot you wish to reach, you shall go there. Now, as the present open water affords an opportunity too good to be lost, return to your ship, secure our hawser in such a way that we may put a big strain upon it without damaging the vessel, and send a trustworthy hand aloft into the crow's-nest to look out for the best channels. We will tow you to the northward as long as a channel can be found through the ice, and at seven o'clock I hope you will give us the pleasure of your company on board here to dinner, when we will drink 'many happy returns of the day' to Florrie in the best champagne the *Flying Fish's* cellar affords."

The captain of the whaler returned to his own ship in a state of such mingled astonishment and elation that his people were at first inclined to think he had suddenly gone demented. However, the order which he gave them to secure the towing hawser in such a manner as would enable the ship to withstand a heavy strain was intelligible enough; it told them that, with the assistance of their strange rescuers, a supreme effort was now to be made to reach those prolific fishing-grounds which had from the first been the goal of their voyage; and that, best of all, that effort was to be unaccompanied by any of the usual harassing labour of working the ship to windward through the ice, and they set to with a will. A sufficient length of the hawser was hauled on board to enable them to take a couple of turns round the barrel of the windlass and two more round the heel of the foremast, the eye of the hawser being further secured by tackles to every ring-bolt in the ship capable of bearing a good substantial strain; and then, the skipper himself going aloft to the crow's-nest, the signal was given for the *Flying Fish* to go ahead.

Chapter Ten
The "Humboldt" Glacier

The two ships were at this time floating in a tolerably broad expanse of open water; but at a distance of some seven miles ahead the pack-ice stretched, apparently unbroken, across their track for miles. The skipper of the whaler, however, shouted down to them from his elevated perch the intelligence that a somewhat intricate but continuous channel extended through this ice in a northerly direction as far as the eye could reach. Toward this channel, then, away they went at a speed of something like sixteen knots per hour, the barque with her string of colours still fluttering bravely in defiance of the adverse gale, and the *Flying Fish* with the white ensign of the Royal Yacht Squadron, of which Sir Reginald was a member, streaming from her ensign staff in honour of little Florrie. It was a strange sight, even in that region of fantastic phantasmagoria, to see the two ships, one of which, moreover, wore such an unaccustomed shape, dashing rapidly along through the black foam-flecked water, with ice in every conceivable form heaped and piled around them, and their bright-hued flags fluttering against the dark and dismal background of a stormy sky; and the skipper of the whaler possesses to this day a spirited water-colour sketch of the scene, executed on the spot by the colonel, which he exhibits with becoming pride whenever he relates the story of his wonderful escape from the threatening icebergs.

Half an hour later they entered the channel through the ice. Narrow and tortuous at first, it gradually widened out, and, after a journey of some fourteen or fifteen miles, turned sharply off in a direction almost due west. About the same time the gale broke, the sun made his appearance through the rifted clouds, and by seven o'clock that evening, at which hour Florrie's father duly put in an appearance on board the *Flying Fish*, the engines having been temporarily stopped to receive him, they found themselves in open water, or rather in a straight channel some twelve miles in width and entirely free from ice, with a clear sky overhead, a light easterly wind blowing, and the evening sun lighting up the snow-clad peaks of the extensive island called North Devon. An hour later, dinner having been postponed on account of their near proximity to the land, the two vessels entered a commodious natural harbour called Hyde Bay, and anchored there for the night, in order to give the whaler's exhausted crew an opportunity to snatch a few hours of much-needed rest.

The master of the *Walrus*, who answered, by the way, to the name of Hudson, though only a bluff hearty seaman, and somewhat shy for the first half-hour or so in such unaccustomed company as that of his four well-bred easy-mannered entertainers, gradually thawed out under the genial influence of the baronet's champagne, and proved himself a tolerably well informed and by no means disagreeable companion. He possessed a fund of interesting anecdote and information with respect to the peculiarities of the region his hosts were now visiting for the first time, and imparted to them many valuable hints as to the best means of protecting themselves from the ice; but, as they did not see fit to inform him of the aerial capabilities of the *Flying Fish*, he laughed to scorn their project of reaching the North Pole, which he assured them most solemnly was an utter impossibility. They duly drank the unconscious Florrie's health, treated her father to some excellent music, gave him a file of the latest newspapers they had brought with them, and sent him back to his own ship at midnight a thoroughly happy man.

On the following morning about half-past eight, whilst the party on board the *Flying Fish* were sitting down to breakfast, the sound of oars was heard close alongside; and a minute later Captain Hudson, ushered by George, made his appearance in the saloon. He was in a great hurry and almost breathlessly explained that he had come on board to repeat his thanks and those of his crew for their rescue of the previous day, and to say "Good-bye," as he was about to weigh and proceed to sea in chase of a large school of whales which had just been seen spouting at a distance of some twelve miles in the offing. The baronet was good-natured enough to offer to tow him to the scene of action; but this service he gratefully declined, saying that there was a fine fair wind blowing and that his anchor was already a-trip. The party therefore shook hands heartily with him, wishing him "Good luck," and he departed, leaving Sir Reginald and his friends to finish their meal at their leisure.

An hour later the *Flying Fish* also weighed and stood out to sea after the *Walrus*, now nearly hull down, to witness the sport.

The engines had scarcely begun to move when the whaler was seen to heave to; and when the *Flying Fish* ranged up alongside her, some ten minutes afterwards, three whale-boats were in the water and pulling lustily toward a school of some forty whales which were lazily sporting, apparently quite unconscious of danger, about two miles away.

"Those whales do not appear in the least alarmed at the presence of the boats," remarked Mildmay; "evidently they have not been chased for a considerable period. If we only had the means of killing a few, now, what a splendid opportunity there would be to do that poor fellow Hudson a good turn."

"Well thought of!" exclaimed the professor. "Follow me, gentlemen; we can do our friend a good turn, and, at the same time, test the powers of our large-bore rifles with explosive shells for big game."

The party hurried below to the armoury, and each selected one of the weapons indicated by the professor, providing himself at the same time with a supply of cartridges from a large chest near at hand.

The rifles were truly formidable, being repeating weapons each capable of firing ten shots without reloading. The barrels were not very long, measuring only three feet from breech to muzzle, but they were of one-and-a-half-inch bore and fired a conical shell four and a half inches in length. Notwithstanding their somewhat ponderous appearance they were very light, being constructed of aethereum throughout.

When the party returned to the deck they had the satisfaction of seeing that, though each of the whale-boats had succeeded in fastening to a fish, the remainder of the school manifested very little alarm, the stricken whales having started to "run" in different directions and quite away from their companions.

The *Flying Fish* was moved as gently as possible into the very centre of the herd, the huge monsters taking no apparent notice of her, and perhaps mistaking her for one of themselves. They were swimming lazily about, rolling over on their sides until their pectoral fins appeared above the surface, and occasionally throwing themselves entirely out of the water.

The engines being stopped the four sportsmen took up their positions, two on each side of the deck, and, having loaded their weapons, waited for a favourable opportunity to use them.

The baronet was the first to fire. He had selected for his victim a huge bull, fully eighty feet in length, and this creature he patiently watched, hoping for an opportunity to inflict a fatal wound. It soon came. The animal rolled lazily over on its right side, exposing the whole of its left fin, and before it could recover itself Sir Reginald had levelled and discharged his piece. There was a very faint puff of thin fleecy vapour, but no report or sound of any kind save the by no means loud click of the hammer, above which could be distinctly heard the dull thud of the shell. The whale shuddered visibly at the blow, and made as though about to "sound" or dive; but before it had power to do so the shell must have exploded, for the immense creature made a sudden violent writhing motion, half leapt out of the water, and rolled over on its side, dead. The professor scored the next success, closely followed by the colonel, Lieutenant Mildmay signalising his first essay with the new arm by making a palpable miss, much to his disgust. His failure, however, taught him a valuable lesson, and he succeeded in killing two whales before either of the others had been able to secure another shot. In ten minutes eight whales had been killed, and the professor, who was very rigid in his objection to the wanton sacrifice of life, then suggested that probably as many had been killed as the whaler could successfully deal with at one time, especially as the boats now had signals flying which showed that each had killed her fish. The *Flying Fish* was accordingly ranged up close alongside the *Walrus*, and the baronet hailed:

"*Walrus* ahoy! how many fish can you 'cut in' at one operation?"

"I wish I had the chance of trying my hand upon half a dozen," was the reply, given, the baronet thought, in rather a sulky tone.

"Well," returned Sir Reginald, "there are eight which we have killed and three taken by your boats, making eleven altogether. Can you handle any more? because, if so, we will kill them for you; but, if not, we think it best not to disturb them further."

"Do you mean to say that you've killed those fish on my account, then?" asked Hudson with great animation.

"To be sure we did. You surely did not suppose that we wanted them for ourselves, did you?"

The whaling skipper muttered a few unintelligible words to himself, and then shouted back in unmistakably hearty tones:

"Thank'ee, gentlemen, thank'ee with all my heart. That's another favour I'm in your debt. That being the case, I think, if it's all the same to you, I'd rather that the rest of the school be left to go their ways in peace. I don't want them to be frightened; and eleven fish is as much as we can well handle at one time."

"In that case, then," returned Sir Reginald, "we will wish you 'Good-bye,' and a prosperous voyage."

"Thank'ee, gentlemen; the same to you, and best thanks for all favours," replied Hudson.

And with mutual hand-wavings and dipping of colours the two craft separated, the *Walrus* bearing up to intercept her boats, and the *Flying Fish* heading northward at a speed of about twenty knots.

For about a couple of hours the adventurous voyagers were able to maintain that speed; but toward noon they found themselves once more surrounded by ice; and they had no choice but either to materially reduce their speed and slowly thread their way through narrow and tortuous channels, or once more take flight into the air. They chose the latter alternative; and for the next two hours the flying ship sped northward through Smith's Sound, for the most part over an unbroken field of pack-ice which, to any ordinary vessel, would have opposed an utterly impassable barrier. At two o'clock in the afternoon, however, the Greenland shore suddenly trended to the north-eastward; and after following it for a short time the ice once more began to be intersected with water channels, short and narrow at first, but wider as they proceeded, until at length they found themselves once more able to descend in a water lane some four miles in width.

"And now," said the professor, as they were nearing a bold rocky headland on their starboard bow, "we are about to be introduced to one of *the* sights *par excellence* of the Arctic regions."

"What is it?" was the question which burst simultaneously from the lips of his three companions.

"Wait and see," answered the professor, nodding mysteriously.

Sure enough, the moment that the *Flying Fish* rounded the point a magnificent spectacle burst upon the travellers' enraptured gaze. It was neither more nor less than an immense cliff of the clearest crystal ice, towering some three hundred feet above the water's edge, and extending so far northward along the coast that its northern extremity lay far below the horizon. It was the magnificent Humboldt Glacier. The afternoon sun was shining full upon its rugged face, causing the enormous mass to flash and gleam like a gigantic diamond. As they coasted slowly along, at a distance of about half a mile from its face, the dazzling flashes of light were reproduced one after the other, changing rapidly from one colour to another through every conceivable tint of the rainbow, until the beholders' eyes fairly ached with the contemplation of so much splendour, all of which was reflected with the most charming variation in the mirror-like surface of the deep still water below. The wind had died away to a dead calm, as if to give the bold explorers an opportunity of witnessing this unrivalled sight to the best advantage; and every now and then the still air resounded with the sharp rifle-like *crack* which told that, though apparently so motionless and solid, hidden forces were at work within the heart of the glacier, slowly but surely tending to its ultimate dismemberment.

Suddenly a crashing report, so loud that it resembled the simultaneous discharge of a whole army of rifles, smote upon their ears; and then, as they stood in a trance of breathless expectation, wondering what was about to happen, an immense section of the icy cliff was seen to be in motion. Slowly at first, but with ever-increasing rapidity, it slid downward into the water, with a continuous roaring reverberating crash, to which even the awful pealing of thunder was as nothing, until in a wild turmoil of madly leaping and foaming surges it disappeared entirely below the water. The sea rushed irresistibly after it from all sides, pouring like a foaming cataract into the hollow watery basin it had left, and dragging the *Flying Fish* helplessly toward the yawning vortex. Then the inward rush suddenly ceased; a gleaming white crest of ice reappeared above the foam, and with a mighty upward rush and a resounding roar the gigantic submerged mass once more upreared itself above the again maddened waters, swaying heavily to and fro, whilst a thousand gleaming torrents poured down its sparkling sides. And, as a fitting *finale* to the thrilling spectacle, a huge wall of water suddenly heaped itself up about the rocking mass and began to rush rapidly outward in an ever-widening circle, its towering crest surmounted by a roaring curling fringe of snow-white foam. Increasing in height and in speed as it advanced, it rapidly attained an altitude of fully sixty feet, bearing down upon the *Flying Fish* so menacingly that, for a few seconds, the party in the pilot-house stood paralysed with consternation, expecting nothing less than that they would be helplessly overwhelmed. The first to recover his presence of mind was Mildmay, who, springing to the rods which controlled the air-valves, pressed them powerfully down, throwing them all wide open and at once ejecting from the hull both the water and the compressed air, and causing the ship to rise until she floated lightly as an air-bubble on the water. He then injected a dense body of vapour into the air and water chambers, completing the vacuum; and the ship rose into the air just in time to avoid the gigantic surge, which went hissing and roaring close beneath them with a power and fury which fully revealed to them the extent of the disturbance from which they had so narrowly escaped. Other surges followed in quick rotation; but each was less formidable than its predecessor, and in another ten minutes the surface had once more subsided into a state of comparative calm.

As the *Flying Fish* once more settled down upon the water and the air-pump was set going, the professor turned to his companions and remarked:

"We have especial reason to congratulate ourselves and each other, gentlemen, for we have to-day not only looked upon the magnificent Humboldt Glacier under most highly favourable conditions, but we have been also permitted to witness that even rarer sight, *the birth of an iceberg!*"

They had indeed witnessed the birth of an iceberg, and that too of quite unusual size; for, as soon as they dared, they approached the newly fallen mass of ice closely enough to make a tolerably accurate measurement of it; and they found that it was of nearly square shape, measuring fully three-quarters of a mile along each of its four sides, and towering to an average height of about three hundred and fifteen feet above the surface of the water. The visible portion of the berg constituted, however, only a small portion of its entire bulk, since fresh-water ice floating in salt water shows above the surface only one-eighth of its entire depth. This enormous berg, therefore, must have measured in its entirety about four thousand feet square by about two thousand five hundred feet deep! And its weight must have approximated closely upon two thousand millions of tons! Bergs of equal, or even greater dimensions, have occasionally been encountered in the Arctic seas; but how few of earth's inhabitants have ever been privileged to witness the disruption of so enormous a mass from its parent glacier!

After witnessing so thrilling a spectacle as this—probably the grandest and most impressive which the Arctic regions can exhibit—it is perhaps not to be wondered at that even the beauties of the glacier itself appeared somewhat tame and uninteresting to the voyagers. But their interest was once more awakened when, having at length coasted along the face of the glacier for a distance of not less than *sixty miles*, they reached its northern extremity and found the succeeding Greenland coast to be magnificently picturesque, the greenstone and sandstone cliffs in some cases towering abruptly from the water's edge to a height of a thousand feet or more, not in a smooth unbroken face, or even with the usual everyday rugged aspect of a rocky precipice, but presenting to the enraptured eye an ever-varying perspective of ruined buttresses, pinnacles, arches, and even more fantastic architectural semblances. In one spot which caused them to pause in sheer admiration, the crumbling *débris* at the foot of the cliff had shaped itself into the likeness of a huge causeway such as might have been constructed by one of the giants of fabulous times, leading into a deep wild rocky gorge rich in soft purple shadows, at the further edge of which rose a gigantic rock hewn by the storms of ten thousand winters into the exact similitude of a castle flanked by three lofty detached towers all bathed in the dreamy roseate haze of the evening sunshine. And, somewhat further on, they came to a single greenstone cliff the skyline of which was boldly chiselled into the likeness of the ruined ramparts of an extensive city, whilst at its northern extremity, at the edge of a deep ravine, a solitary column nearly five hundred feet high, and standing upon a base or pedestal nearly three hundred feet high, shot straight and smooth up into the deep blue of the northern sky.

Tearing themselves unwillingly away from this region of weird enchantment, the voyagers pushed onward along Kennedy and Robeson Channels, sometimes winding their way through intricate water lanes in the ice, and sometimes skimming lightly a few yards above the surface of the solid pack, until they reached the latitude of 82 degrees 30 minutes North, when the land abruptly trended away to their right and left, and they found themselves hovering over an immense field of pack-ice which extended in an unbroken mass as far northward as the eye could reach.

Up to the present, from the time of their passing Disko Island, the voyagers had seen plenty of seals and walruses, with an occasional white bear, a few Arctic foxes, a herd or two of reindeer, and even a few specimens of the elk and musk-ox, to say nothing of birds, such as snow-geese, eider and long-tailed ducks, sea-eagles, divers, auks, and gulls. Moreover, they had been favoured with, on the whole, exceptionally fine weather—due as much as anything, perhaps, to the fact that they had been fortunate enough to enter the Arctic circle during the prevalence of a "spell" of fine weather, and that they had accomplished in a very few days a distance which it would occupy an ordinary craft months of weary toil to cover. But, on passing the edge of this gigantic ice barrier, they left all life behind them; even the very gulls—which had followed them in clouds whenever the speed of the *Flying Fish* was low enough to permit of such a proceeding—after wheeling agitatedly about the ship for a few minutes with discordant screams, as of warning to the travellers not to venture into so vast and gloomy a solitude, forsook them and retraced their way to the southward. The weather, too, changed, the sky becoming overcast with a pall of dull grey snow—laden cloud accompanied by a dismal murky atmosphere and a temperature of ten degrees below zero. The wind sighed and moaned over the icy waste; but, excepting for this dreary and depressing sound, there was absolute silence, the silence of a dead world.

The ice bore at first the same appearance as all the other ice which they had hitherto encountered, but by the time that they had advanced a distance of thirty miles into the frozen desert they became conscious of a change. The hummocks were not so lofty as heretofore, the hollows between them having the appearance of being to a considerable extent filled up with hard frozen snow; the ice itself, too, instead of being a pure white, was tinged with yellow of the hue of very old ivory; the sharp angles, also, were all worn away as if by long-continued abrasion; the ice, in fact, bore unmistakable evidence of extreme age.

At the professor's suggestion a pause was made and a descent effected, in order that he might carefully investigate the nature of the ice; and, warmly clad in furs, the entire party left the ship for this purpose.

"It is as I feared," said von Schalckenberg, after they had toiled painfully over the surface for some time; "we have reached the region of paleocrystic or ancient ice; and my cherished theory of an open sea about the North Pole vanishes into thin air. Look at this ice here, where a portion of the original hummock still remains bare—it is yellow and rotten, not with the rottenness which precedes a thaw, but with extreme age. See, it crumbles at a kick or a blow, but the fragments do not melt; it is years—possibly *ages*—since this ice was water. And look at the edges of the blocks; they are rounded and worn away by the constant abrading action of the wind, the snow, the hail, and possibly the rain, which has beaten upon them through unnumbered years. It is no wonder that this is a lifeless solitude; there is nothing here capable of sustaining the life of even the meanest insect. Let us return to the ship, my friends, and hasten over this part of our journey; we shall meet with nothing worthy of interest until we reach the Pole, which itself will probably prove to be merely an undistinguishable spot in just such a waste as this."

The professor was, however mistaken; a most interesting discovery awaited them at no very great distance ahead. They returned to the ship oppressed with a vague feeling of melancholy foreboding for which they could not account, but which was doubtless attributable to the gloomy cheerless aspect of their surroundings, and, releasing the ship from the hold of her grip-anchors, resumed their way northward at the *Flying Fish's* utmost speed.

Half an hour later, however, they suddenly checked their flight and diverged a mile to the eastward of their former course to examine an object which Mildmay's quick eye had detected. The object—or objects rather, for there were two of them—proved to be short poles or spars about twenty-five feet apart, projecting about twelve feet out of the ice, and surmounted by the skeleton framework of what seemed to have been at one time small bulwarked platforms. Wondering what they could possibly be, and by whom placed in so out-of-the-way a region, but thinking they might possibly mark cairns or places of deposit inclosing the records of some long-lost expedition, they resolved to stop and institute a thorough examination.

They were fortunate enough to find a smooth and level spot suitable for grounding the *Flying Fish* upon, at a distance of barely a quarter of a mile from the objects of their interest; and it being by that time six o'clock in the evening, and too late to do any good before dinner, they secured the ship there for the night—taking the precaution of fully weighting her down with compressed air in addition to mooring her firmly to the ice by her four grip-anchors. It was a most happy inspiration which impelled them to take this precaution; for when they arose next morning a terrific gale from the northward was blowing, accompanied by a heavy ceaseless fall of snow; and, well secured as the ship was both by her weight and by her anchors, she fairly trembled at times with the violence of the blast. Had she been dependent only upon her anchors and her own unassisted weight—which the reader will remember was very trifling notwithstanding her immense dimensions—she would infallibly have been whirled away like a bubble upon the wings of the gale. The highly-compressed air, however, held her securely down upon her icy bed, and, beyond imparting an occasional tremor, as already mentioned, the tempest, fierce as it was, had no power to move her.

In such terrible weather it was of course useless to think of pursuing their investigations; it would, indeed, have been the sheerest madness to have attempted to face the furious gale, with its deadly cold and the blinding whirling snow. The travellers were therefore compelled to spend an inactive day. For this, however, they were by no means sorry; they had been keeping rather late hours since entering the Arctic circle, and this interval of inaction afforded them an opportunity of securing their arrears of rest. Besides this there were sketches to complete, and a thousand little odd matters to attend to—to such an extent, indeed, that when they once began work they wondered at their own thoughtlessness in not having attended to them before. Thus employed, with occasional interludes of meditative gazing out upon the ceaseless whirling rush of the snow, the day passed rapidly and pleasantly away, wound up by an hour or two of vocal and instrumental music after dinner. They retired early to their warm comfortable state-rooms that night, and were lulled to sweet dreamless slumber by the howling of the gale outside.

The four following days were spent in the same manner—the gale lasting all that time with unabated fury, accompanied by an almost ceaseless fall of snow. But on the fifth day the weather moderated; the snow ceased, or at all events fell only intermittently; the wind backed round and blew from the south-west; and the exterior temperature, which during the gale had fallen to thirty-three degrees below zero, rose twenty degrees. The sky was still overcast and lowering, it is true, and the cold was still intense. But notwithstanding this the weather, compared with that of the preceding five days, seemed positively fine; and, wrapping themselves up in their warmest clothing, and arming themselves with pick and shovel, they set out to discover if possible what lay concealed beneath the two queer-looking poles.

Chapter Eleven
An Interesting Relic

They issued from the ship through the trap-door in her bottom; and no sooner did they find themselves in the open air than an almost uncontrollable impulse seized them to go back again. The contrast between the warm comfortable temperature of the ship's interior and the bitter piercing cold without was so great that at first the latter felt quite unendurable. They, however, persevered; and, after perhaps ten minutes of intense suffering, the severe exercise of scrambling over the rotten slippery hummocks somewhat restored their impeded circulation, and they began to feel that, perhaps, after all, they might be able to do something toward the execution of their self-imposed task. The mere act of breathing, however, continued to be exceedingly painful; and when they at length reached the spot of which they were in search, they were able to fully realise, for the first time in their lives, the incredible difficulties attendant upon the exploration of the regions within the polar circles.

On a nearer inspection of the two poles they proved to be stout spars about the thickness of a man's leg; and, from the appearance in each of a sort of sheave-hole, Lieutenant Mildmay declared his conviction that they were the masts of a small ship. They were very rotten, however, and, if Mildmay's surmise was indeed correct, the craft must have been under the ice for a very long time. The mere suggestion was enough to fully arouse their curiosity; and, forgetful for the moment of the intense cold, to which they were already in a measure growing accustomed, they set to work with a will plying pick-axe and shovel upon the ice with such small dexterity as they possessed.

The task to which they had devoted themselves was, after all, not a very difficult one, the ice, especially that of ancient formation, yielding readily before the vigorous strokes of their picks; and it soon became evident that they could work to greater advantage by dividing themselves into two gangs of two each; one gang breaking up the ice with the pick, and the other shovelling away the débris. The low temperature, however, made the work very exhausting; and by lunch time they had only succeeded in excavating a hole some twenty-five feet long — or the distance between the two masts — by six feet wide and four feet deep. They had widened this excavation by a couple of feet and sunk it some four feet deeper by six o'clock that evening; and then they knocked off work for the day, returning to the *Flying Fish* stiff, and exhausted with their unwonted exertions, but with more voracious appetites than they ever remembered experiencing before.

In this way they laboured day after day for ten days; being greatly hindered in their operations by frequent showers of snow, which filled up their excavation almost as rapidly as they made it, until, beginning to lose patience at their slow progress, they resolved to run a little risk, and the professor was induced to employ a minute portion of his explosive compound in blowing away the sides of the pit to a sufficient extent to allow of the snow drifting out with the wind instead of lodging in the bottom. This engineering feat was successfully accomplished without apparent damage to the object they sought to bring to light; and, thus encouraged, they further cautiously employed the compound in breaking up the ice, with the triumphant result that, on the evening of the thirteenth day before giving up work, they succeeded in uncovering the deck of a craft measuring eighty feet long over all by sixteen feet beam. They were now intensely excited and elated, as they had every reason to believe that—judging from certain peculiarities of build which had already revealed themselves—they had discovered a most interesting relic.

The next morning was most fortunately as fine as they could reasonably expect it to be in that stormy and desolate region; and, commencing work at an early hour—having, moreover, by this time acquired quite a respectable dexterity in the use of their tools—they succeeded by lunch time in laying completely bare the entire hull of what proved most unmistakably to be a veritable ancient Viking ship.

This intensely interesting relic was, as already stated, eighty feet long by sixteen feet beam; with a depth of hold in midships, as they now found, of eight feet; she must therefore have been at the time of her launch quite a noble specimen of naval architecture. She was of course built of wood, and was beautifully moulded fore and aft; her stem and stern-posts were carried to a height of five feet above her rail; and the former was finished off with a rather roughly hewn but vigorously modelled horse's head, whilst the latter terminated in an elaborately carved piece of scroll-work. She was fully decked, with a sort of monkey-poop aft, about two and a half feet high and twenty feet long, beneath which was her principal cabin. Her bulwarks and rail were very solidly constructed; the former being pierced with rowlock holes for sixteen oars or sweeps of a side, in addition to holes abaft, one on each side of, and near the stern-post, for the short broad-bladed steering paddles. Both of these paddles, together with twenty-three oars and two square sails, shaped somewhat like lugs and still attached to their yards, were found stowed fore and aft amidships on the vessel's deck. They were all in an excellent state of preservation, as were also the lower portions of the masts; indeed it was only that portion of these spars which had been long exposed to the air which showed signs of rot, the upper extremities being most rotten, whilst the parts close to the deck were perfectly sound.

Having fully satisfied their curiosity with regard to the exterior of this interesting craft, they next essayed to penetrate below by forcing open the after hatch. On removing the cover a small and almost perpendicular ladder was revealed, down which Mildmay rapidly made his way. On reaching the bottom he found himself in a small vestibule or ante-room, the floor, sides, and ceiling of which were thickly cased with smooth glassy ice, long icicles of varying thicknesses also depending from the beams and deck planking overhead. He could trace the existence of a door in the middle of the bulkhead facing him; but it was hermetically sealed with the thick coating of ice before mentioned, and the removal of this occupied over half an hour. Whilst he was thus engaged the rest of the party at his suggestion returned to the *Flying Fish* for the small electric lamps used in their diving operations; and when they returned he was just about ready to force open the door of the after cabin. This was accomplished without much difficulty, and a faint sickly odour at once became apparent, issuing from the interior of the cabin.

Consumed by curiosity, the party pressed eagerly forward through the doorway, and a most extraordinary sight at once revealed itself. The cabin was a tolerably roomy apartment for the size of the vessel, having for furniture a solid handsomely carved oaken table in the centre, shaped to suit the narrowing dimensions of the vessel abaft, and side benches or lockers all round the sides. The walls or inner planking of the ship were thickly covered with seal, walrus, and white bear skins, evidently hung there to prevent, as far as possible, the penetration of the extreme cold through the ship's sides; and upon large nails, driven through these and into the planks, were hung various trophies of weapons, such as long two-handed swords, small shields or targets, maces with heavy iron-spiked heads, short-handled battle-axes, spears, unstrung bows, and quivers of arrows. But it was not these objects, interesting as they were, which first riveted the attention of the intruders; it was upon *the occupants of the cabin* that their startled glances fixed themselves. Yes, strange as it may seem, the four nineteenth-century travellers found themselves face to face with some at least of the hardy crew who had stood on the deck waving their last good-bye to wives, children, or sweethearts—who shall say how many years ago?—when that stout galley swept out of harbour with pennons flying, oars flashing, and arms glancing, maybe, in the brilliant sunshine, as she started on the enterprise of wild adventure from which she was never to return. The inmates were four in number. Three of them were reclining on the lockers, their heads pillowed upon, and their bodies thickly covered with skins, whilst the fourth, doubtless the master spirit of the expedition, sat as in life at the narrow or after end of the table, his body supported in a massive quaintly carved oaken chair.

The bodies, the floor, the table, and every article in the cabin were thickly coated with frost-rime, which glittered with a diamond-like lustre in the cold keen light of the electric lamps, and the first act of the visitors was to carefully remove and clear away this frost coating. To their intense satisfaction this task was accomplished by gentle brushing without the slightest difficulty, and they were then able to minutely inspect the bodies of these ancient sea kings. They were in a state of surprisingly perfect preservation, and indeed had the appearance of having only recently fallen asleep, the intense cold having seized upon them with such fierce rapidity that their bodies had completely congealed before even the primary stages of decay had had time to manifest themselves. Indeed, judging from appearances, they had succumbed, in the first instance, to starvation, and, overcome by weakness, had been frozen to death. They were all of lofty stature and muscular build, with fair hair and tawny beards and moustaches, the latter worn extremely long. They were fully clad, all in garments of the same general character, excepting that those of the seated figure appeared to be of somewhat finer material than those of his companions. These garments, the outer ones, that is to say, consisted of a thick leathern tunic confined at the waist by a broad belt, and leather drawers reaching from the waist to the ankles, thick leather socks or stockings, and sandals laced to the feet and legs by leather thongs. The tunic of the chief was elaborately embroidered on the breast in silk, a winged black horse being the central and most conspicuous design. The trophy hanging at the back of the sitter's chair consisted of a small circular shield, with a formidable axe, double-handed sword, and mace crossing each other, behind it, the whole being surmounted by a handsome bronze headpiece, or helmet without a visor, having a large pair of finely modelled wings starting from the sides and near the crown. The helmets of the other three occupants were of similar shape, but without ornament of any kind. Two drinking horns were upon the table, one being plainly mounted in bronze, and the other elaborately mounted in silver and supported upon three legs modelled after those of the horse, the fourth leg being lifted in the attitude of pawing the ground.

But perhaps the most interesting object of all was a sheet of parchment which lay stretched upon the table before the sitter, and which he had evidently been studying when the drowsiness of death seized him, and, sinking back in his chair, he had closed his eyes for ever. This parchment was, of course, stiff with the frost of centuries; but by exercising the utmost care the finders succeeded in conveying it intact to the *Flying Fish*, and in thawing it out, when it was found to be covered with a rude but vigorously drawn sketch or chart, representing with surprising accuracy of outline—but without much attention to scale—the whole of the channel between the west coast of Greenland and the east coast of America, and showing, at the top or northern margin, an irregular line *evidently intended to represent land*. And in the top left-hand corner of the chart was a square space marked off as a separate and distinct chart, the centre of which was occupied by an island, the southern coast-line of which corresponded in shape with the line drawn next the northern margin of the main or principal chart. Rudely drawn figures of the whale, narwhal, walrus, seal, and polar bear were sketched here and there upon the chart, as though to indicate spots where these animals had been seen by the author of the document; and on the island shown in the small subsidiary chart, great numbers of animals were drawn, among those represented being hares, foxes, deer, seals, and *elephants*, besides others which the travellers failed to identify. There was also a sketch of a ship—very similar in appearance to the craft from which the chart had been taken—represented as *sailing away from the island*. This particular sketch was the source of much speculation on the part of the quartette; Sir Reginald and the colonel being disposed to regard it as an insertion for the purpose merely of giving a more effective appearance to the chart, whilst the professor and Mildmay were of opinion that it was intended to convey an intimation that the mysterious island had actually been visited.

The above particulars, it need scarcely be said, were ascertained and the surmises discussed after dinner that day; the party not leaving the galley until they had effected a thorough and exhaustive examination of her from stem to stern. They found little else of interest on board her, however, except ten more bodies in the large fore-cabin or forecastle of the craft. The store-rooms occupied the central portion of the vessel, being accessible only from the after end, and the fact that they were clean swept of everything which could by any possibility have served for food, tended to confirm the impression that the expedition had perished of starvation. One or two documents and a massive vellum-bound book were discovered, and these, together with some of the armour and weapons found on board, were taken possession of, but the documents and book proved to be written in a tongue wholly unknown to either of the discoverers, and they were therefore destined to remain for some time longer in ignorance of the history of the long-lost expedition. One fact only was it possible to discover in connection with it, which was that the hardy and resolute crew had undoubtedly cut their way for a very considerable distance into the heart of that vast field of everlasting ice. This was most conclusively ascertained by Sir Reginald and his friends, who, on board the *Flying Fish*, were able to follow quite unmistakable traces of the channel cut by the unknown explorers for a distance of fully forty miles to the southward of the galley itself.

The examination of this strange and interesting craft being at length completed, the cabin doors were closed, the hatches replaced, and the ship, with all that she contained, left to the mercy of the weather, there being no doubt that the excavation so laboriously accomplished would soon be again filled up by the almost ceaseless snow-fall, and the ship again concealed in all probability for ever.

The first thing after breakfast on the following morning, the northward journey was resumed in the face of a perfect hurricane from the northward, accompanied by so tremendous and incessant a fall of snow that it was utterly impossible to see anything at a distance of more than twenty feet in any direction. It was, of course, quite out of the question for anyone to venture outside the door of the pilot-house in such terrible weather; and the cold even inside on the steering platform was so intense that the breath of the travellers was condensed on their moustaches, and, instantly congealing, rapidly formed into a mass of ice which effectually prevented the opening of their mouths. An attempt was made to elude the storm by rising into the higher regions of the atmosphere; but the cold there proved to be so unbearable, notwithstanding the protection afforded by the stubbornly non-conducting material of which the *Flying Fish* was built, that they were compelled to descend once more, and their journey was continued at about a height of one thousand feet above the ice, and at a speed of ninety miles per hour, at which rate of travel they considered that they were stemming the gale, and perhaps actually progressing to windward some ten miles or so every hour.

The dreary day lagged slowly on, with the occurrence of no event of importance, until about four o'clock in the afternoon, at which time the travellers became conscious of a decided rise of temperature. By five o'clock the cold had so greatly diminished that they were compelled to throw off their thick fur outer clothing; and half an hour later, the thick dreadnought jackets, which constituted their ordinary outer covering in bad weather, were also discarded; the snow meanwhile giving place to sleet, and the sleet in its turn yielding to a deluge of driving rain. And, whilst they were still wondering what this singular phenomenon might portend, a hoarse low muffled roar, accompanied by an occasional grinding crash, smote upon their ears through the heavy *swish* of the rain; the dull white monotonous expanse of the ice-field was abruptly broken into by a jagged irregular-shaped black blot ahead; and, almost before they had time to·realise the extraordinary change, the *Flying Fish* had swept beyond the northern boundary of the immense expanse of paleocrystic ice, and was careering northward, at an elevation of about a thousand feet, above the surface of a liquid sea which raged and chafed and tossed its foamy arms to heaven under the influence of the fast-diminishing gale.

"Hurrah!" ejaculated the professor; "hurrah! Scoresby and Kane spoke the truth; and my pet theory turns out to be correct, after all. Gentlemen, look round and feast your eyes upon the glorious spectacle of *an open Polar Sea!*"

Whether it actually *was* an open sea, or only an unusually wide channel between two ice-fields, was now the question to be settled. It certainly looked like the former; it was completely free of floating ice, large or small, except the cakes which were broken away by the waves from the edge of the enormous floe just left behind, and they were kept by the wind close to their parent mass; the sea ran so high and was so regular as to convey the idea of a very considerable extent of "fetch;" and, lastly, there was neither ice nor ice-blink to be seen anywhere along the whole stretch of the northern horizon.

Impatient to solve this momentous and interesting question, the *Flying Fish* was pushed to her utmost speed, causing her to make headway over the ground, and against the fresh breeze still blowing, at a pace of about ninety miles per hour. A quarter of an hour later the rain ceased, and the flying ship plunged into the midst of a dense fog, so thick that it was impossible to see even so far as the guard-rail on either side of the deck. The temperature had by this time, however, risen to *thirty-three degrees above zero (Fahrenheit),* and the travellers therefore at once resolved to again brave the rigours of the upper atmosphere. An immediate ascent was accordingly made, with the satisfactory result, that at an elevation of three thousand feet above the sea-level they found themselves once more clear of the fog, with no perceptible fall of the thermometer, and with a clear view ahead. Twenty minutes more of travelling, and the northern skirts of the fog-bank were past, the clouds broke away, and the westering sun cast his ruddy beams upon the surface of the heaving waters. The sea was still without a vestige of ice, and the horizon was perfectly clear ahead.

Consumed with enthusiasm and impatience, the travellers now effected a descent to the surface of the sea, that having been proved to be the situation in which the *Flying Fish* made her greatest speed, and the journey was promptly proceeded with. A further run of twenty miles found them beneath a cloudless sky, with the wind, soft and balmy, fallen to the gentlest of zephyrs, and the temperature risen to the extraordinary height of forty-five degrees above zero. Their delight, especially that of the professor, was excessive at this wonderful change in their surroundings within so short a time; indeed von Schalckenberg became positively extravagant in his demonstrations, dancing about the deck like a schoolboy, laughing, cheering, clapping his hands, and uttering the most extraordinary prophecies as to what awaited them at the now not far distant pole. The moment was favourable for an astronomical observation; and the ship, notwithstanding their eagerness to press forward, was accordingly stopped for a few minutes to take the necessary sights, after which "Northward ho!" again became their watchword. A few minutes sufficed Mildmay to complete his calculations, and then, amidst vociferous cheering on the part of his companions, he announced to them the gratifying intelligence that they had approached to within a distance of *only one hundred and sixty miles of the North Pole.*

At the moment when this announcement was made it was exactly ten minutes after six o'clock p.m. The speed gauge showed that the *Flying Fish* was then making her way through the water at the rate of one hundred and fifty miles per hour; in a trifle over one hour more, therefore, if nothing prevented, they would reach the goal of their northward journey. Their enthusiasm became almost painful in its intensity; and as the *Flying Fish* rushed at headlong speed through the rippling waters, tossing the wavelets aside in a great outward-curling fringe of sparkling foam, and as the minutes lagged slowly away, the eyes of the quartette in the pilot-house were strained with ever-increasing intensity in their vain efforts to pierce the mysteries of the horizon ahead.

At exactly twenty minutes to seven o'clock, Mildmay electrified his companions, and put the finishing touch to their excitement, by raising an exultant shout of:

"Land ho!"

"Where?" "Show it me!" "I can't see it. You must be mistaken!" exclaimed his companions in chorus, after a breathless moment of vain peering into the pearly northern horizon.

"There it is, directly ahead, looking just like the edge of a flat grey cloud showing above the water's edge," was the reply.

Sure enough it *was* land; for when once their eyes had been directed to the proper point there was little difficulty in discerning it. Moreover, as the ship sped on, it rose rapidly above the horizon, the grey tint growing every moment darker and more distinct, and a few minutes later other land, more sharply defined in outline and more distinctive in colour, rose above the horizon immediately below it, showing that the table-land first made out lay at some distance from the southern shore.

And at this auspicious moment the sea began to exhibit signs of the life which teemed within its depths. An accidental glance astern showed an enormous school of whales spouting on the southern horizon; porpoises undulated sportively to windward; a troop of dolphins suddenly appeared for a moment alongside the ship, evidently straining every nerve to keep pace with her; and an occasional sea-otter rose now and then to the surface of the placid sea, to dive out of sight again the next instant in quite a ridiculous state of consternation at so unwonted a sight as the rushing form of the *Flying Fish*. Flocks of sea-birds of various, and indeed some of hitherto unknown, kinds next made their appearance, industriously pursuing their avocation of fishermen, and—unlike the sea-otters—paying little or no attention to their strange visitors. And finally, as they drew nearer in with the land, seals of various kinds were passed, sportively chasing each other, and pausing for a moment to raise their heads inquisitively and turn their mild glances upon the flying ship.

When within some ten miles of the land, it was deemed advisable to rise out of the water and to complete the journey at a few feet above its surface, thus taking the most effectual of precautions against accidental collision with a sunken rock. As the ship drew in still closer with the land, her speed was reduced; and, at a quarter after seven o'clock on that calm July evening, she once more settled down, like a wearied sea-fowl, upon the surface of the water, and let go her anchor in a depth of twelve fathoms, at a distance of half a mile from the shore, in a fine roomy well-sheltered bay of crescent form, the two horns or outer extremities of which rose sheer out of the water in the form of a pair of bold rocky spurs, backed up on the landward side by a sweep of low grassy hills, crowned, at a short distance from the shore, with a forest of majestic pines.

"Well!" ejaculated the professor, as he finally turned away and went below to dinner, after feasting his eyes on the splendid landscape, gloriously lighted up by the rays of the evening sun, "I was prepared to see many unexpected sights in the event of our reaching the North Pole, but grass and trees!—well, I was *not* prepared to find *them*."

Chapter Twelve
Another Startling Discovery

Notwithstanding the state of excitement which the travellers had been thrown into by the successful accomplishment of this, the first, and, perhaps, the most difficult part of their novel enterprise, they managed to secure a tolerably sound night's rest—if one may venture to term night any part of the twenty-four hours at that season and in that region, where the sun had never once sunk beneath the horizon since the twenty-first of the preceding March, and where the day had still two months more to run before it should wane into the long six-months' night of winter. But, as might be expected, they were up bright and early on the following morning, eager to explore this strange new polar land, and scarcely patient enough to sit down and consume with becoming leisure the appetising breakfast which the still imperturbable George had provided for them.

The meal, however, like most other matters, had an end at last; and the travellers felt themselves free to follow the bent of their impatient inclinations. But the expedition upon which they were about to enter was one not to be undertaken without due foresight and preparation. It was only to be a preliminary exploration, it is true, only a journey of some three or four miles into the interior; but the country and the climate having already proved so extraordinarily at variance with all their preconceived ideas, who could say what new and strange forms of animal life might not possibly be lurking within those vast forest depths? It therefore behoved them to adopt at least a reasonable amount of precaution, and so to equip themselves that, in the event of their encountering new and hitherto unsuspected dangers, they might not find themselves in a wholly defenceless condition.

The question of the kind of clothing to be worn was soon settled. The temperature stood at the extraordinary height (for that latitude) of fifty-seven degrees Fahrenheit; and the air, actually cool and bracing, felt almost oppressively warm to them after the rigours of the paleocrystic ice-field; they therefore donned a suit of rough serviceable cloth of moderate thickness, and stout waterproof leather walking boots. Then, for arms, as they were merely going on a reconnoitring and not a hunting expedition, they decided to take their large-bore repeating rifles, which, with the explosive shells constituting their ammunition, would enable the explorers to face anything. And lastly, as accident or design might cause them to extend their ramble beyond its originally intended limits, they adopted the precaution of providing themselves each with a small light knapsack of provisions. Thus equipped they proceeded on deck, raised the two boats with their davits out of the snug below-deck compartments in which they had hitherto been concealed, and, lowering the smaller boat of the two, stepped into her, and were quickly conveyed to the shore.

It was with a curiously mingled feeling of awe and exultation that they sprang from the boat to the strand, and planted their feet for the first time upon this hitherto unknown and unvisited ground.

"Behold!" exclaimed the baronet, pointing to their footprints in the sand; "behold the first human footprints ever impressed upon this soil." And stepping rapidly forward until he had passed beyond the high-water mark, he unfurled a small union-jack which he carried in his hand, and, forcing the butt-end of the staff into the yielding sand, exclaimed:

"In the name of her most gracious majesty Victoria, Queen of Great Britain and Ireland, I annex this land as a dependency of the British crown!"

Then they all took off their hats and gave three cheers for the queen; after which Colonel Lethbridge proposed that the newly-discovered country be called "Elphinstone Land," a proposition which was carried with acclamation by a majority of three to one, the dissenting voice being that of the baronet, who modestly disclaimed the honour of having the country named after himself.

But *were* theirs, after all, the first human footprints which had ever been impressed upon that soil? A decided answer in the negative awaited them; for they had not advanced very many yards from the shore when they came upon an object which, upon examination, proved to be an ancient and much-rusted spear-head broken short off but with some six inches of the haft still attached to it. The travellers felt, greatly disconcerted at this discovery; it robbed them at once irretrievably of the honour of being the first discoverers of the North Pole, and showed them that, at some unknown period in the remote past, there must have existed a man, or more probably a body of men, who, not only without the exceptional facilities offered by the possession of such a ship as the *Flying Fish*, but with, in all probability, ships infinitely inferior to the worst of those used by modern explorers, had actually achieved the hitherto deemed impossible feat of piercing the great ice-barrier and actually reaching the northern pole of the earth.

Who were they? Of what country could they possibly have been natives? And why was the fact of their important discovery suffered to sink into oblivion? Such were the questions which at once rose to the minds of the baronet and his companions, and to which their lips spontaneously gave utterance.

"I think there can be little doubt as to who and what they were," remarked the professor. "They were *Vikings*; and their leader it must unquestionably have been who drew the chart found by us in the Viking ship buried in the ice of the paleocrystic sea. It is his ship which we see delineated upon the chart; this is the land from which she is represented as sailing triumphantly away; and it was doubtless this land which the Viking ship, discovered by us, was making so desperate an effort to reach when death claimed her crew as its prey. The other question, as to why the discovery of this land was suffered to remain an unknown fact, is not by any means so easy to answer. Perhaps the man before whose dead body the chart lay spread open upon the table may have been its author and the original discoverer of this land; perhaps the ship represented on the chart and the ship discovered by us may have been one and the same; she may have been on her homeward voyage; and, finding the channels to the southward completely blocked with ice, may have been attempting to force her way back into the open Polar Sea when her fate overtook her."

"But, admitting for the moment that such may possibly have been the case," remarked the baronet, "how do you account for the fact that, whilst she must necessarily have forced her way twice through the ancient ice, she should have failed in her third attempt?"

"Her third attempt may have been made late in the season," answered the professor. "But it is just possible that her final attempt may have been to force not a *third* but a *second* passage through the ice. She may have been attempting to return *southward* instead of northward, as I just now suggested. My impression, with respect to the vast field of paleocrystic ice, is that at certain seasons—as when, for instance, two or three very mild winters have occurred in succession in the Arctic circle, followed possibly by exceptionally hot summers—it undergoes partial disruption, splitting up, in fact, into several lesser fields which drift for longer or shorter distances out into the open Polar Sea. The fact that Scoresby, Penny, and Kane all beheld, at different periods, an open Polar sea, tends to confirm this impression; and the circumstance that the bows of the galley discovered by us were pointing to the northward may be due, not to the fact that she was actually making her way north when finally frozen in, but to the accident of that portion of the field by which she was surrounded being subsequently turned completely round whilst adrift. But what object do I see yonder? Surely it is not a human habitation?"

It was, however, or at least had been, at some more or less distant period. It was the roofless ruin of a once most substantially built log-hut, measuring some twenty-five feet long by sixteen feet broad. The roof had fallen in; the log sides were decayed and moss-grown; and the interior was overgrown with long grass and brambles, with a stately pine springing to a height of some ninety feet from the very centre of the structure—all of which incontestably proved its antiquity; but that it was the work of man—most probably those who had left behind them the rusty spear-head—there could be no possible doubt.

The party minutely inspected this interesting ruin, but without making any further discovery, and then pressed forward through the heart of a belt of pine forest which they had by this time reached.

The walking was not difficult and they made tolerably rapid progress. That the country was not absolutely tenantless they soon had abundant proof, for they had not advanced more than half a mile before an Arctic fox was discovered gliding rapidly away before them. A little further on they came unexpectedly upon a herd of moose-deer. The behaviour of these animals—naturally extremely shy—conclusively proved that they had never before met such an enemy as man, for, instead of bounding rapidly away, as is their wont, they merely ceased feeding for a moment to stand and gaze curiously upon the new-comers, and then went on browsing again with the utmost composure. Their fearlessness offered a strong temptation to such inveterate sportsmen as Sir Reginald and the colonel; but not being in actual need of their flesh, and being, moreover, anxious not to disturb them just then, the party passed quietly on without firing a shot. A huge brown bear was the next animal encountered, and this time the baronet's love of sport overcame his humanity, bruin falling an easy victim to the noiseless but deadly percussion shell of Sir Reginald's large-bore rifle. A solitary prowling wolf next fell before the equally deadly weapon of the colonel; and then the explorers emerged on the other side of the forest-belt, and found themselves on the borders of an extensive tract of tolerably level country intersected here and there by low hills, with occasional patches of marshy land, the high flat table-land, which had been the first object sighted by them when approaching these shores from the southward, looming up, still misty and grey, at a long distance in the extreme background of the landscape.

Heading directly for this mountain, as a conspicuous landmark, the party again pressed forward, and were speedily delighted to observe several flocks of ptarmigan busily feeding on the crests of the low hills which here and there crossed the route. These birds proved rather shy, though not so much so as to have prevented the sportsmen making a very decent bag had they been provided with fowling-pieces. As it was, however, the birds were, of course, permitted to go free and undisturbed. A mile further on a small drove of musk-oxen were seen grazing in the distance, and, whilst some of the party were watching the animals and discussing the possibility of stalking them, Mildmay, who had been intently gazing through his binocular in another direction, startled his companions by exclaiming, in an almost horrified tone of voice:

"What on earth are those immense creatures moving slowly about in the valley away yonder? Surely they *can't* be elephants?"

"Elephants! my dear fellow, don't be absurd," remonstrated the baronet. "Where are they? Oh, ah! now I have them," as he brought his glass to bear in the right direction. "By George, they *are* elephants, though, and monsters into the bargain. And, I declare, it seems to me that they are covered with a thick coat of shaggy hair. Why, I never saw such a thing in my life."

"*Elephants? Covered with hair?*" exclaimed the professor in a voice so eager that it almost amounted to a scream. "Lend me a binocular, somebody; with my usual luck I have left mine at home—on board, I mean. A thousand thanks, Mildmay, my dear fellow. Now, where are these elephants of yours? Quick, show me where to look for them. Good heavens! if it should really be so. Ah! now I see them. Yes—yes—they are—they *must* be—Gentlemen, as I am a man of science, I solemnly declare to you the stupendous fact that those extraordinary animals are neither more nor less than living Mammoths. I congratulate you, gentlemen—I congratulate myself. Ach, himmel! to think that it should ever be my good fortune to actually behold, not only one, but a whole herd of living mammoths! I cannot believe it— yet—yes, there they are; it is no freak of a disordered imagination, but an actual, positive, undeniable reality."

The worthy professor was so excited that he could scarcely hold the binocular firmly enough to look through it, and it was really laughable— to his companions—to hear his "Ach's" and "Pish's" of impatience as he vainly strove to steady his trembling hands and get another good look at the herd of hitherto believed extinct monsters, which were quietly feeding at a distance of about two miles away. At length he, with a comical gesture of despair, restored the borrowed binocular to Mildmay, and, turning to his companions, exclaimed in a voice of feverish earnestness:

"Come, my dear friends, why do we stand idly gaping here and wasting valuable time, when we really have not a moment to lose? We may never have such a priceless opportunity again. Let us press forward, then, and at all risks secure a specimen of so unique an animal as the mammoth. If we were to achieve this and nothing more our success would be ample repayment for all the anxious thought devoted to the designing of our vessel, and all the money spent in her construction."

His excitement was contagious, and the baronet, after briefly arranging with the colonel a plan of operations, invited von Schalckenberg to follow him; Lethbridge and Mildmay going off in another direction, with the object of getting on the other side of the animals, and, in co-operation with the other party, driving them, if possible, within easy distance of the harbour in which the *Flying Fish* lay at anchor.

To do this a wide détour was necessary, and it was nearly an hour and a half later when the four men found themselves in a proper position to commence the operation of "driving." They had arranged themselves in the form of a semicircle round the herd, at a distance of about a quarter of a mile away, and, at a signal from the baronet, all hands advanced toward the huge creatures, shouting and gesticulating to the utmost extent of their several powers.

The mammoths, utterly unsuspicious of danger, had been quietly feeding among the long grass during the approach of their enemies; but on the baronet's first signal shout they paused, and, facing rapidly round in the direction of the noise, raised their trunks in the air and waved them slowly from side to side as though scenting the air. The hunters now redoubled their exertions, fully expecting that, on seeing them, the animals would wheel about and shamble off in the required direction. But, to their dismay, the creatures, instead of doing this, no sooner caught sight of the party than, with upraised trunks and harsh trumpet-like screams of rage and defiance, they charged furiously straight down upon them. The herd numbered ten individuals, four of which appeared to instantly constitute themselves the defenders of the party; and each of these promptly selected his own particular enemy, occupying his attention so fully that the remaining members of the herd were afforded every facility for escape.

It was a nervous moment for the hunters, who, never having faced such a creature before, had not the most remote idea of its fighting tactics; moreover, the aspect of the monsters, with their towering stature of fully fifteen feet, their thick shaggy coats of rusty brown hair, their enormous spirally curving tusks, and their small eyes blazing with fury as they rushed forward to the attack, all combined to produce such a hideous *tout ensemble* as might well strike terror to the boldest heart. But neither Sir Reginald nor the colonel were the men to shrink from an encounter when game was before them; Mildmay possessed all the cool daring and recklessness of the British seaman; and as for the professor, he would willingly have faced a thousand deaths to secure so new and rare a specimen of natural history as the creature before him.

LIEUTENANT MILDMAY RUNS FOR HIS LIFE.

The four sportsmen pulled trigger almost simultaneously. The baronet and the colonel had each selected the same spot, the eye, as the object of their aim, and both had been equally successful, the shell in each case passing upward through the eyeball into the brain, exploding there and causing instant death. The professor's fascinated gaze being riveted upon the wide-open mouth of his own particular adversary, he seemed to think that the yawning cavern thus revealed would be as good a place as any to empty his rifle into; and he did so—just in bare time to bring down his game and save himself from being trampled to a jelly. Mildmay, however, was not so fortunate. He seemed to think that it mattered very little where he directed his aim, so long as he made sure of hitting the brute *somewhere*, and he therefore fired point-blank at the chest of the mammoth which was menacing him. The shell sped true, but, encountering the thick shaggy coat and the enormously tough hide of the creature, failed to penetrate the body, and, exploding outside, only inflicted such wounds as further excited the already angry monster to a perfect frenzy of rage. Even at this critical moment there was time for another shot; but Mildmay most unfortunately forgot that he had nine loaded chambers still available, and instead of firing again he flung away his piece and ran for his life. The race was a disastrously short one, however; he had not run more than twenty yards when the huge creature was upon him. The great uplifted trunk gave one whirl in the air and descended with force enough to slay an ox. It struck poor Mildmay on his right side, and, but for the fortunate accident of his having at that moment tripped and fallen forward, the lieutenant would there and then have lost the number of his mess. As it was, he was sent whirling through the air like a cricket-ball, to fall senseless, and bleeding from the nose and mouth, fully forty feet away. The vindictive brute instantly turned short off with the evident intention of trampling his victim to death; but before he could reach the prostrate body a shell from the colonel's rifle sent him crashing lifeless to the ground. The remainder of the herd, evidently dismayed at the slaughter of their companions, now abandoned a half-formed intention which they had at first manifested to stay and fight it out, and went off in full retreat with horrible trumpetings of anger and alarm.

The colonel was the first to reach the side of his unfortunate friend, the professor and the baronet joining him as speedily as their legs could convey them to the spot. Very fortunately von Schalckenberg, among his other multitudinous acquirements, possessed a very fair knowledge of medicine and surgery; and his skilful fingers were soon at work removing the lieutenant's clothing so far as was necessary to investigate the nature and extent of his injuries. Singularly enough these were found to be comparatively trifling, a fractured rib and several very severe bruises being the sum of them. A little brandy forced between the lips of the sufferer soon restored him to consciousness, and he was able to sit up.

On attempting to rise to his feet, however, he experienced such severe pain that it was then and there resolved to let him remain where he was, two of his companions also remaining to mount guard over him and see that he came to no harm; whilst the third was to hurry back with all speed to the ship and bring her out on to the plain close by the spot where the accident occurred, when it would be a comparatively easy matter to convey the lieutenant from the spot where he then lay to his own bed on board the *Flying Fish*.

The professor, having first made Mildmay as easy and comfortable as circumstances permitted, volunteered for the service of moving the ship, explaining to his companions that, in the event of an attack of any kind, they, as seasoned sportsmen, would be able to far more effectually defend the wounded man than he could possibly hope to do; and then, Sir Reginald and the colonel quite concurring in this view, he set off for the bay, shouting back an assurance as he went that he would not be absent one moment longer than should prove absolutely necessary.

The worthy scientist was as good as his word; for in less than an hour from the moment of his departure the immense bulk of the *Flying Fish* was seen to rise into the air beyond the tops of the distant pine-trees, and, with her polished hull gleaming and flashing in the rays of the sun, to sweep gracefully round until she was heading straight in the direction of the anxious watchers. Under the professor's able pilotage she was soon brought to the ground and secured within a dozen yards of the spot occupied by them, when it was the work of a few minutes only to convey the injured man to his own stateroom, where his hurts were at once properly attended to and himself made thoroughly comfortable.

As soon as luncheon was over Sir Reginald and the colonel set out for the spot were they had shot the bear in the morning, one of them being armed with a large-bore rifle and the other carrying a fowling-piece; and on their return somewhat late in the afternoon they bore not only the skin, skull, and claws of the defunct bruin, but also a goodly bag of ptarmigan. During their absence the professor had also been very busy, dividing his attention pretty evenly between Mildmay and the finest specimen of the slain mammoths, the latter of which he had succeeded in nearly half-denuding of its skin. With the assistance of his two able-bodied friends this task was completed by dinner-time; and by the corresponding hour next evening not only was the enormous hide undergoing the first stage of preparation for the taxidermist, but the indefatigable labourers had also succeeded in hewing out the tusks of the other slaughtered mammoths. For health's sake the ship was then moved about a mile further inland, and the carcasses were left to the wolves, which had already gathered in large numbers in the vicinity.

Under the skilful treatment of the professor Mildmay made steady and rapid progress toward recovery from the very first; the baronet and the colonel had therefore no hesitation about carrying out a project which had been under discussion between them for the last two or three days, and which was neither more nor less than a pedestrian excursion to the far distant table-land which they had first sighted from the sea. They estimated that this goal of their journey, upon which they expected to find the actual site of the Northern Pole of the earth, must be about sixty miles distant from the ship; and they considered that the trip there and back would occupy them about six days. It would of course have been very much easier, and more convenient in every way, to have made the journey on board the *Flying Fish*; but the professor was busy with the preparation of his mammoth, the skin of which he had carefully stretched and pegged out on the ground alongside the ship, and was so averse to the losing sight of it, even for a few hours, that it was soon decided the *Flying Fish* must not be moved for the present. After all, the journey would probably not involve any very great amount of hardship; it simply meant camping out for five or six nights, or at least those hours of the twenty-four which did duty for night. And this the two seasoned hunters looked forward to as rather a pleasant change than otherwise.

The necessary preparations were all made on the previous evening, and after breakfast on the appointed day the two adventurers set out, taking leave of Mildmay—who was already out of bed again—and of the professor, who, to tell the truth, was heartily glad to be left to the uninterrupted prosecution of his task.

They were in light marching order, having resolved to carry nothing which they could possibly do without; their previous experience of the country had taught them that game was pretty plentiful, and that they might safely depend upon their guns for the supply of their larder; and their stock of provisions consisted solely, therefore, of a few biscuits and a substantial flask of brandy each. The temperature was decidedly mild, and had been so ever since their arrival at "Elphinstone Land," with settled fine weather, and they therefore carried nothing in the shape of extra clothing save a light macintosh each, which they bore securely strapped on the top of their knapsacks. The remainder of their *impedimenta* consisted of a double-barrelled gun for each man—one barrel being rifled and the other a smooth bore—two cartridge belts, one for the waist and the other for the shoulder, fully stocked; a formidable double-edged hunting knife each; a capacious waterproof bag containing a reserve supply of cartridges, and a small stock of matches and tobacco.

Their road for the first five or six miles led up a gentle acclivity, just sufficient to make itself felt, but not steep enough to render walking difficult or fatiguing. Then came a stretch of flat country, bounded on each side by the projecting spurs of a range of rugged hills of fantastic outline which stretched immediately across their path at a distance of some three or four miles or so. The pedestrians had not progressed very far across this plain before their attention became arrested by a curious phenomenon. The atmosphere immediately behind the range of hills last mentioned was thick with fleecy vapour, now so thin that the distant table-land could be dimly seen through it as through a veil, and anon so dense that it assumed a decided cloud-like shape upon which the unsetting sun shone with dazzling brilliancy. This thickening of the vapour seemed to occur at tolerably regular intervals of about twenty minutes each, and was immediately preceded by a sudden silvery gleam succeeded by a most brilliant and perfectly formed rainbow. The periodical recurrence of this singular phenomenon under a perfectly cloudless sky of course greatly excited the curiosity of the pedestrians, and they pushed rapidly forward, eager to ascertain the cause.

As they advanced, the encircling hills thrust their projecting spurs further and further into the narrowing plain, their slopes became steeper and more rugged, and rocks began to crop out here and there with increasing frequency through the lessening soil. A corresponding change of course occurred in the character of the landscape; it grew increasingly picturesque and wild at every step, and at length the travellers found themselves at the mouth of a narrow rocky boulder-strewn gorge bounded on either side by titanic masses of volcanic rock, rugged and moss-grown, with little patches of herbage here and there, or an occasional stunted pine growing out of an almost imperceptible fissure. The only signs of life in this wild spot consisted of a diminutive musk-ox here and there cropping the scanty herbage half-way up the apparently inaccessible height in spots from which it appeared equally impossible for the creature to advance or to retreat.

Plunging into this defile, the travellers advanced with steadily increasing difficulty, the boulders with which their path was strewed growing ever larger and more numerous until at length the narrowing road became completely choked with them, and the only mode of progression was that of a slow, toilsome, dangerous scramble. Still the pair pushed resolutely on, every minute hoping that the difficulties of the journey would come to an end, and every minute less willing to turn back and again encounter the obstacles already surmounted. At length the path became so narrow that one enormous boulder sufficed to completely block the way, whilst the perpendicular rocky walls of the chasm towered so far aloft that only the merest thread of sky was visible; the air grew chill and damp, and so deep a twilight gloom pervaded the place that it was difficult to distinguish any object more than half a dozen yards distant.

The weary travellers looked at each other in dismay. Was this to be the ineffectual ending of that long and toilsome scramble through the ravine? There was just one single narrow crevice between the huge boulder which blocked their way, and one of the precipitous walls which pressed so closely in upon them—a crevice left by the irregular shape of the block, and affording barely space enough for a man of robust proportions to squeeze himself through—and they determined that, before retracing their steps, they would at least satisfy their curiosity so far as to creep through this crevice and see what lay on the farther side. The baronet with some little difficulty squeezed through first, and his exclamation of astonishment quickly took the colonel to his side.

The pair found themselves in a narrow rent between the two vertical faces of rock—the projections of the one accurately corresponding with the indentations of the other, and clearly demonstrating that, at some distant period of the earth's history, that mighty chasm had been suddenly torn open by a great natural convulsion awful in its intensity beyond all power of imagination. The rent was roofed in as it were by boulders which thickly hung suspended and jammed in at varying heights between the almost touching walls of the rift; and the adventurous explorers could not repress a shudder as they glanced aloft at these huge masses and thought of the consequences to themselves which would ensue should a projecting corner just then yield and suffer its parent rock to come crashing down to the bottom. Their first impulse was to beat a precipitate retreat; their second, to go forward; for at only a few yards' distance before them the rift closed altogether, except at the very bottom, where a low cavern-like fissure dimly appeared. A hasty consultation passed between them, resulting in a determination to go forward and explore the fissure.

Fortunately for their purpose they had, at an early stage of their difficulties, provided themselves with a couple of stoutish pine branches— wrenched from their parent stems and hurled into the ravine perchance by some winter storm—to aid them in surmounting the difficulties of the way, and these they now determined to utilise if possible as torches.

With some little difficulty the smaller ends of these brands were induced to kindle; but, once fairly ignited, they blazed up bravely, and thus provided with the necessary lights the adventurers boldly pushed forward and plunged into the recesses of the fissure.

Chapter Thirteen
At the North Pole

The opening was so low and so narrow, that for the first fifty or sixty feet the explorers were I obliged to creep forward on their hands and knees; then it widened and became gradually higher, so that by the time they had penetrated a couple of hundred feet they were able to resume a perpendicular attitude. The cavern, if such it could be called, still however remained so narrow that it was only here and there possible for them to walk side by side. It was also very tortuous; and the heights varied momentarily, at one time compelling them to stoop almost double in order to pass beneath some immense projection, and anon increasing so greatly that the light of their torches failed to reach and reveal the roof. They observed several rifts or crevices to the right and left of them as they pressed forward, but, with one or two exceptions, these were quite impassable, and those which were not so were still so cramped that they offered no inducement to deviate from the main passage.

Groping thus in semi-darkness over painfully rough and broken ground, a full hour was spent, and the colonel was just expressing his conviction that they must have traversed a distance of fully two miles when a faint glimmer of daylight revealed itself on one of the rocky walls of the passage; and, turning sharply round an angle, the pair suddenly found themselves once more within a few yards of the open air.

Emerging into broad daylight a most wonderful spectacle greeted the two adventurous explorers. They found themselves standing on a narrow strip of coarse sandy beach at the bottom of an immense basin, measuring fully a mile in diameter, the sides of which were formed of lofty precipitous cliffs of volcanic rock, so smooth and so nearly vertical that nowhere, at least in their immediate neighbourhood, could they discover a spot capable of being scaled. Before them, and occupying the whole bottom of this enormous basin, stretched a placid lake, the water of which was as clear as crystal. A thin filmy veil of vapour rose everywhere from the surface of the water, softening the hard outlines of the more distant landscape, and imparting an aspect of dreamlike witchery and unreality which it would certainly have otherwise lacked.

"Why, the water is tepid!" exclaimed Sir Reginald, plunging his hand into the lake and raising a small quantity of its water in his palm, to ascertain by taste whether it was fresh or salt.

The colonel thereupon thrust *his* hand down, and satisfied himself by experiment of the truth of his companion's statement. It was even more than tepid, it was positively *warm*.

The two were still discussing the probable reason for this phenomenon when their attention was suddenly arrested by a curious movement of the water in the centre of the lake. First a few tremulous ripples appeared, spreading outward from the centre; then the disturbance became more pronounced, until, within a minute, an area of some thirty or forty yards in diameter had assumed an appearance of violent ebullition. Suddenly a jet of steam and spray shot up out of the centre of this disturbed spot; and then, before either of the two bewildered spectators could find time to remark upon so curious a phenomenon, an immense column of purest crystal water shot into the air to a height of at least two hundred feet, and, gleaming and flashing in the sunbeams as it soared away above the level of the encircling cliffs, spread out into a dome-like sheet, and, leaving behind it aloft a dense cloud of vapour of dazzling whiteness, fell again into the lake in the form of a shower of boiling water.

"A geyser!" exclaimed the baronet. "A geyser! and of such grandeur that the Great Geyser of Iceland, which I have seen, sinks into the utmost insignificance compared with it."

"You are right," acquiesced Lethbridge. "I too have seen the so-called Great Geyser, and admired it immensely; but after this—"

He finished with a shrug of the shoulders so expressive that there was not the slightest need for words to explain his meaning.

"We must bring the professor to see this," he continued after a slight pause. "And—look here, Elphinstone—if you wish to intensely gratify the worthy man, call this geyser after him—'The Von Schalckenberg Geyser'— eh? It doesn't sound half bad, does it?"

The baronet laughingly consented to his friend's proposal, the more readily as he knew that what Lethbridge had said as to the professor's gratification was perfectly true; and then the wanderers resumed their journey, passing along the narrow strip of sand which divided the edge of the water from the base of the cliffs.

"There is no doubt, I think, that this geyser produces the cloud of vapour and the sudden flashing gleam, at tolerably regular intervals, which so aroused our curiosity this morning," remarked the baronet as they plodded somewhat wearily along side by side over the sand.

His companion assented, and then they both paused, and finally flung themselves down upon the sand to witness a repetition of the eruption, the premonitory signs of which at that moment made their appearance. Then, when it was over, finding themselves very comfortable—and very hungry—they concluded to take luncheon before again moving; and, this being followed by a pipe, it was after four o'clock in the afternoon when they once more made a move.

A saunter for three-quarters of an hour along the margin of the lake enabled them to reach a spot almost directly opposite that where they had emerged into daylight from the interior of the cavern; and here they found the point of overflow from the lake. The chain of hills, which from their first point of sight had appeared to completely surround the sheet of water, was here pierced by a narrow valley, through which a small shallow stream, emanating from the geyser lake, made its devious way. As the course of this valley appeared to trend generally in a northerly direction, or toward the high table-land of which the travellers were in quest, and as, moreover, the valley appeared to offer the only exit from the lake basin in a northerly direction, the travellers decided to follow its course, which they did by keeping close to the margin of the stream. This mode of procedure, whilst it afforded them tolerably easy walking, also enabled them to estimate more accurately than they had hitherto done, the enormous quantity of water projected into the air by the geyser; for whilst the stream normally consisted of a body of water some ten feet wide by three or four inches deep, it was swollen—at regular intervals of twenty minutes each, corresponding with the periodical discharge of the geyser—into a rushing and foaming torrent of about ten feet wide and four feet deep, lasting thus for about a minute, when the stream again rapidly subsided to its previous depth.

For a distance of about two miles the stream wound its way over a bed of exposed rock, beyond which occurred a considerable stretch of coarse gravelly soil, thickly overgrown with long grass. The constant flow of water for untold ages through this bed of gravel had scoured out a channel nearly forty feet wide by half that depth; the banks being perfectly vertical, except in a few places where the gravel had crumbled away to a rather steep slope.

It was whilst the wanderers were passing one of these places that— the sun being by this time in the western quarter of the heavens, and his level rays falling directly upon the right bank of the stream—the baronet's attention was arrested by the appearance of several bright sparkling gleams emanating from among the *débris* of the crumbling bank. He directed the colonel's attention to these, whereupon the latter, seized with sudden excitement, scrambled down the bank, waded across the shallow stream, and in another instant flung himself down upon his knees on the gravel. Before the astonished baronet could follow him he leaped to his feet again, and, whilst he waved some glittering object above his head, shouted:

COLONEL LETHBRIDGE DISCOVERS A DIAMOND MINE.

"Hurrah! hurrah! Elphinstone, my dear fellow, we are in luck to-day. Here is a fabulous fortune for every one of us, to be had merely for the trouble of picking up. *This is a bed of diamondiferous gravel.*"

Sir Reginald hastened across the stream, and, scrambling half-way up the bank, joined his companion on the spot where the latter had halted.

"Look here!" exclaimed Lethbridge, holding out for inspection a crystal as large as a pigeon's egg; "what think you of that for a first find? And it is of the first water, too."

The baronet took it in his hand and examined it critically. Then he handed it back with the remark:

"Well, my dear fellow, I am no judge of diamonds, at least in their natural uncut state; but if your supposition—that you have discovered a 'bed' or 'pocket,' or whatever you call it, of diamonds—be correct, I most heartily congratulate you."

"You—congratulate—*me*?" gasped the colonel. "Why, my dear Elphinstone, what on earth do you mean? I am much obliged for your congratulations, certainly; but whether the diamonds here be many or few, we shall of course all share alike, so you may also congratulate yourself and our absent friends at the same time. And as to my supposition being correct, I have had too much experience at the South African diamond-fields to make a mistake in such a matter. Why," he continued, looking round and picking up two or three more stones, "they are positively sown broadcast just here—an hour's diligent work in this spot will make us all rich beyond the power of computation."

"If that be the case," returned the baronet, "then here goes to help you. But, mind, I am a rich man already; and not a single stone will I accept until all three of you are perfectly satisfied that you have abundantly sufficient for all your requirements."

"Very well," said the colonel. "Go ahead with that understanding if you like. I feel pretty confident that, even upon such terms, you will be able to take back to England, if all goes well, sufficient gems to make the future Lady Elphinstone—should there ever be such a personage—a diamond suite which shall cause her to be the envied of all beholders."

Sir Reginald laughed gleefully. "I have never yet met a woman charming enough to induce me to yield up my freedom of action and movement for her sake, and I do not think it likely I ever shall," he said.

Lethbridge shook his head a little doubtfully, but he was just then so busy digging down into the gravel with his hunting-knife that he had no breath to waste in the words of a disclaimer.

The baronet moved away to a distance of some twenty feet, and began poking about the gravel in a very careless, half-hearted sort of way, occasionally picking up and slipping into one of his capacious pockets such crystals as he thought likely to be of value.

Half an hour of this work sufficed him; and, rising to his feet, he cried: "Spell, ho! as our friend Mildmay would probably observe. Now, Lethbridge," as he sauntered up to his companion, "let us compare the results of our labour."

With this he flung himself down upon the gravel, and, plunging his hand into his pocket three or four times, produced a goodly little heap of gems of all sizes, ranging from that of a pea up to stones of fully one ounce in weight. Meanwhile the colonel brought his collection to light, and a very fine one it was, the stones being nearly twice as many as those gathered by the baronet, though many of them were much smaller.

"Is that all?" asked Sir Reginald.

"*All*?" echoed Lethbridge; "why, my dear sir, what would you have? If, after we have quite exhausted the ground here, my share amounts to such a handsome collection as this, I can assure you I shall be exceedingly well satisfied. You have made a most excellent haul too, but I think mine is the more valuable of the two."

"Perhaps," said the baronet, "*this* will go some way toward equalising our finds." And as he spoke he quietly slipped his hand into his pocket and smilingly produced a stone fully as large as a hen's egg.

The colonel took it into his hands and critically examined it for several minutes. It was most unmistakably a diamond, and that, too, of the very finest water, without the faintest trace of a flaw of any kind. He remained silent so long that Sir Reginald grew impatient and finally blurted out:

"Well, man, what is it? Is it a diamond, or is it merely a worthless piece of crystal? Why don't you speak?"

"Simply," said the colonel as he took a final look at it against the light and then handed it back, "because I am at a loss for words to express my admiration. It *is* a diamond, and, so far as I know, the finest that has ever yet been brought to light. Its value must be simply fabulous, and I heartily congratulate you on its discovery. Where did you find it? Was it deep in the gravel?"

"Come with me and I'll show you," was the reply; and, leading the colonel back to the spot, Sir Reginald quietly pointed to a hole about eighteen inches deep which he had excavated, and wherein lay, side by side, seven other gems equally as fine as the one he had produced.

"Help yourself, my dear fellow," he said with a laugh, "and then let us be moving; we have our dinner to find yet, you know."

Lethbridge fairly gasped for breath as his eyes first fell upon the magnificent jewels; but he lost no time in transferring them to his pocket, and then he turned to the baronet and asked what would be the best thing for them to do next.

"Let us simply continue our journey," answered the baronet. "Of course if these stones which we have found are really diamonds, which I do not doubt, since you assure me that they are, I am as fully alive as yourself to the fact that a mine of incalculable wealth lies here at our feet. But it will not run away within the next few days. Let us finish our exploration and return to the *Flying Fish*. We will then move her to this spot, and all hands of us can then go to work at diamond-hunting in good earnest. Meanwhile, if these large stones are of such inestimable value, it seems to me that they are likely to prove, after all, practically valueless, for the simple reason that nobody will be found willing to spend the enormous sum which would enable him to become a purchaser."

"That is very true," answered the colonel with a laugh. "The stones of moderate size are what we must hope to realise upon; nevertheless, I shall not pass over such large ones as may happen to thrust themselves under my notice, for if we should fail to dispose of them, they will still come in handy as ornaments for our future wives, in which, notwithstanding a remark you made a little while ago, I somehow have a profound belief. Now, if you are ready to march, so am I."

The pair accordingly shouldered their guns, and, turning their backs for the time being upon the diamond mine, continued their course down the valley.

Half an hour later a herd of reindeer was discovered browsing upon the lichens and mosses which grew plentifully on the rocky spurs of the range of hills from which the travellers were now emerging, and one of these was soon afterwards killed with little or no difficulty by means of a bullet from one of the rifles. To such experienced hunters as Sir Reginald and the colonel the task of "breaking up" the deer was an easy one, and, that done, they went into camp on the spot, and feasted royally that night upon reindeer tongue and marrow-bones.

The two following days passed uneventfully, that is to say the travellers met with no adventure specially worth recording. They passed through extensive tracts of pine forest, and saw plenty of game, to say nothing of such valuable fur-bearing animals as the sable and ermine, both of which animals seemed to be extraordinarily abundant, and late on the evening of the third day they found themselves at the base of the table-land, after a somewhat fatiguing but most enjoyable tramp.

The next day was devoted to a thorough examination of the somewhat remarkable object which they had set out to visit. It proved to be an enormous mass of rock, nearly circular in shape, about three miles in circumference, and towering aloft from the surface of the surrounding plain to a height of between three and four thousand feet, as nearly as could be measured without the aid of instruments. Their idea had of course been not only to reach this enormous rock, but also to ascend to its summit, but this they found to be quite impracticable, a journey round it demonstrating the fact that on all sides its cliffs rose perpendicularly and without a single break from the base to the flat summit. For that time at least they were defeated; but when they finally turned their backs upon "Mount Mildmay," as they determined to name it, it was with a fixed resolve that, before many days were over, they would reach the summit with the aid of the *Flying Fish*.

Their journey back to the ship was marked by no more noteworthy incident than the sighting in the distance of a herd of mammoths, apparently the identical animals with which they had already had an encounter. They followed a somewhat different route from their outward one, making a détour round the group of hills which inclosed the "Schalckenberg Geyser," and arrived at the ship late on the evening of the sixth day from their departure, weary and somewhat foot-sore it is true, but in all other respects in the very best of health, and with thoroughly pleasant memories of their journey.

They were of course welcomed with open arms by the two friends they had left behind them. Mildmay, under the professor's skilful treatment, was rapidly advancing toward complete recovery; and as for the scientist himself, he was jubilant in the highest degree over the fact that he had been thoroughly successful in his preparation of that gigantic "specimen," the mammoth. A great deal of desultory conversation of course took place within the first hour of the wanderers' return; but at last the party settled down, and then followed a recital by Sir Reginald of the particulars of the journey. Both the professor and Mildmay were of course intensely interested in the story, but in different ways. Mildmay's interest was merely that of the ordinary travelled man of culture, but von Schalckenberg was disposed to regard everything from the scientist's view-point, and incessantly broke the continuity of the narrative by a whole string of questions which neither Sir Reginald nor the colonel could possibly answer. He was extravagantly delighted with both the description of the geyser and the sight of the diamonds, and it was difficult to say which pleased him most; perhaps the most gratifying circumstance to him was the information that the geyser had been named after him, at all events he begged most pathetically that the projected visit to this most interesting object might be allowed to take precedence of that to the diamond mine.

Such being the case, it will readily be understood that no pen of mere ordinary graphic power could hope to adequately portray the ecstasy of enthusiasm with which the worthy man, two days later, actually viewed the geyser itself from so advantageous a stand-point as the deck of the *Flying Fish*; such a task is utterly beyond the powers of the present narrator and must be left to the vivid imagination of the indulgent reader. For over two hours did that amiable and learned scientist sit immovably in his deck chair with a meerschaum of abnormal dimensions in his mouth, and with his eyes beaming in a rapt admiration, which was almost adoration, upon the magnificent spectacle; and it was not until he had been solemnly assured by the others that he would be excused from all participation in the task of diamond-hunting and have full liberty to return to the geyser and spend there the whole of the time during which the rest of the party might be so engaged, that he consented to leave the spot at all.

Three days were spent at the diamond mine; and, with the aid of proper tools obtained from the ship, this time proved sufficient for the accumulation of such a hoard of priceless gems as would, if disposed of at even half their market value, realise a magnificent fortune for each of the lucky finders.

The next move was to the summit of the flat tableland, which was of course easily reached by the *Flying Fish*. It proved to be, as had already been surmised, merely an enormous mass of bare rock, without a scrap of soil or vegetation of any kind about its surface, and useful only as a citadel, into which, had it been planted in some more accessible spot on the earth's surface, it would undoubtedly have been converted, in which case it would have eclipsed even Gibraltar itself in the matter of impregnability. Useless as it was, however, where it stood, its summit afforded an admirable look-out; and from that point of vantage the travellers made the discovery that "Elphinstone Land" was an island, the horizon at that elevation being bounded by the sea on every side. The rock was roughly circular in shape, with a circumference of about three miles, and the travellers made the circuit of the summit in about an hour and a half, pausing at frequent intervals to admire and enjoy the magnificent panorama of woods and hills and streams which lay spread out beneath them. Herds of elk, reindeer, and musk-oxen were seen dotted about here and there on the plains below, as well as a skulking wolf or two, a few Arctic foxes, and other wild animals. The herd of mammoths—apparently the only herd in the island—was also seen; and, with the aid of their telescopes, the travellers were also able to make out, far away at sea, certain dark moving spots which, from their alternate appearance above and disappearance beneath the surface, they judged to be whales.

The chief business of the travellers, however, on the summit of "Mount Mildmay" was to ascertain whether or no the North Pole of the earth was or was not situated within its circumference. This was rightly regarded as a matter of such great importance that several days were unhesitatingly devoted to its settlement; and Mildmay, the professor, and Colonel Lethbridge were busy from breakfast time in the morning until dinner-time at night, making the most careful observations and working out the necessary calculations. These were at length satisfactorily completed—not one moment too soon, for the sun was daily dropping nearer and nearer to the horizon—and the trio were enabled, not only to say that the North Pole *was* contained within the limits of the summit, but to plant their feet upon it and to say unhesitatingly and authoritatively:

"This is the North Pole!"

The position having thus been accurately determined, the next thing was to mark the spot.

With this object a large triangle was first described about it, and a point was carefully marked off on each of its sides in such a position that a line tightly strained from such point to the opposite angle of the triangle would pass directly through the pole. This done, an excavation six feet deep in the solid rock was made, and in its bottom was deposited a tightly-sealed bottle containing a small parchment scroll, on which was inscribed a brief statement of the circumstances connected with the discovery of the spot, with the date, and the signatures of the joint discoverers. This bottle was carefully packed in and buried up with small fragments of rock, and made finally secure by a covering of excellent concrete, the materials for compounding which had been carefully and with infinite labour prepared by the professor. Then, when the concrete had become properly hardened, a substantial flagstaff of aethereum was stepped into the hole in a position accurately corresponding with the North Pole of the earth, and also made secure by being built in or "set" in concrete, which completely filled the hole. The professor next, with the aid of a diamond, engraved on the staff, in bold conspicuous characters, at a height of five feet from the ground, the words:

"*This staff marks the exact position of the North Pole of the earth.*" And finally, amid cheers from the rest of the party, Sir Reginald Elphinstone ran the Union Jack up to the staff head and knotted the halliards so that it would remain there, thus formally claiming for the British nation the honour of actual discovery.

Chapter Fourteen
Southward Ho!

So important a matter as the localisation of the Pole having thus been satisfactorily disposed of, it was next resolved to effect a thorough exploration of the entire island, including its circumnavigation. This, with the aid of the *Flying Fish*, was pretty effectually accomplished in a fortnight, after which the ship returned to her original anchorage in the harbour, on the south side of the island, now named Lethbridge Cove.

Both the forests and the adjacent waters of this favoured hyperborean land were found to be literally swarming with game and other animals, some of which afforded in their flesh a welcome change from the preserved meats with which the ship's larder was stocked, whilst the chief value of others lay in their "pelts" or skins; and, the hydrographic features of the island having been carefully ascertained and recorded, the party, with the exception of von Schalckenberg, now gave themselves up unreservedly to the pleasures of the chase. The professor's tastes lay more in the direction of geology, mineralogy, and botany, though he was also an enthusiastic naturalist, and thus, whilst he sallied forth every morning armed with gun, hammer, specimen box for his botanical treasures, and bag for his minerals, the three others went their several ways, either armed with traps and guns in search of game, or in one of the boats, duly provided with dredger, net, and line, in quest of ocean spoils.

Thus employed, the short remainder of the Arctic summer swiftly passed away; the sun daily sank nearer and nearer the horizon; the temperature fell; frost made its appearance, hardening the soil beneath the tread and coating the pools and puddles and morasses with an ever-thickening sheet of ice and the vegetation with a delicate tracery of silver; and at length the day came when the anchor was lifted and the *Flying Fish* moved some few miles out to sea to enable her occupants to witness the final disappearance of the sun beneath the southern horizon. Some anxiety had been experienced by the travellers for the last few days, as clouds had been gathering in the sky, with every indication of a speedy change of weather, and it was feared that the sight, which they had long been promising themselves, would, after all, be denied them; but at the last moment, or rather at the last hour, fortune proved favourable to them; the cloud-bank broke up along the south-western horizon, the vapours grouped themselves into a series of imposingly picturesque masses, all aflame with the most gorgeous tints of sunset, and from a little after eleven o'clock until shortly after noon the thin golden upper edge of the luminary's disc was visible sweeping imperceptibly along the purple horizon, until finally, as it reached the point of disappearance, it glimmered feebly for a moment, and, whilst the travellers stood watching it bare-headed, sank out of sight. The Arctic day was over, and the six months of night and winter had set in. Not, it must be understood, that darkness set in immediately—far from it; for several succeeding days there ensued a weird, delicious, magic, and ever-deepening twilight; but by the eighth day after the sun's final disappearance this also had vanished, and night reigned with undisputed sway.

And now, too, winter laid its icy hand with unrelenting grasp upon this beauteous polar island; not, however, to desolate it with storm and howling tempest and the deadly cold with which he visits less favoured climes, but only to add newer and more unaccustomed beauties to the scene. It is true that for the first fortnight after the disappearance of the sun the weather wore a more or less unsettled aspect. The sky became overcast with a canopy of cloud which, light and fleecy at first, steadily increased in density; and at length, on the travellers emerging from the pilot-house one morning after breakfast, they found the motionless air thick with falling snow, which, settling noiselessly down, had already covered the deck to a depth of some three inches. The darkness was of course intense, so much so, indeed, that it was impossible to see for a distance of half the length of the ship, and for all that they could see of the land it might as well have been a hundred miles distant.

This state of things lasted without intermission for the ensuing four days and kept the travellers close prisoners on board their ship. This, however, they in nowise regretted; indeed this short breathing space was positively welcome to them, for they had plenty of work to do; and, shut up warm and snug on board the *Flying Fish*, with all her saloons, cabins, and corridors brilliantly illuminated by the electric light, they busied themselves in carefully preparing and curing the many unique specimens of natural history and the various choice skins and furs they had already accumulated.

But on the morning of the fifth day they found that another change of weather had taken place, and, on going out on deck, a glorious spectacle greeted their delighted eyes. The snowfall had ceased, the sky was once more cloudless, and the deep sapphire blue was studded with countless myriads of scintillating stars that gleamed with the cold sharp lustre which is seen only in periods of very severe frost. But it was not the brilliant starlight, beautiful though that was, which drew ejaculations of wonder and delight from the lips of the entranced beholders; it was another and a rarer sight which excited their admiration. As they looked, the sky immediately overhead, and for a distance of some twenty degrees all round from the zenith, became tinged with the softest and most delicate rose-colour, bordering which there suddenly appeared a broad circle of flashing rays of light, blood-red at the inner rim of the circle, and merging from thence through the richest purple into brilliant blue, and from thence, through green of every conceivable tint, into a clear dazzling yellow at the points of the rays. These superbly-tinted rays were animated by a constant motion; now withdrawing themselves into the main body of the circle as into a sheath, and anon darting out again until they almost reached the horizon; and so delicately transparent were they that, notwithstanding their brilliant colour, the stars were distinctly perceptible through them. This magnificent spectacle continued for a full hour with ever-increasing brilliancy, suffusing sea and land with a quivering glow of prismatic light, and imparting an aspect of magic, unearthly, indescribable beauty to the scene. Then the colours gradually faded, the flashes became more feeble, and the darting rays ever shorter and shorter, until they finally faded completely away, to be succeeded shortly afterwards by the keen silvery radiance of the young crescent moon which slowly rolled upwards from the horizon, and, shedding her subdued light upon the snow-clad landscape, invested it with an air of bewitching mystery and unreality which was distinctly heightened by the profound impressive silence of the long Arctic night.

With nature thus presenting herself to the travellers in so novel and attractive a guise a month swiftly passed away, during which they tended their traps or prosecuted their hunting expeditions under the glorious light of the aurora, the cold steel-like radiance of the silver moon, or the dim mysterious starlight; alternating these open-air employments with assiduous devotion to their easels, in sufficiently clever but altogether unsuccessful efforts to adequately transfer to canvas the entrancing beauties of the Arctic scenery and phenomena which constantly charmed their delighted eyes.

Toward the end of October, however, the temperature had fallen so low that ice had begun to form all along the coast-line of Elphinstone Land, and the weather had taken a decided change for the worse. Moreover, the party had accumulated so much extra weight in the shape of valuable skins, natural history specimens, and other curiosities, as to seriously affect the buoyancy of the *Flying Fish* as an aerial ship; and they therefore at last—more than half-reluctantly—came to the determination to desert the enchanted region of the Pole and wend their way southward.

Accordingly, on the morning of the first day of November the anchor was hove up; the vapour was turned into the air and water chambers, producing an almost perfect vacuum; and, rising into the air to an altitude of about ten thousand feet, the *Flying Fish* turned her nose southward, and, illumined by the dazzling effulgence of the most glorious aurora the voyagers had ever seen, was sent ahead at the utmost limit of her speed.

It was determined to return to England forthwith, and without pause or stoppage of any kind, unless some unforeseen necessity should arise, the object being to dispose of their various acquisitions previous to a renewal of their wanderings. The elevation at starting was therefore maintained, and the ship pursued her headlong flight to the southward with only one man—Mildmay—in the pilot-house to take charge and enact the part of look-out; the remainder busying themselves in packing up their various treasures for transference to safe-keeping on shore. The pilot-house, like every other habitable portion of the ship, was maintained at a comfortable temperature by means of pipes communicating with the vapour-generating chamber in the engine-room below; and, reclining at his ease in a most luxurious lounging chair, the lieutenant had nothing to do but maintain a vigilant lookout through the circular windows, and solace himself with his pipe meanwhile. The ship's speed through the air was about one hundred and twenty miles per hour; and by their calculations they expected to overtake the sun in about latitude 79 degrees 49 minutes north; if, therefore, the *Flying Fish* maintained her speed, the sun ought to appear once more above the horizon in four hours thirty-five and a half minutes from the time of starting—Lethbridge Cove being situated in exactly 89 degrees 0 minutes North latitude. It was exactly nine o'clock in the morning when they started; consequently, if their calculations were right, the sun ought to make his appearance at thirty-five and a half minutes past one; and it was this phenomenon for which Mildmay was chiefly watching, his companions being anxious to have the unique experience of seeing the luminary rise an hour and a half past mid-day. And it was for this reason, and in order that they might not on the one hand be taken by surprise by being hurried southward on the wings of a favouring gale, or on the other hand be delayed by a possible adverse one, that the elevation of ten thousand feet had been selected, this being well within the limits of the *neutral belt*, or zone of motionless air.

Not to be caught napping, Mildmay extinguished the electric light in the pilot-house as the musical gong of the clock suspended therein struck the hour of one; after which he rose to his feet and took a good look round on all sides. There was, however, nothing to be seen save a vast sea of cloud beneath his feet and on all sides, as far as the eye could reach, softly illumined by the light of the star-studded heavens above. But even as he looked a just perceptible paleness in the deep velvety blue of the sky to the southward attracted his attention. He looked more intently. Yes, there could be no mistake about it; that pallor of the southern sky was undoubtedly the first faint indication of the approaching dawn; and he at once struck two strokes—the appointed signal—upon the great mellow-toned bell which hung in the pilot-house.

The call was promptly answered by the appearance of his three fellow-voyagers, who, abandoning whatever they had in hand, rushed helter-skelter up the saloon staircase and into the pilot-house, anxious to lose no scrap of that, to them, now novel sight, sunrise.

Rapidly yet imperceptibly the pale dawn stole upward into the sky; the lustrous stars waxed dim before it, and one by one twinkled out of sight; a faint roseate flush tinged the sky along the horizon, brightened first into a rich orange, then into purest amber, the colours being faintly reflected on the most distant edges of the vast cloud-bank floating below; and at length, just as the hands of the clock marked thirty-five minutes after one, an arrowy shaft of pure white light shot upward into the sky, swiftly followed by another and another; and then, with a dazzling flash of golden light, the upper edge of the sun's disc rose slowly into view, soaring higher and higher until the whole of the glorious luminary was revealed, whilst the rolling sea of cloud above which the *Flying Fish* skimmed glowed softly beneath his beams with varying tints of the most exquisite opal.

This return to the realms of day had a curious effect upon the travellers. They had not been conscious of the least depression of spirits consequent upon their sojourn of more than a month in the region of uninterrupted night, but it must have affected them, however unconsciously, to no inconsiderable extent, for now, at the first glimpse of sunshine, their spirits rose to an extravagant height; they felt as though they had just effected their escape from some terrible doom, and they were irresistibly impelled to shake hands with each other, to exchange congratulations, and to talk all together, laughing uproariously at even the feeblest attempt at jocularity.

The thoughts of the quartette were, however, speedily diverted by the ever-imperturbable George, who now sounded the gong for luncheon, and the whole party at once trundled below, leaving the ship to take care of herself, as they very safely might, seeing that she was now travelling down the "first" meridian, or that of Greenwich, with no land ahead nearer than the Shetland Islands, more than a thousand miles distant.

After luncheon, however, the whole party returned to the pilot-house, where they spent the time smoking and chatting, talking over their past adventures, and maturing their further plans, until sunset, when, their short day having come to an end, they once more retired below to complete their preparations for a flying visit to London previous to a resumption of their wanderings.

The question of the disposal of the *Flying Fish* during the short period of their absence from her had greatly exercised their minds for a time. They were anxious still to avoid for the present, if possible, anything approaching to notoriety or the attraction of public notice to their proceedings, and they felt that this could scarcely be done if they ventured to take so singularly modelled a ship into any British port, however insignificant; moreover, there are very few harbours or havens on the British coast capable of receiving a ship with such an excessive draught of water—namely, forty feet—as that of the *Flying Fish*. So they finally decided to sink her off the Isle of Wight (first of all, of course, taking the precaution to accurately ascertain the bearings of her berth), and to proceed to Portsmouth in the two boats, taking with them the spoils of their polar expedition, and trusting to their own ingenuity to evade such suspicions and speculations as might be engendered by the somewhat singular circumstances connected with their arrival, especially as the hour—about half-past four o'clock on the following morning—at which they would reach the Wight would be favourable to the execution of their plan.

The night was intensely dark, with a fresh north-easterly gale blowing, accompanied by frequent rain-squalls, as the voyagers found on descending to within about a thousand feet of the level of the sea at midnight, in order to discover, if possible, their whereabouts. But they could see nothing save the lights of a few ships and fishing craft dotted about here and there; the appearance of the latter indicating that they had already approached to within a short distance of the land; nor did they sight anything by which to fix their position until first the light on Flamborough Head and then that on Spurn Point flashed into view out of the murky darkness. Then indeed, having satisfactorily identified those lights, they knew exactly where they were; the course was altered and shaped anew directly for the spot of their intended descent, and the ship once more soared to her former elevation.

At twenty minutes after four o'clock a.m. a second descent was made, when it was found that they were passing over hilly country which they surmised to be that situated about the borders of the three counties of Surrey, Hants, and Sussex; and almost immediately afterwards the lights on the forts in progress of construction at Spithead came into view, together with the anchor-lights of two or three men-o'-war in the roadstead, and they knew that the first part of their journey was almost accomplished.

Precisely at half-past four o'clock the *Flying Fish* took the water about two miles to the eastward of the "Noman" fort, and her occupants at once began the search for a suitable berth for her—a berth, that is to say, in a position where she would not be likely to be discovered by the fishermen, and where the depth of water would be sufficient to permit of the largest man-o'-war passing over her submerged hull without striking upon it. To discover such a spot proved by no means an easy task; but it was accomplished at last, though at a distance considerably farther out to sea than they had bargained for, and at half-past five o'clock her anchor was let go in the selected berth. Cross bearings were then most carefully taken and entered in each of the travellers' pocket-books, after which the next task was to get their varied spoils into the boats and the boats themselves into the water. This was soon done, and then all hands, including George and the *chef*, but excluding the professor, entered the boats and shoved off a few fathoms from the ship's side, where they anchored.

The first faint signs of dawn were just appearing in the eastern sky when it became apparent to those in the boats that the huge bulk of the

Flying Fish was disappearing. Steadily but imperceptibly she settled lower and lower in the water until her deck was awash and nothing but her pilot-house remained visible in the dim ghostly light of the early morning. A minute more and this too had disappeared, and, as the waves washed over its top, the baronet carefully lowered over the side of his boat a rope-ladder, well weighted at the bottom and with an unlit electric lamp attached to it in such a position as to hang suspended at a height of about six feet above the bed of   the sea. This lamp was of course attached to a battery in the boat, and as soon as Sir Reginald felt the weights at the foot of the ladder touch bottom he sent the current through the insulated wire, a patch of vivid white light, like a patch of moonlight, immediately shining out beneath the waves and showing that the lantern was properly performing its duty. Then they waited.

THE PROFESSOR APPEARS AFTER BERTHING THE "FLYING FISH."

Not for very long, however. An interval of perhaps five minutes elapsed, and then a quivering jerky motion became communicated to the rope-ladder, followed a minute later by the appearance of von Schalckenberg in his suit of diving armour. He stepped quietly into the boat, and whilst he busied himself in doffing his glittering panoply, the lamp was extinguished, the ladder hauled inboard, the anchors tripped, and the two boats made their way slowly to the westward, heading in for Nettlestone Point and the Solent.

They arrived at Portsmouth about half-past seven o'clock, and Sir Reginald at once made his way to the Custom House to get the boats' cargoes cleared. He was fortunate enough to find in the collector a man with whom he had had several previous transactions, and who was consequently pretty well acquainted with him. This facilitated matters greatly, and by half-past eight the duty (a very considerable sum) had been paid and the goods passed, so that nothing further remained but to land everything and have it conveyed to the railway-station for transmission to town. This done the two boats were taken into "The Camber" and put under the care of a trustworthy man, after which the party breakfasted at the "George," proceeding to town directly afterwards by the twelve-o'clock express.

Chapter Fifteen
A Troop of Unicorns

A week later, the four friends once more found themselves beneath the roof of "The Migrants'", where it had been arranged that they were to meet and take luncheon together prior to their journey down to Portsmouth to rejoin the *Flying Fish*. On comparing notes it was found that each had, according to his own views, made the best possible use of his time, the professor having not only placed the mammoth's skin in the hands of an eminent taxidermist, but also prepared and read before the Royal Society a paper on "The Open Polar Sea," which had created a profound impression on the collective mind of that august body; Lethbridge and Mildmay had seized the opportunity for paying a too-long-deferred visit to their respective mothers; and Sir Reginald had, acting upon the best obtainable advice, conveyed the four parcels of diamonds belonging to the party over to Amsterdam, where they had been left in the care of a thoroughly trustworthy diamond merchant, with instructions that certain of the jewels were to be cut and set in the handsomest possible manner, whilst the rest were to be disposed of as opportunity might offer. The furs were also satisfactorily got rid of; some of them having been sold, and the remainder (consisting of all the choicest skins) placed in the hands of the furriers to be cured and taken care of until their owners should return to claim them.

The luncheon was a very lively meal; the conversation naturally turning to the last occasion upon which the travellers had met there; and upon its conclusion the four friends chartered a couple of hansoms, which conveyed them to Waterloo station in good time for the Portsmouth express.

On their arrival at the Harbour station they found George and his French friend, the cook (both of whom had been granted a week's leave), dutifully awaiting them on the platform. The boats, under the care of the man who had been placed in charge of them, were lying alongside the adjacent slipway, in accordance with a telegraphed arrangement which had preceded the travellers; and, entering these, the party at once proceeded down the harbour, past Southsea and its castle, and out toward Nettlestone Point. It was by this time quite dark, save for the light of the young moon, which was already near her setting, and the boats were consequently at once urged to their full speed in the direction where the *Flying Fish* had been left.

Having originally taken their cross bearings wholly from the shore lights, the voyagers had now no difficulty whatever in placing the boats in their proper position. Arrived on the spot, a sounding-line was dropped over the side, and the first cast showed that they were floating exactly over the submerged ship. The boats were therefore allowed to drift with the tide until they were clear of the *Flying Fish*, when Sir Reginald dropped his anchor and ladder, and the professor, who had already routed out from the stern locker and donned his diving armour, stepped over the side, adjusted his weights, and quietly disappeared beneath the surface of the water. A lapse of perhaps a minute occurred, when the ladder was found to be hanging limp and loose; a bright white light flashed upward through the water for a moment, as a signal from the professor that he had reached the bottom all right; and then the luminous beam was seen moving slowly forward over the bottom in the direction of the submerged ship. Suddenly the light vanished.

"He has reached the ship," the baronet reported to those in the other boat, who were alternately drifting with the tide and moving up against it to maintain an easy speaking distance from their consort. A quarter of an hour passed, and then a brilliant, dazzling flood of light streamed out for about ten seconds at apparently no great distance below the surface, then vanished again.

"All right," remarked Sir Reginald as soon as he saw this; "he has reached the pilot-house. Now, George, up with the anchor, my good fellow, and we will back off a few yards out of harm's way."

The boats accordingly did so, von Schalckenberg allowing them ten minutes for the operation; then, with a sudden rush and swirl of water, the huge bulk of the *Flying Fish* appeared above the surface, looming black, vast, and mysterious against the faintly luminous horizon. A moment more, and the windows of the pilot-house shone out a series of luminous discs against the darkness, showing that the professor had lighted up the interior, and that individual himself appeared on deck hailing the invisible boats with:

"It is all right; everything is just as we left it, and you may come on board as soon as you like."

Ten minutes later the boats had been hoisted in and stowed away, and the *Flying Fish*, at an elevation of some three hundred feet above the sea-level, was moving to the southward and eastward across the placid waters of the Channel, at the moderate rate of some five-and-twenty miles per hour. At midnight, however, after a little music and conversation, the pace was quickened to about one hundred miles per hour; the altitude was at the same time increased to ten thousand feet; the course was set to south, by compass, and the travellers, with a feeling of perfect security, retired to rest, confident that the professor's clever automatic devices would not only maintain the ship at her then elevation, but would also steer her straight in the required direction.

On the following morning at daybreak the travellers found themselves hovering over the blue Mediterranean, with the African coast at no great distance, and a town of considerable size directly ahead. This town was soon identified as Tunis (near which is the site of ancient Carthage), and they shortly afterwards passed over it, not unnoticed by the inhabitants, who, with the aid of the telescope, could be seen pointing upward at the ship in evident consternation. Then on over the chain of hills beyond the town, and they once more found themselves with the sea beneath them, the ship's course causing her to just skirt the Gulf of Hammamet, whilst they obtained a splendid view of Lake Kairwan and the three streams which it absorbs. Then past Capes Dimas and Kadijah, across the Gulf of Cabes, and so on to Tripoli, which was reached and passed soon after the party had risen from breakfast. At this point the Mediterranean was finally left behind, and the ship's speed was shortly afterwards reduced to a rate of about fifteen knots through the air; her altitude being also decreased to about one thousand feet above the ground level.

The course was now altered to about south by west (true), and the travellers passed slowly over the Fezzan country, the borders of the Libyan Desert, the Soudan, and Dar Zaleh; the prospect beneath and around them varying with every hour of their progress, from the most fertile and highly cultivated district, dotted here and there with straggling villages, to the most sterile and sandy wastes. They saw but little game during this portion of their journey, and only descended to the ground at night, when the vessel was secured by her four grip-anchors during the hours which her crew devoted to rest.

This uneventful state of affairs continued until they arrived in ten degrees of north latitude and twenty degrees of east longitude, when they found themselves fairly beyond the limits of even the most rudimentary civilisation, and in a country of alternating wooded hill and grassy, well-watered plain, which had all the appearance of a very promising hunting district. The country was very thinly populated, the native villages being in some cases as much as fifty or sixty miles apart, whilst in no instance were two villages found within a shorter distance than twenty miles. The inhabitants were, as far as could be seen, fine stalwart specimens of the negro race, evidently skilled in the chase and, presumably, also in all the arts of savage warfare; but it was not very easy to form a reliable opinion upon their habits and mode of life, as whenever the *Flying Fish* appeared upon the scene they invariably took to their heels with yells of terror and sought shelter in the thickest covert they could find.

As the travellers penetrated further in toward the heart of this district, their anticipations in the matter of game became ever more abundantly realised; vast herds of antelope of various descriptions, and including more than one new species, being constantly visible from the ship's deck whenever she was raised a few hundred feet in the air. And, in addition to antelope, a few elephants, an occasional herd of buffalo, a troop or two of wild horses, a rhinoceros, a family of lions, a skulking leopard, or a gorilla, was a by no means unusual sight; to say nothing of the countless troops of monkeys and other unimportant game with which the country seemed to be literally swarming.

Such a district seemed to be the very realisation of a sportsman's or a naturalist's dream of paradise; and it was quickly decided that a halt should be called, and at least a few days devoted to the pursuit of game and the collection of natural history specimens. A suitable spot in which to bring the *Flying Fish* to earth was accordingly sought for, and found in a small open space of about thirty acres, almost entirely surrounded by bush, and in close proximity to a tiny streamlet which emptied itself into a small shallow lake about half a mile distant from the selected site.

Here they hunted with moderate success for a week, not killing any very large amount of game—for they soon discovered that they could do very little without horses—but managing, by patient stalking and the secreting of themselves in artfully devised ambushes, to secure a few choice and rare skins and horns, besides the tusks of eight elephants and the plumage of over a dozen ostriches.

On the day of their departure from this temporary halting-place, however, a piece of surprising and wholly unexpected good fortune befell them. It was one of those especially glorious mornings which are never encountered anywhere but in the tropics. A very heavy dew had fallen during the night, revivifying the vegetation parched by the fervid heat of the previous day, and causing foliage and flowers to glow for a brief period in their brightest and freshest tints, whilst they exhaled their choicest odours; and a light cool northerly breeze imparted a temporary freshness to the early morning air, as yet uninfluenced by the scarcely risen sun.

They had "broken camp," and had risen to a height of about one thousand feet above the ground level, preparatory to the resumption of their southward journey. An awning was spread over the deck, fore and aft, under the protecting shade of which they proposed to take breakfast; and whilst waiting for the meal to be served, the travellers, each seated in a deck chair, were amusing themselves by inspecting the magnificent prospect which lay spread out around and beneath them, the more distant parts of which were being diligently investigated with the aid of their telescopes.

They were thus engaged when George announced that breakfast was served; and the professor was just on the point of laying down his instrument, preparatory to seating himself at the table, when a small group of animals, which were grazing upon the crest of a distant eminence, swept for a moment across his field of view. A certain something of peculiarity and strangeness in the appearance of the creatures caused the motion of the telescope to be arrested in mid-sweep, and in another instant von Schalckenberg, deaf to the calls of his companions and the respectful reminder of the faithful steward, had his instrument focused full upon the group of animals. They were, however, a long way off, and the mist was now rising so thickly from the surface of the ground that it was impossible to clearly distinguish them; so the professor contented himself by going to the pilot-house and directing the ship's head straight toward the point occupied by the animals. After which he carefully noted the time, made a little mental calculation, and seated himself at the breakfast table, with his watch carefully propped up before his plate.

His friends were, by this time, so accustomed to the professor's little peculiarities that no one thought of asking any questions, feeling sure that an explanation would come all in good time. Neither did they make any remark or evince any surprise, beyond a shrug of the shoulders and an amused elevation of the eyebrows, when the *savant*, glancing at his watch, hastily rose from the table, and, in his absent-mindedness carrying with him a fork with a morsel of venison-steak impaled upon its prongs, hurried away to the pilot-house. A moment or two later a gentle jar was felt as the ship came to the ground; but the mist was by this time so thick that it was difficult to see objects more than a couple of hundred feet distant, and all that could be clearly made out was that they had stopped close to a clump of bush of considerable extent.

By the time that breakfast was over, the morning mist, true to its proverbially evanescent character, had completely passed away, and the travellers found that they had come to earth on the crest of a slight eminence, from which an uninterrupted view, of several miles extent over the surrounding plains, could be obtained in every direction save one, namely, that between which and the ship stretched the belt of bush.

And now came the professor's explanation:

"You have, doubtless, wondered, gentlemen," said he, "why I have thus early, and without warning, interrupted our journey. I will now tell you. I have lately been glancing through the book which, you will remember, I succeeded in recovering from the wreck of the *Daedalus*, and therein I met with a passage of a most surpassingly interesting character. This passage related to the rumoured penetration into this region of a certain unnamed traveller who is stated to have positively asserted that he here saw, on more than one occasion, an animal absolutely identical with the fabled unicorn. This remarkable statement at once reminded me that I had, many years ago, seen a paragraph in a Berlin paper to a similar effect. The statement was accompanied by an expression of strong doubt, if not of absolute incredulity, as to its veracity; an expression which impressed me at the time as being most cruel and unfair to the claimant for the honours of a new discovery in natural history; since the discovery was alleged to have been made in a region which had never before—nor, indeed, has since, until now—been penetrated by civilised man; or from which, at all events, no civilised traveller has ever again emerged, if indeed he had been successful in penetrating it. Such being the case, as the course we were pursuing would take us through the very heart of this unknown and unvisited region, I resolved to maintain a most careful watch for these creatures. I have done so, and I am sanguine that I have this morning actually seen a troop of them. Unfortunately, the mist and the distance together prevented a clear and distinct view of the animals to which I refer; but, whatever they may be, I have an idea that they are at this moment feeding at no great distance on the other side of this belt of bush. Should such be the case, we have the wind of the animals and ought to have no great difficulty in stalking them; a proceeding which, if patiently and cautiously executed, ought to enable us not only to secure a specimen or two, but also to obtain a slight insight into the habits of the creature."

The trio addressed felt, one and all, slightly incredulous as to the realisation of von Schalckenberg's sanguine surmises; but, remembering the mammoths, they prudently kept their own counsel, and hastened away to secure their rifles and to make their preparations for a possibly long and tedious stalk. They exchanged their suits of dazzling white nankeen for others of a thin, tough serge of a light greenish-grey tint, which admirably matched the colour of the long grass through which the stalk would have to be performed; and, in about a quarter of an hour from the commencement of their preparations, found themselves standing outside the huge hull of the ship, and in its shadow, making their final dispositions for the chase. These arrangements were soon made. Sir Reginald and the professor were to constitute one contingent, Lethbridge and Mildmay the other; these last being impressively instructed by von Schalckenberg to take up the most advantageous position possible for intercepting the flight of the game, but on no account to shoot until the others had first opened fire.

The two parties then went their several ways, reaching, at about the same moment, the opposite extremities of the bush belt. The utmost caution now became necessary in order to avoid startling the game, if indeed the professor was right in his conjectures, and the hunters sank down upon their knees and began a slow and tedious progress through the long grass. The professor was fairly quivering with excitement, and all his companion's efforts were ineffectual to prevent his rising cautiously to his feet as soon as they had cleared the bush sufficiently to allow of his obtaining a view beyond. For a moment or two he glared anxiously around him, then dropped to his knees again as if shot.

"They are there," he gasped almost inarticulately, "sixteen of them; not more than half a mile away."

"And what do '*they*' actually prove to be?" murmured the baronet. "Not unicorns, of course?"

"Yes, *unicorns*! Animals with only one horn—the males, that is to say. Some have no horns, and those I take to be females."

This was too much for Sir Reginald's curiosity. He, in his turn, rose to his feet, ignoring the professor's agonised entreaties for caution, and, sure enough, within half a mile of where he stood was a herd of animals so closely resembling the unicorn which figures as one of the supporters of the royal arms of England that he could hardly credit his eyes. He counted the creatures, and found that, as the professor had stated, there were sixteen of them, all apparently full-grown. They very closely approached the zebra in general shape, but were considerably larger animals, standing about fourteen hands high. They were of a beautiful deep cream colour, their legs black below the knee, and they had short black manes, black switched tails very similar to that of the gemsbok, and, in the case of four of the animals then in view, were provided with a single straight black pointed horn projecting from the very centre of the forehead, just above the level of the eyes.

At length, yielding to the professor's entreaties and remonstrances, the baronet again sank to his knees and the stalk was resumed.

Soon, however, it became apparent that, from some cause or other, the animals were growing restless and uneasy. They frequently ceased feeding suddenly and gazed about them with an anxious, inquiring look, as though suspicious of but unable to detect the approach of danger, and instead of steadily cropping at the grass in one particular spot they would snatch a few hasty mouthfuls and then move on some ten or a dozen yards. And, as it unfortunately happened, their progress was directly away from the hunters, so that the latter soon found they were booked for a very long, tedious, and wearisome task. The stalkers were at first disposed to regard the uneasiness of the game as due to their own presence, yet, upon further reflection, this seemed scarcely possible, for, in the first place, they were all, even to Mildmay and the professor, tolerably experienced hunters, and were conducting the stalk in the most approved and sportsmanlike manner, and, in the next place, they were dead to leeward of the animals, and it was consequently impossible that the creatures could have scented them. Both Sir Reginald and the colonel were thoroughly puzzled; and at length they— almost simultaneously, as it afterwards appeared—arrived at the same conclusion, namely, that the unicorns were being stalked by somebody or something besides themselves, or else that a storm was brewing.

In support of the first idea there was no evidence beyond the mere fact of the animals' restlessness; but the aspect of the heavens soon became such as to strongly favour the second. Whilst the hunters had been sedulously pursuing their task the sky had gradually lost its pristine purity of blue and had become a pale colourless grey, in which the sun seemed to hang like a ghastly white radiant ball, shorn of his beams. The distant landscape first became unnaturally clear and distinct in all its details and then became veiled in a sort of murky haze. Presently a sharply defined ridge of cloud made its appearance above the south-western horizon, spreading rapidly toward the zenith, and the hunters began to realise that they were in for a thorough wetting, if for nothing worse. Mildmay, indeed, who was perhaps better acquainted than anyone else in the party with the character of the tropics, strongly urged upon his companion, Lethbridge, the desirability of abandoning the chase and returning with all speed to the ship; and the latter, impressed by the lieutenant's earnestness, once rose cautiously to his feet with the intention of signalling a return to the other contingent, but the baronet and the scientist were at that moment invisible, so the colonel sank once more on all-fours and the chase went on.

Suddenly a sound like a low growling roar, closely followed by a shrill scream, came floating down to the hunters upon the wings of the almost stagnant breeze, and, springing hastily to their feet, they saw that a magnificent leopard had sprung upon the back of one of the hornless unicorns, and was tearing savagely at its neck and throat with its teeth and claws, the rest of the herd, with one exception, being in full flight. The exception was a fine male unicorn, which, with bristling mane and half-averted body, stood motionless save for a quick angry stamping of his fore-feet upon the ground, watching the unavailing struggles of his hapless companion. These were of very short duration, a staggering gallop of a few yards sufficing to exhaust the victim's strength, when she reeled and fell headlong to the ground with her savage rider still clinging tenaciously to her back. This, apparently, was the moment which the male unicorn had been waiting for. Bounding forward at lightning speed and with lowered head he charged full upon the prostrate pair, and, as the leopard faced round toward him with an angry snarl, the long straight pointed horn was levelled and in another instant the great cat was hurled ruthlessly from the quivering body of his victim, transfixed through eye and brain by the formidable weapon of his vengeful antagonist. The unicorn stood for a moment tossing his head, apparently half stunned with the tremendous shock; but he quickly recovered, and was evidently preparing to renew his terrible onslaught when his quick eye detected the presence of the hunters, who, completely carried away by the exciting spectacle they had just witnessed, were standing at their full height in the long grass, fully exposed from their waists upward, and with the light glancing brightly from the polished silver-like barrels of their rifles. A moment's pause was sufficient for the unicorn; some subtle instinct doubtless taught him that in the strange beings who had thus unexpectedly revealed themselves he beheld enemies more dangerous than the most deadly of his four-footed foes; and, wheeling quickly about, he uttered a curious barking kind of neigh and dashed off at a headlong gallop in the direction already taken by the rest of his companions.

"Good Heavens, we have lost them!" groaned the professor in a perfect agony of despair.

"Yes," assented the baronet, who next turned to his more distant companions and hailed them with:

"We have had our trouble for nothing, after all. The best thing we can now do is to make our way back to the ship with all speed, when we can renew the pursuit, unless, as seems only too probable, we are about to have our hands full with the coming storm. We have not a moment to lose, I should say; so I would suggest that each of us put his best foot foremost."

"Ay, ay," replied Mildmay, "crowd sail we must; for, unless I am greatly mistaken, we are about to have a regular tornado."

"A tornado!" gasped the professor. "Run—run for your lives; I verily believe *I forgot to moor the ship!*"

Forgot to moor the ship! Could such fatal carelessness be possible? If so, they must indeed run for their lives; for should the storm burst before they reached the ship she would be whirled away over the plain like an empty bladder before the blast, to what distance and with what results it was difficult just then to foreshadow; but among the possibilities which instantly presented themselves to the mind was that of death to the two inmates of the ship, irreparable damage to the craft herself, and four persons left to shift for themselves in the very centre of Africa, with nothing but the clothes they wore, the rifles they carried, and about a dozen rounds of ammunition apiece. The prospect was appalling enough to send a momentary spasm of horror thrilling through the stoutest heart there, but it also at the same time endowed them with a temporary access of almost supernatural energy; and the four men at once started for the ship at a speed which, even at the moment and to themselves, seemed incredible.

The distance they had to traverse was but short, a mere half-mile or so perhaps; but to the runners it seemed, notwithstanding their speed, as though they would *never* reach their goal. The grass was long and tangled, and rapid progress through it was possible only by a series of leaps or bounds; any other mode of progression would simply have resulted in their being tripped up at every other step. This, to men unaccustomed to such exercise, was in itself a sufficiently fatiguing process; but in addition to this they had to contend with the stifling heat of the stagnant atmosphere, which had been oppressive enough even whilst they had been in a condition of comparative inactivity; now it seemed to completely sap their strength and cause their limbs to hang heavy as lead about them. Then, too, the air had become so rarefied that it seemed impossible to breathe, whilst the blood rushed to their heads, and their hearts thumped against their ribs until it seemed as though nature could bear the tremendous exertion no more, and that the runners must drop dead upon the plain. Still, however, the men sped on, the portentous aspect of the heavens serving as an effectual spur to their flagging energies. The dark slate-coloured cloud had already reached the zenith, deepening in tint meanwhile until it had grown almost literally as black as ink. Presently a few great drops of hot rain splashed down upon the panting runners; and, as they rounded the end of the bush clump and came within view of the *Flying Fish*, a blinding flash of lightning blazed out from the sable canopy overhead, accompanied by a deafening peal of thunder which rattled and crashed and boomed and rumbled and rolled until its echoes gradually died away in the distance. A perfect deluge of rain almost immediately followed, wetting the runners to the skin in an instant as effectually as though they had been plunged into the sea. This lasted for perhaps ten seconds, during which every object, even to the racing figures of their companions, was hidden from view by the dense volume of falling water. Then the rain ceased as abruptly as it had begun, the travellers finding themselves at the same instant close to the towering hull of the *Flying Fish*.

"Last man in, close the trap!" gasped the baronet as he dashed up first to the opening in the ship's bottom. The others were only a few yards behind him and heard his command; so he wasted no more time in conversation, but bounded up the long spiral staircase leading to the pilot-house, having reached which he laid his hands upon the engine lever and tiller, and gaspingly awaited the signal shout which should tell him he might move the ship, gazing anxiously out through the windows meanwhile on the watch for some sign of the bursting of the hurricane.

He had not long to wait. Almost before he had found time to remove his hat and wipe the perspiration from his brow a shout came echoing up the staircase shaft from the bottom of the ship, announcing the fact that the trap-door was securely closed; and Sir Reginald instantly raised the ship from the ground, sending the engines gently ahead at the same moment, and putting the helm hard over so as to bring the *Flying Fish* stem-on to the direction from which he expected the hurricane.

Chapter Sixteen
A Battle on Lake Tanganyika

The ship had risen about one hundred feet from the ground,
engines had just completed a single revolution, when the black pall
cloud suddenly burst apart on the south-western horizon, revealing
patch of livid coppery-looking sky behind it; and at the same m
low moaning sound became audible in the breathless air. A dul
grey veil of vapour seemed at the same time to overspread the mor
features of the landscape in that quarter, and through it the baronet
three companions, who had now rejoined him, saw the trees and fo
the most remote clumps of bush bowing themselves almost to the
before some mighty invisible force. The moaning sound rapidly in
in power and volume, the cloud of vapour rushed down toward the
appalling speed; the long billowy grass was flattened down to the e
if under the pressure of a heavy roller; the successive clumps of bus
seen to yield one after the other to the resistless power of the hurrica
the air in that direction grew dark with the leaves and branches whic
torn from the trees.

"Raise the ship higher. Lift her above the power of the hu
altogether if you have still time to do so," shouted the professor
Reginald's ear, as the roar of the approaching tornado thundered i
ears with almost deafening intensity.

"No," shouted back the baronet; "I am going to try the experim
seeing how she will bear the stroke of the gale. Hold on tight all of yc

And as he spoke he sent the engines ahead at full speed, and dro
ship forward right in the teeth of the hurricane.

The next instant, with an appalling burst of sound, the gale was
them. Contrary to their expectations, there was scarcely any perce
shock, but the ship's speed was rapidly checked much as is the speed
express train when the brakes are suddenly and powerfully applied, a
some six seconds, though the engines were still going ahead at their u
speed, the progress of the *Flying Fish* over the ground was as effect
checked as though she had been lying at anchor.

Meanwhile the air was one vast volume of awful sound, and thick with ~~the~~ clouds of dust, and tufts of grass, and leaves, and hurtling branches ~~which~~ were being whirled furiously along upon the wings of the tornado, so ~~that~~ the inmates of the pilot-house could neither hear each other speak nor ~~see~~ any object beyond a quarter of a mile away on either side. This lasted for ~~perhaps~~ three minutes, when the wind suddenly lulled, and the ship at once ~~began~~ to forge rapidly ahead. The lull lasted perhaps half a minute, and ~~then~~ ensued a repetition of all that had gone before, excepting that perhaps ~~the~~ wind was not *quite* so strong as at the first outburst. But it was of longer ~~duration~~, the second instalment of the gale lasting fully half an hour, after ~~which~~ the wind gradually dropped to a gentle breeze, the sky cleared, the ~~sun~~ reappeared in all his wonted splendour, and the air resumed its usual ~~transparency~~.

But what a sight was now presented to the view of the travellers; what scene of devastation was that which lay outspread around them! The ~~long~~ grass was pressed so flat to the ground that it would scarcely have ~~afforded~~ cover to the smallest animal; stately trees were lying prostrate, ~~either~~ uprooted altogether, or their massive trunks snapped short off, whilst ~~others~~ still retained their upright position indeed, but stood denuded of ~~every~~ branch. Other trees again, whilst less mutilated as to their branches, ~~retained~~ only a few straggling leaves here and there, and the same thing ~~applied~~ to those dense patches of creeper-like tangled growth known as ~~"~~bush," the upper portions of which presented merely a bristling array of ~~leafless~~ twigs. And in some spots could be seen huge clumps of "bush" ~~which~~ had been torn bodily out of the ground and swept remorselessly ~~along~~ for perhaps miles of distance.

But the strangest sight of all was presented by the animals. From a ~~height~~ of one thousand feet, to which the *Flying Fish* had by this time risen, ~~a~~ very wide extent of the plateau below could be surveyed, and on this in ~~every~~ direction could be seen the wild creatures of the forest, the jungle, and ~~the~~ plain, many of them suffering from injuries more or less severe, received ~~during~~ the progress of the tornado, and all of them exhibiting unmistakable ~~and~~ in some instances surprising evidences of demoralisation and terror. ~~Deer~~ and antelopes of various species lay crouched upon the ground ~~palpably~~ quivering with fear, or limped painfully about on three legs, the ~~fourth~~ being doubtless injured through the creature having been hurled ~~violently~~ to the ground, or struck by some falling branch. The lion and his ~~mate~~ could be seen here and there wandering harmlessly and aimlessly to ~~and~~ fro in the midst of hundreds of creatures which on ordinary occasions ~~would~~ afford them a welcome prey, but which were now too completely ~~overcome~~ with terror to notice their presence. In one place a fine elephant

lay prostrate, his massive spine apparently broken by the fall of an enormous tree, the trunk of which had pinned him to the ground; and in another, an immense assemblage of animals of the most mixed and antagonistic species were seen huddled promiscuously together under the lee of an immense belt of bush, where they seemed to have found a shelter from which they were evidently still afraid to venture.

At length, having seen enough to afford them a tolerably clear idea of the destruction wrought by the storm, the professor suggested the retracing of their steps with the object of again finding, if possible, the troop of unicorns. The ship was accordingly put about, and in a short time the spot was reached on which still lay the carcasses of the leopard and the female unicorn. Here she was again brought temporarily to the ground in order that the party might secure the two skins, which was done; but the hide of the unicorn was so dreadfully lacerated by the claws of the leopard that the professor was plunged into the lowest depths of chagrin and despondency. The pursuit of the lost animals was now once more taken up; the ship rising to a height of five thousand feet into the air and then going ahead dead slow in the direction taken by the unicorns, the four gentlemen, armed with their most powerful telescopes, posting themselves in advantageous positions on deck and minutely examining every yard of the ground over which they passed. This method of proceeding was continued until nightfall without result; and it then became evident that the animals of which they were in pursuit had somehow eluded them.

"Well," said the professor, endeavouring to put a good face upon his disappointment, as, the ship having been carefully brought to earth and securely moored for the night, the party left the pilot-house and went below to take their evening bath previous to dinner, "it is disappointing, but it cannot be helped. Perhaps we shall be fortunate enough to encounter them or others to-morrow as we wend our way southward. And, à propos of our next destination, I have a suggestion which I should like to make, and which I will lay before you when we meet at the dinner-table."

Accordingly, when they had fairly settled down to the meal that evening, Sir Reginald called upon the scientist for his suggestion or proposal.

"I must preface it," said von Schalckenberg, "by informing you that I have again been diving into my lamented friend's note-book, which I may say en passant is the most remarkable volume I have ever come across. And in it I find, under the heading of 'Africa,' a most clever and scholarly disquisition on 'the site of ancient Ophir,' the place from which it is recorded that David obtained gold for the building of Solomon's temple. I need not inflict upon you the various arguments and authorities which are cited in the endeavour to identity the position of this most interesting spot; suffice it to say, that I am morally convinced I can lay my finger upon it on the map. The principal, indeed I may say the *only* reasons why the region has never yet been explored are, first, its extreme difficulty of access except by sea; and secondly, the fact that all recorded attempts to penetrate it have been thwarted by the inhabitants, who are a most jealous, warlike, and savage race of people. *We*, however, are fortunately possessed of exceptional, or I should rather say unique, means of approach to this unknown country; and my suggestion is that we should—"

"Do it," interrupted the baronet. "Most certainly we *will*, my dear sir, and I am exceedingly obliged to you for the proposal. The adventure will doubtless possess a piquant flavouring of danger about it, but I presume that will scarcely be regarded by any of us as a drawback?" glancing across the table to the colonel and Mildmay.

"Scarcely," echoed Lethbridge lazily, as he held his glass of wine up critically to the light.

"Did you say 'danger?'" laughed Mildmay. "This craft of yours is so confoundedly safe, Sir Reginald, that upon my word I have almost forgotten what danger is; so if you really think you can find a place where we may once more come within hail of it, pray take us there without loss of time. For my part, I am becoming positively effeminate, and unless I can speedily have a chance of getting my head broken I shall be utterly ruined for 'the service' when I go back to it."

"So be it," said the baronet. "Ancient Ophir is our next destination; and we will start to-morrow morning. You, professor, I know will not shrink from danger when the solving of so interesting a question is concerned."

"Ah, ah! try me," laughed the professor joyously—"try me, my friend, and you shall see."

Accordingly, on the following morning after breakfast a general adjournment was made to the pilot-house, where, with map and chart spread out before them, and the professor's treasured volume beside them for reference, the probable site of ancient Ophir was at length definitely located; when the course and distance were ascertained, and a start made.

Being anxious to see as much as possible of the country during their passage over it, a low rate of speed—averaging about twenty miles per hour—was maintained; the day's journey beginning at six o'clock in the morning, and terminating at the same hour in the evening, when a halt was called and the ship brought to earth for the night.

On the fourth day of this part of their journey, shortly after effecting their morning's start, they came within sight of an immense lake; and a slight deviation from their prescribed course was made in order that a thorough examination of it might be effected. A long range of hills, which had been sighted on the previous day, lay on their left hand; and, on clearing the southern spurs of these, they found that another large body of water lay beyond or to the eastward of them; a river connecting the two lakes, afterwards identified by them as lakes Albert Nyanza and Tanganyika. Rising in the air to a height of about ten thousand feet, they slowly traversed the latter from its northern extremity, reaching its widest part—which they estimated to be about sixty miles across—at mid-day.

And here a most exciting scene presented itself. An hour previously a dark mass had been sighted near the western shore of the lake, which mass had at first been taken for an island; but, on a nearer approach, the supposed island had resolved itself into an immense fleet of canoes, in number about three hundred, manned by from four to twenty men in each, rapidly making its way toward the western shore. So large a concourse of craft, coupled with the fact that the crews were elaborately "got up" with paint, feathers, and skins, and were well provided with bows and arrows, spears, shields, and clubs—to say nothing of a few very antiquated-looking muskets which the travellers' glasses revealed here and there—seemed to point to the conclusion that a hostile expedition was afoot, or, rather, afloat; and the explorers resolved upon a temporary pause in order to watch the course of events.

The natives were so intent upon their paddling that—facing forward as they all were, with the *Flying Fish* somewhat in their rear and nearly a mile above them—not one of them seemed to have detected the near vicinity of the aerial ship; and the fleet diligently pursued its course landward, the short broad-bladed paddles moving to the time of a deep, sonorous, but somewhat monotonous song, which, issuing as it did from the throats of probably quite two thousand warriors, was distinctly audible on board the *Flying Fish*, and really had quite an impressive effect.

The flotilla had reached within about four miles of the shore, and of a tolerably extensive native settlement built thereon on both sides of a river which at that point emptied itself into the lake, when a sudden confused beating of drums and blowing of horns seemed to indicate that the menaced tribe had at last become awakened to the unpleasant fact that an invasion of their territory was imminent. The summons was responded to with very commendable celerity, the men swarming out of the settlement like ants out of an ant-heap; and in less than ten minutes nearly a hundred canoes were launched and manned, and advancing boldly to meet the enemy, whilst the laggards pushed off by twos and threes as soon afterwards as they could get down to the beach, all making the most strenuous efforts to join the main body.

To the observers on board the *Flying Fish* it seemed that the attacked party had made a grave mistake in thus taking to their canoes and advancing in them to meet the enemy; the colonel's impression being that they would have done better if they had awaited their foes on the beach and harassed them during their attempt to effect a landing. But it soon became evident that the threatened tribe knew perfectly well what they were about, their canoes being larger and steadier than those of their opponents, and their method of handling them greatly superior.

The opposing forces encountered each other at a distance of about two miles from the western shore of the lake, when a simultaneous discharge of arrows was poured in by both sides, after which the two fleets closed, and a most determined and sanguinary battle commenced. The invaders outnumbered their opponents nearly in the proportion of two to one; yet the latter not only gallantly held their own, but actually appeared now and then to gain some slight temporary advantage. Spears were thrown and arrows were shot by hundreds; the heavily-knobbed war-clubs were wielded with untiring activity and terrible effect; and, occasionally, a flash and a faint puff of smoke followed by a report told that one of the ancient muskets had been brought into play. The shouting of commands, the cries of anguish or defiance, the shrieks of the wounded, and the yells of triumph united in the creation of a most deafening din; and that it was not noise only, but work as well, was speedily manifested by the numerous bodies, splashing and struggling in the agonies of death, or floating quiescent on the surface of the lake.

"How stubbornly the rascals fight!" remarked Lethbridge at last, when the battle had been hotly raging for fully three-quarters of an hour without yielding to either side any decided advantage. "I wonder what the quarrel is all about?"

"It is difficult to say," answered the professor, who seemed to consider the question as addressed to himself; "it may be a simple case of tribal animosity; it may be an attack of retaliation; or it may be a slave-hunting expedition. It is pretty sure to be one or the other of those three, but it is impossible to say which."

"Well," remarked Mildmay, "whatever the cause of the fight, my sympathies are all with the weaker side. Cannot we help the poor wretches a little? A shot or two from our rifles—"

"Would ensure to either party a victory," interrupted the baronet. "Yes; that is quite true. But how can we tell which party—if either—is fighting in the cause of right and justice? We cannot take the part of either the aggressors or the defenders without a certain lurking doubt that in so doing we may perhaps be unwittingly giving aid and encouragement to the evil-doer. My sympathies are, like yours, on the side of the defenders; but I am afraid we must let them fight it out unaided."

And fight it out they did in the most gallant manner, the invaded baffling all attempts on the part of the invaders to get even a small portion of their force between them and the shore; and finally, by what looked like a last supreme and desperate effort, putting the foe to flight, and pursuing him triumphantly and persistently in his retreat, harassing his rear, cutting off and capturing stragglers, and in every possible way worrying and annoying him so thoroughly that, to those on board the *Flying Fish*, it looked unlikely in the extreme that the attack, whether provoked or not, would ever be repeated.

The combatants had evidently been far too busy to notice the extraordinary apparition floating in the sky above them; but just as the battle was about to commence a crowd of women and children, with a few decrepit old men, had assembled on the beach, seemingly to watch the conflict; and on bringing the telescopes to bear on these it soon became apparent, by their gestures and cries of amazement, that they had seen the ship.

"Yes," said the professor, peering through his telescope, "they see us undoubtedly, but they can detect neither form nor details. The sun is immediately behind them, you will observe; consequently, as it is shining full upon our burnished hull, those people, in the position they now occupy, will be able to see nothing but a shapeless blaze of dazzling effulgence, which they will doubtless take as an outward manifestation of their particular deity's favour, and an indication that he is present to crown their cause with victory."

And indeed there was plenty of evidence to support this singular opinion, for the people, though evidently astonished beyond measure, manifested delight rather than fear at what they saw, stretching out their hands, palms upward, by way of greeting and salute, whilst many were seen to hurry away to the village and back, bringing with them offerings of fruit, goats, and fowls, which they ranged in a line ("in order to make the most of them," as Mildmay suggested) along the margin of the lake. The proffered offering was, however, unaccepted, and, the battle being over, the *Flying Fish* resumed her course along the centre line of the lake, reaching its southern extremity in time to select a halting-place before sunset.

The fourth day following found them within easy distance of their destination; and the disappointment of the travellers, arising from the fact that no more unicorns had been seen, was to a very great extent swallowed up in curiosity as to what lay before them. Shortly after effecting their morning's start the fertile region over which they had hitherto been travelling came abruptly to an end, and they found themselves passing over an arid sandy desert, utterly destitute of even the feeblest suggestion of vegetation, without a trace of water or even of moisture, and of course with no sign of a living creature anywhere upon it. So uninteresting a region offered no temptation for loitering or dalliance, and the speed of the ship was accordingly increased to about sixty miles an hour over the ground, the pace being maintained until two o'clock in the afternoon, when a low range of rocky precipitous hills was reached, beyond which fertility and life once more resumed their sway. The travellers computed the stretch of desert over which they had passed as being fully three hundred miles in extent, and they could therefore fully understand the difficulty—not to say impossibility—of approaching Ophir, at all events from a north-westerly direction. Speed was now once more reduced, the ship gently gliding through the hot afternoon air at the rate of about eighteen knots, over a somewhat rugged, well-wooded country, watered by numerous streams, with native villages dotted here and there along the banks, in the midst of well-cultivated maize and tobacco fields, with an occasional patch of sugar-cane. Large herds of cattle were also frequently passed, and it soon became evident that to the natives in charge of these, and indeed to the inhabitants generally, the apparition of the aerial ship was productive of a vast amount of curiosity, excitement, and wonder. These natives appeared to possess the same power or gift attributed to the Montenegrins, namely, that of projecting the voice for incredible distances through the air; and it was speedily apparent that the arrival of the monster aerial visitant to the country was being orally telegraphed forward in the direction of her course. Mounted men were seen dashing madly along until they reached some eminence favourably situated for the exercise of their powers, when, dismounting, the messenger would raise his hands to his lips, and, in a peculiar high-pitched tone of voice which seemed to have the power of penetrating the air for an immense distance, send his message echoing forward over hill and dale, to be instantly caught up and repeated by another. So smartly was this novel system of telegraphy performed, that the message actually outsped the ship, and the   travellers found the inhabitants of every village along their route awaiting *en masse* their appearance, which was instantly greeted with loud shouts of astonishment. At one village or settlement, which, from its size, appeared to be of more than ordinary importance, they found, in addition to the general inhabitants, a squadron of about fifty mounted warriors awaiting them, fully armed with bow, spear, and shield, and upon the appearance of the *Flying Fish* these troops most pluckily ranged themselves directly across her course and prepared to treat her to a shower of arrows.

A SQUADRON OF MOUNTED WARRIORS PUT TO FLIGHT.

"Now is our time to create a wholesome impression of our invincibility upon these fellows," remarked the baronet, and hurrying to the pilot-house he caused the ship to sink well within range of the projected salute.

In an instant every bow was drawn to its utmost tension, a second or two sufficed the warriors to steady their aim, and then, with a simultaneous *twang* of bowstrings, the fifty arrows sped through the air, and, rattling harmlessly against the ship's gleaming hull, glanced off and fell to the earth again. The baronet smartly raised the fore end of the tiller, and, obedient to her helm, the *Flying Fish* made a sudden swoop earthward in the direction of the audacious cavalry, who, already disconcerted at the utter failure of their attack, at once wheeled short about, and, with piercing yells of terror, took headlong flight, jostling and overthrowing each other without the least compunction in their frantic eagerness to escape.

"There," remarked the baronet, as, steadying the helm, the ship once more soared to her former elevation, "I hope that will suffice to convince them that we are not to be attacked with impunity. If not, we shall be compelled to read them a sharper lesson."

After that no further attempt at molestation was ventured upon, the inhabitants simply congregating in close proximity to the doors of their huts to see the ship go past, watching her stately progress in silent, awestruck wonder, and obviously holding themselves ready for an instant dive beneath the fancied shelter of their thatched roofs in the event of any hostile demonstration on the part of the Mysterious Visitant.

At about half-past five in the evening the hilly character of the country gave place to that of a wide-stretching level plain, thickly overgrown with long rank grass, with occasional isolated clumps of bush, and here and there a tall feathery palm, or a grove of wild plantains or bamboo. The faint grey glimmer of the sea appeared on the utmost verge of the distant horizon, and certain huge shapeless irregularities in the extreme distance gradually revealed themselves as the colossal remains of what must at one time have been a city of extraordinary extent and magnificence. The ship was brought to earth and secured exactly at six o'clock, at a distance of some eight or nine miles from the sea, and the travellers then found themselves surrounded on all sides by gigantic ruined walls, arches, columns, erect and overturned, huge fragments of pediments, shattered entablatures, ruined capitals, splintered pedestals, and crumbling mutilated statues of men and animals, all of colossal proportions, the buildings being of a massive but ornate and imposing style of architecture, quite unknown to civilisation. The ship had found a resting-place as nearly as possible in the centre of the ruins, which extended all round her for a distance of nearly three miles, the eastern half being all aglow with the golden radiance of the sunset, whilst the western half loomed up black, imposing, and solemnly mysterious against the clear orange of the evening sky.

"Well," said the professor, as the party slowly paced the deck, watching in almost silent rapture the swiftly changing glories of the dying day, the rapid but exquisite gradations of tint on the mouldering ruins which accompanied the fading light, and the almost instantaneous appearance of the stars in the darkening heavens—"well, I am equally surprised and delighted at the result of our resolve to come hither. Here we find ourselves in the very heart of savagedom surrounded by the vast remains of a remote but civilised and evidently highly cultivated race; and though at present we have nothing more than the merest surmise to help us to their identification, I have little doubt that the result of our explorations and investigations will be to satisfy us that we have in very deed found in these ponderous ruins the remains of Ancient Ophir."

Chapter Seventeen
A Native Chieftain's Visit to Cloudland

The travellers, safely shut up in that impregnable fortress, the hull of the *Flying Fish*, passed the night in peaceful slumber, undisturbed, in the confidence begotten of a sense of perfect security, by the weird cries of the night birds, the incessant howling of the jackals, the maniacal laugh of the prowling hyena, the occasional roar of the lion, the loud *whirr* of myriads of insects, the croaking of bull-frogs, and the other multitudinous nocturnal sounds which floated in through the open windows of their state-rooms. They were early astir in the morning, eager to commence their investigations as are school-boys to plunge into the enjoyments of a long-anticipated holiday. Moved by a common impulse, they all went out on deck to witness the ruins under the effect of sunrise previous to their plunge into the matutinal bath; and it was whilst they were admiring the exquisite beauty of the scene that the keen-eyed colonel became conscious of the fact that they were beleaguered by a host of lurking savages.

"Umph!" he commented, "I expected as much."

"You expected as much as what? What is it, Lethbridge?" asked Sir Reginald.

"Look there," was the reply; "and there, and there, and there. Do you notice anything peculiar in the appearance of the undergrowth about us, especially where it is thickest?"

"N–o, I can't say that I do—unless you refer to those occasional quick gleams which come and go here and there. What are they? At first I thought it was the flash of the sun on the dew-laden grass and leaves as they wave in the wind, but it can hardly be that, or we should see more of it."

"No," said the colonel, "it is not that; it is the occasional glint of the sun on a native spear-head. I have been through the Kaffir war, and have seen the same thing before, though not so distinctly as now, our present towering height above the ground giving us an advantage in that respect which we sadly lacked before. We are beset by the natives. You cannot see *one*, I know, but they are all about us, all the same. Ah! look there, just behind that magnolia bush. Do you see a small dark object rising slowly into view? That is the head of a savage, and he is—ah! now he has ducked again, having caught sight of us."

"And what do you suppose the fellows want?" asked the baronet. "They cannot attack us, you know."

"No; but *they* don't know it. Their object is to steal up as close as possible to us in order, in the first place, to satisfy their curiosity, and, in the second place, to make a sudden swoop if they see any fancied chance of being successful."

"Well," said Sir Reginald. "I should like to see the savage who can reach us so long as we stick to the *Flying Fish*. But we don't want to stick to her, so we will leave them undisturbed to satisfy their curiosity to its fullest extent until after breakfast, when we must adopt measures either to conciliate them or to terrorise them into leaving us alone. Come, gentlemen, we shall be late for breakfast. What a superb mass of ruins it is!—beats the Acropolis; don't you think so?"

If the thousand or more savages, who had spent nearly half the night in accomplishing the engirdlement of the *Flying Fish*, could have heard and understood the airy way in which the fact of their close proximity was dismissed by the baronet as a matter of the most trivial importance, they would have been intensely disgusted. Happily for their dignity they were blissfully unconscious of it; and whilst Sir Reginald and his companions were luxuriating in the bath, and afterwards dallying with a light but dainty breakfast, the sable warriors continued to close cautiously in upon the huge white gleaming object which had come into their midst in so unexpected and extraordinary a manner. Slowly, cautiously, with untiring patience, and practising every known art of savage warfare, the band drew closer and closer, until they found themselves within about a hundred feet of the hull, and almost overshadowed by her enormous bulk, when considerations of personal safety prevailed over the ardour of the warrior burning to distinguish himself, and further advance was, as by unanimous consent, checked. The huge monster, with its gleaming silvery skin and its curiously-shaped tail, lay so ominously still and silent, with its enormous circular black eyes so wide open and fixed, that, having heard of its threatening demonstration against the cavalry who attacked it on the previous day, they felt certain it meant mischief, and was only waiting for some foolhardy wight to venture within its reach, to seize and devour him. They had been despatched by a despotic king to capture or kill the creature; but, whilst every man there would have emulated his neighbour in rushing to certain death against the ranks of an enemy, there seemed to be so little glory in furnishing a breakfast to this monster that every individual there inwardly resolved that some other man than himself should be the first to offer himself as a sacrifice. And, equally afraid to advance or to retire, there they remained motionless, and in a state of breathless suspense, waiting for events to develop themselves. And there they were distinctly visible from the lofty stand-point of the *Flying Fish's* deck when the quartette, cigar in mouth, emerged from the pilot-house after breakfast.

The situation was decidedly comical, and the travellers indulged in a hearty laugh at the expense of the discomfited savages. But it was obvious that matters could not be allowed to remain in that condition; the natives must be impressed with the conviction that hostilities were neither necessary nor desirable, and that it would be to their advantage to be on terms of amity with the newcomers. How could this be achieved? A parley offered the most ready solution of the difficulty; and the professor—who was a perfect polyglot dictionary in human form—offered to essay the task of conducting it. This was by no means his first introduction to savages; he had encountered them in various parts of the world before, and had never experienced any very serious difficulty in communicating with them, so that he felt tolerably sanguine of success on the present occasion.

"The matter is very simple, I think," remarked the German, as he led the way to the larboard gangway. "We want these people to understand that we are friendly disposed toward them; that they have nothing whatever to fear from us; that we have not come here to rob them of one tittle of their possessions; that we merely wish to explore and examine these ancient ruins; and that, if they will receive us among them as friends, they will be distinct and decided gainers by the transaction. Is not that so?"

"Certainly," remarked the baronet. "Tell them—if you can—that all we ask is permission to investigate and explore unmolested; and that if they will accord us this privilege they shall be substantially rewarded."

"Very good; I will do my best. And that reminds me that you had better order George to bring on deck and open a small case of those beads and nick-nacks that we provided for such occasions as the present," remarked the professor.

The baronet returned to the pilot-house to give the order; and von Schalckenberg drew out his white pocket-handkerchief, waved it two or three times in the air, and then demanded, in the language he thought most likely to be intelligible:

"What chief commands the warriors who have assembled to pay homage to the four Spirits of the Winds?"

Most luckily for the professor's prestige and reputation as an all-wise Spirit, the dialect he had adopted, though not the language actually spoken by the tribe he addressed, was so far similar that his question was understood; and whilst the astounded blacks started to their feet in dismay at finding themselves at last actually face to face with and addressed by an avowed Spirit, one of them hesitatingly and timorously advanced a few paces, threw himself prostrate on the ground, and, maintaining his posture of humility, stammered out:

"I, Lualamba, am the leader of these warriors, O most potent Spirit."

"Approach, brave Lualamba, and ascend to us by the ladder which we will let down to you. We have that to say which must be heard by your ear alone," commanded the professor, waving his hand majestically.

A rope-ladder was attached to the lower extremity of the side-ladder and let down to the ground; and the chief, in a state of mind about equally divided between the extremity of bodily fear on the one hand and pride at being selected as the recipient of a special communication from the Spirit Land on the other, hesitatingly and falteringly, and with many doubtful pauses, advanced until he reached the foot of the ladder, when his courage failed him, and he came to a dead halt.

"Ascend, and fear not," called out the professor encouragingly; "we are the friends of your nation, and have forgiven the attack which some of your people (not knowing us) made upon us yesterday. We have come hither to shower gifts and benefits upon you—if you are obedient; but if you reject our friendship, beware!"

Upon this the savage, no doubt feeling that, by placing himself at the head of this most unlucky expedition, he had already gone too far to permit of withdrawal, summoned up all his courage, and, with the air of a man who knew himself to be treading on mined ground, scrambled up the swaying ladder, and finally stepped in through the gangway on to the spacious deck of the *Flying Fish*, upon which he prostrated himself on his face, laying his shield and weapons—his most valued possessions—as an offering at the feet of the professor.

The latter, touching him lightly on the shoulder, at once bade him rise; and, as the chief gathered himself up and regained his feet, von Schalckenberg threw round the quaking but gratified savage's neck a string of large opaque, turquoise-blue glass beads, and over his naked shoulders a length of gaudily-flowered chintz. A loud shout of admiration from the crowd of natives below proclaimed the fact that they had witnessed the bestowal of these gifts, whilst Lualamba, notwithstanding the august presence in which he found himself, could not restrain the broad grin of delight which spontaneously overspread his features.

A few judicious questions, artfully put, soon elicited from the savage the information that the travellers were now in the country belonging to M'Bongwele, a fierce, cruel, and jealous despot, so suspicious of foreigners that the most stringent orders were in force to allow none such to cross his borders upon any pretence whatever. This king had been duly apprised, through the medium of the curious voice-telegraphic mode of communication already described, of the mysterious arrival in his dominions on the day previous; and had been so greatly disconcerted and enraged at the news that he had forthwith issued the most peremptory orders for the capture or slaughter of the monstrous visitant; and he was now, according to Lualamba, impatiently awaiting in his palace, a few miles distant, the intelligence that his order had been executed. The chief, during the conversation which elicited these facts, had so far recovered his self-possession and equanimity as to be able to make the best possible use of his eyes; and, being a very shrewd fellow, he was not long in arriving at the conclusion that the gigantic monster on whose back he stood was, after all, nothing more nor less than an inanimate, though unquestionably wonderful, *vehicle* of some sort; and that the fair-skinned beings to whom he was talking, though they claimed to be the four Spirits of the Winds, were very similar in many respects to certain white men whom he had seen only a few moons ago. The wily savage accordingly made up his mind that, if he could only induce these beings to accompany him into the king's presence, he would, after all, have most satisfactorily accomplished his mission; and he forthwith proceeded, with all the craft and subtlety of which he was master, to urge upon them the desirability of an immediate visit to king M'Bongwele, who, averse as he was to the prying visits of strange *men*, would, he assured them, be highly gratified at the honour of having as his guests the four Spirits of the Winds.

This proposition, however, by no means accorded with the views of the travellers; and von Schalckenberg somewhat sternly intimated that, whilst an interview with M'Bongwele was undoubtedly desirable, it was *he* who must visit and pay homage to *them*, and not they to him. They had entered the country with the most friendly disposition toward M'Bongwele and his people, and that friendly disposition would be manifested to the distinct advantage of the entire nation if the king showed himself properly appreciative of the honour done him by this visit. But if not, king and people would be very severely punished for the insult offered to their potent visitors, "and," continued the professor, "in order that Lualamba might see for himself that, in making this threat, they were indulging in no mere empty boast, he would give the chief and his followers a single specimen of their power."

Mildmay having, during the progress of this conversation, received a hint from the professor how to act, had quietly, and as if not particularly interested in what was going forward, sauntered off to the pilot-house, where, stationing himself at the engine and other levers controlling the movements of the ship, he awaited further instructions.

The professor, having promised to give the savages a specimen of their visitors' power, now waved his right hand very slowly and impressively skyward, as a signal to the watchful Mildmay, loudly exclaiming as he did so:

"Lualamba will now accompany the four Spirits of the Winds to yonder cloud," pointing, as he spoke, to a single small white fleecy cloud which was floating at the moment across the sun's disc.

Dexterously manipulating the various valves, Mildmay caused the *Flying Fish* to rise with a gentle and almost imperceptible motion from the earth. So gentle was the movement that Lualamba was utterly unconscious of it, and it was not until some seconds had elapsed that he fully realised what was happening. The savages below, however, no sooner heard von Schalckenberg's exclamation than, to their inexpressible horror, they beheld the huge structure, round which they were standing, lift itself off the earth without the slightest visible effort and begin to rise into the air. Many of them were so overpowered by astonishment that they could only stand, open-mouthed and as motionless as statues, staring at the extraordinary sight; others, however, remembering the stringent orders of the king, and feeling that the prize which they had believed to be so secure was not only escaping them but also carrying off one of their number, rushed forward, and, whilst some fruitlessly attempted to grasp and hold the smooth and polished hull, others seized and clung tenaciously to the rope-ladder. The weight of some seven or eight natives clinging to the dangling ladder had, of course, no visible effect upon the movement of the great ship; and, finding themselves being helplessly dragged skyward, they let go their hold with a yell of dismay when they were some four or five yards from the earth, upon which they dropped back heavily.

The ship once fairly off the ground, Mildmay increased the rarefaction of the air in the air-chambers to an almost perfect vacuum, and the immense structure soared skyward with great rapidity. Lualamba, hearing the shouts of his people from below, stepped to the gangway to ascertain the cause; and it was then that, to his inexpressible dismay, he saw the earth apparently falling from under him, and the upturned faces of his followers rapidly dwindling until they became unrecognisable. In the first extremity of his terror he would have flung himself headlong from the deck had he not been prevented; failing in this he prostrated himself, and for some time lay motionless, with his face hidden in his hands. At length, however, somewhat reassured by the encouraging adjurations of the professor and the apparent absence of movement in the ship, he ventured first of all to uncover his eyes and then to rise slowly to his feet. He glanced wildly about him, but could see nothing, save a thick white mist which completely enveloped the ship (for she had just plunged into the centre of the cloud), with the sun dimly visible through it; and a fresh paroxysm of terror seized him, for the horrible thought at once suggested itself that he had looked his last upon mother Earth. The professor, however, speedily reassured him upon this point, and, leading him to the guard-rail which ran round the deck, bade him look downward. Terrified into the most servile obedience, the wretched chief did as he was bidden, and in a few minutes, the mist growing thinner and thinner, he once more caught sight of the earth at an immense distance below, the gigantic ruins above which they were hovering dwarfed to a mere sprinkling of boulders over the plain; the trees, the clumps of bush, and the meandering streams stretching away to the horizon in almost illimitable perspective, and to the eastward the sea, with just one solitary sail upon it, barely visible above its gleaming rim.

Ignorant savage though he was, Lualamba was quite intelligent enough to appreciate the novel beauty of the scene upon which his eyes now rested; and, forgetting for the moment all his terrors, he leaned upon the rail, lost in wonder and admiration. And when, after a minute or two, he became conscious that the ship was again nearing the earth, his delight knew no bounds, for he felt that, as the hero of so unique an experience as he was now passing through, he must henceforth be a person of much greater consequence among his countrymen than he had ever been before.

Meanwhile the travellers had availed themselves of their recent ascent to sharply scrutinise the face of the country immediately adjacent to the ruins, and had at length discovered, on the summit of a distant hill, an extensive village or settlement, strongly defended by a circular stockade, which they shrewdly suspected to be the headquarters of king M'Bongwele. The single street, which ran through the centre of the village from end to end, was crowded with people all gazing skyward at the unwonted apparition of the aerial ship; and, with the aid of their telescopes, the travellers could see in the central square a small group of persons (who they conjectured to be the king and his suite) similarly engaged, surrounded and protected from the rabble by a phalanx of armed men.

The ship swept rapidly onward until she hovered immediately over the last-named party (just to impress upon the king a wholesome conviction of the utter uselessness of his stockade as a protection against such a foe as the *Flying Fish*), and then, making a majestic sweep, came gently to earth immediately opposite the principal gate in the stockade.

"Now, go," said the professor, addressing Lualamba, "and inform king M'Bongwele that we await him on the spot among the ruins where you found us this morning."

The bewildered chief, scarcely able to realise the fact that he had actually been brought safely back to *terra firma*, lost no time in availing himself of the permission given him to depart, and, scrambling down the ship's side and the rope-ladder, he reached the ground and bounded off like a startled deer toward the gate, which was hastily thrown open to admit him, and as hastily closed and barred again the moment he had passed through. The *Flying Fish* then rose once more into the air and leisurely made her way back to the ruins, passing, *en route*, the force which had been sent out to capture her, and which was now making the best of its way back to the village to report the result of the expedition.

Meanwhile Lualamba made his way rapidly up through the village to the king's palace (which was, after all, merely the largest hut in the inclosure), having gained which he besought an immediate audience with M'Bongwele on a matter of the utmost importance. The king, who had already been made acquainted with the circumstance of the chief's involuntary journey into the upper regions, was, of course, all curiosity to learn the fullest details of the adventure, and the desired audience was accordingly at once granted. Conscious of the fact that, for the first time in his life, he had failed to execute the mission intrusted to him, and extremely doubtful as to the reception which would be accorded to the message of which he was the unwilling bearer, Lualamba deemed it best on this occasion to tell a plain unvarnished tale, and, commencing his narrative at the point where he and his warriors had first come within sight of the huge object of which they were in quest, he described in full detail all his subsequent adventures, with the thoughts, feelings, and impressions resulting therefrom, and wound up falteringly with the message.

His story was received by the king and his suite with ejaculations of wonder and incredulity, interspersed with many sharp commands from the monarch to repeat or to explain more fully certain passages; and when the message was delivered a profound silence reigned for fully an hour. King M'Bongwele was a despot, accustomed to issue his commands in the most heedless manner and to have them executed at all costs; but to *receive* a command was an entirely novel and decidedly disagreeable experience, and he was thoroughly puzzled how to act. His first feeling was one of speechless indignation at the insolence of these audacious strangers; his second, a wholesome fear of the consequences of disobedience. For if these mysterious visitants had the power of soaring into the air by a mere wave of the hand, what might it not be possible for them to do in the event of their being seriously provoked. Besides, he had already received a practical assurance of his impotency so far as they were concerned; moreover, he was consumed by curiosity to see for himself the marvels so graphically described by his lieutenant, to receive a moiety of those magnificent gifts which the strangers seemed prepared to lavish broadcast upon all with whom they chanced to come into contact, and, above all, to satisfy himself with respect to certain conjectures which had flitted through his brain whilst listening to the astonishing narrative of Lualamba. M'Bongwele was an ignorant savage, it is true, but he was possessed of a dauntless courage, a persistency of purpose, and an unscrupulous craftiness and ambitiousness of character which would have won him distinction of a certain unenviable kind in any community. Already his brain was teeming with vague unformed plots of the wildest and most audaciously extravagant description, the possibility of which he was determined to ascertain for himself, and the maturing of which he was quite prepared to leave to time. He therefore ultimately resolved to obey the summons sent him by the strangers; but, remembering his kingly dignity, he postponed obedience as long as he dared, and it was not until four o'clock in the afternoon that he set out for the ruins, attired in all his native finery, consisting of a lion-skin mantle and magnificent gold coronet adorned with flamingo's feathers—the emblems of his regal power—gold bangles on his arms and ankles, a necklace of lion's teeth and claws round his neck, and a short petticoat of leopard's skin about his loins. He was armed with a sheaf of light javelins or assegais, he carried in his left hand a long narrow shield of rhinoceros hide decorated with ostrich plumes, and he was mounted on a superb black horse (which he rode bare-backed and managed with the skill of a finished equestrian). His followers, numbering about five hundred, were also fully armed and excellently mounted, they being, indeed, with the exception of a few court officials, his regiment of household cavalry, the pick of his native warriors and the very flower of his army. He was anxious to make the profoundest possible impression of his power and greatness upon the mysterious beings he was about to visit; and, indeed, the cavalcade, as it swept at a hand-gallop out through the wide gateway which formed the principal opening in the stockade, constituted, with its tossing plumes, its fluttering mantles, its glancing weapons, and its prancing horses, a sight to make a soldier's heart bound with appreciative delight.

Chapter Eighteen
King M'Bongwele is temporarily reduced to Submission

In the return of the *Flying Fish* to her former berth the subject of the reception to be accorded to king M'Bongwele, in the event of his obeying their summons, was somewhat anxiously discussed by the travellers. They had already seen and heard enough to convince them that the individual in question was a sovereign of considerable power, as African kings go, and former experience among savages had taught them that he would, as likely as not, prove to be a crafty, unscrupulous, and slippery customer to deal with. To satisfactorily carry out the object of their visit to this man's country — namely, the examination and exploration of the mysterious and very interesting ruins which surrounded them — it would be absolutely necessary that they should be able to pass to and fro, freely and unmolested, between the ship and the various points selected for examination; and, in order to secure this perfect freedom, it would be necessary not only to conciliate this powerful ruler and his people, but also to so thoroughly impress him and them with the mysterious and wonderful attributes of their unbidden guests that they should, one and all, be absolutely *afraid* to interfere with them. The question was, how could this be most effectually achieved? The first part of the programme, namely the conciliation of sovereign and subjects, appeared simple enough; the obvious pride and delight with which Lualamba had received his flashy presents of beads and Manchester finery furnished a key to the satisfactory solution of this difficulty; but how was the second and equally important part of the programme to be carried out? Lualamba, it was true, had been effectually cowed by the simple expedient of carrying him a few thousand feet up into the air; but something more than the mere repetition of this experiment would be necessary to produce the required impression upon M'Bongwele and the crowd of warriors he would be certain to bring with him. The matter was placed in the hands of the professor for settlement, and he promptly avowed himself to be fully equal to the task.

"Science, my friends," he remarked, "is constantly revealing wonders which surprise and astound even the most cultured minds of the civilised world; how much more capable is it then of overawing the uncultured savage, however shrewd and clever he may be in those simple matters which affect his everyday life! Leave it to me; we have ample scientific means at our command to quell this man and his followers, and to reduce them to a state of the most abject and servile subjection."

Von Schalckenberg then retired to make his preparations, which were soon complete. When next he appeared he carried upon one arm a glittering mass of what at first sight appeared to be drapery, but which, on his unfolding it, proved to be three suits of chain armour (minus helmet and gauntlets), constructed of very small fine links of aethereum, light and flexible as silk.

"I think," said he, "it will be unadvisable to make any change in our outward appearance in preparing to receive this royal savage; any such change would be certainly noticed, and as certainly regarded as an indication of the importance we attach to his visit. Now, our policy is to treat the whole affair as a matter of no moment whatever, and we will therefore (if you agree with my views) continue to wear the white flannel suits in which we received Lualamba this morning. But I would recommend that each of you don a suit of this mail under your clothing (I have already assumed mine), and we shall then be pretty well prepared for emergencies. These savages are often exceedingly treacherous fellows, and it is quite among the possibilities that certain of this king's followers may have received instructions to test our supposed invulnerability by a sly stab in the back or something of that kind; it will be well, therefore, that we should be properly prepared for anything of the kind. I had in view some such occasion as the present when I arranged for the construction of these suits. There is a helmet and gauntlets for each; but we shall scarcely need them today, I think, and it would hardly be politic to wear any *visible* defensive armour."

The luncheon hour arrived and passed without sign or token of the presence of a single savage in the neighbourhood, and as the afternoon waned with still no indication of human vicinity, the travellers—but for the absolute impregnability of the *Flying Fish*—would have begun to feel uneasy. About half-past four o'clock, however, as the quartette were languidly puffing at their cigars, lolling meanwhile in the most luxurious of deck-chairs, a huge cloud of yellow dust rising into the air beyond the ruins announced the approach of the cavalcade, and a minute or two later king M'Bongwele at the head of his cavalry swept like a whirlwind into the open space occupied by the great ship, and, charging in a solid square close up to her, suddenly wheeled right and left into line, and came to an abrupt halt. The evolution was very brilliantly executed, and as Lethbridge lazily scanned the performers through the thin filmy smoke of his cigar, he could not restrain a low murmur of admiration, followed by the remark:

"By George! what splendid soldiers those fellows would make with a couple of months' training!"

"Y–e–s," agreed the baronet, "that was very well done; but I suppose that particular evolution is the one in which they most excel, and of course it was done purely for effect. Ah! the individual now dismounting is, I suppose, our royal visitor."

The baronet was quite right in his conjecture. As the party halted, some ten or a dozen individuals, including Lualamba, flung themselves from their horses, and, advancing reverentially, grouped themselves about the royal charger. Two of them then stepped to the creature's head and grasped the bridle, whilst two more assisted the king to dismount. The horse was then handed over to the care of a warrior, and the king, closely followed by the members of his suite, advanced to the foot of the rope-ladder, which had been lowered for their accommodation; the professor at the same time stepping to the gangway and inviting the party to ascend.

M'Bongwele looked somewhat doubtfully at the swaying ladder for a moment or two, and then essayed the ascent; but the oscillation set up by his movements proved too much for his nerves—or his dignity—and, much chagrined, he was obliged to desist. The professor then in compassion suggested the steadying of the ladder at its foot, when the king, promptly giving the necessary order to his suite, ascended to the deck, leaving those who followed him to manage as best they could.

The first glance of the travellers satisfied them that in king M'Bongwele they had a man of more than ordinary intelligence to deal with. The colour of his skin and complexion was a rich deep brown, he stood nearly six feet high on his naked feet, and, but for his somewhat excessive corpulence, he would have been a man of magnificent proportions. His lips were rather thick, and his nose somewhat flattened, but not nearly as much so as in the case of the genuine negro. His forehead was broad and lofty, though receding, his eyes keen, restless, and piercing, and there was a crafty, cruel, resolute look about the lower part of his face which taught his hosts that they would have to be exceedingly cautious in their dealings with him. He was accommodated with a chair between Sir Reginald and the professor, the former being flanked by Lethbridge (Mildmay, in accordance with previous arrangements, had ensconced himself in the pilothouse); Lualamba and the rest of the suite were quietly allowed to squat in a semicircle before them on the deck.

The king opened the conversation by somewhat abruptly demanding the reason for the strangers' visit to his dominions; to which the professor replied by pointing to the ruins, explaining that they were believed to be the remains of a great city built many ages ago by a very interesting race of people of whom but little was known, and he and his companions were anxious to minutely examine and explore what was left, in the hope of discovering some sculptured or other record bearing upon the origin, habits, and history of the builders.

A few minutes of profound meditation on the part of the king followed this announcement, and then he suddenly demanded where the travellers had come from. The professor replied by a comprehensive sweep of the hand skyward.

"But," objected M'Bongwele, "if you are spirits you should know all that you want to know about these ruins without coming here to investigate. The spirits know everything."

A low murmur of applause from the king's adherents followed this enunciation, showing that they evidently considered their monarch to be getting the better of the strangers, and a smile of gratification flickered for an instant over M'Bongwele's features.

"Not everything," corrected the professor. "We know a great many things, but not everything. And what we know we have been obliged to find out by investigation. We spend the greater part of our existence in passing from place to place investigating and finding out things."

"Then I have been misinformed, and the spirits are neither so wise nor so powerful as I thought them to be," retorted the king.

"Perhaps so," quietly remarked the professor. "Nevertheless we are very powerful—sufficiently so to destroy you and your whole army in a moment, should we choose to do so. Would you like to witness a specimen or two of our power?"

M'Bongwele glanced somewhat nervously about him for a second or two, and then with an obvious effort answered:

"Yes."

"I see that some of your followers here are armed with bows," continued the professor. "Are they good marksmen?"

"The best in the world," answered the king proudly.

The professor in his turn hesitated an instant; he was about to make a dangerous experiment. Then he drew from his pocket a small crimson silk rosette, and, placing it in M'Bongwele's hand, said:

"I will attach this to any part of my dress you choose to point out; then order one of your archers to shoot an arrow at it, and observe the result."

The king took the rosette in his hand, examined it carefully, and passed it round among his suite for inspection. On receiving it back he suddenly wheeled round in his chair, and, reaching over, laid his finger on Lethbridge's breast exactly over the heart.

"Fasten it *there*," he said with a scornful smile, "and I will shoot at it myself."

The professor was disconcerted. The danger of the experiment consisted in the possibility that the archer, instead of aiming at the rosette, would select an eye or some part of the head for a mark, in which case the result would be fatal. He was quite willing to incur the risk himself, trusting that the archer's vanity would impel him to aim at the right spot; but he had never contemplated the turn which affairs had now taken.

Lethbridge, however, with a languid smile and a shrug of the shoulders, rose to his feet, and, nonchalantly flicking the ash off the end of his cigar, waited for the professor to affix the rosette.

A happy inspiration just then occurred to von Schalckenberg. "It is a very small mark," he murmured confidentially to M'Bongwele; "I do not believe you can hit it. Shall I get something larger?"

The king would not listen to any such proposal; he was evidently anxious to exhibit his skill; and the professor, reassured, attached the rosette to Lethbridge's coat in the exact spot indicated, M'Bongwele and his companions watching the operation with the keenest interest.

The colonel, glancing round for a good background against which to place himself, noticed a large clump of trees with olive-green foliage growing at a short distance directly astern of the ship. Against these his white-clad figure would stand out in strong relief. He accordingly stepped leisurely out to a suitable position on the deck, and, with one hand in his pocket and his smouldering cigar in the other, patiently awaited the decisive moment. M'Bongwele in the meantime snatched a bow from one of his followers, and, selecting a long straight arrow from the sheaf, retired to the other end of the deck, a distance of about one hundred and fifty feet from his living target. He strung the bow carefully, adjusted the arrow to the string with the utmost nicety, drew it to the head, and then paused for a full minute, apparently waiting for some indication of flinching on Lethbridge's part. In this, however, he was disappointed, not the faintest suggestion of uneasiness could be detected in the colonel's face—indeed, he seemed to be absorbed in a critical contemplation of the smoke which lazily wreathed upward from the end of the cigar. Suddenly the bow twanged loudly, the arrow whizzed through the air, and, striking fair upon the rosette, fell in splinters to the deck. Lethbridge somewhat contemptuously kicked the fragments aside, unpinned the rosette from the breast of his coat, and sauntered back to his former seat. The group of chiefs gathered on the deck glanced at each other and uttered suppressed ejaculations of dismay. As for M'Bongwele, he was thoroughly discomfited; he had been shrewd enough to suspect in the professor's proposal some preconcerted arrangement, which he flattered himself he had skilfully baffled; instead of which his *ruse* had simply redounded to his own more complete confusion.

The professor rose and picked up the pierced rosette, which he handed to the king.

"You are very skilful," he remarked, pointing to the puncture; "I compliment you." Then, changing his tone, he continued: "We have allowed you to do this in order that you may be thoroughly convinced of the impossibility of injuring us. Now you shall have a further example of our power. Order your warriors to dismount and try their best to lift this ship from off the ground."

The king turned to Lualamba and gave him the necessary order; whereupon the chief, descending the ladder to the ground, advanced to the troops, and, dismounting them, assembled them all round the hull; then, at a given signal, the entire body exerted themselves to the utmost to lift the immense fabric from the ground—of course without effect, as her chambers were full of air.

"Now," said the professor when the savages had pretty well exhausted themselves, "let all but one man retire."

This was done, Mildmay meanwhile exhausting the chambers until the gauge showed that the ship weighed only a few pounds. The professor glanced carelessly at the pilot-house, caught the signal that all was in readiness, and said to the king:

"Now order that man to lift the ship on to his shoulders."

M'Bongwele duly repeated the order, without the slightest expectation that it would be fulfilled; and the man—who would have plunged into a blazing bonfire if he had been so ordered—advanced, and, to the unutterable astonishment of himself, the king, and in fact the whole concourse of natives, raised the gigantic structure to his shoulders and held it there with scarcely an effort.

"Now, tell him to toss us into the air," commanded von Schalckenberg, shouting down from the gangway to Lualamba.

And in another second the terrified king and his suite felt a slight movement, and saw the earth sinking far away beneath them. This was altogether too much for the suite, who grovelled on the deck in mortal fear; and even king M'Bongwele felt his courage rapidly oozing away as he sat uneasily in his deck-chair convulsively gripping its arms and glancing anxiously about him.

The ascent was continued to a height of about fifteen thousand feet, at which altitude the wretched savages were shivering even more with cold than they had hitherto done with fear. The ship was then headed straight for the sea, which she soon reached, and, speeding onward at the rate of thirty miles an hour, her course was continued, accompanied by a gradual descent until the land was lost sight of; when a wide sweep was made, and, at a height of only one hundred feet above the waves, the return journey was commenced. This experience proved sufficient, and more than sufficient, for M'Bongwele; he was completely cowed; and when he found himself hovering over the illimitable sea, without a sign of land in any direction, he flung himself upon his knees before the professor and piteously entreated to be restored to his home and people, abjectly promising that he and they would be the willing slaves of the White Spirits for ever; and as for the ruins, the Spirits might do whatever they chose with them, freely and without let or hindrance. This was all very well, but von Schalckenberg had not yet fully carried out his programme; he had still one more item in the entertainment which he was determined to produce, and which he fully believed would render M'Bongwele's subjugation not only complete but permanent.

Accordingly, on returning to their starting-place (by which time it was nearly dark), the demoralised warriors, who had all but given up their king as lost, were set to work by von Schalckenberg's orders to collect wood for a gigantic bonfire. This was soon done, and the fire was kindled; but, much of the wood being green, an immense cloud of smoke was raised, with very little flame, which exactly suited the professor's purpose. When the fire was fairly alight, the troops were re-formed in line as close to the ship as possible, and M'Bongwele and his suite were arranged in position on the deck immediately beneath the pilot-house walls. By this time it was perfectly dark, save for the starlight and the flickering gleam of the bonfire; and the air was stark calm.

Gradually and imperceptibly the dense cloud of smoke which hung motionless over the smouldering pile became faintly luminous. The radiance grew stronger and stronger, and presently an immense circular disc of light appeared reflected on the slowly-rising cloud of vapour, in which a host of forms were indistinctly traceable. Another moment and a loud ejaculation of astonishment burst from the savage spectators, for, with another sudden brightening of the luminous disc there appeared the phantom presentment of M'Bongwele's troops drawn up as they had appeared a couple of hours before, when the king had first boarded the *Flying Fish* So clear and vivid was the representation that it met with instant recognition, amid loud murmurs of amazement from the beholders; the king being quite as strongly moved as any of his subjects.

"Do you recognise the vision?" demanded the professor sternly of M'Bongwele.

"I do, I do. Those are the spirits of my bravest soldiers," murmured the king. "Truly the Spirits of the Winds have wondrous powers."

"You say well," answered von Schalckenberg. "Now, look again and you shall see a few of *our* warriors."

As he spoke the picture became blurred and indistinct, prismatic colours began to come and go upon the curtain of vapour, and suddenly out flashed the image of a wide-stretching sun-lit plain, upon which were drawn up on parade, in illimitable perspective, a countless host of British troops, infantry, cavalry, and artillery, with bayonets, swords, and lance-points gleaming in the sun, with colours uncased, guns limbered up, and all apparently ready and waiting for the order to march. So realistic was the picture that even the baronet and Lethbridge could scarcely repress an exclamation of astonishment, and as for M'Bongwele and his people, they were perfectly breathless with surprise. The picture was allowed to remain clear, brilliant, and distinct for some ten minutes, then the radiant disc rapidly faded until it vanished altogether, and nothing remained but the red glimmer of the smouldering fire.

A heavy sigh issued from M'Bongwele's breast, and he rose to his feet.

"It is enough," he said. "Let me go home."

He advanced gropingly to the gangway (for it was now very dark), when, in an instant, every one of the electric lights in the ship flashed out at their fullest brightness, brilliantly illuminating the deck, and turning night into day for fully a mile round, and, under the clear steely radiance thus unexpectedly furnished him, the king slowly made his way to the ground, mounted his horse in silence, and galloped away at the head of his followers. The illumination of the ship was maintained until the cavalcade was well clear of the ruins, when the side-ladder was drawn up, the lights extinguished, and M'Bongwele was left to make the remainder of his way as best he could in the darkness.

"Well," said the professor as the quartette wended their way below to dinner, "how have I managed?"

"Admirably," answered Sir Reginald and the colonel together. "Never, surely," continued the latter, "was African king so completely overawed in so short a time as this fellow has been to-day."

"We all, and I especially, owe you thanks, colonel, for the sublime *sang froid* with which you stood up and allowed yourself to be made a target of to-day," said von Schalckenberg. "Believe me, I would never have made the proposal I did had I suspected that the part of target would have been so cleverly transferred to someone else. But the crafty fellow evidently suspected what you English call 'a plant'—a prearranged plan—and he thought that by adopting the course he did he would have us at advantage."

"Oh," laughed the colonel scornfully, "that was a mere trifle, less than nothing. I saw that the fellow was confident of his skill as a marksman and anxious to show off, so I felt perfectly easy in my mind. Had it been one of our own men, now—" An expressive shrug of the shoulders finished the sentence.

"Yes," remarked the baronet reflectively, "what a pity it is that they are not trained to individually select and aim at a particular object. If they were, no troops in the world could stand up for ten minutes before them. But, speaking of troops, professor, what a master-stroke that was of yours to give the darkies an opportunity of comparing their own soldiers with ours. How on earth did you manage it?"

"Oh, easily enough," laughed the professor. "A magic lantern and a couple of slides did the whole business. The throwing of the pictures upon the smoke-wreath certainly enhanced its effectiveness a good deal, but it is quite an old trick, which I have often done before with excellent results. Everyone who is going much among savages ought to include a lantern and an assortment of good startling slides in his outfit if possible."

"But how did you get the first of your two slides? That was surely a representation of M'Bongwele's own people."

"Certainly. And our friend Mildmay very cleverly secured it with a camera which I set up and prepared for him in the pilot-house. He only had to release a spring at the right moment, and the thing was done. He developed the picture whilst we were making our little excursion out to sea and back. Well, the whole thing was a farce; but I believe it has effectually secured us from interruption during our researches among the ruins; and if so, it was worth playing."

Chapter Nineteen
King M'Bongwele turns the Tables upon his Visitors

In reaching his palace that night king M'Bongwele dismissed his followers with but scant ceremony, and at once retired to rest. He passed a very disturbed night of alternate sleeplessness and harassing fitful dreams, and arose next morning in a particularly bad temper. He was anxious, annoyed, and uneasy in the extreme at the unexpected and unwelcome presence of these extraordinary visitants to his dominions—these spirits, or men, whichever they happened to be, who had taken such pains to show him that they despised his power, and were quite prepared to ride rough-shod over him unless he slavishly conformed to all their wishes; who had frightened and humiliated him in the presence of his immediate followers and most powerful chiefs, and entailed upon him a loss of prestige which it would be difficult if not impossible to recover. He was childishly jealous of the slightest interference with his supreme authority, and he fretted and chafed himself into a state of fury almost bordering upon madness as he reflected upon the veiled menaces to himself which had been only too distinctly recognisable in every manifestation of these strangers' extraordinary power on the preceding day. He recognised that their deliberate intention had been to show him that during their sojourn in his country he must in all respects conform to their wishes, and model his conduct strictly in accordance with their ideas of what was right and proper, or take the consequences. And what were those consequences likely to be? Judging from what he had already seen, his dethronement and utter humiliation seemed to be among the least severe of future possibilities. Instead of remaining the irresponsible autocrat he had hitherto been, he would, during the sojourn of these strangers in his vicinity, be obliged to carefully weigh and consider his every word and action, in order that he might neither say nor do anything which could by any possibility prove distasteful to them. And if this state of servile, abject, slavish submission was to be his condition during the period of their stay—which might last the Great Fetisch himself only knew how long—his life would not be worth having, it would simply be a grinding, insupportable burden to him.

As these unwelcome reflections thronged through his mind he grew so madly ferocious that he issued orders for the instant execution of certain white prisoners which had fallen into his hands a few months before, countermanding the order almost immediately afterwards—and, happily, in good time—partly because they were women, and he still hoped, notwithstanding present difficulties and frequent former failures, to add them to his harem; and partly because he was under the apprehension that, among their other attributes, his mysterious visitors might possess that of omniscience, and, getting knowledge of the execution, object to and call him to account for it. It was a similar consideration alone which deterred him from solacing himself by the impalement of half a dozen or so of his principal ministers, the entire suite having an exceedingly lively time of it that morning, and being infinitely thankful when they were at last dismissed with whole skins.

The question which harassed and perplexed M'Bongwele for the remainder of that day was: could the visit of these extraordinary beings be by any means shortened or terminated? And, if so, how? Or if the visit could not be cut short, was there any possibility of subjugating the visitors? This particular African monarch possessed at least one virtue, that of perseverance under difficulties. He was not at all the sort of man to sit down and tamely submit to evils if he thought there was even the most remote and slender possibility of overcoming them. He had, on a previous occasion, encountered certain fair-skinned men so similar in appearance, and in every other respect, except dress, to these present troublesome visitors of his that they might well have been taken for beings of the same race; yet *they* had proved so thoroughly mortal that he had had no difficulty whatever in disposing of them. True, he had shot an arrow at one of these visitants yesterday, striking him fair upon the breast, and the arrow, instead of piercing him through and through, had fallen splintered to pieces at his feet. Yet this very extraordinary incident was not, to M'Bongwele, wholly conclusive evidence as to their invulnerability. Lualamba had on the previous day made certain suggestive remarks tending to strengthen his monarch's belief that if these persons could by any means be separated from the huge structure which seemed to be their home they might possibly prove to be very ordinary mortals after all. He was inclined to believe that a great deal, if not the whole, of their power was centred in the gigantic fabric which they called a ship. And, if that should indeed prove to be the case, all that they had done on the previous day could be done by anyone into whose hands the ship might happen to fall. It could be done by *him*. As this reflection flashed across his brain he pictured to himself the immense accession of power and prestige which would come to him with the possession of that wonderful structure; of the conquests it would enable him to make, and of the boundless extension of his dominions which it would enable him to secure; and his eyes flashed and his bosom heaved with unsuppressed excitement as he inwardly vowed that he would achieve its possession or die in the attempt. All the conditions of his life, he angrily told himself, had been violently and permanently disarranged by the incidents of the previous day; he had been publicly threatened; publicly terrified into a cowardly and disgraceful state of submission; and it was quite impossible that he could permanently continue as he then was. He must fully recover all his lost prestige and add immeasurably to it, or must be content to see some ambitious chief rise up and wrest the kingdom from him. These presumptuous strangers had forced him into enmity against them, and they must take the consequences.

Lualamba was one of M'Bongwele's most trusted chiefs, and shortly before sunset he and the head witch-doctor were summoned to a special conference with the king.

Meanwhile the travellers, having enjoyed a most excellent night's rest, rose betimes in the morning and prepared for a thorough systematic investigation of the ruins. They bathed and breakfasted in due course, and then, armed to the teeth, set out upon a tour of general inspection, the professor carrying his camera, and Sir Reginald his sketch-block and colour-box, whilst Mildmay and the colonel, provided with a box-sextant and a light measuring chain, set themselves the task of making a rough survey of the ruins and a portion of the surrounding country. The tour of the ruins, the taking of an occasional sketch or photograph, and the making of the survey, kept the party fully occupied for the whole of the first day; and they returned to the ship just before sunset, tired and hungry, but thoroughly satisfied with their day's work, and fully convinced that their success in penetrating to this interesting spot would alone more than repay them for all the trouble and expense connected with the outfit of the expedition. One important fact at least had been clearly ascertained by them in the course of the day, which was, that the ruins were extremely ancient, their antiquity being demonstrated by the circumstance that during successive ages the soil had gradually accumulated about the ruins until they were nearly half buried. The most interesting discovery made by them during the day was that of an enormous block of ruins, which, from its extent and the imposing character of its architecture, they felt convinced must have been a temple or other public building, and it was resolved that their investigations should commence with it. It was situated about a mile distant from the spot occupied by the *Flying Fish*, and their first intention had been to move the ship somewhat nearer; but an inspection of the intervening ground had shown it to be so encumbered with ruins that it was soon apparent that she must be left where she was.

A very large amount of excavation—much more than they could possibly manage alone—would be necessary before the lower portion of the walls and the pavement of the building could be laid bare, and they decided to go over to M'Bongwele's village on the following morning and arrange with him if possible for the hire of some fifty or a hundred men. This, however, proved to be unnecessary, for whilst they were at breakfast next day the sound of a horn was heard without, and, going on deck, they discovered Lualamba below in charge of a party of some twenty women bearing a present of milk (in closely woven grass baskets), eggs, fowls, and fruit, and a message from the king asking whether his visitors required assistance of any kind in the pursuit of their investigations.

"Capital!" exclaimed the baronet when von Schalckenberg had translated the message. "This is as it should be. Lower the ladder, professor, and ask Lualamba to come on deck. We must send back a present to the king in return for that which he has sent us; and we can at the same time forward a message explaining our wants."

Lualamba quickly made his appearance on deck, where, after receiving a further small present for himself and a cast-off soldier's coat, battered cocked-hat, an old pair of uniform trousers, the seams of which were trimmed with tarnished gold braid, and half a dozen strings of beads, as a present for the king, the wants of the travellers were explained to him. The chief shook his head; he feared it would be difficult, if not impossible, to meet the wishes of the illustrious strangers in the particular manner spoken of. The male inhabitants of the village were all warriors, to whom work of any description would be an unspeakable degradation. But he would see what could be done. If women, now, would serve the strangers' purpose as well as men, the thing could easily be arranged.

Had the travellers been less experienced than they were this suggestion as to the employment of women would have come upon them as a surprise; but they were well aware that among many savage races labour is looked upon as degrading, and therefore imposed solely upon the women; so they merely thanked Lualamba for his promise, and intimated that women would serve them equally as well as men. Upon which Lualamba withdrew, promising that a gang of at least fifty should be at the ruined temple—or whatever it was—"before the sun reached the top of the sky;" in other words, before noon. This promise was faithfully fulfilled, for at eleven o'clock the explorers saw the gang of labourers come filing in among the ruins, armed with rude wooden mattocks and spades, and provided with large baskets in which to convey away the soil as it was dug out. They were as unprepossessing a lot of specimens of female humanity as could well be imagined. Naked, save for a filthy ragged skin petticoat round their waists and reaching to the knee, their faces wore, without exception, an expression of sullen stupidity, and they looked as though they had never experienced a joyous moment in their lives; but they were active and muscular, and soon showed that they thoroughly understood how to use their clumsy tools to the best advantage. They were led by and worked under the directorship of a lean, shrunken, withered old grey-haired hag of superlative ugliness, who did no work herself, but went constantly back and forth along the line of workers, bearing in her hand a long thin pliant rattan, which she did not hesitate to smartly apply to the shoulders of those who seemed to her to be doing less than their fair share of the work in hand. This bit of petty cruelty was, however, as a matter of course, promptly stopped by the professor, who thereby won for himself a look of withering scorn from the hag aforesaid, and glances of stupid wonder—in which in some cases could be also detected faint traces of an expression of gratitude—from the unfortunate sisterhood who laboured under her.

The amount of work performed was, as might naturally be expected, nothing approaching to that which would have been accomplished in the same time by the same number of white labourers; indeed, a gang of half a dozen good honest hard-working English navvies would have accomplished fully as much per diem as the fifty women who laboured among the ruins. But the explorers were quite satisfied; they were in no particular hurry; the climate was delightful; M'Bongwele was wonderfully civil, sending large supplies of provisions, fruit, and milk to the ship daily, accompanied by the most solicitous inquiries through Lualamba as to whether all things were going well with his visitors. There was no attempt whatever, so far as they could discover, to pry into their doings, not a single warrior, save Lualamba, having been seen by them since the day of the king's visit, and everything seemed to be favourable to a thorough and leisurely execution of their purpose.

On the fourth day from the commencement of the excavation the explorers were gratified by the uncovering of a yard or two of what appeared to be a magnificent tesselated pavement of white and variegated marble; and by the end of a fortnight fully half of its supposed area was exposed, showing it to be of an entirely novel and exquisitely graceful design, the intricate outline of the pattern being emphasised by the insertion of plates of gold about a quarter of an inch wide between the tesserae. The pavement was smooth, level, and in perfect preservation, and the explorers were in the very highest of spirits at their exceptional good luck.

At the outset of the work the four friends had been in the habit of returning every day to the ship for luncheon, but as time passed on they felt that to do this in the very hottest part of the day was a wholly unnecessary waste of energy, and they accordingly transferred from the ship to the scene of their operations a spacious umbrella-tent (that is to say, a tent with a top but no sides), together with a small table and four chairs. And under the shadow of this tent they were wont to partake of the mid-day meal (usually a cold collation), which they generally finished off with a cup of chocolate or coffee and a cigar, the potables being prepared by a particular one of the women labourers, who speedily developed quite a special aptitude for the task, and who at length fell into the habit of regularly bringing with her, every day, the milk needed for the purpose. The tent being pitched on a spot which commanded a full view of the operations in progress, the quartette gradually acquired the habit of lingering somewhat over their luncheon, and especially over the final coffee and cigar, the inevitable result of which was that, for the next hour or two, they experienced a feeling of delicious languor and drowsiness, and an almost unconquerable disinclination to exchange the grateful shade of the tent for the scorching heat of the afternoon sun. At first they struggled resolutely and manfully against this overpowering temptation to idleness; but finding, or fancying, that they could supervise the work as efficiently from the tent as they could at a yard or two from its shelter, they gradually gave up the struggle, yielding day after day more completely to the seductive feeling of lassitude which seemed to have laid hold upon them.

Finally, one hot afternoon, overcome by the drowsy influence of the warm perfumed air which played about their languid bodies, they all fell asleep.

Unknown to and wholly unsuspected by them, the old crone who was in charge of the gang of female labourers had, for some days past, been keeping a sharply watchful eye upon the investigators, and upon the day in question she had been, if possible, more sharply watchful than ever. So interested in them did she at last become that, turning her back upon the women and leaving them to work or not as they saw fit, she advanced until she entered the shadow of the tent, where she paused, eagerly scanning the features of the slumberers. For some ten minutes or so she stood motionless as a statue, her sunken glittering eyes turning from one placid face to the other; then she stepped to the baronet's side and, seizing him by the shoulder, shook him sharply. The sleeper might have been dead for all the consciousness which he exhibited at her rude touch. Another and more violent shake proved equally unproductive of results. Then she passed on to the colonel, to Mildmay, and to the professor, experimenting in like manner with each. If she wished to arouse them, her efforts were useless; they were, one and all, locked fast in the embrace of sleep—profound, unnatural, death-like sleep. A scornful laugh grated harshly from her lips, and, wheeling sharply upon her heel, she rejoined the gang of excavators, exclaiming:

"Cease this useless labour; there is no further need of it. The witch-potion has done its work, and you may all return to the village. I go to summon the warriors."

The women, without further ado, gathered up their tools and baskets, and, breaking into a low monotonous song, to which their feet kept time, took the trail leading to the village, and soon disappeared among the scattered ruins and the bush which clustered thickly about them.

Ten minutes later a band of dusky warriors, fully armed and numbering about a hundred, made their appearance, and, led by Lualamba, advanced to the tent, which they surrounded. Four grass hammocks, each of which was stretched between two long bamboo poles, were then brought forward, and, by the directions of the chief, the unconscious white men were carefully lifted from their seats and deposited at full length in them. The tent was then struck, and, with its simple furniture, taken in charge by certain members of the band told off for the purpose, when each of the hammocks, with its sleeping burden, was carefully raised from the ground and shouldered by four savages, and, the remainder of the warriors forming round them as an escort, the band took the trail to the village, and marched rapidly away.

On reaching their destination the prisoners (for such they evidently were) were carried to a new hut, which had all the appearance of having been specially constructed for them, and, once inside, the poles of the hammocks were carefully laid in the forked ends of upright posts, firmly fixed in the ground, the whole forming a sufficiently comfortable bed. Four young women then entered the building, and, taking their places, one at the head of each sleeper, proceeded, with the aid of large feather fans, to protect their helpless charges from the attacks of the mosquitoes and other insect torments with which the village swarmed; when the hammock-bearers filed out, and the white men were left to sleep off, undisturbed, the effects of the potent drug which had been artfully mingled with the milk with which their coffee had that day been prepared.

The hut in which our four friends were thus left had been erected in a spacious palisaded quadrangle which surrounded the king's palace, so that M'Bongwele might, as it were, always have them under his own eye; and the fact that, having got them into his power, the king was determined, if possible, to keep them there, was made manifest by the presence of a strong cordon of guards, who, on the passage of the prisoners within the portal, immediately ranged themselves round the hut outside. The hut was only some twelve feet square, and entirely open at one end, the open end being, however, protected from the sun by a continuation of the roof in the form of a broad verandah supported at the eaves upon two stout verandah-posts; and round this diminutive structure were ranged twenty picked men, facing inward, fully armed with bow, spear, and shield; it was pretty evident, therefore, that, unless the prisoners had the power to render themselves invisible, or of paralysing their guards, there was little probability of their effecting their escape.

The posting of the guard having been effected to Lualamba's satisfaction, he entered the palace to make his report to the king, who was anxiously expecting him. M'Bongwele listened attentively to all the details of the capture, and, upon its completion, rose and, accompanied by the chief, made his way to the hut, which he cautiously entered, placing himself at the foot of each hammock in succession, and long and anxiously regarding the countenances of the sleepers. He had been successful in his bold enterprise beyond his most sanguine hopes; but it was evident that even in the very moment of his triumph he was anxious and disturbed in his mind. He trembled at the audacity which had led him to pit himself against these extraordinary beings, and the very ease with which he had accomplished his purpose frightened him. Had these men—if men they were—been encountered and overcome awake, and in the full possession of their senses, he would have been happy, for he would then have felt that his own power was superior to theirs. But they had been surprised whilst under the influence of a subtle and potent drug prepared by the chief witch-doctor; and when they awoke and discovered what had been done to them, what might not the consequence be? But what was done was done; he had now gone too far to retreat; besides which, his ambition overmastered his fears, and he determined to go on and risk the consequences.

Having obtained possession of the persons of these formidable beings, obviously the next thing would be to secure that wonderful thing which they called a "ship;" and this M'Bongwele determined to do at once: who knew but that its possession might give him a much-needed and decisive power over its former owners? He accordingly retired from the prison hut, and gave orders for the immediate assembling of all his available cavalry; at the head of which he soon dashed off in the direction of the ruins, leaving Lualamba in charge of the guard and of the prisoners, a position of responsibility which that chief by no means coveted, and which he accepted with much inward perturbation.

Proceeding at a gallop, the impatient M'Bongwele and his troopers soon reached the *Flying Fish*, which they immediately surrounded. The king then dismounting, and summoning some fifty of his most famous braves to follow him, cautiously approached the ship, with the purpose of boarding her. But the rope-ladder, by means of which he had on a former occasion accomplished this feat, was no longer there; and, as he glanced upward at the gleaming cylindrical sides of the towering structure, it began to dawn upon him that the task he had undertaken was, after all, not without its difficulties. Presently, however, a brilliant idea occurred to him, and, selecting a dozen men, he gave them certain orders which sent them scurrying off at a gallop. Half an hour later they returned, dragging behind them two long stout bamboos and a considerable quantity of tough pliant "monkey-rope" or creeper. With these materials the men, under M'Bongwele's instructions, proceeded to construct a ladder, which, when completed, they reared against the side of the ship; and by this means the king and his fifty chosen warriors ascended and triumphantly reached the deck.

M'Bongwele now regarded himself as completely successful; he had gained possession of the wonderful structure; and all that remained was to make use of it in a similar manner to that of its former owners. He accordingly advanced pompously to the gangway, and ordered his troopers to first remove the ladder from the ship's side, and then return to the village with all speed, adding exultantly that he and those with him on the "flying horse's back" would be there long before them.

Resolved to give the cavalcade a good start, he watched it disappear in a cloud of dust among the ruins, and then, assuming his most commanding attitude and manner, raised his right hand aloft and exclaimed:

"We will now return through the air to the village—keeping as close to the ground as possible," he added with some trepidation as he nervously grasped the guard rail in anticipation of the expected movement.

The ship, however, remained motionless. Something was evidently wrong, but what it might be he could not imagine; surely he had not forgotten or misunderstood the formula as stated to him by Lualamba? He now most heartily wished that he had brought that trusty chief with him, and provided against all possibility of error; however, the omission could not be helped, and he would try again, adopting a somewhat different form of words. This time he stamped rather impatiently on the deck, exclaiming:

"Take us back to the village, good flying horse, but gently, and not very far above the ground."

Still no movement. The king began to look puzzled, and to feel as vexed as he dared, with the consciousness weighing heavily upon him that he was playing with frightfully keen edged tools. He did not know what to make of this persistent immobility; it was uncanny, sinister, portentous, almost appalling. He would try again. He *did* try again, not once but nearly a dozen times, varying the form of words, more or less, every time; and, of course, with the same ill success. At length, in chagrin and disgust, he gave up the attempt to move the ship, and turned his attention to an examination of her interior. He advanced to the pilot-house, complacently reflecting that here, at least, he could not possibly be beaten; he had only to walk up to the door and enter. But here, again, surprise and confusion awaited him; for, after *twice* making the circuit of the building, he was unable to find a door; there was no perceptible entrance anywhere excepting the circular windows, which, however, were all open. Summoning his followers to his assistance, he made them give him a "back;" and, scrambling up on their shoulders, he at length contrived to raise himself to the level of these openings and to look in. He saw a great many levers, and knobs, and buttons, and short lengths of insulated wire; in fact, he got a glimpse of pretty nearly all the apparatus contained in the pilothouse; but that did not help him in the least, for he had not the most remote idea of what all these things were for; and when he essayed an entrance by one of the windows he was again foiled; it was much too small. At length, after a great deal of ineffectual wriggling and struggling—which occasioned serious inconvenience and anxiety to the human supports who were with the utmost difficulty maintaining a state of very unstable equilibrium beneath his feet—his patience completely failed him, and, in a fit of childish anger and spite, he sent a series of truly blood-curdling yells echoing into the interior of the pilot-house. These cries were of course distinctly heard by George and the *chef*, but (acting upon a concise code of instructions furnished to them when they were first engaged for the voyage, and which provided for almost every conceivable emergency), neither of these individuals condescended to take any notice of them. Having thus given vent to a portion of his spleen, king M'Bongwele, paying but scanty attention to the comfort or dignity of his supporters, scrambled down from his elevated position to the deck, and sat down to reflect upon the next steps to be taken. He would gladly now have left the ship and made the best of his way back to the village, even though the journey would have had to be performed on foot; but the ladder had, by his own command, been removed, and his retreat was thus effectually cut off, a drop of about forty feet from the bottom of the metal accommodation ladder to the ground being a something not to be thought of.

Chapter Twenty
The History of certain Distressed Damsels

Meanwhile Seketulo, the chief in command of king M'Bongwele's household cavalry, returned to the village in due course, and lost no time in dismissing his men, chuckling to himself as he reflected that, after all, he had beaten his monarch in the race homeward.

Time passed on; the sun set; the evanescent twilight faded out of the sky; the stars twinkled forth in all the mellow radiance characteristic of the tropics; and still the adventurous M'Bongwele and his wondrous prize came not. Hour after hour lagged slowly away; and at length the expectant villagers, who had poured into the open air to witness the triumphant arrival of the king, returned to their huts—their transient enthusiasm overcome by their habitual apathy and indolence—and surrendered themselves willingly enough to the blandishments of sleep. All, with the exception, that is to say, of the guard detailed to watch over the prisoners, the anxious Lualamba, and Seketulo. These were all wakeful enough, the latter perhaps even more so than any of the others. For, as the night waxed and the great full moon rolled slowly upward into the sky, the powerful chief, who had won for himself the envied position of commander of the king's cavalry (a position equivalent to that of commander-in-chief of the whole army), felt the hope growing within him that the foolhardy king and those with him had been carried off to the nether regions for a permanency by the wondrous Thing of which they had so audaciously sought to secure the possession. And in that case (M'Bongwele being without sons, and having, in order to avoid possible future complications, carefully slaughtered all his brothers and other relations on his accession to the throne) there would be a vacancy in that particular country for a king, which vacancy Seketulo believed himself powerful enough to secure and fill.

Giving free rein to these ambitious ideas and aspirations, the chief paced thoughtfully to and fro in a retired corner of the village until about ten o'clock that night, when his impatience could no longer be curbed, and he felt that he *must* sally forth to ascertain, if possible, the fate of M'Bongwele and his party. Accordingly, mounting his horse, he took his way out of the village, passing through the principal gateway, and heading for the ruins at a gallop. He was greatly disconcerted, on reaching his destination, to discover that the *Flying Fish* still peacefully reposed in her usual berth; and his disgust was supreme when he further noticed, crouched on her lofty deck, a disconsolate-looking group, which his fears only too truly assured him must be the king and his companions. His first impulse was to retire and leave them to their merited fate; but the unwelcome reflection suggesting itself to him that they might possibly be discovered and rescued in the morning, he altered his purpose, and, making a virtue of what was almost a necessity, advanced with the intention of proffering a respectful inquiry as to whether any unfortunate accident had delayed the royal return. He was, however, forestalled by the king and his party, who, the instant they saw him, hailed his appearance with joyous shouts and an almost piteous entreaty to him to replace the ladder. This he, still making a virtue of necessity, at once attempted to do; but the clumsy construction proved too much for his strength. A happy idea, however, now flashed through the mind of one of the party; and, unstringing their bows, they joined the strings together into one continuous line, which, luckily for them, reached the ground; and Seketulo bending the lower end on to the ladder, the latter was soon, by the exertions of all hands, reared into position. The party, thoroughly crestfallen, now lost no time in making their way to the ground, when M'Bongwele at once requisitioned Seketulo's horse, and galloped off homeward at top speed, the chief and the rest of the party being left to plod back to the village at their leisure and as best they could.

Notwithstanding this most dismal failure, M'Bongwele still entertained hopes of being able to possess himself of the coveted ship; and early next morning every available man and woman was marched to the scene of the preceding day's discomfiture to attempt the task of *carrying the Flying Fish to the village!* This attempt, it is scarcely necessary to say, also resulted in complete failure, and with this failure king M'Bongwele was at last compelled to recognise himself as beaten. It became clear to him that the mysterious beings whose persons he had so rashly seized possessed certain peculiar and wonderful powers; and the only course now open to him seemed to be to make the best terms he could with them for their co-operation in the furtherance of his schemes. And he felt heartily glad—pluming himself at the same time upon his prudence—that he had not taken advantage of their seemingly helpless condition, when brought to the village, to attempt the putting of a period to their existence.

Meanwhile, Seketulo, though greatly chagrined at the turn of affairs, by no means abandoned hope. He felt that though disappointment had for once overtaken him, it by no means followed that such would always be the case; and if his ambitious dreams could not be realised in one way, they still might be in another. The king, unfortunately, had not been carried off to perdition; but, figuratively speaking, that seemed to be his ultimate and speedy destination. For, had he not pitted his own power against that of the mysterious strangers, and lost the game? He had inflicted a most grievous outrage upon them, and had ineffectually attempted to seize their wonderful ship; yet not a particle of gain or advantage of any description had been secured, and the wrath of these strangers had yet to be faced; the penalty of his audacious deeds had yet to be paid. Did not all this point to M'Bongwele's speedy downfall? And if such a state of things should happily be in the near future, would it not be worth his (Seketulo's) while to approach the strangers in a friendly spirit and (after cautiously feeling his way) with offers of assistance? He decided that it undoubtedly would, and that he would forthwith adopt that line of policy, cautiously, yet without losing a single favourable opportunity.

So far as M'Bongwele was concerned, he found himself in a greater strait than ever. He had not only failed completely in his ambitious schemes, but he had also lost prestige with his own people and had made enemies of the strangers. His situation was distinctly worse than if he had done nothing at all; and how to make his way out of the imbroglio he knew not, nor could any of his ministers advise anything. He now fervently wished he had adopted other and more friendly measures with his visitors; but it was too late; he fully recognised that, with the odium of failure fresh upon him, any attempt at conciliation would be utterly hopeless; the only course still open to him appearing to be that of "masterly inactivity." This would, at all events, leave time for events to shape themselves, and afford him an opportunity of regulating his conduct in accordance therewith; and this course he accordingly determined to pursue; at the same time issuing the most imperative orders that the prisoners were to be treated with the utmost courtesy and consideration consistent with their safe-keeping.

In accordance with these orders, the prisoners found that, after the second day of their seizure, they had very little of which to complain beyond the actual loss of their liberty. They were abundantly supplied with provisions of all kinds within the resources of the village; the four young women originally detailed to watch over them during their drugged slumber were permanently appointed to attend upon them, do their cooking, keep their hut clean, and so on; and they were allowed to take unrestricted exercise within the bounds of the compound. Their attendants and guards were allowed to answer any questions except such as related to the king's recent attempt to possess himself of their property; and hints were freely offered to the effect that M'Bongwele was most anxious to secure their friendship, and would gladly afford them an audience whenever they might desire it. But they had no intention whatever of seeking an audience with the king; they had a very shrewd suspicion of what had actually taken place; and having by this time formed a tolerably accurate estimate of the royal character, they felt convinced that their only chance of advantageously dealing with M'Bongwele lay in forcing upon *him* the character of a suitor to *them*.

Thus matters stood for nearly a fortnight from the date of their seizure—Seketulo doing his best to effectually ingratiate himself in the strangers' favour before venturing to tender his proposed offer of assistance; and M'Bongwele waiting with daily growing impatience for overtures from his prisoners—when an event occurred which, simple though it seemed at the moment, was destined to have an important bearing on the fortunes of certain other white prisoners then in the king's power.

It happened thus. The quartette were sitting under the verandah of their hut one morning, whining away the very last remains of their carefully hoarded stock of tobacco, when a soft thud, followed by a low startled cry of pain and terror from one of their female attendants caused them to glance hastily round. The sight which then met their eyes was startling enough to make them spring instantly to their feet. A snake fully seven feet long, and of the most deadly venomous kind (which had evidently just dropped out of the thatch of the hut), had flung its coils round the bare leg of one of the women, and, before help could be rendered, had struck its fangs deep into the flesh. The cruel heart-shaped head, with its wicked eyes glowing like a couple of carbuncles, was already drawn back to repeat the stroke when Lethbridge sprang forward, and, seizing a small pliant rattan which happened to be handy at the moment, dealt the reptile a swift downward cut across the body, dividing the creature almost in two; following up the blow by a rapid dart of his hand, grasping the reptile by the neck and tearing the quivering coils away from the wounded limb. Another second, and the head was being fiercely ground into the dust under the thick solid leather of his boot-heel, the wounded body twisting and writhing in the most horrible contortions meanwhile.

Two out of Lethbridge's three companions stood helplessly aghast whilst this tragedy was in progress; but the professor, ever alert in the interests of science, promptly compelled the wounded girl to lie down, and instantly applied his lips to the wound made by the poisonous fangs of the snake, sucking vigorously until he had induced as copious a flow of blood as could reasonably be expected from the two tiny punctures. Then, fumbling in his waistcoat pocket, he drew forth a small stick of lunar caustic (with which he had some time previously provided himself in anticipation of possible snake-bites) and effectually cauterised the wound. The result of which prompt treatment was that the girl, after enduring some three hours' slight suffering and inconvenience from the pain and subsequent swelling of the wound, recovered, and in a day or two was as well again as ever.

This incident was, as might be expected, much talked about in the village, and it very soon reached M'Bongwele's ears. That monarch happened, just then, to be plunged into a state of serious domestic affliction; and, inspired by the above occurrence with a brilliant idea, he, after much painful cogitation, resolved to seek the aid of his prisoners. Briefly stated, the difficulty was this. His youngest and favourite wife had just added another to his already too numerous family of daughters, thus disgusting and seriously disappointing the king, who had confidently looked forward to being this time blessed with a son. This was by no means the first disappointment of the kind that the monarch had been called upon to endure; and it had been his wont, on such occasions, to banish the offending wife from his presence, replacing her with a new one. He proposed to follow the same rule upon the present occasion; and the only difficulty which lay in his way consisted in suitably filling up the vacancy. There were, of course, hundreds of sable damsels within the limits of his dominions who would gladly have accepted the responsibilities of the position, but that would no longer suit king M'Bongwele; the women of his own race had, one and all, so far as he had tried them, failed disgracefully in their duty of providing him with an heir, and he was now determined to try elsewhere. He happened to have in his possession, as prisoners, four white women, one of whom was somewhat elderly, whilst the remaining three were young, and, though by no means sufficiently *embonpoint* to be strictly handsome, from an African savage's point of view, still attractive enough to justify his choice of either of them as a wife. The difficulty with these women was that they were unfortunately all insane—a circumstance which (in accordance with one of the many superstitious beliefs of the natives, and quite apart from the equally important objection of consequent unsuitability) effectually precluded any resort to threats or compulsion for enabling the king to carry out his plans. And it was for the purpose of securing these unfortunate creatures' restoration to reason that M'Bongwele now resolved to invoke the potent aid of his new prisoners. When making up his mind to this course he was at first greatly puzzled as to how he should approach the individuals he had so basely betrayed, and how explain and excuse his conduct; but at last the happy idea suggested itself of ignoring his ill-behaviour altogether; and acting upon this, and without giving himself time for further consideration, he hurried off to the hut and presented himself before his prisoners.

Seating himself jauntily upon one of the bedsteads, he opened the negotiations by explaining that he had come to express his admiration of, and his thanks for, the wonderful manner in which the woman had been saved from the deadly effects of the snake-bite; and then, without affording an opportunity for interruption, he went on to state, in full detail, his further business.

The indignation excited in the breasts of his listeners by the cool impudence of the king soon subsided under the influence of the interesting news that four white women were captives in the village; and when M'Bongwele closed his explanation and proffered his request, the professor, instead of loading his captor with reproaches, followed the latter's example of ignoring all cause for unpleasantness, and simply stated that no promise of any kind could be made until the four friends had been afforded an interview with the afflicted women. To this proposition the king eagerly assented, overjoyed at so unexpected a measure of success, indeed he volunteered to personally conduct the quartette into the presence of his female prisoners; but this was promptly negatived, the professor declaring that if he and his friends went to see the women at all they must go entirely unattended, and at such time as might be most convenient to themselves. It would have suited M'Bongwele very much better to have been present at this interview, for he was suspicious to a really absurd degree; but, finding the white men firm upon this point, and, apparently, wholly indifferent in the matter, and being also unable to discover any cause for suspicion in their conduct, he at length yielded his assent and retired, giving the necessary instructions to the guard as he passed out of the hut.

The next morning, about eleven o'clock, having previously talked this curious matter carefully over together, they paid their promised visit; the women's prison (to which they were carefully escorted by their entire guard) being situated close to the principal opening in the palisading which surrounded the village; the same guard being apparently made to serve for both the prison and the gateway. The building was an almost exact facsimile of their own place of confinement, both in shape and dimensions; but at the very threshold the visitors encountered evidences of female delicacy and refinement in the shape of finely woven grass curtains or *portières* across the otherwise unclosed entrance, and these trifling elegances were multiplied a hundred-fold in the interior, converting the little building into a veritable miniature palace in comparison with their own unadorned domicile.

But these little interior adornments did not attract the visitors' notice until later on; their whole attention was at once claimed, upon their entrance, by the occupants of the building, or at least by the fairer portion of them. There were eight altogether—four white and four black, the ebony damsels evidently filling the position of attendants. Of the white women three were young—that is to say, they apparently ranged between nineteen and twenty-five years of age—whilst the fourth seemed to be somewhere between forty and fifty. This lady was of medium height, with a figure slightly inclined toward stoutness, brown hair with just a single streak of silver discernible here and there amongst it, a complexion still in fairly good preservation, a pair of keen but kindly grey eyes, an excellent set of teeth, shapely hands and feet, and a pleasant smile which at once prepossessed the beholder in its possessor's favour. Of the three younger women, two, aged respectively twenty-one and nineteen, were sisters; whilst the third, aged twenty-five, was their cousin, the elderly lady being aunt to all three.

On entering the hut, in response to the cry of "Come in" which followed their knock on the framework of the portal, the visitors at once found themselves face to face with the four ladies, who had risen to their feet to meet them; the sable attendants crouching at the rear end of the apartment with a grin of sympathetic curiosity overspreading their shining visages.

"You are most welcome, gentlemen," said the elderly lady, advancing and offering her hand to each of her visitors in succession. "We have been expecting you. Allow me to perform the ceremony of introduction. I am Mrs Scott, widow of Brigadier-general Scott of her majesty's forces in India. This lady is Miss Sabine, my niece and the only daughter of Major-general Sabine; and these are respectively Miss Rose and Miss Lucilla Lumsden, the daughters of an Indian judge."

The gentlemen bowed low as each name was mentioned, and, upon Mrs Scott making a somewhat significant pause, the baronet took up his parable, remarking:

"We are greatly honoured and delighted, ladies, at thus unexpectedly making your acquaintance in this out-of-the-way spot, and we sincerely hope that the acquaintanceship will redound to our mutual advantage. I am Sir Reginald Elphinstone. This gentleman is Colonel Lethbridge; this is Lieutenant Mildmay, of her majesty's navy; and, last but by no means least, this gentleman is Professor von Schalckenberg, an eminent German scientist, a most delightful companion, and a man clever enough, I firmly believe, to help us all out of our present difficulties."

A general shaking of hands ensued; and then Mrs Scott laughingly invited the gentlemen to seat themselves on the four bamboo pallets which occupied opposite sides of the apartment, apologising at the same time for the lack of suitable sitting accommodation.

"And now," said Mrs Scott laughingly, "to which of you gentlemen are we to look for the cure of our madness?"

"It is expected, I believe," said Sir Reginald, "that we shall each aid, to the best of our ability, in the good work. But," he continued in a lower and more cautious tone of voice, "is it not rather imprudent of you to behave in so very sane a manner before these women?"

"Oh," said Mrs Scott, "they are all right. They are perfectly trustworthy—indeed, they are actively aiding and abetting us in the exceedingly disagreeable but necessary deception we are practising upon king M'Bongwele. The wretch!" she continued, starting indignantly to her feet. "Would you believe it? He actually has the audacity and impudence to—to—to—"

"To aspire to a matrimonial alliance with one, if not all, of you. Yes, I am aware of his ambition," said the baronet with a smile; "and whilst we are here to-day, at his request, to remove the obstacle which your most deplorable insanity interposes, I hope that the ultimate result will be your speedy deliverance, with our own, from his power. We are, like yourselves, prisoners, but we are by no means hopeless of escape, and I pledge you my word that we will not leave until we can take you all with us."

Mrs Scott shook her head somewhat doubtfully. "We are all infinitely obliged to you for your generous promise," she said with a sigh; "but I greatly fear you are somewhat overrating your powers. The difficulties of escape—in the first place, from this village, and, in the next place, from the country itself—are so formidable that we have almost given up all hope. May I ask what strange accident brought you hither?"

"Assuredly," answered the baronet. "And when I have informed you of the facts, you will see that the difficulties of escape are, after all, not so very enormous, and I trust that you will all take heart once more."

Sir Reginald then proceeded to give a detailed description of the *Flying Fish*; and of his own and his companions' adventures in her; winding up with an account of their capture—so far as they were aware of its details—and a recital of the grounds upon which they founded their hopes of escape.

The ladies listened to Sir Reginald's singular story with an astonishment which they vainly strove to conceal, and had it been uncorroborated, they would probably have suspected in him a touch of the same malady with which they were supposed to be afflicted; but, as matters were, they had no choice but to credit the tale, and very much gratified they were to learn that there existed a means of conveyance affording, if they could but once gain access to it, a safe, easy, and speedy escape from the realms of king M'Bongwele.

Sir Reginald, having brought his story to an end, requested that he and his companions might be favoured with an account of the manner in which the ladies had fallen into the hands of the savages, which request Mrs Scott complied with, somewhat in the following terms:

"It is, to a great extent, my fault that these poor girls find themselves in the unfortunate position which they occupy to-day. I have been a widow for nearly seven years; but, having been early left an orphan, with no friends in England and many in India, I did not, as many newly-made widows do, turn my face homeward immediately on my husband's death; on the contrary, I determined rather to remain in the country of my adoption, and, being left in tolerably comfortable circumstances, made arrangements to reside alternately in Delhi and Simla. These arrangements I duly carried into effect, and nothing occurred to disturb them until about a year ago, when my brother, Sir James Lumsden, died, leaving his motherless daughters—Rose and Lucilla here—in my care, with an earnest entreaty that I would convey them, at my earliest convenience, home to their grandfather, who owns a very fine place in Hampshire, and who would, doubtless, be glad to receive them. I, of course, very willingly undertook the duty—not the less so, perhaps, from the fact that I was myself somewhat ailing, and had been strongly urged by my medical adviser to try the effect of change and a long sea voyage. Our preparations were soon completed, and we journeyed down to Bombay, at which place I happened to meet my brother-in-law, General Sabine. He, poor man, was in a great difficulty just then, being under orders to proceed at once to Afghanistan, and not knowing what to do with his daughter, who, I ought to explain, has been motherless from her infancy. The best way I could see out of the difficulty was for her to take the trip home to Europe with us, and, upon my making the proposal, it was joyfully adopted. So far all was well; but at this point our difficulties were to begin. We, unfortunately, took passage for London in a sailing ship for my health's sake. We, or the ship rather, had to call at the Cape, and, three weeks after we sailed, the captain died. The chief mate then assumed the command of the vessel, and in a few days afterwards we found that he was giving way to drink. That was, doubtless, the cause of the disaster which followed, for on a dark and stormy night, whilst the chief mate—or captain, rather, I suppose I ought to call him—was lying in his berth in a state of almost helpless intoxication, and the ship was flying before the rising gale under all the sail the sailors could spread, *we struck!* the masts snapped short off at the deck, and in a moment all was confusion and panic. The mate, or captain, staggered up on deck to see what was the matter, and he had scarcely reached the poop when a breaker swept down upon the wreck and washed the unhappy wretch overboard, never to be seen again. The next officer—a brave energetic young fellow - then took command, and by his coolness and courage soon restored order among the crew.

He commanded the lead-line to be dropped overboard, and by its means ascertained that the ship was being rapidly driven shoreward by the force of the waves. Meanwhile the shocks of the ship striking against the ground gradually grew less and less severe, until they ceased altogether, and the vessel became motionless save for an occasional sickening lurch when an exceptionally heavy wave struck her. By this time it was ascertained that the hold was nearly full of water, a circumstance from which the young officer in charge came to the conclusion that the hull was irretrievably damaged, and he then gave orders to lower the boats. This task the sailors with great difficulty accomplished, and then, there being at the moment no immediate prospect of the wreck going to pieces, the boats were secured under the shelter of the ship, and it was determined to defer until daylight our attempt at landing, when the dangers of the enterprise could be distinctly seen and more easily avoided. About two hours elapsed between the first striking of the vessel and the launching of the boats, during which time I and my nieces were on deck in our night-dresses, supplemented by such wraps as we had been able to hastily snatch on the moment of the first alarm. But when the boats had been safely lowered into the sea and secured, Mr Snelgrove (the young officer who had last assumed the command) came to us, and, in the kindest manner possible, begged us to retire to our cabins, assuring us that we might do so with perfect safety, and that we might depend on him to summon us in good time to attempt a landing with the rest of the crew. We accordingly took his advice, glad to get back to the shelter of the saloon, where we at once discarded our wet garments and proceeded to make ourselves as comfortable as the circumstances permitted. Day broke at length, and then Mr Snelgrove made his appearance in the saloon, informing us that the weather had moderated, the sea gone down a good deal, and the tide had ebbed, rendering it a favourable moment to attempt a landing, which he believed might be effected without much danger; he further added that the seamen were then passing provisions and water into the boats, and that he would allow us ten minutes wherein to select and pack a small bundle of such clothing and effects as might be deemed by us most necessary. At length the eventful moment arrived for us to pass down into the boats, and though we were assured by the sailors that there was no danger, I never was so thoroughly frightened in my life, for the sea was still very rough, leaping, curling, and foaming all round us. However, we all managed to embark without accident, and then our boat (which was the second to make the attempt) pushed off and made for the shore. The breakers were appalling, and the boat was turned round with her bow pointing seaward, and 'backed'—I think they called it—toward the shore. The sea broke over us several times, half filling the boat; but two men were kept constantly baling with buckets, and at length—thanks to Mr Snelgrove's admirable management—we safely reached the beach, but wet to the skin as a matter of course. Meanwhile, the first boat, in charge of the boatswain, had discharged her cargo on the beach, and was now sent back with four men to the wreck to bring on shore the remainder of the crew and whatever of value they could lay their hands upon. This going to and fro between the beach and the ship lasted nearly all day, and by nightfall we had quite a large quantity of provisions, water, canvas, spars, and other matters, and last, but not least, all my nieces' and my own boxes. The sailors constructed two tents in a sheltered spot high up on the beach—one for themselves and one for us—and we at length retired to spend our first night in the character of castaways.

"About an hour before daybreak we were rudely awakened—to find ourselves in the power of the savages. I am of opinion that we must have been watched during the whole of the previous day, for the surprise of the camp was complete; we had been noiselessly surrounded, and, whilst we unfortunate women were spared, the equally unfortunate men were, for the most part, slain in their sleep; not one had escaped—at least we never afterwards saw any of them alive. The camp was of course ransacked, and when every man had possessed himself of whatever happened to take his fancy, we were placed in the centre of the band and conveyed to this place, where we have been detained close prisoners ever since. The scattered contents of the camp must afterwards, I fancy, have been collected and brought to this village, for a few days later our boxes—broken open and the contents in a dreadfully soiled and disordered condition—were brought to us, and upon our replying in the affirmative to the questions put to us by signs as to whether they were our property, were left in our possession. I have only to add that the wreck, and the horrors which succeeded it, proved too much for poor Lucilla in her then somewhat weak state of health, and she fell into a low fever with delirium, which prostrated her for nearly three months, and from the effects of which she has even now not wholly recovered. It was during this dreadfully anxious period that those four poor black creatures were appointed to attend upon us. They have been most zealous and faithful in their efforts to help us; they have instructed us to some extent in their simple language; and they have informed us, not only that they are cast-off wives of the king, but that he was, and still is, anxious to secure one (if not more) of my nieces for a wife, and that the only hope of escape from such a fate lay in our simulating insanity, which, most reluctantly, we have been compelled to do whenever M'Bongwele or any of his emissaries have visited us. But, beyond our close confinement and this horrible ever-impending danger, we have no very great cause for complaint, all our expressed wants being instantly satisfied so far as the resources of the king will permit."

Mrs Scott having thus brought her story to an end, the gentlemen expressed their sympathy and condolences, and the conversation gradually grew more general. At length, much as they would have liked to prolong the interview, they felt that they had already lengthened it out almost beyond the bounds of prudence, so they rose to take leave, uttering a few encouraging remarks, which Sir Reginald rounded off with an exhortation to them to be ever on the watch, and to hold themselves in readiness for flight at a moment's notice, adding that one or other of the gentlemen would visit them as often as possible and keep them well informed upon the progress of events.

Chapter Twenty One
Retribution overtakes King M'Bongwele

King M'Bongwele had evidently been keenly on the watch for the return of the four prisoners, for they had scarcely had time to enter their hut when the monarch presented himself before them, and, with some little impatience of manner, began his interrogations with the single word:

"Well?"

"We can cure them," briefly answered the professor.

"Good!" ejaculated the king, his impatience yielding to almost childish delight. "When is the cure to be performed?"

"Within one span of the sun's journey through the sky after we have administered a certain medicine, which we must procure from the ship. Provide us each with a horse to go and fetch this medicine, and I promise you, that before you see the stars to-night those women shall be in as full possession of their reason as you are."

"No," said the king, eyeing the professor keenly, "I will arrange better than that. You shall tell Lualamba where to find this wonderful medicine, and he shall fetch it for you."

"That will not do at all," answered the professor. "Lualamba could never find the medicine; he could not even gain access to the ship. We must fetch it ourselves."

M'Bongwele rested his chin in his hand for some minutes, pondering deeply. Then he rose to his feet and stalked out of the hut again without vouchsafing a word, either "yea" or "nay."

"He is not quite such a fool as he looks," was the baronet's sole comment upon this strange behaviour, and then they sat down to luncheon.

The king, upon re-entering his palace, at once sent for Lualamba, and, upon that chief making his appearance, issued strict orders that every available man, woman, and child, not only in the village but in the entire district, should be mustered by noon next day, to make one grand and final attempt to move the ship to the village, pending which the king decided to hold no further communications with his prisoners. The attempt was made in due course, and, like the others, it proved, as might be expected, a miserable failure. Poor M'Bongwele was now completely at a loss; he knew not what to do. He was most anxious to have the white women cured; but he had a powerful presentiment that if those singular beings, whom he certainly to some extent had in his power, once again set foot upon that curious thing they called a "ship," his power over them would be gone for ever. And in such a case he felt that his fate was certain; he had laid unholy hands upon them, and dire would be his punishment. No; he was convinced that at all costs they must be debarred from access to that terrible "ship," unless he could first of all gain their forgiveness, amity, and good-will, and interest them in his fortunes to the extent of securing their active co-operation in his schemes of conquest and aggrandisement. How to do this was, however, the question which puzzled king M'Bongwele; and it puzzled him so long that—but stay, we must not forestall the story.

Thus engaged in a futile endeavour to discover a way out of his dilemma, the king kept himself strictly secluded in his palace day after day, allowing no one access to him unless upon business of the utmost urgency and importance. Meanwhile, Seketulo, deeming the period a favourable one for the furtherance of his own schemes, first exhibited an increased amount of precaution in the proper posting of the guard over the prisoners, and then a gradually growing disposition to converse with the prisoners themselves. From this he proceeded to develop an interest, which, after a suitable lapse of time, was allowed to merge into anxiety for their welfare and greater comfort, and, finding these cautious advances well received, he then set to work in real earnest upon the delicate task of unfolding his proposals. He was so very cautious, however, and took so long a time about this, that he missed his opportunity altogether, and that, too, through a very simple accident.

It happened one night that, after an unusually long, disjointed, and desultory conversation with this same chief, Mildmay failed to get to sleep with his usual promptitude, and he lay tossing restlessly upon his pallet until he became impatient and finally exasperated at his want of success. The hut felt hot and stuffy to the verge of suffocation, and the lieutenant at length came to the conclusion that there was no hope of his getting to sleep until he had taken a turn or two up and down the compound, in the comparatively cool night air.

He accordingly scrambled to his feet, and, groping his way in the intense darkness, made for the verandah. Here he paused for a moment, glancing upward to the sky, which he found to be obscured by a dense canopy of heavy black cloud, portending rain, which sufficiently accounted for the pitchy darkness. His eyes at length becoming accustomed to the obscurity, he looked round for the guard; and he eventually discovered the various members faithfully occupying their posts, but, one and all, squatted upon the ground evidently fast asleep. He stalked out toward the centre of the compound and took two or three turns up and down its length, his footsteps falling noiselessly upon the light sandy soil, and not one of the savages manifested the slightest consciousness of his presence. Then he gradually extended his walk until he reached the gate in the palisade, and here too the guard was fast asleep. An idea presented itself to him; and he was about to make an attempt to noiselessly remove the bars and open the gate, when prudence suggested another and a better plan. He tiptoed lightly back to the hut, and, gently awakening each of his companions in turn, whispered in their ears:

"Up at once! There is an opportunity for us to effect our escape!"

The aroused sleepers instinctively comprehended the situation and sprang to their feet. Another minute, and four shadowy shapes stole noiselessly across the compound, to vanish almost instantly in the deeper shadows of the palisading. The closed gate was reached and passed, and presently the fugitives found themselves in the angle of the compound most distant from the slumbering guard. Here Mildmay offered a "back" to the baronet, whispering:

"You go first."

Without a word Sir Reginald complied, clambering first upon his companion's back and thence noiselessly to the top of the palisading. In another second a faint thud on the outside told that the first adventurer had successfully scaled the barrier. "You go next," whispered Mildmay to the colonel, "and remain on the top of the palisade to give the professor a hand."

Up went the colonel, and up after him went the professor. The latter, with the baronet's assistance from below on the outside, accomplished his descent in safety; and then the colonel, reaching as far down as he could, assisted Mildmay to the top. The rest was easy; and a minute later they were cautiously making their way up the road to the top end of the village, or that which was most thinly inhabited. At this moment down came the rain, a regular tropical deluge, which was undoubtedly a most fortunate circumstance for the fugitives, as they could otherwise have scarcely hoped to escape the vigilance of the numerous prowling curs belonging to the village, who, as it was, were driven by the rain to take refuge in their masters' huts.

Five minutes sufficed the travellers to reach the stout lofty palisade which inclosed the village; and this, the framework all being on the inner side, they were easily enabled to surmount. Once outside this obstacle, Mildmay assumed the leadership, confidently declaring his ability to find the ship, though he had only once before, consciously, passed over the ground between the village and the ruins.

The party made their way in the first place along the outer side of the palisading until they reached the main entrance gate to the village; and from this point Mildmay "took his departure." A well-defined pathway led for some distance down into the plain, and this they traversed until the lieutenant believed he had reached the point at which to turn off. Here he paused for a full minute, looking about him and peering into the darkness. The rain was still pelting down, though not so heavily as at first; and away to the eastward the clouds were already beginning to break, allowing a star to peep through here and there. At length Mildmay thought he had got his bearings right; and, selecting a star to steer by, away he plunged into the long thick wet grass, his companions following closely behind. A few minutes later the rain ceased, the clouds vanished from the sky, and the stars shone calmly out in all their beauty, affording an ample sufficiency of light to distinctly reveal to the wayfarers the nearer clumps of bush, trees, and other large objects. Mildmay now paused again, and, shading his eyes with his hand, once more keenly surveyed the horizon.

"All right," he murmured. "We are going just right, I believe. I can indistinctly make out something away there on the horizon, just ahead, which I feel certain must be the ruins. Come along, my hearties; heave ahead!"

Again they pushed forward, dripping wet, drenched to the skin with the recent shower, and stumbling every now and then as their feet became entangled in the long matted grass; now swerving to the right to avoid a clump of bush, then to the left for the same purpose; but ever keeping one particular star, low down on the horizon, as nearly straight ahead as possible. Though the rest of the party felt themselves utterly lost, without the faintest notion of where they were going, and though neither of them could distinguish anything even remotely resembling the ruins, Mildmay still persisted that he was right; and he continued to press rapidly forward, the rest following him, since they could do no better. At length they struck a narrow path through the grass, and Mildmay at once announced his intention of following it.

"It is a little off our course," he said, "but the walking is so much easier here that we shall gain more than we shall lose by following it; and I should not be surprised to find that it leads to the ruins."

Half an hour later a brilliant star suddenly appeared in the dense darkness ahead. It shone steadily for nearly a minute, disappeared, and almost instantly appeared again.

"Hurrah!" ejaculated the lieutenant joyously, "there is the ship's light. Now we *know* that we are right. Another hour's tramp will, if all be well, take us alongside. How I wish I had a pipe of tobacco!"

"Don't mention it!" fervently ejaculated the professor, who was an ardent lover of the weed. "However, in another hour, as you say—ah!"

The professor's "ah!" was so very expressive of anticipated pleasure that his companions with one accord burst into a hearty laugh, which, however, was abruptly cut short by a low savage growl and a sudden rustling in the grass close by.

"What was that?" was the simultaneous inquiry as the party came abruptly to a dead halt.

"Push on, push on!" urged the professor. "It is some nocturnal animal prowling in search of prey. At this moment he is more frightened than we are; but if we wait here until he has regained his courage he will perhaps spring on one of us."

The march was accordingly resumed, with perhaps some little precipitation; and at length Mildmay's companions began to be conscious of the presence of certain shapeless blotches of blackness rising up against the sky ahead of them and occasionally obscuring for a few seconds the now brilliant light which gleamed from the top of the *Flying Fish's* pilot-house. These shapeless blotches of blackness increased in size with almost startling rapidity; and in a few minutes the travellers, still following the footpath, found themselves in the midst of them, winding in and out between great blocks of masonry which suddenly rose up in front of them in the darkness, and stumbling over loose boulders and fragments of stone. At length they found themselves in the clear open space occupied by the *Flying Fish*; and in another quarter of an hour the party passed into the black tunnel formed by the bilge-keel and the side of the ship, and began to feel with their feet for the open trap-door. This was soon reached; the party entered the opening, closed the flap, and, with a murmured "Thank God, we are safe at last!" began to feel for the button which was to open the door giving access to the interior proper of the ship. Another second and this door swung open, and the party found themselves at the foot of the cylindrical staircase, in the full blaze of the electric lamps.

"Now," said the baronet, "ten minutes in which to strip, rub down, and don dry garments, and then we will   be off to the rescue of those poor women, after which I think we must give our friend M'Bongwele a salutary lesson on the evil and impolicy of treachery."

THE "FLYING FISH" DESTROYS KING M'BONGWELE'S PALISADE.

The allotted ten minutes had not quite expired when the professor, the last of the party, made his appearance in the pilot-house, by which time the *Flying Fish* was some five hundred feet in the air, with her nose pointing in the direction of M'Bongwele's village, and her propeller driving her ahead at full speed. The electric lights of the ship were all called into requisition for the illumination of the landscape, producing a weird and ghostlike effect as the trees and clumps of bush first caught the light and then brightened into full radiance as they flashed past, to instantly fade again into obscurity. A startled howl or two smote upon the ears of the travellers, and the forms of hastily retreating animals were momentarily caught sight of; but all eyes were intently directed ahead in anxious expectancy of catching sight of the village, and presently it came into view. The speed was at once reduced and the vessel's flight directed earthward, and in another moment she dashed through the palisade, shivering the principal entrance gate to splinters, and (as was intended) frightening the guard clean out of their senses. With one shrill, piercing scream of terror, as they caught sight of the dazzling bow lights of the ship, the sable warriors took to their heels and vanished in the darkness, whilst the *Flying Fish* was dexterously brought to earth close alongside the hut tenanted by Mrs Scott and her nieces. That appalling yell effectually awakened the entire occupants of the hut; and whilst they were sitting up on their pallets, rubbing their eyes and wondering what the terrible sound might portend, the portière was pushed aside and the professor, bearing a hand-lamp, unceremoniously made his appearance before them with an earnest request that they would dress with all speed and join him on the outside of the hut, where he would await them, the hour of their deliverance having arrived.

A quarter of an hour later the bewildered ladies were conducted by von Schalckenberg in through the trapdoor in the bottom of the *Flying Fish* and up the cylindrical staircase to the saloon, where they were warmly welcomed by the other three gentlemen, who, after a few congratulatory remarks on their fortunate escape, retired to secure and convey on board the boxes containing the remainder of their guests' wardrobes. This done, Mrs Scott and her nieces were conducted to the cabins assigned for their use, and the gentlemen then retreated to the pilot-house, where, over a keenly enjoyed pipe, a hasty council was held as to what should be done with M'Bongwele.

This question was settled just as the first faint streaks of approaching dawn began to brighten the eastern horizon, when the ship was moved up into the great square before the king's house, where the whole of the king's body-guard were drawn up under arms, and, beyond them, the remaining inhabitants of the village, a dense, surging, excited, squabbling crowd.

On the approach of the *Flying Fish* the latter flung themselves face downwards, in abject terror, to the ground, and the armed and mounted warriors betrayed a disposition to stampede which was only with the utmost difficulty checked and restrained by Seketulo. Even this chief found himself unable to wholly conceal the feeling of nervousness which agitated him; but he in this trying moment enjoyed a consciousness, unshared by any other man there present, of having done his best to make the erstwhile prisoners comfortable.

As the huge ship settled quietly down in the centre of the great square a profound and deathlike silence suddenly succeeded the confused babbling sound which had hitherto prevailed, and when the four travellers stepped out from the pilot-house to the deck and appeared at the gangway a visible shudder ran through the entire concourse of people there assembled. They dreaded they knew not what, and their fears were only in a very trifling degree allayed by the promise of intercession on their behalf which Seketulo had made to them.

The professor was of course to be spokesman for the occasion; it was he, therefore, who broke the terrible silence by exclaiming, in a loud, commanding tone of voice:

"Seketulo, we are your friends. Advance, therefore, and listen to the commands which we are about to lay upon you!"

The reassured and now happy chief struck with his spurred heels the sides of his charger, and the animal, bounding and caracoling, advanced to within a few yards of the ship's side, where his rider dismounted and, with bowed head and bended knee, waited for such communication as might be vouchsafed him.

"Listen, O Seketulo!" continued the professor. "We entered this country animated by feelings of the most amicable nature to its king and to every one of its inhabitants. We showed this by distributing presents of beads, cloth, and other matters when Lualamba and his warriors first visited us. And we asked for nothing in return save permission to examine and explore the ruins on yonder plain; offering to pay promptly and liberally for whatever assistance we might need. Is not this the truth?"

"It is, O most mighty wizard," answered Seketulo humbly; some of the braver warriors also venturing to murmur:

"It is! It is!"

"And how have we been treated?" asked the professor. "Your king, not satisfied with our friendship and the presents we gave him, wickedly and treacherously devised a scheme to get us into his power—a scheme which, in order to try him, we permitted to succeed. And, having done that, he further attempted to gain possession of this ship,"—this fact having leaked out in Seketulo's previous conversations—"profanely and audaciously thinking he could subdue her to his will and control her as we do. Now, therefore, be it understood by all present that, for his base treachery, *M'Bongwele is dethroned*, and Seketulo will, from this moment, reign in his stead. Let a detachment of the guard enter the palace and bring M'Bongwele forth to hear his sentence!"

In an instant Lualamba—anxious above all things to please the powers that be, and having, moreover, in revengeful remembrance many little gratuitous slights and insults which he had suffered at the king's hands—dismounted a squadron of the guard, and, surrounding the palace, himself entered the building at the head of half a dozen men. Two or three minutes later the party reappeared with the dethroned monarch in their midst. They advanced until almost level with the spot occupied by Seketulo, when, at a sign from the professor, they halted; the guards disposing themselves round M'Bongwele in such a manner that, whilst to escape was an utter impossibility, he could still see and hear the individual who, perched far aloft in the gangway of the ship, was about to address him.

M'Bongwele never, perhaps, looked more kingly than whilst he thus stood to receive his sentence of dethronement. He was fully conscious of his treacherous behaviour to his guests, but he felt no shame thereat, for he had been schooled in the belief that treachery, falsehood, ay, even deliberate, cold-blooded murder, was perfectly justifiable in the pursuit of power. His only feeling was that he had played a bold game for a high stake and had lost it. The moment of reckoning had now arrived, the penalty of failure had to be paid, and though he knew not what that penalty might be—though his brain was teeming with all sorts of possible and impossible horrors— he never for a moment forgot that he was a monarch, that the eyes of his people were on him, noting his every look and gesture, and he summoned all his fortitude to his aid, in order that, since fall he must, he should fall as becomes a king.

So there he stood in the bright sunlight of the early morning—an unarmed man, surrounded by those who, whilst they would yesterday have poured out their heart's blood at his command, were now prepared to hew him in pieces at the bidding of a white-skinned stranger—with arms folded across the muscular naked chest which throbbed visibly with the intensity of his hardly repressed emotions, his head thrown back, his brows knitted, his lips firmly closed over his rigidly set teeth, and his eyes unquailingly fixed upon the group of white men whom he recognised and tacitly acknowledged as his conquerors and judges. And when the sentence of dethronement, separation from his family, and instant banishment for life from his country, was pronounced upon him, he offered no plea for pardon or mitigation of his punishment; he urged nothing in extenuation or justification of his conduct, but simply bowed his head in token of his submission to the inevitable, and begged a respite of a few minutes in which to bid farewell to his family before setting out upon his journey to the frontier, whither he was to be escorted by a small well-armed party, in whom Seketulo knew he could place implicit trust.

This somewhat painful scene over, the troops and people there present were required to swear allegiance and fidelity to their new king, which they readily did with all the formalities customary among them on such occasions; after which the crown of gold and feathers worn by M'Bongwele was brought forward and placed upon Seketulo's head; and the new king was then invited on board the ship to confer with—and in reality to receive instructions respecting his future policy and conduct from—the men who had raised him to the supreme dignity. The advice—given with sufficient firmness and emphasis to constitute a command—comprised many valuable hints for the wise and humane government of the nation, and was concluded with a powerful exhortation to treat with fairness, justice, humanity, and hospitality all strangers who might be brought by accident or otherwise into the country; to succour, nourish, and carefully protect them from molestation or spoliation of any and every kind whilst within its borders; and to afford them every help and facility to leave whensoever they might desire. And, finally, a satisfactory arrangement was made whereby the baronet and his companions were enabled to continue and complete their exploration and examination of the ruins.

The *Flying Fish* and her inmates remained in the country for rather more than three months from that date; quite long enough to satisfy the party that they had really acted wisely, and for the benefit of the nation, in deposing M'Bongwele; and long enough to enable them to make several most surprising and interesting discoveries among the ruins—discoveries which it is not necessary to describe or particularise here, since the professor has prepared, and is now revising for the press, an elaborate and exhaustive treatise upon the subject.

Chapter Twenty Two
An Adventure on the Top of Mount Everest

Leaving the country at last—to the very great regret of the inhabitants, who found that every little service rendered to the white strangers was munificently rewarded by a present of beads, buttons, party-coloured cloth, or perhaps a small hand mirror—the travellers made the best of their way to Bombay, at which place Mrs Scott and her nieces were anxious to be landed, and there they bade their fair guests a reluctant adieu. Thence, starting under cover of night and rising to a height of about ten thousand feet above the ground surface, the travellers made their way across the Indian peninsula in a north-easterly direction, travelling at a speed of about one hundred miles per hour, and arriving about eight o'clock the next morning at the foot of Mount Everest, the summit of which—towering into the sky to the enormous altitude of twenty-nine thousand feet above the sea-level, and believed to be the most lofty spot of earth on the surface of our globe—they intended attempting to reach.

Here, on a magnificent grassy plateau surrounded by trees, and with not a single sign of human life at hand, the *Flying Fish* was brought to earth and temporarily secured whilst the party took breakfast.

"Now," said the professor as they rose from the breakfast-table, "in seeking to plant our feet upon the topmost peak of Mount Everest we are about to enter upon a task of no ordinary difficulty and danger, and it is desirable that no avoidable risks should be run. The danger arises from two causes—the excessive cold, and the highly rarefied state of the atmosphere at so enormous an elevation. The first can be guarded against by suitable clothing; the second can only be overcome by the assumption of our diving dresses. The latter, no doubt, seems to you a strange precaution; but it is a fact, that on the top of Mount Everest the air is too thin to support life, at all events in comfort, and for any but the briefest possible time; so we must take up our air with us. Let us therefore go and make these necessary changes of costume before we attempt moving the ship from her present position."

Half an hour later, the party, accoutred in their diving armour—between which and their ordinary clothing they had interposed stout warm flannel overalls—and armed with small ice-hatchets, mustered in the pilot-house; the ship was released from the ground, a vacuum created in her air-chambers, and upward she at once shot into the clear blue cloudless sky. A few minutes only sufficed her to soar to the height of ten thousand feet, after which her progress upward, as indicated by the steadily falling column of mercury in the tube of the barometer, gradually decreased in velocity. At the height of twenty-nine thousand feet the mercury ceased to fall, or the ship ceased to rise, which amounted to the same thing, and Mount Everest lay before them, its snowy peak glistening in the sun ten miles away, and its topmost pinnacle still towering somewhere about five hundred feet above the line of their horizon.

"Well," said the professor, remarking upon their failure to attain a greater altitude, "I anticipated this; I was quite prepared to find that here, where the sun is so much more nearly vertical than it is with us in England, we should meet with a more rarefied atmosphere. However, we cannot help it. We must do what we can; and if we fail to reach the summit we shall simply be obliged to descend again, rid ourselves temporarily of a few of our more weighty matters, and then renew the attempt. Perhaps we may be enabled to *force* her up that remaining five hundred feet by the power of her engines. Let us try."

The engines were sent ahead at full speed, and the *Flying Fish* rushed toward the glittering peak, the professor so adjusting the helm as to give the ship's bows a slight upward inclination. The experiment resulted in partial success, an additional elevation of some two hundred feet being attained, but beyond that it was found impossible to go; even then it was necessary to keep the ship moving at full speed, and to maintain the upward inclination of her bows, in order to preserve the slight additional height gained, her tendency being to sink immediately upon any relaxation of speed. It was resolved to be satisfied with this, to effect a landing somewhere, and to attempt surmounting the remaining three hundred feet by climbing. A landing-place was next sought for, and this was at length found on the northern side of the mountain, on a sidelong slanting snow-bank, which seemed to have accumulated between two projecting crags. It was by no means a desirable spot on which to effect a landing, the area of the bank being very small, and the surface sloping most awkwardly; however, it was the best place the travellers could find, and they were therefore obliged to rest content with it; so the ship was headed toward it, and in another second or two a harsh grating sound, accompanied by an upward surge, showed that she had taken the ground, or rather the snow-bank. The engines were then stopped, and the grip-anchors brought into requisition to secure her in her somewhat precarious berth.

"Well, here we are," exclaimed the baronet; "and the next thing, I suppose, is to land and commence our climb without loss of time. What a wild-looking spot it is, to be sure; if I were to stand looking at it long I believe I should lose my nerve and shirk the task."

"Better not look at it any longer, then, until we can contemplate the prospect from the peak away up aloft there," remarked the practical Mildmay. "But," he continued, "I don't half like the idea of going out upon that sloping slippery surface of frozen snow that the ship has grounded upon; a single slip or false step and away one would go over the edge, to bring up, perhaps, on a rock a thousand feet below. I shall hook on the rope-ladder, and endeavour to make a start from yonder naked spur of rock."

The others also seemed to think this the wisest plan, and in a few minutes they were making their way cautiously down the rope-ladder one after the other, the baronet, an experienced mountaineer, leading, and Mildmay bringing up the rear.

The adventurers soon found that their task was likely to be a great deal more difficult and hazardous than they had at all contemplated. The snow-bank upon which the *Flying Fish* rested proved to be the only even approximately level spot at that elevation; the rocks rising almost sheer above them everywhere, with only an occasional crevice here and there by way of foothold, and in many places the precipice was coated with treacherous frozen snow, sometimes tenacious enough to afford a momentary support, but more often crumbling away beneath the weight of the body. Slowly and steadily, however, they worked their way upward— now occupying perhaps five minutes to advance as many feet, and anon hitting upon a favourable spot where twenty or thirty feet might be gained in a single minute. At length, after a toilsome and hazardous climb of more than an hour's duration, the baronet found himself clinging to a slender pinnacle of rock about seven feet high and four feet in diameter, upon the top of which he next moment triumphantly seated himself. The colonel, the professor, and Mildmay speedily followed, and there they sat, undoubtedly the first human beings who had ever reached the topmost pinnacle of Mount Everest.

Having accomplished the ascent, they now settled themselves down as comfortably as they could upon their narrow perch to enjoy at leisure the magnificent view spread out around them, a view such as no human eye had ever before looked upon, and which even *they* would probably never have another opportunity of beholding. The atmosphere, most fortunately, was exceptionally clear and transparent, not a vestige of cloud or vapour being anywhere visible; the view was therefore unobstructed to the very verge of the horizon, which extended round them in a gigantic circle measuring *four hundred and eighteen miles in diameter*.

Northward of them stretched the vast plains of Thibet, the only object worthy of notice being the river Sampoo, which, although sixty miles distant, was distinctly seen as it issued from the purplish-grey haze of the extreme distance on their left, meandering along the plain beneath for a visible distance of nearly two hundred miles before its course became again lost in the haze on their right hand. Eight and left of them stretched the vast mountain chain of the Himalayas, their wooded slopes and countless peaks and cones presenting a bewildering yet charming picture of variegated colour, sunlight and shadow, as they dwindled away on either hand until all suggestion of local colouring was swallowed up and lost in an enchanting succession of increasingly pure and delicate soft pearly greys, which merged and melted at last into the vague shapeless all-pervading purple-grey of the horizon. Glancing immediately around and beneath them their blood curdled and their brains whirled with the vertigo which seized them as they peered appalled and shrinkingly down upon the sharp crags, the sheer precipices, the steeply-sloping snow-fields with their lower edges generally overhanging some fathomless abyss, the great glaciers, the awful crevasses spanned here and there by crumbling snow bridges—the effect of the scene being heightened and intensified in its impressive grandeur by the deathlike silence which prevailed, broken only by the occasional thunderous roar of an avalanche far below. The scene was absolutely fascinating in its appalling sublimity; but it was a relief to turn the eye further afield until it rested to the eastward upon the grandly towering mass of Everest's rival, snow-capped Kunchinjinga, which reared its giant crest aloft to a height of twenty-eight thousand five hundred feet above the sea-level, and which, though it was eighty-five miles away, appeared to be almost within rifle-shot. And still more was it a relief to turn the eye in an opposite direction, and to allow it to rest upon the glittering summit of Dhawalagiri, which, at a distance of no less than *two hundred and forty miles*, gleamed faint and softly opalescent out of the western haze. And, lastly, to the southward of them they beheld the fertile province of Nepaul, watered by countless tributaries to the mighty Ganges; and, beyond it again, the still more fertile province of Oudh. The professor, totally forgetful of his exceedingly perilous position, was enthusiastically expatiating, after his usual manner, upon the marvellous extent and beauty of the prospect, and interrupting the flow of his eloquence at short intervals to assure his companions that a—to them— invisible object on the far horizon *must* be the town of Patna, when a terrific crackling crash just below them drew the eyes of the party in that direction, just in time for them to see the supposed projecting crag—in reality an enormous mass of ice—which supported the snow-bank on which the *Flying Fish* rested, break off and go thundering down into the unfathomable depths below. The spectators clung to each other in helpless nerveless terror at so appalling a spectacle as the falling of this mass, weighing probably millions of tons; but the full significance and import of the catastrophe did not present itself to their dazed and bewildered senses until they beheld the *Flying Fish*, after following the falling mass for a couple of hundred feet, recover herself and float jauntily in the air, *adrift*, at a distance of fully two thousand feet from the mountain side. Then, indeed, the full horror of their position began to slowly dawn upon them, and they looked at each other with eyes in which could be read a despair too deep and too complete to need or find expression in words. Their long search for a landing-place that morning had unconsciously impressed upon them a fact which now—and not till now—took intelligible shape within their brains, and it was this: they could descend the mountain as far as the spot at which they had left the *Flying Fish, but no further*; beyond that point further descent, with the means at their disposal, was impossible. Which meant, in plain language and few words, that, sooner or later, they would try to get down, and either be dashed to pieces in the attempt or perish miserably of starvation upon the edge of some ghastly impassable precipice.

It took but a moment for these ideas to shape themselves intelligibly, and then a general movement was made to commence the descent and thus cut short a state of suspense which would soon become unbearable.

But at this moment the colonel interposed with a word of caution.

"One moment," said he. "Before we start let each one of us clearly understand that perfect coolness and presence of mind is imperatively necessary if we would emerge from this strait alive. We *may* perhaps find a way down after all, but in order to do so we must have our wits completely about us; let no man move, therefore, until he has fully recovered the control of his nerves; when all have done so we will make a start, and I will go last."

"And I first," exclaimed the baronet, "because, next to you, I believe I am the most experienced mountaineer of the party."

The colonel's little speech produced a most beneficial effect upon the nerves of the whole party, his own included; and now, without further ado, a general start was made, the baronet going first and directing and helping the professor, who followed him; Mildmay going third, also helping von Schalckenberg, and being helped in his turn by Lethbridge, and the latter bringing up the rear.

The descent, owing to the perpendicular precipices over which they had to pass, and the extremely dangerous character, generally, of the road, proved to be even more tedious and difficult than the ascent; and within the first quarter of an hour (during which they had accomplished only about one hundred feet of perpendicular descent) every one of the party had experienced at least one narrow escape from certain death.

Steadily, however, they toiled on; foot by foot they crept down the face of the icy precipice, and at length they reached a ledge nearly a foot in width, upon which the entire party were enabled to pause for a minute or two to rest and relieve their tired and quivering muscles.

When their feet were safely planted upon this ledge Mildmay spoke.

"I may now venture," he said, "to call your attention to a fact which I feared to mention before, lest it should upset the balance of your nerves and produce a catastrophe. It is this. The *Flying Fish*, floating undisturbed in this motionless air, is, in obedience to the law of gravitation, slowly but steadily being drawn in toward the side of the mountain; and if—which God grant—it remains perfectly calm up here for another quarter of an hour, she will be once more alongside, and we may yet regain access to her. To do this, however, we must edge away more toward the eastern side of the mountain, where I fear we shall encounter even greater difficulties than we have yet met with. We can but try, however, and I think the sooner we push on the better."

"Forward, then, at once," cried the baronet; "and take heed to your steps, my friends, for this ice is terribly smooth and slippery."

Once more was the journey resumed, the baronet availing himself of the ledge, as far as it extended, to work his way round the shoulder of the hill in the required direction; and by the time they reached a point where actual descent had again become necessary, they had once more come within sight of the ship, and had the satisfaction of seeing that she had drawn sensibly nearer to the cliff.

"All right," exclaimed Sir Reginald cheerfully, "I see the spot we must aim for—that pinnacle of bare rock yonder, and there is a tolerably easy road down to it, moreover."

Away they now went, their spirits at the very highest pitch of exhilaration, and their nerves by so much the steadier, and such rapid progress did they make that ten minutes later saw them clustered together clinging to the rocky pinnacle before mentioned. And a gruesome-enough looking spot it was—a sharp projecting point of rock overhanging a sheer precipice some two hundred feet deep, with a narrow snow-bank immediately beneath, and then another frightful abyss of unknown depth beyond. And, to the right and left of it, an almost vertical face of bare rock coated with smooth, slippery, transparent ice, any attempt to traverse which would be courting death in its most horrible form.

The *Flying Fish* seemed to be drifting steadily in toward this pinnacle of rock, though at a depth of some twenty feet below it, and it was resolved to pause there and allow events to develop somewhat before exerting themselves further.

Slowly, very slowly, the *Flying Fish* drifted nearer and nearer in; the little party clustered upon the rock watching her with bated breath, and every moment dreading that a faint air of wind might after all waft her beyond their reach. But nothing of the sort occurred; in she steadily came, until at last her starboard gangway was immediately underneath the party.

"Now or never!" exclaimed Sir Reginald. "I am going to make a jump for her. We shall scarcely have a better chance; and breeze may at any moment sweep round the face of the rock and carry her away from us. Lethbridge and Mildmay, let me steady myself by your shoulders whilst I stand on the extreme point of the rock. Stand firm, now; I am about to jump. Are you ready? Then—one—*two*— **three** !"

The body of the baronet darted outward from the face of the rock, Mildmay and the colonel retaining their footing with the utmost difficulty under the recoil from the outward impulse; and then the three men left behind on the rock craned their necks over the precipice to watch the result.

The sight which met their eyes caused their hair to bristle and their blood to curdle with horror. Sir Reginald had either miscalculated his distance, or his foot had slipped in the act of springing, for instead of alighting upon the ship's deck, as he had intended, he had fallen on the circular bilge of the vessel, from whence, after an unavailing struggle to secure a footing, he slid off, and, with a piercing scream, went whirling downward until he alighted on the narrow snow-bank some two hundred feet below. His horror-stricken companions fully expected to see him rebound and go plunging over the edge of the next precipice, but luckily the snow upon which he had fallen was so deep that his body sank into it, and there he lay, motionless.

"Merciful Heaven, he is killed!" ejaculated the colonel with stammering lips.

"Perhaps not," returned Mildmay; "at all events we will hope for the best. Let me see if I can do better. *Quick*—out of the way—ah! The wind after all! We are too late!"

And even as he spoke the bows of the *Flying Fish* swung slowly round, and her hull was swept gently away from the face of the cliff by a capricious zephyr which just then came creeping along the mountain side.

Chapter Twenty Three
How the Adventure terminated

The silence of despair again settled upon the three remaining travellers; they had lost one of their party, and were a second time left stranded upon that terrible mountain top, from which it now began to appear that there was no possibility of escape. One thing at least was certain, which was, that on their side of the mountain there was no means of further descent; the pinnacle of rock upon which they then stood was the lowest accessible point; there was no possible way even of reaching poor Sir Reginald's body, and the way downward, if indeed such existed, must be sought elsewhere.

They crouched where they were, in helpless bewilderment, watching the ship until she slowly drifted out of sight round a projecting bluff; and then, in a dazed, halfhearted way, and with nerves all unstrung by disappointment and the dreadful accident which had befallen the baronet, they began to slowly retrace their steps, in the faint hope of stumbling upon some means of escape.

Led this time by the colonel, Mildmay bringing up the rear, the little party at last made their way back to the narrow ledge where they had previously paused to rest, and here they again made a momentary halt, afterwards following the ledge in the other direction until it terminated abruptly in an almost perpendicular wall of smooth rock. Another ledge was here discovered, about eighteen feet further down, but it was certainly not more than a foot wide, with apparently a vertical fall of several hundred feet beyond. This ledge extended right and left beyond their range of vision, and had evidently been traversed by them in their original ascent, for their footprints were plainly visible in the snow with which it was covered; if, therefore, they could reach it, it would at least be possible to return to their original starting-point, which would certainly be something gained. But how to get down to it was the question. They had grown bewildered in their gropings round about the summit, and knew not in which direction to go to regain the lost path. They might, of course, go on climbing until they were once more at the very top of the mountain, and commence their descent afresh, but this was a task so full of difficulty and peril as not to be thought of, save as a last resort. Besides, the day was already on the wane, and it was of the utmost importance that they should reach some place of comparative safety before nightfall. At length Mildmay hit upon a bold though terribly dangerous mode of mastering the difficulty.

"Look here," he said, "it is no use hesitating here; we shall never do any good at this rate. Let me offer a suggestion. I will lower myself down over the ledge until I hang from it by my hands alone; then you, Lethbridge, must climb down over me, using my body as a ladder (or a rope, rather), and when you are hanging at arm's-length from my feet there will only remain a very trifling drop to the lower ledge, which you can surely accomplish in safety. That done you must stand by to steady me and prevent me, if possible, from going backward over the precipice; and, with us two safely on the ledge, we are surely men enough to catch the professor when he makes the drop. What say you to the plan?"

"It is frightfully dangerous, but it is perhaps worth trying—if you think you have the strength for it. What say you, professor? Have you nerve enough to make the drop, trusting to us to catch you?"

"Anything is better than this," answered the professor. "Your own and Mildmay's are the most difficult portions of the task. If you are equal to your parts I will perform mine; but my strength is not sufficient to justify my offering to change places with either of you."

"Then let us try it," exclaimed the colonel decisively. "Will you go first, Mildmay, or shall I?"

"You go first," answered Mildmay. "I am pretty strong in the arms, and think the method I have proposed the safest, on the whole."

"All right, then. I am ready whenever you are."

"Stand firm, then, and let me steady myself down over the ledge by your leg—we shall be down, one way or another, all the sooner. Now, look out, I am going!"

The colonel braced himself as firmly as possible against the strain, and Mildmay lowered himself cautiously down until he hung from the ledge by both hands. Then, without wasting a moment, Lethbridge carefully placed himself in position, got down on his knees, lowered one foot until it rested on Mildmay's shoulder, then the other; firmly grasped the ledge with both hands, outside Mildmay's; got his knees down on Mildmay's shoulders, and then, warning the lieutenant to hold firm, grasped him by both wrists and proceeded as rapidly and carefully as possible to slide down his body until he hung to him by a firm hand-grasp round the ankles. The muscles of poor Mildmay's hands and arms quivered and fairly cracked with the terrible strain thrown upon them during the latter part of this manoeuvre; but he set his teeth hard, remembering that the lives of the whole party depended upon him just then, and hung on. It was not for long. The colonel paused only for a moment to give one downward glance at the spot upon which he was about to drop, and then let go. He pitched fairly on the ledge, slipped, staggered for a moment, *almost* went over, but recovered himself and stood firm. Then moving a little to one side he prepared to receive Mildmay, and gave him the word to drop. It came none too soon, for the lieutenant's quivering muscles were already failing him, his nerveless fingers were already relaxing their grasp, and he felt that he must let go, whether or not, in another moment. At the cry from Lethbridge he released his hold, and next moment, with the colonel's arm thrown firmly round his waist, stood safely on the ledge.

It was next the professor's turn; but now that the critical moment had arrived for him too to drop from one ledge to another, the unwelcome discovery was made that his nerves were unequal to the task, and for some time persuasion, cajolery, entreaties, and threats proved equally unavailing to tempt him to the enterprise. At length, however, in a fit of desperation he essayed the task, hurried over it, missed his hold, and went whirling outward from the face of the cliff. In another instant he would have been over the precipice, and plunging headlong downward to the death which awaited him thousands of feet below, but most fortunately both Mildmay and the colonel saw the mishap, and made a simultaneous snatch at him; the former succeeded in grasping him by the arm, and, before either of the trio had time to fully realise what had actually happened, poor von Schalckenberg was dragged—pale, breathless, and completely unnerved— in upon the ledge.

A few minutes were allowed the unhappy professor in which to recover his presence of mind, and then the little party cautiously worked their way downward along the ledge, finally arriving half an hour later on the narrow platform of ice which was now all that remained of the plateau whereon the *Flying Fish* had been grounded.

It had been the intention of the unfortunate adventurers to make a temporary halt here, for the purpose of recruiting their exhausted energies so far as it might be done by taking a few minutes' rest, but the ice was so shivered by the shock of its recent rupture as to present a very insecure appearance, and they were therefore constrained to keep moving notwithstanding their fatigue. Very fortunately the breaking away of the snow-bank had, in one place, laid bare the surface of the rock, which here was very jagged and uneven (which would probably account for the original accumulation of the snow in that spot), and these irregularities were promptly utilised as a means of further descent. By their aid an additional two hundred feet of downward movement was slowly and painfully accomplished, and then Mildmay (who was now leading the way) found himself within a foot or two of the lower edge of an almost perpendicular slope overhanging an awful abyss of unfathomable depth, his further progress downward being barred by the fact that beneath him the rock sloped *inwards!* A single downward glance sufficed not only to reveal to him his appalling situation, but also to wring from his lips such a piercing cry of horror as effectually warned his friends from following him any further. Then he pressed his body close to the face of the rock, and clung there convulsively with feet and hands to the trifling irregularities of surface which alone afforded him a hold, his blood curdling and his brain reeling at the thought of the horrible deadly danger which menaced him. A single slip of hand or foot, a momentary failure of a muscle, the slightest seizure of cramp or vertigo, and he would go whirling headlong downward at least five hundred feet sheer through the air before reaching the ground below. He was so unnerved that he was actually incapable of replying to the colonel's anxious hail as to what was the matter.

It was whilst he stood thus vainly striving to recover his self-control — a growing conviction of the impossibility of escape meanwhile forcing itself with momentarily increasing intensity upon him — that a huge moving mass suddenly swung into view round a projection on his left, and a simultaneous cry of surprise from his two waiting and wondering companions told that they too had caught sight of it. It was the *Flying Fish* slowly drifting round the mountain, stern on, and that too so closely that her propeller actually touched the rocky projection, some thirty feet off, as she passed it. The force of the contact, though very gentle, was sufficient to give her a slight outward impulse; and though she continued to drift round toward the rock to which the adventurers were clinging, it appeared as though she would pass it at such a distance as would *just* preclude the possibility of their reaching her.

"We must shout," exclaimed Mildmay, finding his voice all at once; "we must shout to George. Perhaps our cries may reach him and bring him on deck, in which event we shall be able to tell him what to do."

And shout they did, simultaneously, and at the full power of their lungs; but it was of no avail — George and the cook were both at that moment in the innermost recesses of the ship busily engaged on their respective avocations, and in all likelihood profoundly ignorant of the state of affairs. At all events there was no response, and the ship went drifting slowly past. She was floating almost level with the little party clinging there desperately to the face of the naked rock, the boss of her propeller being at just about the same height as the colonel's head. As she drove almost imperceptibly along it seemed to Mildmay that she was also being drawn inward toward the face of the rock; and he began to ask himself whether an active man might not, after all, be able to overleap the intervening space and grasp one of the propeller-blades. The craft was so tantalisingly close that it seemed to him almost a cowardly thing to let this chance pass; yet, when he glanced downward at the darkening abyss over which he hung, he shudderingly confessed to himself that the leap was an impossibility, and that they must retreat upward with all speed to gain some comparatively secure spot upon which to pass the night now gathering about them. He was about to put this thought into words, and to propose an immediate upward movement, when he turned to take (as he believed) a last parting glance at the *Flying Fish*, now immediately behind him. In doing so his fingers slipped and lost their grip upon the rock, and before he could recover his hold he found himself going over backwards. He felt that he was lost; but, with the instinct of self-preservation, turned quickly on his feet, and as they too were slipping off the minute projections on which he had been supporting himself, he made a vigorous desperate spring outward from the face of the rock, reaching forward into space toward the curved end of the propeller-blade which he saw in front of him. Despair must have leant him extra strength when making that last awful leap, for, though the distance was fully twenty feet, he actually reached and succeeded in grasping the end of the blade. To swing himself up astride upon it was the work of a moment; and then he paused to rest and recover from this last shock to his nervous system. Not for long, however; he knew that his companions must be nearly exhausted, and that their lives now probably depended solely on his activity and the celerity with which he might be able to go to their rescue; so he pulled himself together, shouted to them the encouraging news of his success, and then devoted himself in earnest to the difficult and perilous task of reaching the deck of the ship. He had hardly begun this task before he realised that it was one which would tax his strength, energy, and ingenuity to their utmost extent. The propeller-blade upon which he was perched happened to be at the very lowest point of its revolution; and his first task must be to reach the boss, which was about seventeen feet above his head. The peculiar shape of the blades rendered it impossible for him to achieve this by climbing up the edge of any one of them; his only chance consisted in working his way from one to the other. The blade to his right seemed to him the most easily accessible, and he forthwith set about the work of reaching it. To do this he had to climb about ten feet up the fore *edge* of the blade upon which he was perched, and to anyone but a sailor this would have been an impossibility. Even to Mildmay it proved a most difficult as well as hazardous feat; but after a couple of failures success crowned his efforts, and he found himself high enough to reach the point of the next blade. This was so far away, however, that he could only touch it with his finger-tips, and in order to grasp it—even with *one* hand—he found that he would be obliged to overbalance himself so much that, if he missed, a fall must inevitably result. The risk had to be taken, however; and he took it, fortunately with success. This left him swinging by *one* hand from the point of the propeller-blade; but in another second he had grasped it with his other hand, and, after a struggle or two, managed to get fairly astride the edge. His next task was to work himself in along the edge until he was abreast the after edge of the blade he had just left, when he had to reach over to the utmost stretch of his arms, grasp the blade, and in that awkward position scramble to his feet. This he also managed, when a further comparatively easy climb enabled him to reach the boss. He now found himself standing on the boss and leaning against the smooth elliptical stern of the vessel. His next task was to climb up over this smooth rounded surface and so make his way along the upper surface of the hull to the superstructure, when he would soon find means to reach the deck. This also, though a task of immense difficulty, he actually accomplished; finally reaching the deck in so prostrate a condition that he fell insensible before he could gain the pilot-house.

His fit of insensibility, however, did not last long—the latent consciousness of responsibility effectually prevented that; and he was soon able to rise and stagger to the pilot-house. Once there, he forthwith made his way below and availed himself of the stimulus afforded by a glass of neat brandy, after which he felt equal to the task which yet lay before him. Having swallowed the brandy, he at once returned to the deck and shifted the rope-ladder over to the larboard gangway. He then looked about him to ascertain the whereabouts of the ship, which he found to be about half a mile distant from the spot where he had left his friends, and gradually drifting further away under the influence of a gentle night-breeze which had just sprung up—thus proving indubitably that, had he not reached the craft when he did, she would probably have been lost to them all for ever. Having attached the ladder securely, Mildmay next entered the pilot-house, and—night having by this time completely fallen—turned on the electric lights; after which he set the engines in motion and returned to the side of the mountain in search of the two companions he had left clinging in so dangerous a situation. These were found just as he had left them, and were speedily taken on board—they too being completely overcome by the revulsion of feeling following upon their rescue.

A glass of brandy each quickly revived them, however, and then they devoted their united energies to a search for the baronet. With some little difficulty the scene of the accident was discovered; and a minute or two later Sir Reginald was observed, not dead, as they had feared to find him, but sitting up on the snow-bank upon which he had fallen, a prisoner to the spot, from the fact that there was no possible way of retreat from it either upward or downward; but in other respects very little the worse for his terrible fall, the snow, happily, proving so deep that it served as a cushion or buffer, allowing the baronet to escape with only a few somewhat severe bruises. The adventure being thus happily terminated, the ship was quickly navigated to the berth she had occupied on the preceding night; and the party then sat down to dinner, over which meal they came to the conclusion that they had had enough mountain-climbing that day to suffice them for the remainder of their lives.

Chapter Twenty Four
The Foundering of the "Mercury"

The nerves of the adventurers were so shaken by the vicissitudes of their day's adventure that they found it impossible to obtain sound and refreshing sleep that night, notwithstanding their terrible fatigue; their slumbers were broken by horrible dreams, and further disturbed by the cries of wild beasts of various descriptions which kept the forest in a perfect uproar the whole night long. So great, indeed, was the disturbance from the latter cause, that, on comparing notes over the breakfast table next morning, the party came to the conclusion that they must be in a district literally swarming with big game, and that it might be worth their while to spend a few days there hunting. This they did; with such success that their stay was prolonged for nearly a month, by which time they had collected such a quantity of skins, horns, tusks, skulls, and other trophies of the chase that even they, inveterate sportsmen as they were, acknowledged themselves satisfied. The professor, meanwhile, had devoted himself enthusiastically to the forming of a collection of rare birds, beetles, and butterflies, in which pursuit he had been fully as successful as his companions in theirs; so that when the time came for them to leave this delightful spot they did so in the highest possible state of health and spirits; the remembrance of their ugly adventure on Everest disturbing them no more than would the memory of a troublesome dream.

Their next destination was the island of Borneo; and they arranged their departure so as to pass over Calcutta and enter the Bay of Bengal during the hours of darkness, their intention being to make the latter part of the trip by water rather than by air.

They descended to the surface of the sea at daylight, the land being at that time invisible from the elevation of ten thousand feet at which they had been travelling during the night. Not a sail of any description was in sight; the sparkling sea was only moderately ruffled by the north-east monsoon; and appearances seemed to warrant a belief that the passage would be a thoroughly pleasant one. The travellers were in no hurry whatever, and they were, moreover, longing for a sniff of the good wholesome sea-breeze; the *Flying Fish* therefore proceeded very leisurely on her course, her engines revolving dead slow, which gave her a speed of about sixteen knots through the water.

They proceeded thus during the whole of that day and the succeeding night, finding themselves at daybreak next morning within sight of one of the lesser islands of the Andaman group. And at this point of their journey a gradual fall of the mercury in their barometers warned them that they were about to experience a change of weather. The atmospheric indications remained unchanged, however, until about two o'clock in the afternoon, when the wind lulled, the mercury experienced a sudden further fall, and a great mass of murky cloud began to bank up in the south-western quarter. This rapidly overspread the sky, until the whole of the visible heavens became obscured by a thick curtain of flying scud. The sea, inky black, suddenly became agitated, and formed itself into a confusion of irregular waves without any "run," but which reared themselves tremblingly aloft, and then subsided again, only to be instantly succeeded by others. The wind fell away to a dead calm, which continued for about a quarter of an hour, during which an alarmingly rapid fall of the mercury, combined with a low weird moaning in the atmosphere, seemed to forebode the approach of some dire disaster. This was followed by a sudden blast of wind from the eastward—which came and was gone again in an instant—and which preceded a brief but terrific downpour of rain. This lasted for perhaps three minutes, when it ceased as suddenly as it had commenced.

"Now, look out for the wind," exclaimed Mildmay. "Ah! here it comes—a regular hurricane! Thank Heaven, there is no sail to shorten on board the *Flying Fish*!"

He might well say so; for sore indeed would be the plight of the unwary seaman who should find himself under similar circumstances, unprepared. A long line of white foam suddenly appeared on their starboard bow, racing down toward them and spreading out right and left with frightful rapidity, until the whole horizon, from some four points on the larboard bow right round to broad on their starboard beam, was marked by a continuous line of flying foam and spindrift. They watched with eager curiosity this remarkable phenomenon, noticed the astounding rapidity with which it travelled, and saw that the sea on their starboard hand, ay, and even well on their starboard quarter, was lashed into a perfect frenzy by the hurricane before it reached the ship. Then, with a wild rush and a deafening roar, the gale struck them, and the *Flying Fish*—stout ship as she was—fairly shuddered under the force of the blow. In an instant the air became so thick with the driving scud-water that every window in the pilot-house had to be closed to prevent the inmates being drenched to the skin. In less than five minutes the deck was wet fore and aft with the flying spray; and before a quarter of an hour had elapsed the *Flying Fish* was pitching her fore-deck clean under water.

At its commencement the gale blew from about south-east, or dead in their teeth; and the revolutions of the engines were increased to a rate which, under ordinary circumstances, would have given the ship a speed of some twenty-five knots, but which now drove her ahead at the rate of only some fifteen knots against the gale. As the afternoon wore on, the wind gradually "backed," until, at four p.m., it was blowing from due south. This confirmed Mildmay in his suspicion that they had fallen in with one of those most terrible of storms—*a cyclone!*

At half-past four o'clock—at which time the gale was raging with hurricane force—a sail was made out, bearing about one point on the *Flying Fish's* port bow, and about four miles distant. As well as could be made out, she appeared to be barque-rigged; and, on approaching her more closely, this proved to be the case. She was a vessel of some four hundred tons register, pretty deep in the water; and—though she was hove-to under close-reefed fore and main topsails—was making frightfully bad weather of it, the seas sweeping clear and clean over her, fore and aft, every time she met them.

The moment that the stranger was first sighted, Mildmay opened one of the windows—at the risk of getting drenched to the skin—and brought a telescope to bear upon her. He had scarcely brought her within the field of vision when he exclaimed agitatedly:

"Good Heavens! what is the man about? He has hove-to his ship *on the port tack*; does he not know he is in a cyclone?"

"What does it matter which tack the vessel is hove-to upon?" asked Sir Reginald with a smile at Mildmay's excitement.

"All the difference in the world, my dear sir," was the reply. "We are in the Northern Hemisphere; in which—as you have already had an opportunity of observing—cyclones *invariably* revolve *against* the apparent course of the sun. A knowledge of this fact teaches the wary seaman to heave-to on the *starboard* tack; by doing which his ship dodges *away from* the fatal centre or 'eye' of the storm. This fellow, however, by heaving-to on the port tack, is steadily nearing the centre, which must eventually pass over him, when his ship will be suddenly becalmed, only to be struck aback a few moments later, when she will—almost to a dead certainty—founder with all hands. For Heaven's sake let us bear down upon him and warn him ere it be too late. And we have no time to lose about it either; for, if I may judge from the fury of the gale, the centre of the storm is not far off."

The speed of the *Flying Fish* was promptly increased, her course being at the same time so far altered as to admit of her intercepting the barque, and a few minutes later she passed under the stranger's stern and hauled close up on her weather quarter, the travellers thus having an opportunity of ascertaining the name of the vessel, which proved to be the *Mercury* of Bristol. They were now also able to realise more fully than they had yet the tremendous strength of the gale and power of the sea; the unfortunate barque careening gunwale-to under the pressure of the wind upon her scanty canvas, whilst the sea deluged her decks fore and aft; the whole of her lee and a considerable portion of her weather bulwarks having already been carried away, together with her spare spars; whilst every sea which broke on board her swept something or other off the deck and into the sea to leeward. The long-boat and pinnace, stowed over the main hatchway, were stove and rendered unserviceable; and, even as the *Flying Fish* ranged up alongside, their destruction was completed and their shattered planks and timbers torn out of the "gripes." The crew of the ship had, for safety's sake, assembled aft on the full poop; and among them could be seen a female figure crouching down under the meagre shelter of the cabin skylight evidently in a state of extreme terror.

"You go out and hail them, Mildmay; you know what to say," remarked Sir Reginald, as he steered the *Flying Fish* into a favourable position for communicating.

The lieutenant needed no second bidding; he felt that the crisis was imminent; and, stepping out on deck, where he had to cling tightly to the lee guard-rail to escape being washed overboard, he hailed:

"Barque ahoy! do you know that you are in a cyclone, and hove-to on the wrong tack? I would very strongly advise you to wear round at once and get the ship on the starboard tack. If the eye of the storm catches you you will surely founder."

To his intense astonishment an answer came back—from a great black-bearded savage-looking fellow—couched in the words, as nearly as he could make them out for the howling of the wind and the rush of the sea:

"You mind your own business! Nobody on board this ship wants your advice."

"But I am giving it you for your own safety's sake, and that of the ship," persisted Mildmay.

The answer was unintelligible, but, as it was accompanied by an impatient wave of the hand and a turning of the speaker's back upon him, Mildmay rightly concluded that the individual was one of those obstinate, pig-headed people, who, having once made a mistake, will persist in it at all hazards rather than take advice, and so admit the possibility of their having done wrong; he accordingly turned away somewhat disgusted, and made his way back to the shelter of the pilot-house.

The lieutenant was in the act of describing to his companions the unsatisfactory nature of the foregoing brief colloquy, when suddenly— *instantaneously*—there occurred an awful pause in the fury of the hurricane; the wind lulled at once to a dead calm; the air cleared; the sea, no longer thrashed down by the gale, reared itself aloft as though it would scale the very heavens; and the canvas of the barque flapped with a single loud thunderous report as she rolled heavily to windward.

"Now, look out!" gasped Mildmay. And, even as the words escaped his lips, down came the hurricane again in a sudden mad burst of relentless fury; but *now* the wind blew from the *northward*, the point of the compass exactly opposite that from which it had been blowing a minute before.

The *Flying Fish*, having neither sails nor spars exposed to the blast, received this second stroke of the gale with impunity; but with the devoted barque it was, alas, very different. She was struck flat aback and borne irresistibly over on her beam-ends, gathering stern-way at the same time. The crew, at last fully alive to the extreme peril of their situation, scrambled along the deck and made their way to the braces in a futile attempt to haul round the yards, the helmsman at the same time jamming the wheel hard down that the ship might have a chance to pay off. The yards, however, were jammed fast against the weather rigging, and could not be moved; neither would the ship's head pay off; meanwhile, her stern-way was rapidly increasing, the sea already foaming up level with her taffrail; and presently it curled in over her lee quarter, sweeping in a steadily increasing volume along her deck. The catastrophe which followed took place with startling rapidity. The stern of the barque, now buried beneath the surge, seemed at once to lose all its buoyancy, and, powerfully depressed by the leverage of the topsails on the masts, plunged at once deeply below the surface of the hungrily leaping sea, the rest of the hull following so quickly that, before the horrified spectators in the *Flying Fish's* pilot-house fully realised what was happening, the entire hull had disappeared, the masts, yards, and top-hamper generally only remaining in sight a moment longer, as though to impress upon them unmistakably the fact that a ship was foundering before their eyes.

"Come back and close the door!" thundered Sir Reginald to Mildmay, laying his hand upon certain valve-handles as the lieutenant sprang out on deck, urged by some indefinite purpose of rendering help where help was obviously no longer possible.

Mildmay stood for a moment, as one in a dream, watching the submergence of the ill-fated *Mercury's* jib-boom end and fore-topgallant mast-head (the last of her spars to disappear) beneath the swirl where her hull had just vanished, and then, dazedly, he obeyed the baronet's sharply reiterated command.

No sooner did the door clang to than Sir Reginald rapidly threw open all the valves of the water chambers, and the *Flying Fish* at once began to follow the barque to the bottom. In less than five seconds the travellers found themselves clear of all the wild commotion raging on the surface, and descending silently, rapidly, yet steadily deeper and deeper into the recesses of the cool twilight which prevailed around them, deepest blue below and an ever-darkening green above. They quickly overtook the *Mercury* and continued the descent almost side by side with her, watching, with awe-struck curiosity yet overwhelming pity and horror, the death-struggles of those who were being helplessly dragged down with her. They observed, with a feeling of intense relief, that the struggle for life ceased, in almost every case, in less than a minute, the expression of horror on the dying men's faces passing away still earlier and giving place to one of profound peace and contentment; thus confirming, to a great extent the current belief that death by drowning is a painless mode of dissolution.

The crew had, without exception, at the moment of the barque's foundering, grasped some rope or other portion of the vessel's equipment, the death-clutch upon which was in no single instance relaxed; hence they were, one and all, dragged hopelessly to the bottom with the wreck. With the female, however, it was different. She had been crouching in a kneeling attitude upon the deck, under the imperfect shelter of the cabin skylight, and when the poop deck became submerged she was swept forward, still in the same attitude, with her hands clasped as in prayer, until her body was washed clear of the poop rail, when the suction of the sinking ship dragged her below the surface. As the hull of the barque settled down it gradually recovered its balance and assumed an almost level position, due, to some extent, no doubt, to the pressure of the water upon the sails; and, with every fathom of descent, the downward motion grew increasingly slower. The wreck had sunk to a depth of perhaps twenty or five-and-twenty fathoms, when the absorbed spectators in the *Flying Fish's* pilot-house were startled by observing a sudden convulsive motion in the body of the female. Her hands were unclasped, her arms were flung wildly out above her head, and her body was slowly straightened out. At the same moment the space between her and the sinking wreck widened; the vessel was sinking more rapidly than the body. The descent of the *Flying Fish* was instantly checked, and in another moment it became apparent that the body *was rising to the surface.*

In eager, breathless anxiety the watchers noted the steady downward progress of the *Mercury's* spars and cordage past the now struggling form of the woman, victims of alternate dismay and hope as they saw the body now fouled by some portion of the complicated net-work of standing and running gear between the main and mizzen masts, and anon drifting clear of it again. A few seconds, which to the quartette in the pilot-house seemed spun out to the duration of ages, and the last of these perils was evaded, upon which the body, still feebly struggling, resumed its upward journey.

With a great sigh of intense relief, echoed by each of his companions, Sir Reginald swiftly backed the *Flying Fish* astern, causing her at the same time, by a movement of the tiller, to swerve with her bow directly toward the body, now some five or six feet above the level of the deck. Then, quick as thought, the ship was sent ahead until her deck was immediately beneath the body, when, the valves of the air and water chambers being simultaneously thrown open, she rushed upward to the surface, overtaking the drowning woman and carrying her upward also.

In another instant, a vacuum having been created in the air-chambers, the *Flying Fish* broke water with a tremendous rush and swirl, and, without a moment's pause, rose into the air, the senseless body on deck being prevented from washing off again only by the guard-rail which stood in place of bulwarks.

"Take charge, please, and do not rise too high," hurriedly exclaimed the baronet to Mildmay, springing, as he spoke, for the door of the pilot-house, which he flung open, rushing out on deck and seizing the body as though fearful that it might yet be snatched away from him.

Gently raising it in his arms he turned and bore the slender form to the shelter of the pilot-house, at the door of which he was met by the professor, who felt that his medical skill might yet perhaps serve the unfortunate girl in good stead. Together they conveyed her below to one of the state-rooms, and, without a moment's loss of time, the most approved methods of resuscitation were vigorously resorted to. For fully half an hour their utmost efforts proved all unavailing; but von Schalckenberg so positively asserted life was not extinct that they persevered, and at length a slight return of warmth to the body and colour to the lips, followed by a fluttering sigh, assured them that success was about to reward their endeavours. Another minute, and a pair of glorious brown eyes were disclosed by their opening lids, a faint moan escaped the quivering lips, the head moved uneasily upon the pillow, and the sufferer murmured a few inarticulate words.

"Thank God, we have saved her, I believe," ejaculated Sir Reginald, in a whisper, to the professor. "Now, doctor, I will retire and leave you to complete her restoration, so that the poor girl may be spared embarrassment as far as possible on the full recovery of consciousness. But I shall establish myself outside the door of the state-room, within easy reach of your voice should you need anything; and do not forget that the whole resources of the ship are at your absolute disposal."

"All right," answered the professor. "Now go, for the patient is coming to herself rapidly."

Half an hour later von Schalckenberg crept out on tiptoe, his kindly face beaming and his eyes sparkling with exultation.

"It is all right," he whispered in his broadest German-English. "I have fully restored the circulation, and the young patient is now in a sound sleep, from which she must not be disturbed on any account. I shall keep watch by her side, and when she awakes you shall all be duly informed of the circumstance. You may now go about your business, my good friend, your services are no longer required here."

The worthy professor kept sedulous watch over his patient until satisfied that she was completely out of danger, presenting her to his companions only when they assembled in the saloon for dinner some four-and-twenty hours after the catastrophe which had thrown her into their society.

The colonel and Mildmay were stricken absolutely, though only temporarily, dumb with astonishment and admiration at the vision of remarkable beauty which met their gaze as the saloon door opened, and von Schalckenberg, stepping hastily forward with a most courtly bow, met the fair stranger at the threshold, taking her hand and leading her forward into the apartment preliminary to the ceremony of introduction. Even Sir Reginald, though he had not failed to notice the beauty of the pale and apparently lifeless girl he had raised from the wet deck and borne so carefully below on the preceding evening, was startled at her radiant loveliness as she, somewhat shrinkingly and with a momentary vivid blush, responded to the introductions and congratulatory greetings which immediately followed. All night long, and throughout the day, she had been haunted by the dreamy recollection of another face than that of the kindly professor who had so assiduously nursed her back to life—a bronzed handsome face, with tender pitiful blue eyes, close-cut auburn hair clustering wavily about the small shapely head, and luxuriant auburn moustache and beard, bending anxiously over her as she lay weak, helpless, suffering, and with the feebly-returning consciousness of having recently experienced some terrible calamity; of having passed through some awful and harrowing ordeal; and now, as she gave her hand to Sir Reginald, and shyly glanced up into his handsome face and read the tender sympathy for her expressed by the kindly blue eyes, she recognised the embodiment of the vision which had haunted her so persistently, and knew that she had not been merely dreaming. The circumstances in which she thus found herself placed were certainly somewhat embarrassing; but, with the tact of a true gentleman, Sir Reginald at once led the conversation into a channel which soon made the poor girl forget her embarrassment, and almost immediately afterwards the party sat down to dinner.

During the progress of this meal—which, however, their guest scarcely tasted—the gentlemen were made aware of the circumstances which led to this lovely girl being thrown, helpless and friendless, into their society and upon their hospitality.

Her name, she informed them, was Olivia D'Arcy. She was an orphan. Her brother, formerly a lieutenant in the royal navy, had been compelled by straitened circumstances to quit the service and enter the mercantile marine, in which he had without much difficulty succeeded in securing a command. By practising the most rigid economy he had contrived to maintain his only sister, Olivia, and educate her at a first-class school, and on her education being completed he had decided, as the simplest way out of many difficulties, financial and otherwise, to take her to sea with him. This had been her first voyage with him, as it had been his first in command of the *Mercury*. The ship had been to Manilla, and at the time of her loss was homeward-bound, with instructions to call at Madras *en route*. The voyage had been an unfortunate one in many respects, even from its commencement, and Olivia thought the climax had been reached when, a week before her wreck, the *Mercury* had been attacked by pirates in the Straits of Malacca, and her brother slain by the pirates' last shot, as they retired defeated. The cruel shot, she declared in a burst of uncontrollable grief, had robbed her, in her brother, of her sole relative; and whilst she was deeply grateful to those she addressed for preserving her life, she felt that it would perhaps have been better for her had she been allowed to perish.

Such a story was calculated to excite the deepest sympathy and commiseration in the breasts of those who listened to it; and it did; in Sir Reginald's case, indeed, the feeling was even warmer than either of those mentioned, especially when he learned, upon further inquiry, that Olivia's

brother had been none other than the George D'Arcy who, in the days of their mutual boyhood, had fought many a battle on his behalf at Eton when certain first-form bullies had shown a disposition to tyrannise over the then delicate curly-headed "Miss Reggie" (as Elphinstone was dubbed when he first entered the school), and the sorrowing girl was assured that, so far from being friendless, she would find in her then companions four men upon whom she might always rely for the warmest sympathy, the most kindly counsel, and the most substantial help so long as their lives might last.

The accession of such a guest as Olivia D'Arcy to the little party on board the *Flying Fish* occasioned, it will readily be understood, a complete and immediate change in all their plans. In the first moment that they gave to the consideration of the matter they saw that it would never do for a young, beautiful, and unprotected girl to accompany them hither and thither in their wanderings, even were she willing to do so, which they felt well assured she would not be. Two alternatives then presented themselves to the choice of the party: the one being to land her at the nearest port, and, furnishing her with the necessary means, leave her to make her way to England alone and unprotected as best she could; the other alternative involving the temporary abandonment of their further projects and the immediate return of the *Flying Fish* to England. The first project was named only to be abruptly and unanimously rejected by the entire party, the second being gladly adopted by Sir Reginald upon his receiving from his three friends the assurance of their hearty approval and acquiescence.

This decision was arrived at shortly before midnight on the evening following Olivia's formal introduction by the professor to the remaining members of the party, and thereupon—the *Flying Fish* being at the time afloat and making her way leisurely southward toward the Straits of Malacca—an ascent to the upper regions of the atmosphere was at once made, and the ship's head pointed homeward. The distance to be traversed was considerable, but it was calculated that by travelling at the ship's utmost speed along the arc of a great circle (the shortest possible route between any two places on the earth's surface), the journey might be accomplished in about forty-five hours, which, allowing for the difference of longitude in time between their then position and the English Channel, would enable them to reach the latter place at about two o'clock in the afternoon of the day but one following. This was rather an awkward time, if they still intended to maintain their secrecy of movement and avoid observation, but under the circumstances they resolved to risk it. Soaring, therefore, to a height of ten thousand feet—the elevation which experience had taught them to be most suitable for the performance of long-distance journeys—the *Flying Fish* was put to her utmost speed, and, with the gentlemen keeping watch by turns in the pilot-house, the journey was commenced.

Swiftly the wonderful fabric sped forward upon her homeward way, and, without incident of any kind worthy of mention, and almost at the very minute calculated upon, the waters of the English Channel were sighted; an unobserved descent being effected some twenty miles seaward of the little town of Saint Valery on the French coast. A course was now shaped for the Isle of Wight, and, a few hours later, one of the boats belonging to the *Flying Fish* quietly glided into Portsmouth harbour in charge of Lieutenant Mildmay. Three passengers—Olivia D'Arcy, the professor, and Colonel Lethbridge—landed from her without attracting any attention, and found themselves just in good time to take the London express, which they did, Mildmay making his solitary way out of the harbour again immediately.

In accordance with arrangements previously made by Sir Reginald, Miss D'Arcy was escorted by her two cavaliers straight to the town residence of a certain aunt of the baronet's, and handed over to the care and protection of the old lady, with whom (to make short of a long story) for the ensuing twelve months she found a most comfortable and happy home; Sir Reginald and Mildmay turning up in town two days later laden with their African spoils, the equitable division of which, and their ultimate disposal, occupied the party for several months.

Thus ended the cruise of the *Flying Fish*. What remains to be told may be said in a very few words. Will the sagacious reader be very much surprised to learn that Sir Reginald Elphinstone suddenly discovered, in the aunt who had kindly taken Olivia D'Arcy under her protection, an old lady whose good graces were worth the most assiduous cultivation? Such, at all events, was the fact, and, this much having been stated, the aforesaid sagacious reader will perhaps be not altogether unprepared to learn that, about a year after the return of the *Flying Fish* to England, a wedding took place from that old lady's house; in which ceremony Olivia enacted most charmingly the part of bride, with Sir Reginald as bridegroom, supported by the three staunch friends who had shared with him so many perils.

And what about the *Flying Fish*, does somebody ask? When last heard of she was—where she probably still is—lying safe and unsuspected at the bottom of the "Hurd Deep," in the identical spot where she made her first descent into the waters of the English Channel.

Whether she will ever again be put into commission—and, if so, under what circumstances—time alone will show.